Benjamin
and the
Time Machine

C. C. Cairns

Benjamin
and the
Time Machine

Vanguard Press

VANGUARD PAPERBACK

© Copyright 2024
C. C. Cairns

A CIP catalogue record for this title is
available from the British Library.

ISBN 978 1 80016 698 1

Vanguard Press is an imprint of
Pegasus Elliot Mackenzie Publishers Ltd.
www.pegasuspublishers.com

First Published in 2024

Vanguard Press
Sheraton House Castle Park
Cambridge England

Printed & Bound in Great Britain

Chapter One

Ben opens his eyes to the sound of his father's voice calling his name. 'Ben, it's time to get up.'

He looks up at the blank ceiling above him and pulls the duvet tightly around his neck to keep out the cold. The bedroom is veiled in semi-darkness which makes it all the more difficult to determine whether the voice he heard was for real or just part of a vague recollection from a dream he may have had. Ben closes his eyes again knowing all too well that it's a Saturday morning and not a school day, so he doesn't need to get up. *'Ben!'*

The sound of his father's voice echoes around his room like a clap of thunder causing him to sit up and stare at the silhouetted image of his father standing in his doorway.

'What?' Ben defensively calls out.

'You've got five minutes,' his father informs him before disappearing out of sight.

From the tone of his father's voice, Ben knows he needs to get up. The fact that he can't remember why his father has woken him so early is not important at this moment. Ben throws back the duvet and slides his feet out of bed. He looks at the crumpled pair of jeans and tee shirt that he wore yesterday on the bedroom floor and proceeds to put them on. As a twelve-year-old boy, he's never been into fashion and as far as he's concerned, whatever clothes his mum buys for him, he wears, even when they're creased and full of dirt stains from playing in the garden and climbing trees. The only time he's ever been told by his mum to change his clothes was when he wore the same pair of socks for nearly two weeks. 'What's that smell?' his mum asked, then immediately sent him up to the bathroom to wash his feet and put on a fresh pair of socks. To this day, Ben has not been able to work out how his mother knew. Ben slips his feet inside his trainers and quickly ties up the laces before making his way downstairs to the dining room.

Mum and Dad have nearly finished their breakfast while his sister Jess is playing with her food at the table. 'Take your time won't ya,' Jess sarcastically says as he enters the room. Ben ignores his older sister and takes his usual seat at the table.

'Dad, why did we have to get up so early; it's not a school day?' Ben nervously asks, having noticed his father's stern expression.

'We explained why last night: we're going round to Granddad's house to sort through his things before his house is sold.'

Ben suddenly remembers the conversation he and Jess had with their parents just before bedtime last night. Granddad died just over a week ago from a heart attack or old age or something. He vaguely remembers Mum telling them that Granddad had just turned eighty before he died and that they shouldn't feel sad because he had a good and long life. Ben remembers how upset they were. Jess burst into tears more or less straight away while Ben managed to excuse himself before going upstairs to his bedroom before he gave way to tears. The mention of Granddad always brought back memories of how Ben and Jess were always dropped off at Granddad's house every week on a Saturday morning. He thinks Mum and Dad thought it best to kill two birds with one stone by letting them stay with Granddad for the morning while they went shopping. That way, the children got to see Granddad while Mum and Dad could concentrate on getting the weekly food shopping without being harangued by their children demanding sweets and presents.

Ben picks up the box of cornflakes from the centre of the dining table and begins sprinkling the orange flakes into his bowl. Jess sees an opportunity to get her brother into trouble as she usually does and reaches across and prods him in his side, causing the flakes to scatter across the table.

'*Jess!*' Ben protests.

'What's going on?' Dad calls out in his firm voice from the kitchen doorway. Ben looks over at his sister who's now sitting upright in her chair, looking as though butter wouldn't melt in her mouth. He knows it would be futile to try to blame his sister because he knows she's "Daddy's little girl".

'Sorry Dad, I think I had a muscle spasm or something,' Ben quickly answers before placing the cereal box back down on the dining table, scooping up the scattered flakes with his hands and depositing them into his cereal bowl. Dad gives him a stern look and points to his watch indicating that he'd better get a move on with eating his breakfast. Ben gives his father a partial smile and immediately picks up the milk container before pouring the cold liquid over his cereal. Ben notices his sister giving him her usual victory smile so he casually looks across at her and glares, so she knows he's not happy. She's only two years older but she acts like she's an adult. A few years ago, when Jess was twelve, she suddenly changed from being a quiet obliging sister to a loud, irritating and devious sister from hell. Ben heard all the derogatory remarks from all of Mum and Dad's friends telling them about "teenagers" and how their children can be so sweet and loving, but once they reach that certain age, they turn into little monsters. Jess is not exactly a monster. She is, however, devious, unscrupulous and very underhanded and deceitful when it comes to how she treats her brother. Ben continues to eat his breakfast as quickly as he can while watching his parents collect all that they need for their trip to Granddad's house. He spoons the last of his cornflakes into his mouth just as his father opens the front door indicating to everyone that it's time to leave. Ben picks up his bowl and quickly carries it into the kitchen and deposits it in the sink ready to be washed later. He jogs to the opened front door and joins the rest of his family in the car.

Chapter Two

Ben stares out of the rear car window at the semi-detached house that belonged to Granddad as they reverse the car up to the front of the house. Seeing the house again and knowing that Granddad's not there anymore suddenly brings a sense of sorrow adding to the gloominess of the occasion. Ben remembers the last time they were here; it was only two weeks ago and as far as he was concerned, everything was just how it had always been. Granddad greeted them at the door with a big smile on his face. He was a good-looking man with a full head of grey hair, which was always combed back flat on his head with a slightly off-centre parting, and he was dressed in his usual corduroy brown trousers, white cotton shirt and green thick knitted cardigan.

'Good morning, my favourite grandchildren,' Granddad would always say, although Ben could never understand why, because he and Jess were his only grandchildren as far as he knew. Ben would give his grandfather a hug before entering the house and his sister would do the same.

They'd always go into the kitchen because Granddad would undoubtedly have made a sponge cake of some description and he would offer them a slice of cake alongside a cold drink before they were allowed to play in the conservatory until Mum and Dad returned from shopping.

Dad turns the engine off and they all climb out of the car and head for the front door feeling subdued at the prospect of having to rifle through all of Granddad's stuff. Dad stops at the front door and turns round to them.

'Children, Mum and I will check the downstairs rooms and we want you two to check the upstairs. If you find anything of value like money, jewellery, or suchlike, bring it down and place it on the table in the hallway. Do you understand?' he asks while staring directly at them to see if they're paying attention. Jess and Ben look up at their father and nod.

'If you find anything that you're not sure about, but you think it may be valuable, just bring it down and put it on the table. Your mom and I will check through them after we've checked the downstairs rooms. Do you know what you've got to do?' Dad asks.

'Yes Dad,' they reply in unison.

'Good.' He opens the front door and they all step through into the hallway. Ben notices a strange smell in the house; it's not the usual smell he'd always smelt. No, this was a kind of musty smell from an unventilated house which he didn't like.

'Phaw! What's that smell?'

'Do not concern yourself about the smell; just open a bedroom window when you get upstairs and we'll leave the front door open to air the house,' Mum tells them. Mum and Dad go into the lounge while Jess and Ben quickly rush upstairs and head for the first room to their left. They'd never been allowed to venture upstairs in Granddad's house before so the prospect of exploring the upstairs seems so exciting, yet disconcerting at the same time. Jess quickly opens the bedroom door and comes to a complete standstill on the threshold to the room. Ben stops just behind his sister as they peer into what appears to be a storage room crammed full of toys and games.

'You've got to be kidding me; I never knew Granddad had so much stuff!' Jess exclaimed.

Remembering back, it all makes sense now; whenever Jess and Ben would visit, Granddad would always take them through to the conservatory where a selection of toys would already be laid out for them to play with. Each week, the toys and games would change. One weekend they'd play with toy cars and a dolls' house with miniature dolls for Jess. Another time it was a Lego set and a couple of Sindy dolls. One time Granddad set up a huge train track on the floor. The track would run around the edge of the large conservatory and then turn into the centre between a couple of dining chairs and a coffee table. The track would invariably loop back out from under the coffee table into a station, where other tracks would run out and back around the room forming an inner circle. Jess and Ben were always amazed at how many accessories Granddad had. There were miniature people, trees, dogs, sheep, cows and signs. There was so much to play with and do with the train set that it soon became their favourite toy.

Ben looks up at his sister wondering what she's decided their game plan should be, considering there's so much stuff as every conceivable space has been filled. They can just make out a single bed under a mass of toy boxes on the left-hand side of the room with toys, games and cuddly toys stacked all around. A wall-to-wall bookshelf on the right-hand side seemed to be packed with bric-a-brac. Ben recognises a Punch and Judy, then an Action Man figure, and a Sindy Doll lying on top of a red double-decker London bus. More toy cars and trains were crammed inside the small spaces designed for books.

'Ben, you check the boxes on the left and I'll check the shelves on the right,' Jess suggests.

Jess squeezes through a stack of toys to the large shelf unit and Ben steps forward to the nearest stack of toys just inside the doorway to his left. Ben lifts down a box balanced on top of the first stack of toys and stares at the label: Monopoly. Immediately Ben remembers the last time he'd played the game with Jess and Granddad and how he managed to buy Park Lane and Mayfair and how his sister reminded him that he'd wasted his time and that nobody would land on his property. Ben had ignored his sister and sure enough, Jess landed on his property not once but three times in a row, making her bankrupt. It was probably the only time Ben had ever beaten his sister so to him, it was a special and memorable occasion he wouldn't forget. Ben sees his sister searching through the plethora of toys over to his right, which immediately reminds him that he needs to get a move on. Ben looks at the game and notices how old and damaged the outer box is. He places the game down on the only available clear space on the floor and lifts off the lid to the game. Looking at the contents, he notices how old and shabby they are. The corners of the board are battered and split; the playing cards look old and worn and the small plastic houses appear to be grubby and stained. Ben replaces the lid and stacks the game on the floor to his left, to form a rubbish pile. He picks up the next game Jenga which also, from the look of the outer cover, appears to be in the same condition as the Monopoly game. Without opening the lid, Ben stacks the game to his left and picks up the next game from his right. This one, called Operation, also ends up on the rubbish stack. Bingo, Buckaroo, Kerplunk and the Game of Risk all follow the same path, onto the rubbish pile.

Ben moves slightly to his right and checks the games in the next stack. He starts a new rubbish pile just to his left and continues to lift off the old games from his right and stack on the left.

Finally Ben reaches the far wall, having searched through all the games he'd been assigned to. He turns around to see how his sister is getting on.

The space between Ben and his sister has suddenly been filled with a mountain of toys piled up on the floor. Ben sees a rag doll being tossed in the air from the other side of the room and landing on the heap of toys in the middle adding to the height of the mound. Ben can only assume the pile of toys in the middle must represent the rubbish pile. Jess suddenly appears behind the huge stack as she stands up.

'Have you found anything you want to keep?' Jess asks.

'No it's all old stuff.'

'I found the old train set in a box but several pieces are broken so I don't think it's worth keeping. Shall we look in the other bedroom?' Jess asks. Without waiting for Ben's reply, she walks out of the spare bedroom and turns left towards Granddad's bedroom. Ben walks out onto the landing and sees his sister standing in front of Granddad's closed bedroom door.

'Please, please let there be no toys in this room,' Ben hears Jess say. He's not sure whether she's talking to him or praying to God. Jess opens the door and they enter the room to an audible sigh of relief from them as they see a normal bedroom, free of clutter. The room is much larger than the spare bedroom and has the usual bedroom furniture. Ben and Jess see a large double bed neatly made up with a cream-and-blue checked bedspread and matching pillows, centrally positioned against the far wall. Two pine single drawers, bedside cabinets with storage shelves underneath at either side of the bed, with matching small blue ceramic lamps with cream shades. A large three-drawer pine chest of drawers stands tucked away in the left corner with a pine double wardrobe next to that and a writing desk with an overhead wall lamp to our right with a blue leather chesterfield chair underneath.

Jess walks over to Granddad's wardrobe and opens the two large doors to check inside. Ben recognises his cue to start looking, so he goes over to his chest of drawers. He pulls out the top drawer and looks inside. The drawer is full of jumpers and tee shirts perfectly folded and tightly stacked in four perfectly formed piles. Ben closes the drawer and slides open the middle drawer which is also neatly packed with rows and rows of nicely rolled-up socks on the left and boxer shorts on the right.

'Granddad was really neat and tidy,' he tells his sister.

Ben closes the middle drawer and slides open the bottom drawer, revealing another neatly stacked drawer full of bed linen: sheets, duvet covers and pillow cases. 'Nothing in here,' Ben tells his sister just as she closes the wardrobe doors.

'I'll check the desk; you look inside his bedside cabinets,' Jess tells her brother.

Ben closes the bottom drawer and walks over to the bedside cabinet.

He slowly pulls out the only drawer to the small bedside cabinet and catches sight of a large sealed padded brown envelope resting on the top. He takes the envelope out and feels the sealed package realising quickly that there's something concealed inside.

In his excitement, he blurts out, 'Jess I've found something,' sounding victorious at finding something that may turn out to be important. Ben holds the envelope up to show his sister what he'd found.

'What is it?' Jess asks as she turns in the desk chair and spots the brown envelope. Within seconds she's standing by his side and snatches the envelope from his hand.

'Oy Jess, give it back; I found it!' Ben protests. Jess blocks his attempt at trying to retrieve the envelope with her left hand while examining the manila rectangle held firmly in her right hand.

'It's got your name on it Ben; is there one in there for me?' Jess asks, sounding excited that there may be something in the drawer for her. Ben turns around and looks down at the small opening to the drawer.

'I can't see anything.'

Immediately he finds himself being shoved out of the way as Jess pushes forward to look inside the drawer. She reaches inside the small opening and searches with her left hand for another brown envelope. Suddenly she stands up feeling all indignant at not finding anything.

'Give me my envelope,' Ben demands trying desperately to reach across his sister and grab the package now held out at arm's reach. *'Jess!'* Ben screams.

'What's going on?!' The sound of their mother's voice brings them up quickly and they turn to find her standing in the doorway.

'You're supposed to be looking for anything valuable, not arguing!'

'Mum we found this in Granddad's drawer and it's got Ben's name on it,' Jess informs Mum. Mum takes the envelope from Jess and looks at the handwriting on the front.

'Master Benjamin Chapman,' Mum says, reading. 'Well it's definitely Granddad's handwriting.' Immediately Ben holds out his hand expecting the package to be handed back to him when Mum adds, 'Not so fast; I want to know what Granddad's given you.'

She holds the envelope up to her ear and gives it a little shake. Ben and Jess move their heads nearer the package and together they all hear a faint clicking sound coming from within the envelope. Mum stares at the envelope trying to visualise what might be contained inside but from her blank expression Ben realises that none of them have any idea. Mum quickly turns the envelope over and slides her index finger underneath the lip on the sealed edge and tears the end open. She opens the flap wide enough and peers inside. Ben's heart begins to beat faster in anticipation of finding out what Granddad has given him. He and Jess stare expectantly at the envelope with bated breath. Mum reaches inside and lifts out a piece of folded paper and a small metal object attached to a chain. She lays the envelope on the bed and opens the folded paper.

'What is it, Mom?' Ben enthusiastically asks while trying to focus on the metal object held tightly in her left hand. Mom finishes reading the message on the paper before looking at the metal object once more. 'Granddad's left you this watch.' She looks at the small pocket watch and chain and flips it over in her hand, before handing it over to Ben.

The first thing Ben notices about the watch is how heavy it is, compared to the old Mickey Mouse watch he used to have. Ben's uncle on mum's side of the family gave Ben a Mickey Mouse watch as a present after returning from Disney World a few years ago. Ben thought it was the best present he'd ever received and it never left his wrist until last year when it was accidentally broken in gym class at school.

'What does it say?' Jess asks.

'Sorry. Ben, Granddad says: *Dear Ben I was given this watch when I was just a boy by my father and I think his father gave him the watch when he was a boy. This watch is very valuable and holds a secret. Promise me you'll keep it safe and if you ever have a child, you too can pass this heirloom down to him as I am doing for you. I wanted to pass this down to your father but as you may know your father and I fell out many years ago and I don't believe he would be responsible enough to look after such a precious gift. I pray you use it wisely. All my love Granddad Joe xx.'*

Valuable?' Mum says while looking down at the watch again held in Ben's hand. She takes the watch from him and holds it up so she can see it clearly.

'It's not even gold,' she adds and gives the watch back to Ben who quickly tucks it inside his trouser pocket to stop anyone taking it from him again. 'You may as well have this, too.' Mum hands Ben the small letter from Granddad which he takes and squashes inside the same pocket as the watch. 'So have you both checked everywhere?' Mum asks.

'Yes we were just about finished in here,' Jess tells Mum.

'Come on then; Dad and I have finished downstairs and I think Dad wants to get back home for the football.'

Chapter Three

During the afternoon Ben spends a few hours tidying up his bedroom. Not that he wanted to. He'd much rather have played on his computer game or just played outside, but his mom told him that he had to clean up his room because 'it is starting to look like a tip'. He wasn't quite sure exactly what his mother was referring to; even so, he thought it would be best just to do as he was told as he'd learnt from experience not to test the wrath of his parents. He never considered himself to be a messy person, but, having spent the last few hours picking stuff off the floor and putting things away, he could see that he probably was. His eyes scan the room for the fortieth time, searching for anything that's out of place and needs to be put away. He doesn't see anything, so he finally sits down on the edge of his bed to admire his hard work. Sure enough his room now appears to be so much cleaner and to his surprise so much more spacious. Ben gives himself a smile, knowing that his mum's going to be impressed. She'll probably tell him that he needs to keep his room in this condition all the time. Now that it's tidy, he knows it won't take much to keep it that way, so he decides that today is the day to turn over a new leaf and become a clean and tidy person; at least then his mum would be happier. Ben suddenly remembers that his dad is watching football. He likes watching football with his dad because he can be so animated, especially when something goes wrong or his team wins. Ben goes downstairs and walks into the lounge. He sees his dad sitting on the edge of his seat, staring at the TV screen so he knows they must be at a critical point in the game. Ben quietly goes over and sits down next to his dad on the sofa so as not to disturb him.

Dad was born in Liverpool and so became an avid supporter of the Reds. Merseyside have another premiership team named Everton but Ben's not even allowed to mention their name in the house, else Dad would become very angry. He doesn't understand how there can be such rivalry between football supporters; as far as Ben's concerned, they're all English teams, so what's the problem? When England plays in the World Cup, the England team is usually made up of players from other teams like Arsenal and Manchester United and they always cheer them on. So why do they get booed when they play against your home team in the premiership? It just doesn't make any sense.

Ben notices the playing time for the game displayed in the top corner of our TV screen: *90 + 1* which means they must be injury time as the game is normally played for just ninety minutes. Just under the time on the screen is the score: Liverpool 1: Leicester 0. Ben feels his heart start to race because he knows if Leicester scores in the dying minutes of the game, Dad's going to be in a foul mood all evening. *Please, please don't score,* Ben silently pleads.

'Dinner's ready,' Mom calls out from the kitchen. 'Two more minutes darling; they're in injury time,' Dad shouts back while keeping his eyes glued to the screen.

A man in blue runs down the wing, stops and kicks the ball across the pitch to another player in blue, who immediately volley the ball towards the Liverpool goal. *'Noooooooooo!'* Dad screams.

The ball clips the top bar and goes out for a goal kick; just then the ref blows his whistle indicating full time. *'Yes!'* Dad shouts and throws his arms up into the air in a victory salute.

'Did we win then?' Ben asks, knowing all too well that Liverpool did win.

'Too right son; we slaughtered them. Come on, you reds!' Dad replied at the top of his voice.

Ben giggles to himself at the complete exaggeration he'd just heard from his father. 'We slaughtered them.' Which clearly implies that Liverpool thrashed Leicester, yet the score was only one goal to nothing. How can that be a thrashing? Ben asks himself. Oh well, it doesn't really matter. He's just pleased that Liverpool won because that means Dad will be in a good mood tonight.

'Are you two hungry or should we start without you?' Mum asks while popping her head around the door frame.

'We're coming,' Dad tells Mum. Ben stands up and follows his dad through to the dining room and they take a seat at the table while Mum goes into the kitchen to fetch the food that she's cooked for dinner. Mum walks in from the kitchen carrying a hot platter of spaghetti Bolognese and places it down in the centre of the table next to a plate of garlic bread.

Jess reaches across the table and picks up a slice of garlic bread, accidentally knocking over her glass of Coke. In a flash, Dad reaches across the table, picks up the glass, and sits it back down on the table in its upright position.

'Whoa Jess,' Ben calls out and quickly slides his seat back from the table to avoid getting wet from the brown frothy liquid now running off the table. Mum throws a tea towel she has next to her over the spilt Coke which immediately absorbs the liquid.

'Sorry,' Jess says.

'Don't worry darling; I'll get you some more.' Mum wipes the partially damp tea towel across the table to mop up the last of the liquid before taking the now sodden cloth into the kitchen. Seconds later she returns with a half-empty Coke bottle and refills Jessica's glass.

Ben, noticing the table's now clear, slides his chair back towards the table as Mum starts to serve the food.

After dinner, Ben decides to play in his clean bedroom for a bit. Last month his mum and dad bought him a cool present. It was a model of the HMS *Victory* that you assemble yourself using matchsticks; small wooden sticks, about three centimetres long and three millimetres thick. The box came with a huge bag of them; he remembers thinking at the time that there had to be at least two thousand matchsticks in the clear polythene bag, contained in the box alongside a small tube of glue. Ben thought he could build the ship in one day. However, the five hours of applying a dab of glue to a small matchstick and then pressing it against another matchstick until you knew the glue had dried seemed to take forever. Looking at the assembled hull and reflecting on the many hours he's already contributed to the building of the ship he knows it's going to take quite a while before he'll complete it. Ben sits down at his desk and undoes the lid to the nearly empty tube of glue. He picks up one of the small wooden sticks between his forefinger and thumb and applies a small dab of glue to both ends. The trick is not to get glue on your fingers as it makes it even harder to stick the match to the ship when it wants to remain stuck to you. Ben places the glue down on the desk before concentrating on positioning the match exactly where he wants it.

He presses the match down into place and makes the needed adjustments sliding it left, so it butts up tightly against the previous match. He holds it for a few seconds until he knows it's not going to move before slowly lifting his finger and thumb away from the matchstick.

'Yes!' he says to himself.

After half an hour, he squeezes the last drop of glue from the tube and fixes the last match in place for today. He drops the tube into his empty waste basket next to his desk and sits back in his chair to admire the progress of his ship. He stares at the hull for a moment trying to identify the newly fitted pieces. The fifty or so matchsticks he'd only just stuck down, covers just a small section of the ship.

'It doesn't even look like I've done anything,' he says to himself feeling a little deflated. Ben had thought he was doing pretty well today at building his ship but the actual area he'd completed doesn't look much and he begins to wonder if he'll ever complete the thing.

Ben looks around the bedroom wondering what else he could do to pass the time, when he remembers the watch Granddad gave him. He can't believe he'd forgotten all about the watch and the note until now. He reaches inside his trouser pocket and takes out the watch with the folded piece of paper and places them down on his desk. Ben opens the folded paper so he can read the message.

Dear Ben, I was given this watch when I was just a boy by my father and I think his father gave him the watch when he was a boy. This watch is very valuable and holds a secret. Promise me you'll keep it safe and if you ever have a child, you too can pass this heirloom down to him as I am doing for you. I wanted to pass this down to your father but as you may know your father and I fell out many years ago and I don't believe he would be responsible enough to look after such a precious gift. I pray you use it wisely. All my love Granddad Joe xx

Ben stares at the letter, feeling quite emotional. Granddad gave him a present and nobody else. Why did he get something from Granddad and his sister Jess didn't? Was it because he was Granddad's favourite grandchild? The letter said that Granddad was given the watch from his father so maybe it's a boy thing. Maybe the watch has to be in the possession of a male? Ben looks at the wording again to try to get the sense of what Granddad was trying to tell him when his eyes immediately stop at the part that says, *This watch is very valuable and holds a secret.*

'Secret! What does he mean secret?' Just the mention of the word "secret" sets his heart beating faster. Ben continues to scan the message again when his eyes are drawn to the words *precious gift.*' Ben places the paper down on the desk and picks up the watch. 'So, what's so precious about this watch?' he asks himself as he begins examining the small object.

The first thing he notices about the watch is its colour. The pocket watch is encased in a dull bronze-coloured metal that's engraved in a kind of ornate pattern consisting of spirals and small stars. It's quite unusual and it's something he'd never seen before. If Granddad was given the watch from his father and he may have been given it from his father, the watch must be very old. 'Is that why Granddad said it was very valuable?' Ben wonders aloud. 'If that's the case, it may well be hundreds of years old.'

The whole outer casing is smooth except for a small crevice next to the small protruding winder on the side of the watch that's encircled by a hook from which a small chain hangs. Ben digs his fingernail into the crevice and tries to lever the outer casing open. Suddenly the top cover opens out on a small spring hinge on the opposite side to the winder, revealing more engraving on the inside of the cover. Under the lid is a clear flat glass plate protecting the delicate watch hands that stretch out from the centre of its face. A thin, long black hand is pointing to the two and a shorter black hand rests between the eleven and the twelve. A third gold-coloured hand encompassing a small star hangs down towards the number six.

Ben looks at the time on his digital alarm clock which tells him it's ten past six. He decides to set the time on the watch to the correct time so he can use the watch. He pulls the adjuster winder out on the side of the watch and turns it clockwise until the hands are in the correct position. He pushes the adjuster back in and rotates the adjuster in the hope of winding the watch up. Nothing seems to happen. 'This is strange,' Ben murmurs. He holds the watch up to his ear to hear if the timepiece is working but he can't hear anything. He lowers the watch and pulls out the adjuster knob as he did before but this time he pulls it out further until it clicks. Ben slowly turns the adjuster clockwise and immediately notices the gold hand turn back around to the nine. 'This is weird.' He decides to try to pull the adjuster out again as he doesn't quite understand how to wind the watch up. He tentatively pulls on the adjuster hoping that he's not about to break it when he feels that third click. He turns the adjuster slowly while staring at the small hands on the watch face. None of hands move. *This sounds promising*, he thinks as he continues to wind the watch up a few more turns. Ben holds the watch up to his ear and listens to the faint clicking sound. *Tick, tick, tick.* With a sigh of relief he closes the lid and places the watch back inside his trouser pocket.

'*Noooooooooo!*' Ben hears what appears to be his father screaming from downstairs. The sound of his father calling out sends a chill down Ben's spine. *Why is he screaming? What's happened? Has there been an accident and someone is injured?* A multitude of unanswered questions race through Ben's brain sending his anxiety levels through the roof. All he really knows for sure is that he needs to get downstairs to find out what's happened. Ben sprints from his desk to the door, opens it, half expecting to hear his mum or Jess scream, having found Dad injured or something but there's no other sound except the faint sound of the TV. Ben can't understand it; if there's been an accident or if someone's broken into the house, surely he would hear other noises by now. In his confused state, he strides down the stairs missing every other step to get down quicker and rushes into the lounge to see his father standing in front of the TV with both arms raised up in the air.

'Dad what's happened? Are you all right? Ben asks. Dad turns towards Ben and says 'It's okay Ben; I thought they nearly scored.'

'Who scored?' Ben asks.

'Leicester,' his dad replies and points towards the TV screen. Ben stares at the screen feeling totally confused.

'Are you two hungry or should we start without you?' Mum appears at the door and asks them again. 'We're coming,' Dad tells Mum. He picks up the remote control and switches the TV off. He puts the remote down next to the TV and wanders through to the dining room. Ben, feeling like he's just experiencing a déjà vu moment, follows his father through to the dining room. Dad sits down at the table next to Jess, so Ben takes his seat on the other side of Jess as he did less than an hour ago, wondering why they're all sitting around the table again.

Why is the table set up exactly as it was for dinner? Ben thinks as he takes in the plate of garlic bread positioned where it was before with four glasses and cutlery set out for four place settings. Ben looks over at his sister waiting for her to break into a smile or to explain the joke.

'What are you staring at?' Jess says feeling vexed at being stared at. Ben looks away and catches sight of his mother carrying another platter of spaghetti Bolognese as she approaches the table and places the heavy dish next to the garlic bread. Jess reaches across the table and takes a slice of garlic bread and knocks over her glass of Coke again. Dad quickly reaches across and picks the glass up and repositions it upright on the table as he did before.

Ben can't believe his eyes. How does his sister do the same thing she did earlier? She must be the dumbest person in the world.

Ben slides his seat away from the table to avoid the Coke dripping down onto his lap. Mum quickly mops up the spilt Coke with a tea towel as she did before.

'Sorry,' Jess says.

'Don't worry darling, I'll get you some more,' Mum says.

Why are we re-enacting the same scene as before? Ben thinks. He's convinced that everyone's done and said exactly the same thing. He continues to watch Mum as she takes the damp cloth into the kitchen and returns with a half-empty bottle of Coke and begins to refill Jessica's glass.

'What's going on? Haven't we already eaten?' Ben asks, feeling this situation is a little surreal.

'We had lunch at lunchtime, but this is dinner,' Dad tells him. Mom continues to serve the food to everyone as she did before, before sitting down and smiling at Jess and Dad as they eagerly tuck in to their food.

'Mmmm this is delicious, Mum, I've been looking forward to this all day,' Jess says before placing another large forkful of spaghetti coated in tomato sauce into her mouth.

'Thank you sweetie, it's nice that you enjoy my cooking,' Mum replies. Mum picks up a large meatball with her fork and places it into her mouth. Ben just can't believe it; he stares in amazement at the scene in front of him. He's never seen his family eat a second helping within a relatively short space of time. He knows that he's still feeling bloated from the first dinner they ate this evening, so how can they all do what they're doing without throwing up? Ben continues to stare at Jess in awe, because he's never seen Jess eat so much and tonight she's well outdone herself. To be honest, watching his whole family gorge themselves on a second helping is just beyond him, it truly is a wholehearted display of gluttony with which he just can't compete. Ben picks up his fork and coils a single strand of spaghetti around the prongs before placing the small amount inside his mouth. The food tastes nice, so he knows he's not dreaming. Is this all a trick they're playing? Is it some elaborate game where a cameraman will jump out from behind the kitchen door and say 'Gotcha!'? Ben just can't fathom why they're all doing this, and why would they? This charade can't go on much longer so he decides to just go along with it.

Sooner or later, they'll tell him what's going on, he reasons to himself.

'So, what was that scream I heard, just before dinner?' Mum asks Dad.

'Sorry. Leicester nearly scored right at the end of injury time.'

'So does that mean Liverpool won?' Mum asks.

'Of course they did; we're the best team in the premiership. That's why.'

'Where are they now on the football table?' Jess asks.

'We're top, yeah come on you reds!' Dad sings in his best impersonation of Gerry Marsden from Gerry and the Pacemakers, except for the strand of spaghetti dangling from his mouth.

'Darling, not with your mouth full; you don't want the children picking up bad habits,' Mum quickly reminds him.

'Sorry kids.' Dad sheepishly apologises. The three of them finish the food on their plates along with the rest of the garlic bread before Dad glances over at Ben's relatively untouched plate of spaghetti. 'Are you all right son? Are you not hungry?' he asks.

'Not really,' Ben replies.

'Are you feeling sick? Do you need to lie down?' Mum asks, with a look of concern.

'No, I'm fine, thanks,' Ben tells his mother.

'Don't you want the rest of your food then?' Dad asks.

'No, thanks.'

Immediately Dad reaches across the dining table and slides Ben's plate towards him.

'Chris, don't make yourself sick,' Mum tells him. 'I'm not going to let good food go to waste,' he replies. He digs his fork deep inside the mound of spaghetti and after rotating his fork a few times, he lifts the loaded fork up and into his opened mouth.

After dinner, Ben goes upstairs to his bedroom. He closes the door and sits down on the side of his bed feeling a little out of sorts for the moment. He can't understand why anybody hasn't told him about the trick they've been playing. *What's the point in playing a practical joke on someone and not revealing the joke afterwards; how can Dad eat three plates of food; he's never done that before.* Ben finds himself staring into space, not thinking of anything for a few seconds until his eyes fall onto the alarm clock by the side of his bed, which immediately makes him sit up and stare. Why does his clock say it's five forty-five? 'What's going on?' he asks himself. First they played a trick on him during dinner and now someone's gone into his room and changed the time on the clock. Why are they doing this? Ben's eyes quickly scan the room looking for other things that may have changed. Suddenly he spots the tube of glue next to his ship. 'You've got to be kidding,' he mutters. He walks over to the desk and picks up the nearly empty tube of glue and examines it. It looks exactly the same as it did an hour ago. He remembers finishing off the glue and dropping the empty tube into his wastepaper basket so he steps to the side of his desk and looks down at the empty basket. Ben slumps down into his desk chair and stares at the hull of the HMS *Victory* in front of him. His eyes search the hull of the ship for the pieces he glued on earlier. He knows he finished the back end of the hull. He knows it wasn't a huge section but he would swear blindly that he did it, so where's it gone? That whole section is missing. Ben rests his face in his hands feeling like something seriously wrong with him. His eyes start to glaze over and a tear starts to run down his cheek.

'Am I dying? Am I going mad?' he asks himself.

Chapter Four

Another tear makes its way down his cheek along the same path as the first. It reaches his jawline before falling onto the desk. Through his glaze-covered eyes, he sees the tiny splash of liquid impact on the wooden surface directly below him. Another tear begins to fall but this time he quickly wipes it away with the sleeve of his jumper. *There's got to be a simple answer to what I am seeing,* he reasons to himself. He rests his elbow on the desk and supports his cheek with his left hand. His eyes begin scanning the top of his desk, not for any particular reason as his mind is a total blank. He finds himself staring at the slightly different coloured wood grain on the top of the desk. He begins tracing the narrow strip along its length; sometimes the grain would run along a straight course then curve slightly before returning to its original course without any indication of its change of direction. Ben follows the dark line with his eyes to the far side of his desk before moving his gaze to a slightly paler grain next to it and returns his gaze along the line back towards his left elbow. Suddenly something springs to mind.

'Where's Granddad's piece of paper?' He sits up straight in his chair and stares at the top of the desk, searching for the folded piece of paper. *It's gone! I'm positive I left it there, right in the middle of the desk,* he tells himself. Ben slides the chair back and stands up. He stares at the top of the desk clearly seeing that the paper is nowhere to be seen. Ben crouches down and looks under the desk thinking that it might have fallen off the desk. The floor is void of anything after his cleaning spell so he walks around the desk and looks down the gap between the desk and the wall thinking it may have fallen over the back of the desk and is lodged in the gap. Still he doesn't see anything that resembles a piece of paper. Finally, having searched everywhere it may have been, Ben instinctively reaches inside his pocket and pulls out the contents. He looks down at the watch and folded paper resting on his palm and a spine-tingling chill washes over him. He knows the paper shouldn't be where he found it, so why was it back in his pocket when he definitely remembers leaving it on top of the desk. *Has this got anything to do with the secret Granddad mentioned in his letter?* he thinks. Ben places the watch down on top of the desk and unfolds the paper so he can read the message again. He begins reading every word slowly to allow the message to really sink into his mind. Suddenly the words *This watch is very valuable and holds a secret'* hit him like a thunderbolt. 'Holds a secret,' he says to himself feeling very excited. Ben senses his body starting to tremble at the thought of finding out a secret. The small piece of paper in front of him seems to be constantly moving forward and backwards as his right hand begins to shake. He finds it difficult just to focus on the wording because his eyes can't quite focus on the moving object. Ben quickly sits down in his chair to steady himself. He puts the paper down on the desk next to the watch and proceeds to take a deep breath to calm his excitement.

'Come on, Ben, calm down,' he tells himself.

He wipes his eyes with his hands so he can see clearly, and, with trembling hands, he picks up the bronze object. Knowing the watch may be connected to a secret is making him feel exhilarated and a little apprehensive at the same time. He wants to know what the secret is, but there's an uneasiness about the unknown which is making him feel a little anxious. *What if the secret is something scary? What if I don't like what I see? Can I change it? Would I be allowed to reverse whatever I find? Come on Ben, you need to know what the secret is before you can decide if you like it or not,* he tells himself.

Ben opens the cover to the timepiece and stares at the time displayed on its face. The long hand is on the ten and the small hand is between the five and the six. He looks over at his alarm clock, to see how the time compares; it's showing the same time.

'Okay, so the time still works,' he tells himself.

'What about the thin gold second hand?' He looks down at the face of the watch again and stares at the small gold second hand which is still pointing towards the nine. 'What does that mean? Why has the time changed but the gold hand hasn't?' Ben murmurs but his mind seems to be a total blank. Usually he can come up with something when presented with a conundrum but his brain is just not responding. Either his brain has suddenly decided to go to sleep or the problem is just too great for him to comprehend and to produce an answer. Ben decides it's no use trying to solve a puzzle when his brain has stopped working. What he really needs is a few minutes of solitude to gather his thoughts. He closes the cover on the watch and places it back inside his pocket. He pulls out the top drawer to his desk and deposits the paper inside before closing the drawer and walking over to his bed. His head is feeling a little light, so he lies down on the bed and closes his eyes. Ben tries to empty his mind of everything. In the darkness, he concentrates his mind on his breathing. His chest rises slightly as the air rushes in through his nose filling his lungs, his chest cavity drops and the air is thrust out through the small nostrils making a long soft gusting sound. Listening to his breathing has a calming effect and after a few minutes, Ben finds himself feeling very relaxed. He opens his eyes and looks up at the clear white blank ceiling above him. His soft pillow is wrapped around his head half covering his ears causing any external sounds to be dampened. He can vaguely make out a faint musical sound coming from downstairs. He assumes it must be from a TV programme his mother must be watching. Jess usually goes to her room about this time and Dad sometimes washes his car on the drive while it's still light. Ben starts to feel much better now that he had a moment to relax.

'Okay, let's think about this logically,' he tells himself. 'The time on the watch is the same as my alarm clock so that tells me that the watch is working. I moved the gold hand from the six to the nine and that's still at the nine. So why do the black hands move, but the gold one doesn't?' He remembers moving the black hands before he wound the watch up, but he moved the gold hand too. If the black hands tell the time, they would move anyway, so he doesn't need to concern himself with the black hands because they work. He just doesn't understand why the gold hand hasn't moved. Why did Granddad mention the word 'secret'? The watch must be more than a watch if it holds a secret. All he really knows is that time has changed and he doesn't know why.

'That's it!' Ben immediately sits up with his eyes wide open and his hands clasped over his mouth preventing himself from shouting. Suddenly everything starts to make sense: the gold hand is not a second hand as he originally thought; it must have something to do with altering time. Ben feels his heart start to race and all of a sudden he's feeling a little light-headed again from the thought that he may have in his possession a time machine.

'Calm down Ben,' he tells himself. He knows not to get too excited because he may well be jumping to conclusions and his watch may not be able to do anything but tell the time. 'Let's just think this through...' He remembers turning the gold hand anticlockwise from six to the nine which in real time is forty-five seconds if each mark on the outer rim represents seconds. What if the marks represent minutes? That would make it forty-five minutes.

'I don't believe it!' he excitedly calls out. It suddenly dawns on him that he may have turned time back, by forty-five minutes. That would explain everything. That's why he had dinner a second time and it would also explain why the glue was still in the tube and not in the waste bin. He must have jumped back in time by forty-five minutes before he worked on his ship.

Ben sits there in shock. The realisation that his granddad has given him this incredible gift is so unbelievable. Just thinking about it is so surreal. Who gives someone a time machine? This kind of thing is just too marvellous to comprehend. *'I've got a time machine!'*

Chapter Five

Ben turns his head to the side and looks at the time on his alarm clock. The digital display tells him that it's 6.25 p.m. He knows that every Saturday night at six thirty, they all watch a film on the TV as a family. Ben feels too excited to be watching a film but he also knows that this is something his family always does and it's going to be impossible for him to get out of it. He slides his feet off the side of the bed and stands up. His hand slips inside his pocket and his fingers feel the watch wrapped around its small chain. Just feeling the metal object gives him such a thrill. 'I've got a *time machine*!' he excitedly tells himself. 'What could I use it for?

'When would I need to know what happens in the future or why would I need to travel into the past?' Ben asks himself. He's never been in such a situation before and he's not really had much of an opportunity to think about it. Where could he go?

What if I travelled into the future to see myself as a world-famous inventor, or maybe I could go back in time to the birth of Christ or something. What if I travelled back in time and met up with the Wright brothers. I could give them a few hints on how to make a plane. I could become famous. I could be the first boy ever to fly. My name would be recorded in all the history books; I would be famous; I would be a legend in the aviation industry... Ben stops himself. *Wait a minute, maybe I'm getting ahead of myself. What if the watch doesn't work?* He hasn't actually tested it except for accidentally travelling back in time by forty-five minutes, what he needs to do is thoroughly test his time machine to make sure it really works. He knows he should test it again but when? He certainly doesn't want to travel back in time and be forced to eat another dinner, no, twice was definitely enough. So when should he test it? What about tonight? What if he waits until midnight when everyone's asleep, then he could test it without anyone knowing. He could travel back in time, say just for an hour and check the time on his watch to confirm that he actually did travel back; before travelling forward in time to his original time. That way, he would know for sure that it worked and no one else would be any the wiser. He gives himself a smile and agrees to follow through with his plan at midnight.

Ben decides that it would be a good idea to watch a film with his family just to take his mind off his time machine. He slowly goes downstairs to the lounge. His dad is already in his favourite armchair with his feet up on his padded footstool. Jess is in her usual spot on the far left of the sofa texting, someone on her phone, while Mum is busy in the kitchen doing something.

Ben goes over towards the sofa when his mum walks in from the kitchen carrying a tray with three drinks and a selection of snacks for everyone to nibble on while they're watching the film.

'Oh hi, Ben; are you feeling better?' Mum asks.

'Yes thanks.'

Ben sits down in his usual place on the right side of the sofa as far away from his sister as possible. Mum places the tray down on the coffee table. 'Do you want a glass of Coke, Ben, before we start the film?' Mum asks.

'Yes please.'

Mum goes back into the kitchen and returns moments later with a full glass of Coke and places it down alongside the other drinks before taking her seat between Jess and Ben. Dad presses the play button on the remote control to start the DVD.

'What film are we watching?' Ben asks.

'Don't worry son, I picked something I know you'll like.' Dad reaches for his drink and grabs a handful of peanuts before snuggling back into his armchair. Ben grabs a few peanuts and leans against the backrest to make himself comfortable just as the trailers at the beginning of the DVD finish and the main title to the film appears on the screen. *Back to the Future.*

'I don't believe it!' Ben says to himself.

Ben found it difficult to concentrate on the movie because there were just too many references to time travel. One moment he'd be watching Marty McFly crashing his DeLorean car into a barn and then the next scene, he'd see himself walk out wearing a space suit. It all felt so surreal.

What if he could travel back in time to 1955. He knows his dad wasn't alive then, but his granddad would have been. For a moment during the film, he did think of travelling back just to see his granddad as a young man, but then the thought occurred to him that he may not be able to recognise him because he can only ever remember him as an old man. Ben quickly put the ideas to the back of his mind when he noticed his dad giving him a funny stare; possibly because Ben was daydreaming and his facial expression must have been a picture.

After the film finished, Ben made his way up to his bedroom at nine o'clock which happens to be his normal bedtime. Each year their bedtimes would increase by ten minutes, that's why Jess is allowed to go to bed at twenty past nine because she's two years older. Dad told them that they don't have to go to sleep straight away so they can read if they want to, but they're not allowed to watch TV or play on their computers or phones as they need to allow their minds to relax. Ben picks up a book he's reading from his bedside cabinet called *The Adventures of Tom Sawyer* by Mark Twain. His dad recommended it and although he's already halfway through the book, he doesn't think his mind would be able to focus on this fictional character, when his real life seems to be so much more exciting. Ben puts the book back down where he got it. He gets undressed and visits the bathroom to brush his teeth before returning to his bedroom and closing the door. He hears his sister walking up the stairs stomping her feet as she usually does. The pounding steps clonk past his bedroom and straight into the bathroom; the bathroom door bangs closed and the lock on the door clangs shut. Ben gets onto his bed and places the watch on his bedside cabinet next to the alarm clock. He lies down on his bed on his left side so he can see the alarm clock. The digital display illuminates the time as 9.23 p.m. Ben rolls over onto his back and looks up at the ceiling. 'Two hours and thirty-seven minutes to go,' he quietly says to himself. He hates waiting for anything, so having to wait for another two hours and thirty-seven minutes is going to drag on and on. Ben closes his eyes and tries not to think of anything. He knows Jess will be coming out of the bathroom any second now, so he tunes his ear towards the door in the hope of hearing her stomp her way back to her bedroom. With his eyes shut he can faintly hear the sound of traffic way in the distance. Suddenly the sound tapers away and then he doesn't hear anything. After what appeared to be a few moments, Ben changes his position on the bed and rolls over onto his right side. He opens his eyes and immediately notices in the darkened room with the thin bands of light reaching in through the window blinds and stretching across the ceiling to the far side of his bedroom from the street lamp across the road. He can't understand how he'd not noticed those bands of light before. He rolls back over onto his back and turns his head to the side so he can look at the time: 2.19 a.m.

'What!' he calls out in surprise at seeing the time. He quickly sits up and slides his feet off the side of the bed so he's facing his bedside cabinet. Ben gives his eyes a quick rub to wipe away any sleep that may have collected over the past few hours before reaching across and picking up his watch.

Ben holds the bronze object in his left hand with its chain dangling down through his fingers and stares at the watch for a few seconds in the semi-darkened room, feeling a little apprehensive about what he's planning to do. Has this all been a dream? Has he been imagining it all? His mind hasn't fully awakened yet, so he's not sure what to think.

'Come on, Ben, get a grip,' he tells himself in the hope of building up his confidence. He decides it's now or never; he's got to test the watch out and the longer he waits the more anxious he'll get. He reaches over and turns his bedside lamp on so he can see what he's doing. Ben looks down at the watch and tentatively opens the cover with the nail on his right index finger. He wants to know everything that happens so he decides to talk his way through every process so the experience remains in his mind. He looks down at the watch face to check the time. 'Okay, the time on the watch is two nineteen,' he looks over at the time on his alarm clock. 'The time on my alarm clock is two nineteen. What about the gold hand?' he asks himself. He looks at the small gold hand on the watch and says to himself. 'The gold hand is still pointing at the nine. Okay, if I turn the gold hand back around to the nine again, that would mean I should travel back in time for just one hour.' He notices the time on the alarm clock moves forward one minute and is now displaying the time as two twenty. 'The time is now two twenty so I'll travel back in time to one twenty,' he tells himself. He immediately pulls the turner knob out one click and tentatively turns it slowly clockwise. His eyes are fixed on the gold hand as it starts to move anticlockwise from the nine to the eight, seven then six. He glances up at the alarm clock and sees the time change. 2.10 a.m., two a.m., 1.50 a.m. He keeps turning the adjuster knob until he sees the gold hand return back to the nine. He looks back at the alarm clock which is now displaying the time as 1.20 a.m. Ben notices something else has changed: he's no longer sitting on the bed but lying down and the room is back in semi-darkness. 'Wow, what just happened?' he asks himself. 'This is so weird.' Ben reaches across to his bedside lamp and switches it on, when he notices the watch resting on the bedside cabinet as it was an hour ago. 'That was amazing. I can't believe it! I've just travelled through time!' Ben throws back the duvet cover and sits up, he slides his feet over the side of the bed and begins thrusting his arms into the air while silently screaming *Yeahhhhhhhhhh!* in his victory celebration. This has got to be the best day of his life.   'I can time travel; I can travel through time; *I am the doctor,*' he tells himself feeling elated, knowing the watch works. He can't believe his luck; he's just a normal kid who's got this incredible power. Suddenly he starts to feel tired again so he decides to travel one hour back to the future. He gives himself a smile as he remembers the film he watched earlier with his family. Ben looks at his alarm clock and notes the time, now showing 1.21 a.m. He picks up the watch from the bedside cabinet and opens the cover, and sure enough the time on the clock face is now showing one twenty-one and the gold hand is still pointing to the nine. 'Okay, it's one twenty-one and I'm going forward in time one hour so the time will be two twenty-one,' he says. He pulls out the adjuster knob and turns it clockwise. Ben watches the gold hand turn around the watch face from the nine to the ten, then eleven and twelve. He glances up at the alarm clock which is now showing 1.22 a.m.

That's strange, Ben thinks as he notices that the time hasn't changed yet. He continues turning the adjuster until the gold hand is back at the nine before glancing back at the alarm clock: 1.22 a.m. Ben's ecstatic state suddenly plummets to a feeling of anxiety and an overwhelming desire to throw up.

'What's going on? Why hasn't it worked?' he asks himself, feeling quite nauseous. Ben stares at the alarm clock thinking the time will change any moment, but it doesn't; it still remains at 1.22 a.m. He wonders if the alarm clock has suddenly stopped working so he picks it up and gives it a shake to see if anything rattles inside the plastic case. There's no sound from inside the clock so he places it back down on the bedside cabinet and stares at the display wondering if the display has unexplainably stopped working. Thirty seconds or so later, the digital display changes to 1.23 a.m.

Ben immediately looks down at the watch face to see if the time had changed. The long hand is pointing between the four and the five, and the short hand is pointing just to the right of the one. He can't understand it, why hasn't the time changed; it should be two twenty-three now because he turned the gold hand all the way around as he did before; so why hasn't it worked? There has to be a logical explanation to why it worked and then it didn't, but what is it, what's the answer? Is the watch broken?

Just asking the question sends a chill of despair through his entire body. What if he has broken it? It was a gift from his granddad and not only that but it was a precious gift and he's ruined it. Granddad obviously thought Ben could be trusted with such a valuable gift and look! In just one day, he's broken it. Ben can't believe it. At times like this, Ben wishes he had an instruction manual or something to show him what he's done wrong, or at least point him in the right direction. Ben notices the minute hand move forward and suddenly a glimmer of hope appears before him. 'It still works. Okay so if it's still working, why didn't I travel forward in time?' Ben chews on his lip as he contemplates the answer. 'What if I can only use it once a day?' he asks himself. That would explain everything, but it would also mean that he'd have to wait twenty-four hours before he could use the watch again, which sucks. The only way to find out for sure is to do exactly what he did the first time; to see if that made a difference. He's not exactly sure if it's the right thing to do but what other options does he have, apart from waiting twenty-four hours. Ben slowly takes hold of the adjuster knob and begins turning it anticlockwise again as he did the first time and watches the gold hand begin its journey around the watch face moving from the nine to the eight, seven, six, five, four, three, two, one, twelve, eleven, ten, and then back to the nine. Ben tries to glance up at the alarm clock from his seated position on the side of the bed when the sensation of something soft is pressing against his cheek and he finds himself no longer sitting up but lying down under his duvet and the room is back in semi-darkness as it was not long ago. Ben closes his eyes for a moment while the stress from thinking he'd broken the watch drains from his body leaving him in a calm and relaxed state of well-being, knowing the watch is still working. He opens his eyes and throws back the duvet before reaching over and turning the bedside lamp back on. The alarm clock displays the time as 12.23 a.m., which proves that he travelled back in time by one hour. Ben picks up his watch and holds it tightly to his chest as you would with a prized possession. 'Thank you Granddad,' he murmurs while thinking how truly valuable and precious this watch really is; immediately he recalls the words describing the watch in the letter from his granddad, which said the watch was a precious gift. Only now does he truly understand those words. Ben looks at the time on his alarm clock and the sudden realisation of something important dawns on him.

'Poo! That means I can't go forward in time; I can only travel backwards.'

Chapter Six

Through his closed eyelids, Ben notices a bright light in the room. It must be morning but he's still feeling so tired. He's finding it hard to open his eyelids so he gives his eyes a rub with his hands and through squinted eyes he peers out at the bright light streaming in through his window blinds. He uses his hand to screen out the light while he looks towards the alarm clock and sees the time displayed as 8.25 a.m.

'Oh, great, it's morning,' he tells himself. He can't understand why he's still feeling so tired because he usually gets up around this time in the morning. He expels out a large yawn and stretches his arms out to the sides to awaken his muscles from being in the same position for hours when he remembers the extra two hours of sleep he'd enjoyed. 'Wow that means I've slept for... ' his unresponsive brain struggles to calculate the length of time immediately but he eventually reaches the result. 'Thirteen hours, I don't think I've ever slept that long before,' he'd heard people say that you can have too much sleep, but he'd never truly understood what they were implying until now. Having experienced it first-hand has definitely helped him understand the lethargic state he was now in. Ben gives another yawn before throwing back the duvet and sliding his feet off the side of his bed. He stands up and goes into the bathroom to use the toilet and to have a quick wash. He doesn't usually wash in cold water but this morning he thinks he needs that added shock treatment to wake himself up. Ben cups his hands under the cold tap until his hands are full with the cold water and then bends his head towards his hands above the sink and douses his face into his hands. The sudden shock from the cold water covering his face really brings his senses back to life. He lifts his head up and breathes in a deep breath and stares at his revived expression in the bathroom mirror. 'Wow I'm never going to do that again'

He quickly uses the hand towel next to the sink to dry his face before picking up his toothbrush and after loading it with toothpaste, he proceeds to brush his teeth for the recommended two minutes. Ben wanders back into his bedroom and begins to get dressed in his usual jeans and tee shirt which he conscientiously placed over the back of his chair, having tidied up his room yesterday. As he sits in the chair and bends down to do his laces up on his trainers. He suddenly remembers that it's Sunday and his best friend, Paul Hale, has invited him over to play at Paul's house.

Last year Paul's family moved into the area and Paul at the start of the school year began attending the same school as Ben. He remembers seeing Paul for the first time after the first week of term, at the beginning of his English class. Miss Jones introduced Paul to the whole class and told everyone that he'd just moved into the area, so they should all help him get settled in. Nobody likes the idea of sitting next to the new kid because he may well turn out to be a total loser and having a loser sit next to you for the whole year would be a real bummer. Miss Jones looked around the classroom for somewhere to seat Paul when her eyes fell on the only spare seat available which happens to be the desk next to Ben. Ben's shocked expression must have said it all because Paul never once looked at him as he made his way from the front of the classroom past two rows of desks to the vacant seat next to Ben. Miss Jones apologised to Paul because she had an English test planned for the class that day and she felt sorry that Paul had been thrown into the deep end.

'Don't worry, just try your best,' Ben remembers Miss Jones telling Paul. To everyone's surprise, Paul scored a whopping ninety-nine percent in the test. Everyone in the class couldn't believe it when the scores were announced the following week. Ben thought Paul may have actually scored one hundred percent but Miss refused to give him that perfect score because she wanted him to try harder next time. When Miss handed Ben his paper with the score of thirty-seven percent clearly marked on the top, Paul must have noticed, because shortly after class had finished, Paul approached Ben and offered to give him additional help if he wanted it. Ben couldn't believe a fellow student would take the time to help another pupil. The following day, Paul arranged to meet up with Ben in the school classroom allocated for students wanting to do extra work assignments during the lunch break. It was that day that they became best of friends.

Ben quickly ties his laces and excitedly goes downstairs to remind his parents that he's been invited round to Paul's house. He knows he can't tell his family about the watch as they'd take it from him, but he most definitely can tell his best friend when he sees him. Ben rushes into the dining room.

'Mum, Mum! Paul's asked me to go round his this morning.' Ben reminds his mother that he needs a lift. Ben's mum tells him not to run in the house because it's a sure way to have an accident and hurt someone, implying herself. Ben apologises for running and asks his mum if she'll drop him round at Paul's house as he's expecting him. Mum tells Ben to have some breakfast first and that she'll give Paul's mum Linda a ring to confirm that it's still okay. Ben reluctantly takes a seat at the table and proceeds to fill his cereal bowl with cornflakes. He looks over at his mother who's now talking to Linda on the telephone. Ben quickly covers the cornflakes with semi-skimmed milk that's next to the cornflakes box and begins shovelling the breakfast into his mouth and chewing his food as fast as he can. Mum hangs up the phone and notices how quickly Ben's eating his breakfast; tells him off for rushing. Ben slows down a little so as not to appear to be in a rush. He does however load up his spoon with the golden flakes so that he's eating more with every spoonful. The front door opens and Ben sees his dad walk in looking a little puzzled.

'Darling, have you seen my golf shoes?' he asks. 'Yes, they're leaning against the back door.' Dad walks through the dining room to the kitchen door and asks Mum as she's washing up. 'Why are my shoes outside the back door?'

Without stopping, Mum replies, 'Remember last week when you got home from golf, your shoes were caked in mud so you hosed them down in the back garden.'

Dad must have remembered because he sheepishly goes out through the back door and picks up his damp shoes because it had rained in the night.

'Honey, as you're off to the golf course, could you drop Ben off at Paul's house?' Mum asks.

'Sure, but I won't be able to collect him because we're all having something to eat at the clubhouse after the game.'

'That's all right; Linda said Ben can stay for lunch so we won't need to pick him up until much later.'

Dad nods, then takes a plastic bag from the kitchen cupboard and places his damp shoes inside it.

'Okay, have you finished your breakfast?' Dad asks. Ben quickly spoons into his mouth the last of his cereal and rushes the empty cereal bowl and spoon through to Mum, who's still standing at the kitchen sink. Dad walks out the front door and puts his golf shoes in the footwell behind the driver's seat and gets in behind the wheel. Ben opens the front passenger door and gets in. He gives his mum a quick wave before closing the car door and strapping his seatbelt around him. Dad waves to Mum and after putting the car in gear, reverses off the drive and pulls away in the direction of Paul's house.

Ten minutes later, Dad pulls up outside Paul's house and they get out and walk towards the front door. Linda and Paul, having seen them arrive, open the door before they even have time to knock.

Linda's very petite in size; she's kind of a miniature version of Ben's mum but with blonde hair. Seeing them in the doorway, a passing stranger may think they were brother and sister instead of mother and son.

'Hi, is it all right if I collect Ben around three o'clock; sorry to ask, it's just that I'm playing golf and you know how golf games can run a little longer than expected?' Dad says to Linda.

'No problem,' Linda replies.

'That's great, thank you; I'll see you later,' Dad tells Ben before holding his right hand up in front of him so Ben can give him a high five. Ben smacks his right hand against his dad's as his father walks past him and gets back inside his car. He closes the door and quickly drives away down the long narrow street to the end, when he turns left. They all wave until he's out of sight. 'You won't believe what I'm going to tell you,' Ben quickly tells Paul, sounding all excited.

'Okay boys, come back inside,' Paul's mom says. Paul and Ben walk in through the front door and then into the lounge. Linda closes the front door and follows them.

'So, Ben, did you want anything to drink before you both dash upstairs; we have Coke, lemonade or orange juice?'

'Coke please, Mrs Hale.'

'Can I have some as well Mum?' Paul adds.

'Of course you can; I'll just fetch it for you,' Linda says and heads for the kitchen. Paul waits until his mum's out of sight before he asks.

'So what am I not going to believe?' he asks, sounding intrigued.

Ben leans forward towards Paul and with his voice just above a whisper, tells him, 'I can travel through time!' Ben leans back and fixes his eyes on Paul's face in anticipation at seeing his face change to one of astonishment.

Paul's blank expression remains the same as he asks, 'What do you mean, travel through time?'

'You know, time travel; I can travel back in time,' Ben tells him with a slightly raised voice.

'Okay… I've got a new racing game for my PS4. Did you want to play, we could race each other?' Paul asks.

Ben spots Paul's mom coming back towards them holding a tray with two glasses of Coke and a side plate with two cupcakes on it. She stops next to Ben and lowers the tray.

'Here you are; help yourselves to a cake as well.' Ben picks up one of the sponge cupcakes decorated with white swirled icing alongside one of the glasses of Coke. Linda turns to face Paul and he does the same.

'Thanks Mum.'

'Yes, thanks Mrs Hale.'

'You're welcome,' she says with a smile before turning around and slowly walks towards the kitchen carrying the tray by her side. Paul takes a sip from his glass of coke so as not to spill it before slowly making his way upstairs. Ben looks at the cream stair carpet and seeing how full his glass is, decides to do the same. He takes a large swig from his glass, reducing the volume by a third. It's quite warm in the house so the cold, sweet liquid is really refreshing. Ben sees Paul nearing the top of the stairs so he steadily begins his journey up the flight of steps while keeping his eyes fixed on the glass of Coke in his hand. Paul's bedroom is immediately to the left of the landing so by the time Ben reaches the top of the stairs; Paul has already disappeared inside his bedroom. Fortunately, the bedroom door is wide open to allow Ben to carry his cake and drink through without having to contend with turning a door handle to do it. Ben steps inside Paul's bedroom which is a similar size to his own and immediately notices Paul crouching down next to his twenty-one-inch TV screen centrally positioned on his IKEA multimedia wall unit. The wall unit has a base cabinet with three eighteen-inch doors where you can store all your games and anything else you want to hide inside. The shelving units above, have a large space in the centre for a TV to fit with shelving units on either side for any other electrical equipment. Paul has his PlayStation PS4 game console and controllers in one section to the left of the TV. On the right he's stored all his CDs next to a small digital radio and CD player with small speakers above. The rest of the shelving space is basically filled with books and toys.

Paul turns around and holds up a computer game case with the words "Rally Cross" written across the front.

'This is so cool, you'll love it.' Paul says, sounding all excited. Ben puts his drink and cake down on top of the chest of drawers just to his left and looks back at Paul. 'Paul, I'm serious; I can travel through time,' he tells him.

'No one can travel through time; it's impossible,' Paul quickly replies.

'It's not; I did it yesterday and again last night; *twice.*' Ben emphasises the word so Paul will know that he's deadly serious. Paul lowers the Rally Cross game down onto his lap and stares at the floor for a few seconds as he analyses the information Ben had just told him.

He asks, 'Why do you think you can travel through time?'

'Remember I told you that my granddad died.'

'Yes,' Paul replies and wonders where this conversation is going.

'Well, we all had to go round to his house and take out everything that was valuable.'

'Okay, I'm listening,' Paul says.

Ben tells Paul all about finding the brown envelope with the watch and the message telling him about the secret. He explains how he accidentally travelled back in time and hadn't realised it. It was only after seeing everything that happened at the dinner table re-enact itself exactly as it did an hour earlier when he realised that he must have travelled back in time. Paul doesn't say a word, his eyes appear to be wider and his mouth is slightly open as he listens to Ben. Ben finally tells him about waiting until two in the morning to test out his theory and how he checked the time on his watch with the time on his alarm clock before going back in time not just once but twice. Paul continues to stare at Ben without saying a word.

'Paul, what do you think?' Ben asks.

'I... .I'm not sure; where's the watch now?' he asks. Ben reaches inside his pocket and pulls out the time piece. He offers it to Paul who's staring at it as though it's contagious or something.

'It's all right, you can look at it.' Ben offers. Paul stands up and tentatively takes the watch. He turns the watch over so that he can examine the outer casing.

'It looks old; does it really work?' he asks. Ben takes the watch from him and opens the case and shows him the watch face.

'The black hands tell the time and see that gold hand at the back; that's the hand that turns back time,' Ben explains. Paul leans forward and stares at the hands.

'I'll show you if you want?' Ben offers. Paul immediately looks up into Ben's eyes and his facial expression changes to one of trepidation and foreboding. 'O... kay... show me,' Paul says hesitantly.

Ben keeps the watch flat on his left palm while taking hold of the adjuster with his right finger and thumb so Paul can see what he's doing.

'I'm just going to turn it back five minutes, just so you can see that it works,' Ben tells him. Paul stares at the watch half expecting the watch to glow and emit flashing rays of light. Ben slowly rotates the adjuster and they watch as the gold hand moves from the nine to the eight.

Chapter Seven

Suddenly the surroundings change and Ben finds himself standing outside Paul's house waving as his dad drives away along the narrow street to the end then disappearing out of sight as he turns left. It feels really strange that one second he was in Paul's bedroom in subdued lighting and now outside staring at a bright sun shining into his eyes. Ben looks down at his hand still imagining that the watch would still be there, only to find that it's still in his pocket.

'Okay boys, come back inside,' Paul's mum tells them so Paul and Ben walk in through the front door and then into the lounge. Linda closes the front door and follows them.

'So, Ben, did you want anything to drink before you both dash upstairs; we have Coke, lemonade or orange juice?'

'Coke please, Mrs Hale.'

'Can I have some as well Mum?' Paul adds.

'Of course you can; I'll just fetch it for you.' Linda wanders through to the kitchen. Ben waits until he knows Linda's out of earshot before he turns to Paul and says, 'I told you it worked.'

'You told me what worked?' Paul asks, not quite following. Ben looks at Paul expectantly and says, 'T… h… e… *time travel*!'

Paul, now looking totally confused, asks, 'What do you mean, time travel?'

'You know, what I showed you five minutes ago?' 'What, when you arrived with your dad?' Paul asks.

Ben stares at Paul feeling like the conversation they're having is a little disjointed. *Why has Paul suddenly forgotten what they did just moments ago?* Ben thinks. *Surely he should remember; I told him that I was going to travel back in time and…* '

As Ben tries to analyse why Paul can't remember what he told him five minutes into the future, it all becomes clear. He told Paul about the time travel and then travelled back in time before he told him so it's logical that he wouldn't remember, because in his reality, Ben hasn't told him yet.

Arghhhhhhhh, Ben thinks.

'What about time travel?' Paul asks again.

Ben decides it's pointless to bring up a subject that he can't explain.

'Oh nothing, I was just thinking how cool it would be if we could travel through time, that's all.'

'I guess so; so, do you want to play my new game?' Paul asks.

'What, you've got a new game?' Ben asks while trying to sound interested.

'Yes, and I bet you'll never guess what it is!'

Ben gives Paul a smile and says, 'You haven't got Rally Cross have you?'

'*What!* I don't believe it; how did you know? I only bought the game last night and I haven't told anyone,' Paul exclaims.

'That's all right, it was just a guess.'

Linda returns from the kitchen carrying a tray with two glasses of Coke and two cupcakes. After helping themselves to a drink and a cake, Ben and Paul go upstairs to Paul's bedroom. They play on Paul's new game for the next hour or so before Linda calls them down for lunch at twelve o'clock.

'So how have you been, has Paul showed you his new game?' Linda asks.

'Yes, it's really good,' Ben tells Linda.

'So, who's winning?' Linda asks.

'Erm... .. I think it's a draw at the moment.' Paul tells his mum while trying to be diplomatic because he knows he's won the most games but doesn't want to embarrass his friend in front of his mum. Linda smiles at the two boys and for the next few minutes they eat their lunch in silence. The sun is shining so they decide to play in the back garden for a while. Paul has a five-a-side football net at one end of the garden next to the fence so they take turns in being in goal while the other person tries to score. Forty minutes later, they decide to return to the bedroom and play on Rally Cross for the last hour or so before Ben gets picked up by his father. Dad pulls up outside Paul's house in his car exactly at three fifteen and after thanking Linda and Paul for having him over, Ben gets into the front passenger seat and his dad sets off for home.

Ben sits quietly in the passenger seat and thinks about how he travelled back in time at Paul's house and how Paul didn't remember a thing about it. What is he going to do about proving to his best friend that he can travel through time? How is he ever going to convince Paul that he has a time machine when he's already tried to, and failed? It's so frustrating; he's got the best present in the world and can't show it off to anyone. What's the point? he thinks.

'Did you have a nice time at Paul's?' Dad asks. 'Sure.'

'Is everything all right?' he asks, sensing that Ben's not quite his enthusiastic self.

'Yes, just thinking about stuff, that's all,' Ben replies, sounding angry and frustrated. Dad senses that his son's not in a talkative mood so he doesn't ask any more questions for the rest of the journey. Dad drives the car onto their driveway and turns the engine off.

'Hi, we're home,' Dad calls out to Mum. Ben goes straight upstairs to his bedroom and shuts the door behind him.

Chapter Eight

Mum drops Jess and Ben off outside school before continuing on into town to pick up a few food items they're running low on. Jess meets up with a couple of her girlfriends while Ben hangs around the school playground until Paul arrives. Paul's very short for his age which makes him instantly recognisable with his red hair and round-rimmed glasses. Ben did think it may have been one of those distinguishable features that first attracted the attention from the school bully, Tony Vernall. It wasn't long after Paul started to attend Harrogate High School and probably a week after they had become friends that Tony first picked on Paul. Ben remembers seeing Paul upset one morning during their first break of the day. Ben had gone indoors to use the toilet and when he returned to the playground, Paul was visibly upset. Ben asked him if he was all right but his response was a shrug of his shoulders and mumbled, 'Yeah.'
Ben knew something was wrong but as they hadn't been friends for long, he didn't exactly know if something had happened or if it was a mood swing or something that Paul may suffer from.

After school when they were waiting for their parents to pick them up, Paul eventually told Ben what had happened. He explained that yesterday Tony had asked Paul to do his English homework for him every week, but Paul refused. So that morning during their break time, after Ben had gone indoors to use the toilets, Tony and his friends – Simon Dicks, Brian Philips and Andrew Woodhouse – surrounded him near the entrance to the dining hall. They had purposely waited until Ben was indoors before they surrounded Paul. He explained how they were first calling him names and prodding him from all sides. He told Ben that he tried to break free, but they just pushed him up against the wall and held him there while Tony punched him in the stomach. Paul thought about reporting them to Miss Clarke but they told him that if he said anything, he would get severely beaten up.

Ben put his arm around his friend and told him that it's going to be all right.

Ben's not the toughest boy in school, nor does he have a reputation for being the best fighter in school; actually, he's never had a fight in his life. He is however the same height as Tony which seems to make a difference because all the boys Ben had heard have been picked on by Tony, have all been much shorter in height. There may be another reason why Tony hasn't tried to pick a fight with Ben. He may have heard that Ben goes to Karate classes once a week and is now the proud owner of a brown belt for which he's really pleased about. It's taken Ben over two years to rise up the ranks in his karate club, starting at the bottom of the pile wearing a beginners white belt, then gradually moving up to yellow, green, blue then brown, before the final accolade of reaching black which he hopes to achieve within the next year. He took up the sport because his dad told him to, he said it was a good way to keep fit and that one day it might come in handy if he ever got into a fight. He thinks his dad was speaking from experience because of previous conversations his dad has had with his mum.

Ben takes a seat on a wooden balance beam in the play area and looks over towards the school entrance across the playground for Paul to arrive. Within a few minutes Paul walks in through the main entrance gate and stops to see where Ben is. The playground is crowded with learners milling around in the large fifty-metre concrete square communal area between them, so it's difficult for Paul to see Ben seated over the far side of the playground. Ben stands up and waves to try to catch his friend's attention but Paul is now looking in the opposite direction. Ben lowers his arm until he can see Paul look his way when he spots Tony and Simon walk in through the main entrance behind Paul.

'Paul!' Ben shouts to warn his friend but it's too late. Tony shoves Paul hard in the back, sending him flying forward. Paul's legs seem to sprint forward to catch the ground before buckling under him as the weight from his rucksack forces his arched body down towards the hard concrete path. Ben immediately sprints towards his injured friend and calls his name to alert Tony that help is on the way. Tony looks over and notices Ben running across the playground towards him. Tony immediately heads off towards the school entrance and disappears inside. Ben reaches Paul who's now sat up on the path holding his left knee. His rucksack is next to him with half the contents sprawled out across the ground.

'Are you all right?' Ben asks his friend, concerned.

'One of these days, I'm going to get him back,' Paul says as he slowly gets to his feet. Ben crouches down and begins putting Paul's books back inside his rucksack when he notices the tear on Paul's trousers just below his left knee and sees a faint trace of blood on the fabric.

'Your knee's bleeding, and your trouser leg's ripped,' Ben tells his friend. Paul bends forward and looks at the tear in the dark-blue fabric and with his fingers he widens the two-inch gap to inspect his injury. 'It's all right, it's just grazed, but Mum's not going to be happy when she sees my pants,' Paul tells Ben as he stands up shaking his head. Ben holds out Paul's rucksack for him which he takes and swings the bag up onto his back. They turn towards the main entrance just as the school bell starts to ring, sounding the start of class. They go into the school building and head to their classroom. Ben feels a little annoyed with himself that he wasn't there for his friend and has noticed that the attacks on Paul seem to be increasing. What should he do; should he confront Tony during their lunch break and threaten him to stop picking on his friend.

The problem with doing that would be getting Tony alone. At the moment, he seems to be always with his so-called buddies and to be honest, the thought of confronting four of them seems a little bit daunting and bordering on suicidal.

Ben's first lesson that morning was geography and he found it extremely difficult to concentrate on glacier formations and how the shifting ice transforms the landscape because Tony was sitting to his far left on a desk by the window and he felt convinced that he was staring at him. What's he up to? Is he thinking about challenging him to a fight or is he just planning his next attack on Paul in the hope that Ben would step in and they'd eventually end up fighting each other, he wonders. Ben hears the school bell indicating the end of class. He places his geography book back inside his rucksack and casually looks across at Tony, who's now making his way towards the opened classroom door. Tony gives Ben one of his condescending sneers before disappearing out of the classroom. Ben knows something is about to kick off soon with Tony Vernall but as he's got no idea what's going on in Tony's mind, he decides to push any thoughts of him to the back of his mind for the time being. Ben excitedly goes to the science building for his next class because Paul will be there and they usually have a lot of fun in biology.

Mr Thompson tells everyone to settle down and take their seats. Ben and Paul go over to the far side of the classroom and take their seats on two metal legged stools on the far side of a stainless-steel table tucked in the far right-hand corner of the classroom. The noise in the class eventually subsides as all the pupils take their seats and look towards Mr Thompson.

'Good morning class. This morning we've got a practical lesson which I'm sure you'll all enjoy.' He gives everyone a smile. 'Who can remember what we discussed last lesson?'

Brian Taylor quickly raises his hand. 'Yes, Brian?'

'We looked at the anatomy of a frog, sir.'

'Well done Brian, so what do you think we'll be doing this morning?' Mr Thompson asks.

Sally Dickens raises her hand immediately in front of Sir.

'Yes, Sally?' 'Are we going to look at a real… frog, sir?' Sally tentatively asks with her hand partially covering her mouth as though the idea of looking at a real frog would be abhorrent. Mr Thompson smiles at Sally, knowing what he's about to say next is probably going to get a shocked reaction from some of the girls.

'We're not just going to *look* at a real frog, but we're going to *dissect* a real frog.'

'Yuck!' Sally immediately replies, feeling totally repulsed by the whole idea and her protests are quickly added to by a few other students echoing their distaste at the thought. Mr Thompson smiles at the class and turns towards the large refrigerator behind his desk.

'I want everyone to form into groups of four for this lesson,' he instructs the class as he opens the large refrigerator door. Half the class stand up and drag their seats to another table next to them as they organise themselves into groups with four to each table. Paul and Ben remain in their seats as they're already tucked in the corner and can't exactly go anywhere. Susan Mills and Alexis King, who were sitting on the table in front of them, drag their metal stool chairs towards their table and sit facing Ben and Paul, to Ben's utter surprise and shock.

Ben's heart begins to race when he sees Alexis sitting opposite not two feet away. Ben's had a crush on Alexis for just over a year now, ever since he first caught sight of her at the beginning of school last year. You could say it was love at first sight for Ben although Alexis has no idea of his interest because he feels too shy even to acknowledge her. He's all right around other people and doesn't have a problem speaking to them; it's just Alexis. Ben considers her to be the most beautiful girl in the world and well out of his league even to speak to.

'Why would she even want to talk to me?' Ben would occasionally ask himself, only to realise that she wouldn't really, because he's a nobody and has no appealing qualities from what he can tell.

'Hello,' the two girls say as they take their seats. 'Hi,' Paul replies and gives the girls a smile. Ben glances over towards Susan and says, 'Hi' before quickly looking back towards Mr Thompson at the front of class so he doesn't make eye contact with Alexis. He knows if he looks at Alexis, she'll see right through him and immediately discern his infatuation for her. Ben can feel his heart pounding in his chest and his cheeks begin to feel warm so he makes a conscious effort to stare at Mr Thompson in the hope that his body will calm down and his heart and face will return back to normal. Mr Thompson goes around the classroom depositing a dead frog on a small dissecting platter in the centre of each table of four children before making his way back to the front of class. The four of them look down at the green-and-brown lifeless frog, flat on its back next to a small scalpel and a set of tweezers. 'Children, I want you to choose one person in your groups to make the first incision. Don't worry, you'll all have an opportunity to get your hands dirty but for now we're just going to open up the frog's chest cavity and pin back the flesh so we can take a look inside,' Mr Thompson informs the class. Alexis whispers something to Susan and she nods in agreement.

'Ben, why don't you make the first cut?' Alexis suggests while looking over in his direction. Hearing Alexis say his name sends his heart into a state of euphoria. Ben glances up and his eyes lock on to Alexis brown eyes looking right back at him. The girl of his dreams is staring right at him and in that moment, his mind goes a complete blank. He finds himself staring deep into Alexis's eyes and for the next few seconds, he's lost in time. Everything around him fades into obscurity. Ben finds himself alone with the prettiest girl in the universe and grinning from ear to ear.

'Ben, Ben!' the sound of Paul's voice breaks through Ben's utopic world and he suddenly realises where he is. Immediately he feels his face start to turn red again and beads of sweat start to run down the back of his neck. Ben quickly turns to his friend to save him. Paul realises what's happening so he reaches over to the scalpel and picks it up. 'I'll do it.' Ben looks down at the dead frog on the table and fixes his gaze at the lifeless form so he doesn't have to make eye contact with Alexis. For the next thirty-five minutes, Ben tries to remain in Paul's shadow.

Chapter Nine

'She thinks I'm an idiot, doesn't she?' Ben asks Paul during their morning break.

'No, I don't think so, I think she just thinks you're shy, that's all.'

'I should have said something; I've waited all year to talk to her and now I've blown it. I'll never get another opportunity to talk to her!' Ben tells his friend as they sit down on a balance beam in the playing field.

'Not necessarily; it just so happens that I've got a plan,' Paul says.

'A plan? What do you mean you've got a plan?' 'Remember the headmistress telling us about an Inter-School Competition next Friday?' 'What, Miss Clarke? I don't remember that.'

'Because you were staring at Alexis all through assembly, that's why.'

'I wasn't!'

'You were! I saw you; anyway, every year all the schools in the district submit a team of six students to represent their school from years eight and nine, to find out which school has the best students.' Paul explains. 'Okay, so what's this plan?'

'I heard Alexis telling Susan that she's put her name down for the team. So, if you put your name down as well, you'll have plenty of opportunities to talk to her,' Paul says and gives Ben a huge smile while he waits for some praise for his wonderful idea.

'Oh great, that's the dumbest plan I've ever heard,' Ben says, shaking his head. Paul leans back in shock 'What do you mean? It's a great idea! You'll be with Alexis and four others and you'll have team talks and strategy meetings, etcetera. So, there'll be lots of opportunities to talk to her.'

'The problem with your plan is simply this: I'm not clever enough and everyone will find out when I'm asked a question,' Ben explains.

'I don't think they'll ask a specific question to an individual, they normally ask a question to the whole team and the one who knows the answer presses their buzzer and answers,' Paul replies.

'So, you're suggesting that I just sit there for the whole competition and not say a word, while everyone else answers? They'll soon work it out that I don't know anything and then Alexis will never talk to me again.' Paul suddenly realises his mistake.

'You might be right, I just thought, you know…' Paul looks down at his feet, feeling that he'd just let his friend down.

Ben knows Paul was just trying to help and to be honest, the idea was quite good. If Ben was intelligent and one of the top students at school it would be no problem, but he's not.

Ben pulls his watch from his pocket to check the time when an idea pops into his head. He thinks, *I don't need to be clever; I just need to be smarter. What if I knew the answers? In fact, what if I knew the questions before they're asked? I could be the first to press my buzzer and give the right answer and everyone will think I'm a genius!*

'Paul, I've changed my mind. I think I'm going to put my name down for the team,' Ben tells his friend. Paul looks up at Ben rather confused at having just been told that the idea was the dumbest he'd ever heard and now having Ben change his mind and decide to do it. 'Why the sudden change? I thought you said it was a bad idea, and that you don't know anything,' Paul asks.

Ben gives his friend a smile and says, 'That was before, but I have a plan.' Ben gives Paul a smile and a wink before asking, 'So where do I enter?'

Paul takes Ben back inside the school building via the side entrance and heads for the main reception. They reach the small lobby next to the main entrance doors and stop in front of the large noticeboard next to the glass reception desk. They scan the multitude of notices pinned to the board, searching for one advertising the Inter-School Competition. Ben's eyes scan the left-hand side while Paul looks at the right-hand side of the board. Their focus jumps from one A4 and A5 sized notices to another, just catching sight of the main titles advertising book clubs, planned school trips, library opening times and everything else pertaining to school.

'Found it,' Paul says while pointing to an A4 sized poster with the words *Inter-School Competition* at the top with each individual letter coloured a different colour making it stand out like a rainbow. Ben begins to read the entry information at the top of the page.

We are proud to announce the upcoming Inter-School Competition which will be held at Harrogate High School this Friday, the 11th of October in the auditorium at seven p.m. All those interested in representing our school as part of our Elite student team; please add your names to the entrants list below. The best six students from years 8 and 9 will be selected from the list of entrants.'

Ben looks down the list of names already entered for year 8:

Philip Matthews

Avalon Vernall

Alexis King

Andrew Perkins

Simon McDonald

Ben picks up the pen dangling from a piece of string attached to the noticeboard and writes his name at the bottom of the list. He lets go of the pen and looks at his friend.

'If anyone else puts their name on the list; I'm not going to be selected,' he tells Paul. Paul looks around to see if anyone's watching.

'Don't worry, nobody is going to.'

He takes hold of the notice and folds the paper just below the sixth entry position and tears off the bottom of the page. Paul nonchalantly folds the bit of paper into quarters and slips it inside his pocket. Ben stares at the young girl behind the reception window with her back towards them, hoping that she doesn't turn around and see them. Paul gives Ben a wink and pats him on the shoulder to indicate that they should get a move on. They quickly walk down the corridor away from reception and dash out through the side entrance back into the playground.

After lunch Ben invites Paul to take a walk with him around the school sports field. They don't usually go for a walk at lunchtime around the school playing field so Paul's a little intrigued as to why Ben had asked him. They slowly walk to the security fence at the far-right side of the playing area and follow the fence line to the furthest corner on the sports field, just behind a maple   tree. They stop just out of view from other children on the other side of the tree.

'Paul I know this is going to sound weird but what I'm about to tell you is the honest truth and I'll prove it   to you,' Ben says, looking serious.

'Okay… this… is a bit weird,' Paul nervously says. 'Don't worry, it's nothing horrible, it's just that I wanted to explain something. I expect you're wondering why I decided to join the Inter-School Competition after I told you that it was a dumb idea?' Ben asks.

'Yes, I did wonder why you changed your mind.' 'Now this is the bit that's going to sound weird: I can travel through time.'

Paul stares at Ben for a second, waiting for a punchline, but when it doesn't arrive he says while shaking his head, 'You can't.'

Ben looks at Paul's disbelieving face and realises that it's going to take a more detailed explanation to convince him.

'I can and I'll prove it.'

'Okay, prove it,' Paul says and stands back to give his friend room to do something spectacular.

'Let me just explain something first,' Ben says. He tells Paul how he was given the watch by his granddad, and how he accidentally travelled back in time and had to eat two dinners. He explains how he'd travelled back in time in the middle of the night and just so he knew for sure that it worked; he made a note of the time.

Paul doesn't say a word; he just listens intently as Ben continues to explain how he'd travelled back in time at Paul's house the other day after explaining what he was about to do to Paul. He explains why Paul can't remember any of it because he travelled back in time to a point before he told Paul.

'So, you're saying you've travelled a couple of times already?' Paul asks.

'Yes, now listen. This time I'm going to time travel during our history class this afternoon and you'll know because I'm going to answer every question Miss Havelock asks the class.'

'But you're rubbish at history'

'Exactly! I'm going to let someone in class answer the question correctly, then I'm going to jump back in time so when Miss asks the question, I'll know it and answer it before anyone else does,' Ben explains.

Paul slowly contemplates what he's just been told for a few seconds before asking, 'Can you really do that?'

'Yes. I can jump back in time one minute or ten minutes or even longer if I want. I'll just jump back to a time just before Miss Havelock asks the question and then put my hand up and answer it.'

'Wouldn't everyone see you reappear like in *Star Trek* when they teleport?'

'No. I'm not teleporting; I'm just moving back in time. Anyway, don't worry about it. You won't notice anything; all you'll see is me getting every question right.'

'Wow, I can't wait,' Paul says looking all excited. They slowly walk back towards the school playground to join the other children when Ben becomes perturbed by the fact that he's told his friend. Not only that, but he's noticed that Paul hasn't stopped grinning for the past few minutes and looking at him as though he's some kind of superhero. Fortunately, the school bell begins ringing to indicate the start of class so they go into Miss Havelock's history class and take their seats on the third row from the front. Ben casually glances over at Paul sitting two places over to his right and immediately sees him smiling back at him. Ben holds his hand up in a cursory wave before pointing to the front of class, so Paul knows class is about to start. Miss Havelock closes the classroom door as the last pupil enters the room.

'Right children settle down and take your seats,' Miss Havelock says to those not already seated. Within a few seconds all those standing go to their desks and sit down. Miss Havelock walks around to the front of her desk and leans back so she's partially sitting on the corner of her desk.

'This afternoon, we're going to have a ten-minute question-and-answer session to find out how much you remember from what we've learnt over the past month,' Miss Havelock informs them. She picks up a sheet of paper from her desk with a list of questions and answers and holds the paper up so she can read from the list. 'Are you ready?' She looks at the class to make sure they're all paying attention.

Ben sits nervously at his desk knowing that his friend is watching his every move. Surreptitiously he opens up the cover to his watch held in his lap and positions his hand on the adjuster knob. 'So, who can tell me where in the world Aztecs could be found?' Miss immediately sees Ben's hand held high in the air. 'Yes, Ben?'

'Mexico, Miss.'

'Very good Ben.'

Ben looks over to Paul and gives him a wink before looking back to Miss Havelock as she asks the next question.

'Now can anyone remember in which time period they lived and flourished?'

Ben quickly raises his hand and notices Gemma's hand raised over to his left.

'Yes Gemma?' Miss offers Gemma the chance to answer. Ben can't believe it; he knows he put his hand up before Gemma's so Miss should have asked him, but then he realises that he'd already answered, so it's only fair to let someone else answer.

'Was it 1200 to 1350, Miss?' Gemma says.

'Not quite Gemma but a good guess; anyone else, fancy a try?' Miss asks while looking around the classroom for a fresh hand. Nobody else has their hand up so Miss points towards Ben. 'Okay Ben… what do you think?'

'Was it from 1300, to 1521, Miss?' Ben asks. 'Very good, that's exactly right.'

Miss sounds surprised at how accurately Ben answered that last question. Ben confidently leans back in his chair giving the impression that he can answer anything Miss throws at them. The whole class stares at Ben in awe because they've never heard him answer anything correctly in history before. Miss asks the next question to which nobody puts their hand up. Ben waits until Miss tells the class the correct answer before he can jump back in time and answer it correctly. Des Cook tried to answer the next question but gave the wrong answer. Ben waited again for Miss to say the correct answer before answering that question correctly. For the next two questions asked, Ben was the only one with his hand up so Miss allowed him to answer those. As he'd already answered the first five questions correctly, he gets the feeling that the rest of his class have already decided to let him continue. He answers the next four questions before Miss finally says, 'Come on class, this is the last question; can anyone other than Ben please have a go at answering this one?'

Miss Havelock makes a last ditch effort to involve the other class members. She looks at each pupil in class, willing them to offer up an answer but nobody does. Finally, Miss Havelock says, 'Okay Ben. What are the names of the two daughters of Prince Andrew and Sarah Ferguson?'

'Princess Eugenie and Princess Beatrice, Miss.'

Miss Havelock places the question-and-answer sheet down on her desk and then looks over towards Ben.

'Well done Benjamin; another correct answer.' She begins to give Ben a short round of applause and the rest of the class join in while adding a few cheers. Ben is taken back by the applause especially from Miss Havelock and feels his cheeks start to redden in embarrassment so he bows his head and stares at the top of his desk until the applause dies down. Ben slowly turns his head to the side and looks over towards Paul who is looking directly at him with an electrified expression on his face. Ben quickly gives him a thumbs-up sign and Paul reciprocates before they turn their gaze towards Miss Havelock as she returns to her seat. Ben notices Miss jotting something down on a notepad on top of her desk before she lifts her head and stares right into Ben's eyes for a few seconds, almost looking right through him which immediately makes Ben feel uncomfortable. Ben quickly looks down again but this time focusing on his history book to avoid Miss Havelock's penetrating stare.

Why is she staring at me? What have I done wrong? he asks himself, trying to understand Miss Havelock's change from an approachable and amiable person to one with an intimidating demeanour. *What have I done to suddenly cause Miss Havelock to look at me like I'm a criminal?* Then Ben realises that his impressive performance today must appear to be suspicious, because he's never in the past participated in any of the question-and-answer sessions.

Miss continues teaching the class all about the birth of slavery and how it spread throughout the world. Ben tries to appear to be interested and enthusiastic about what they're being taught but he's finding it difficult because he's never had an interest in history and it's difficult to suddenly drum up enthusiasm for something you know nothing about. Finally, the bell sounds for the end of class and the noise in the classroom erupts as everyone stands up and begins to pack away their things. Ben glances over towards Miss Havelock sitting at her desk and notices her eyes staring right back at him. He looks down again and quickly ties the buckle on his rucksack ready to make a speedy exit when he hears his teacher call him.

'Benjamin can I have a word?' Miss Havelock's voice filters through the noise in the classroom. Suddenly everyone in class stops what they're doing and looks over at Ben as he swings his rucksack over his shoulder. Ben's conscience is telling him to make a dash for it but he knows if he does, he'd be in more trouble and the whole class would know he was guilty of something. Miss Havelock stands up and steps to the side of her desk to meet Ben as he goes towards the door. Ben looks round to Paul for moral support but Paul's nowhere to be seen as half the class have already left. Ben slowly walks towards Miss Havelock and stops just in front of her.

'Yes, Miss?' he replies, feeling guilty that somehow Miss knows all about the misuse of Ben's time travel capabilities. Miss Havelock rests her hand on his shoulder and waits until the last pupil has left the classroom.

'I was very impressed with your answers today, Ben.'

'Thank you, Miss,' Ben replies feeling that she's going to tell him off any second now. 'You've never participated in any of my question-and-answer sessions before, so what made you answer today?' Miss asks inquisitively.

'Errrm my mum... said I should.' Ben nervously tells Miss Havelock struggling to get the words out as he couldn't think of what to say. 'That's good advice from your mother. The thing that I don't understand, Ben, is how you managed to answer every question correctly, when nobody else in the class could?' Miss Havelock adds, looking intently at him.

Ben offers an explanation and not quite a convincing one at that. 'I... I... studied every night over the weekend, Miss.'

Miss Havelock leans forward and stares into his eyes for a few seconds, apparently hoping to see the truth. She stands up and gives him a reassuring smile. 'Okay Ben, well done and keep up with the good work,' she tells him. Ben manages a forced smile before turning towards the classroom door and tentatively walks out, feeling totally relieved at not being caught out.

Chapter Ten

Ben felt convinced that Miss Havelock would have had a word with Miss Clarke, about how brilliant he was, during the question-and-answer session the other day. He also knew that Paul modified the entry form for applicants, limiting the space to just six named entries and Ben's name was on that list; so why does he still feel nervous about not being selected to represent the school in the forthcoming competition. Ben and Paul follow the long line of pupils along the corridor and through the door to their right into the assembly hall. The students file into the assembly hall as they usually do every Wednesday. The pupils are directed to fill the seats on the far right of the front row, gradually filling each seat across the row to the left-hand side before moving to the second row and filling those seats. Ben takes his seat on the sixth row from the front, almost central to the stage in front of them; Paul sits down next to him on his right. After a few minutes, all the students in the school have taken their seats and wait patiently while members of the faculty file in from the left of the stage and take their seats facing the school.

Out of the corner of his eye, Ben sees Paul's head shoot forward. His glasses fly off his face and drop down between the seats as a hand immediately retracts back behind where Paul is sitting.

'Arrgh!' Paul cries out as he tries to retrieve his spectacles from the floor.

'Paul Hale, stop fidgeting,' Mr Thompson calls out from the front of the platform.

All eyes turn towards Paul as he resumes his seat. He notices that Tony Vernall is sitting right behind him. Ben looks round at Tony looking innocent with his arms folded across his chest.

'Watch it,' Ben tells Tony before returning his gaze to Miss Clarke as she goes up to the podium positioned towards the centre of the stage to address the school.

'Good morning children. As you are all aware, this Friday will be the annual Inter-School competition and for this year, the competition will be held at our school. As with every year, the faculty has selected from the list of entrants – the best among our pupils from years eight and nine – to represent our school.' Miss Clarke takes a moment to look around the hall, adding a long pause before looking down at the sheet of paper in front of her. 'And here is the list of pupils selected to represent our school for year eight in the Inter-School Competition:

'Philip Matthews. Avalon Vernall. Alexis King. Andrew Perkins. Simon McDonald and...

Benjamin Chapman.'

She looks up again and smiles. 'Congratulations on being selected for year eight and we wish you all the best for the competition.'

Miss Clarke gives a short round of applause and is joined by all those in the audience. Ben looks at Paul feeling enormously relieved that his name was mentioned and whispers, 'I can't believe I'm in the team.'

'Hey stupid, how did they choose you?' Ben hears Tony say behind him. Ben ignores Tony's remark and smiles at Paul.

'He's only jealous,' Ben tells his friend. Paul gives Ben a nervous smile half expecting some sort of retaliation which doesn't arrive.

They turn and face the front again as Miss Clarke continues her announcements. 'Finally, our list of pupils for year nine are... ' Miss Clarke pauses for a few seconds for dramatic effect before continuing to read the list of names for year nine. Ben catches sight of a girl four rows ahead looking round in his direction. He looks at her wondering what she's staring at when his eyes lock on to hers and the sudden realisation dawns on him that she's staring at him. Ben quickly breaks eye contact and looks forward to Miss Clarke in front of him, but in the corner of his eye; he can still see the girl staring.

Why is she staring at me? he thinks. He doesn't know who she is, so why is she glaring at him? He starts to feel uncomfortable that she hasn't taken her eyes off him, when finally, she turns around and looks at Miss Clarke.

After the assembly Ben goes to his locker near the school entrance to collect a book he needs for his next lesson. He removes the books he doesn't need and places them inside his locker before taking out the one book from his locker that he does need. Over his shoulder, he notices the same girl from the assembly approach him with Alexis King by her side. She stops right in front of Ben and folds her arms in front of her as though she means business.

'Hello,' he says, nervously wondering why two girls have cornered him up against his locker.

'What the hell do you think you're doing?' the taller girl says.

'I... I'm getting a book out of my locker,' Ben replies while wondering why this girl is so interested in what he's up to.

'You know what we mean; why are you in the team for the school competition?' Alexis asks. Ben's heart begins to speed up again as he stares at Alexis and for a few seconds, his mind has gone a complete blank as his eyes focus on Alexis's well-formed mouth.

'Hello stupid; we asked you a question!' the taller girl barks.

Ben quickly realises that he hasn't responded to their question, so he tentatively says 'Because... I put my name on the list... and... the teachers picked me and... because I'm clever.'

'We want to *win* the competition, not lose,' the taller girl angrily states.

Ben can't believe that he's being interrogated in front of what now appears to be a large gathering of students. Who do they think they are, telling him that he can't be in the team? Suddenly Ben realises that neither of these girls were in his history class, so they don't know how brilliant he is.

'I'm brilliant at history and you'll be asked questions on history,' he says, trying to reassure them. The tall girl looks at Alexis for confirmation but Alexis just shrugs and shakes her head. The tall girl looks back at Ben and says, 'You'd better be brilliant, else you're history. And when I say history, I mean it. I'll get my brother to kick your arse.'

The two girls turn and walk away through the crowd of spectators. Paul appears in front of Ben looking concerned.

'What was that all about? What did Avalon and Alexis want?' Paul asks.

'Avalon, is that her name?'

'Yes, you know, Tony's sister,' Paul explains. 'You've got to be kidding, Avalon the school bully's sister hates me and the school bully hates you; what's wrong with that family?' Ben says in a bewildered tone.

'So, what did she want?'

'Oh, she just wanted to say that she doesn't want me in the school competition, that's all.'

'Hey, Ben!'

Ben hears someone call his name from across the playground. He looks up from his seated position on the climbing frame and sees Tony Vernall, Simon Dicks, Brian Philips and Andrew Woodhouse walking towards him. Immediately, Ben recalls the last thing Avalon told him yesterday about how she'll get her brother to kick his arse. His body quickly tenses and he fights back the urge to stand up and assumes a karate stance to protect himself against four potential attackers. Instead, he quickly assesses the situation to see whether these boys look as though they're about to start a fight or not. Usually when someone intends to strike out at another person, they look like they mean business and their hands are normally clenched. Tony, who is leading the procession, looks relaxed and his hands are down by his sides so Ben takes this as a sign that they're not going to do anything. He takes a deep breath and sits upright so as to appear relaxed and not threatened by the four of them. Tony stops a few feet in front of him while the others move around to Ben's left and right, possibly to prevent Ben from trying to escape.

Ben looks directly at Tony and says, 'What do you want?' trying to sound confident and unperturbed. 'My sister tells me that you're going to cause them to lose the competition tonight.'

'Did she? Well, you can tell your sister that I'm going to win, and I'm going to do it on my own without any help from her.'

'What do you mean, you're going to win on your own; you're in a team, you idiot?' Tony says looking confused.

'Just wait and see what happens,' Ben tells them. 'Chapman, if you lose tonight, you're dead.'

Tony holds up his clenched fist and shakes it in Ben's direction. The four of them turn around and walk towards the school building.

Ben slumps back down on his seat feeling completely drained. He could literally feel his adrenaline pump around his body in anticipation of something about to happen and now the threat has gone the feeling of relief is so refreshing. Having had four lads confront him in the playground is not something he wants to experience again and the thought that they might come back if he causes Avalon to lose tonight is something of a concern, but he'll just have to deal with it as and when it happens. Ben notices a crowd of boys standing nearby, all staring at him; they'd probably seen the whole thing and, knowing what type of person Tony is, half expected to see Ben being beat up. Ben smiles at the group of lads and tries to give the impression that he's not in the slightest bit fazed about what happened. The boys smile back before resuming their conversation. For the first time Ben starts to get an uneasy feeling about being in the competition. That feeling stays with him during his morning classes causing him to not fully concentrate on his work and he found himself staring into space while thinking the worst scenarios. *What if I mess up? What if someone presses the buzzer before I do and their team end up losing? What if my watch stops working? What if my mind goes a complete blank?* He can see images of him walking out from the competition having caused their team to lose and seeing Tony, Simon, Brian and Andrew waiting for him outside, with Avalon right behind him screaming at her brother to kick my arse. What options does he have? Could he quit at the last moment and let the side down? That might save him from getting a beating but Alexis would certainly hate him because who would they get to replace him at such short notice? Probably no one. Ben hears the sound of the bell for lunch so he packs his books inside his rucksack and goes to the dining room where he sees Paul sitting at their usual table.

'So, how's it going?' Paul asks.

'Oh, I forgot to tell you that Tony and his pals surrounded me this morning when you'd gone to the toilet.'

'Oh yes? What did they want?' Paul asks.

'They said they're going to kill me if I mess up at the competition.'

Paul hears the depressed tone in Ben's voice and looking at his slightly downtrodden expression, decides to spur him on a little. 'You'll be great, Ben, don't worry,' he tells Ben.

'I know but I've been having these negative thoughts like my watch won't work or someone else will be quicker to their buzzer,' Ben nervously tells Paul. 'Ben, you'll be fine. Remember, you've already proved you can do it, when you answered all the questions in our history class. Just do exactly the same as you did then, and our team will win.' Paul gives Ben a confident smile.

'I suppose you're right,' Ben replies, sounding a little happier. He leans forward and takes a bite from his cheese and cress sandwich.

Avalon and Alexis walk over towards them.

'Miss Jones has arranged a team meeting for everyone in the team, straight after lunch in the library,' Avalon informs Ben.

'Okay I'll be there.'

Ben watches Avalon and Alexis go over to Simon on the next table and notify him about the meeting.

'She still doesn't like you, does she?' Paul asks.

'I know; I don't understand it. I haven't actually done anything wrong and yet she's got this chip on her shoulder; maybe she just doesn't like boys.'

'She gets on all right with Philip, Andrew and Simon,' Paul says.

'Whose side are you on?'

'Sorry, I mean they're not as tall as you, maybe she doesn't like boys that are taller than herself.'

'That's better.' Ben gives his friend a smile.

As soon as the lunch break finishes, Ben notices the other team members heading off to the library for the team meeting so he tells Paul that he'll see him later and heads off in the same direction. Ben opens the library door and enters the room to see the rest of his team all sat around a circular table in the centre of the room.

'Hello Ben, please take a seat; we're just about to start,' Miss Jones informs him.

Immediately, Ben senses a chill in the air and a tension you could cut with a knife. Avalon, Alexis, and Andrew are all staring at him. He knows Avalon must have had a word with the other team members, because as he nears the table he sees them all glaring. Ben pulls out the only available chair between Andrew Perkins and Simon McDonald and sits down.

Miss Jones, sitting at the far side of the table, now stands up and addresses the team.

'Thank you all for coming and thank you, Avalon for letting everyone know.'

'That's all right Miss,' Avalon replies looking smug.

Miss Jones continues. 'As head of the English Department, I've been assigned with the responsibility to motivate the team, and to get you ready for the competition tonight. The reason for this meeting is to discuss tactics. Now I'm duly informed that the format for the questions will follow the same pattern as last year. In the first round you'll be up against Richmond High School, which, I'd like to remind you, knocked us out of the competition last year.'

'Booooo!' the other team members immediately reply.

'Yes, my sentiments exactly; however, this year we're going to knock them out of the competition.' 'Yeeeaaah!' everyone calls out.

'Okay children, but before we can do that, we need to make sure that the *right* person answers the *right* questions.' Miss says emphasising the word "right". She continues. 'You will be asked questions on six subjects taught through our syllabus; they are: maths, English, history, chemistry, geography and biology. Like I said, we want the pupil who excels in that subject to answer that particular question, to give us the best possible chance of getting that question right. Do you understand?'

Everyone around the table begins to nod in agreement.

'So how will you know which questions you may answer?' Miss asks.

'I'm answering the maths questions,' Avalon quickly responds.

'No, *I'm* answering the maths questions,' Simon interjects.

'Well, I'm answering questions on geography—' 'Quiet everyone!' Miss Jones shouts above the noise. Everyone stops and looks up at Miss.

'Like I said, we are not leaving this to chance. We've looked at your test scores over the past few months and, having discussed these results with your teachers, we've come up with a plan of action. Now listen carefully.' Miss Jones waits a few seconds before continuing. 'The best mathematician among us, and therefore the one who will be answering all the maths questions will be... Simon.' Simon looks across at Avalon and smiles.

'Alexis will answer all the English questions. Chemistry questions by Avalon. Geography questions by Philip or Avalon. Biology questions by Andrew, Avalon and Alexis. And finally, questions on history by Benjamin after his impressive performance the other day.'

'What impressive performance?' Avalon demands. 'Yes, I forgot to tell you; Ben was amazing!' Philip exclaims.

'What do you mean amazing?' Alexis asks, sounding surprised. Ben leans back in his chair and listens as the conversation unfolds while feeling a sense of relief at seeing Philip defend his corner.

'We had a question-and-answer session with Miss Havelock; you know how she likes to have one every month. Well, you should have seen it; Ben answered every question Miss asked in history class and got them all right.'

'So, did everyone else get them right?' Avalon asks. 'No, that's the thing; no one knew the answers except Ben,' Philip explains.

The other team members all look across at Ben with surprised expressions, having heard this revelation. Ben knows his school reputation is not one to be applauded or praised and he's sure the rest of his team members feel the same so to receive such flattery from one of their own was definitely unforeseen and surprisingly refreshing. Ben smiles at everyone while basking in his own glory.

'Okay children, now that we know that everyone here has earned their place, shall we move on to the next part in our agenda: who will be team captain?' Miss asks. The group immediately erupts as everyone begins chattering with the person next to them, about who they think would be a good captain. Miss quickly interrupts.

'If you can't decide between you, I think the best way to decide would be a secret ballot.'

Miss tears an A4 sheet of paper into eight strips. She hands everyone in the team a piece of paper and discards the remaining two pieces in a nearby waste bin. Everyone is handed a pencil and asked to write down the name of the person they would like to nominate.

Ben shields his slip of paper with his left hand to prevent anyone else from seeing and scrawls his name on the piece of paper; he quickly folds the paper over and hands it back to Miss Jones feeling confident that he'll be chosen to lead the team. Miss Jones collects the last slip of paper from Avalon and shuffles the slips of paper in her hand, so nobody would be able to work out who voted for whom.

'Okay everybody, the person with the highest number of votes will be team captain; and the names are…' Miss Jones opens the first slip of paper on top of the stack and, after giving the team a reassuring smile, reads out loud the name written in front of her. 'Avalon.' Avalon confidently smiles making out that she knew her name would be called although in truth, she probably felt relieved that her name was actually on the list. Miss Jones reads the next name. 'Alexis' then she opens the next slip of paper. 'Ben.' Everyone immediately looks over at Ben in disbelief, but then realises that he must have written his name down so they turn back towards Miss Jones as she reads the next name. 'Alexis.' Avalon's facial expression suddenly changes, reflecting her jealous side as she glares at her friend. Two seconds later she hears, 'Avalon.' Avalon and Alexis look at each other with excitement, knowing that in a moment or two, one of them will be chosen as the team captain. Ben shakes his head as he realises that it's all over for him and that one of the girls will become team captain. For a second he wished he'd voted for Alexis now as he'd much rather her be captain than Avalon. They all wait with bated breath for the final vote to be announced. 'Avalon. Well done Avalon, you'll be the team captain,' Miss Jones announces.

The rest of the team give her a quick round of applause and Avalon duly smiles at being given the privilege.

'Now, as team captain, it will be your responsibility to lead the team onto the stage and you'll take the seat nearest to the judging panel. Alexis will follow you and sit next to Avalon followed by Andrew, Simon, Philip and finally Ben. Are we all happy; any questions?'

'No Miss,' they all reply in unison.

'Okay, for the next few minutes I want to discuss the type of questions that will be asked. For the past few years; ever since I joined the teaching faculty, I made a note of all the questions asked at the Inter-School Competition. Now don't get too excited; they don't ask the same questions.' Miss informs everyone.

'So, what's the point in making a note if they're not the same questions, Miss?' Philip asks.

'The point is; we can get an idea of the type of questions that will be asked, so we can prepare.'

'I don't understand Miss; how can we prepare when the questions are different?' Simon asks.

'Okay Simon, I'll give you an example. They never ask a straight maths question. For instance, they wouldn't ask for the square root of three thousand one hundred and thirty-six. They always ask a mathematical equation, like if an engine uses three litres of fuel every hour, how much fuel will it use in four hours and twenty minutes.'

For the next few minutes, Miss Jones discusses other possible questions that may come up for the other subjects, so everyone has a general idea of what to expect. Miss reminds the team that they'll be facing either York or Preston in the final, after they knock Richmond out of the competition in the first round. 'Now don't worry about how we're going to get on tonight; just enjoy yourselves and do your best. Miss Clarke is very proud of all of you and wishes you all the best in the competition, so make us proud,' Miss Jones says. Everyone gives a little cheer, before Miss Jones concludes. 'Now don't forget, we all need to be back here in the auditorium for six o'clock so we can go through the final preparations before the competition at seven.'

She excuses the team members from their afternoon classes so that they can all relax, prior to the competition tonight.

Ben goes home and spends the next couple of hours in his bedroom to chill out. His mum is downstairs tidying up and getting all excited about seeing her son in the school competition while his dad is still at work. Ben lies on his bed with his head turned to the side so he can look out of the window. The pale blue sky is broken up with small cumulus clouds moving very slowly across his windowed canvas in an ever-changing picture. The relaxing scene in front of him is both hypnotic and calming and also pleasing to the eye, and for a little while his anxiety levels had dropped until two pigeons flew into view, flapping their wings and trying to peck each other in a kind of aerial dogfight. The mid-air battle suddenly brings back the negative feelings he had earlier when he thought he was going to fail somehow and Tony and his cohorts attack him for letting his sister down. Ben quickly sits up on his bed feeling a cold sweat on the nape of his neck. He reaches into his pocket and takes out the watch. Just seeing the watch in his hand has a calming and a reassuring effect. He closes his eyes and breathes deeply in through his nose and out through his mouth.

'Ben, dinner's ready,' he hears his mother calling. It takes him a few seconds to realise that he must have dropped off for a while. He notices the watch is still in his left hand resting by his side, so he tucks the watch back inside his pocket so he knows he's got it for later on. Ben goes downstairs and takes his usual seat at the dining table, between his dad and sister.

'Sorry guys; nothing too exciting for dinner, just sausages, mash and beans I'm afraid,' Mum informs them as she carries through two plates of food and sets them down in front of Jess and Ben.

'I like bangers and mash,' Dad replies. Ben looks up at his father feeling totally confused as to what his dad is referring to, although he assumes it must have something to do with what they're eating. Dad gives Ben a smile and a wink before pointing to the sausages on his plate. Mum brings through two more plates of food and places one down in front of dad and the other she keeps for herself. Ben, still feeling nervous about the competition, finds it difficult to eat anything, so he picks at his food and watches the rest of his family eat theirs. 'So, are you all excited about tonight?' Mum asks.

'I'm not sure. I suppose so.'

'Are you all right Ben?' Mum asks, noticing that he's not touched a thing from his dinner plate.

'Just feeling a little nervous, that's all,' Ben tells them.

'Well don't you worry; we'll be there to cheer you on,' Mum tells Ben hoping that having his family there will make him feel better.

Dad stops the car near the school entrance gate at five to six, to allow Ben time to get to the auditorium before six. Ben waves to his dad as he drives the car down the road for a hundred metres and then turns left down a side street as he goes back home. Ben turns to walk in through the main school entrance when he catches sight of Andrew and Simon in the distance as they appear around the corner of the school property.

'Ben!' Andrew calls out as he sees him waiting by the entrance. Ben waits for a few seconds until they catch him up.

'Hi,' Ben says as they all turn into the school grounds.

'This is exciting; I've never been in a competition before and certainly not in front of the whole school, and our parents,' Andrew says, sounding enthusiastic.

'Me neither. My parents reminded me at dinner,' Ben tells them.

'I couldn't eat dinner; I think I was far too nervous about tonight.' Simon adds.

'I couldn't either,' Andrew says.

'Well, that makes three of us. I just hope we all don't faint from lack of nutrition in front of the whole school,' Ben comments.

'I know, that would be really embarrassing; the whole team from Harrogate High fainting!' Simon says and the three of them all burst out laughing at the thought. They all enter the school building through the main school entrance and are immediately greeted by Miss Jones and Mr French standing in reception with the other members of year eight and nine.

'Okay everyone, now that we're all here, we can see that two other schools have already arrived. Year nine, can you all follow Mr French and he'll take you to your designated waiting area. Year eight, if you'd like to follow me; we'll be waiting in the auxiliary classroom next to the auditorium.'

Six members of year nine turn and follow Mr French off through a door to the left while the rest of Ben's team follow Miss Jones as she leads them to the right side of reception and down a narrow corridor. She stops at the last door on the left and opens it.

'Okay, in you go.'

The six team members file into a smaller sized room that has four rectangle shaped tables placed in each corner along with an appropriate number of chairs for everyone to sit down. Ben notices two other teams assembled in their own little groups. York are all sat together around the table on the far left. They look smart in their blue blazers fashioned with a white trim around their lapels and their traditional shield emblem stitched on their breast pockets. Preston's scholars are all huddled together on the far right in their dark blue blazers with yellow motifs on their breast pockets. Miss Jones directs year eight to the nearside right table where they all take their seats. The noise in the small room begins to rise as each team begins chattering to themselves.

Miss Jones takes a seat between Avalon and Alexis. 'Are we all excited?' she asks.

Andrew and Simon are slightly distracted by the impressive look of the other teams while Philip seems to be smiling at a pretty blonde girl member from Preston. 'Don't worry about the other teams.' Miss Jones raises her voice to get the attention from the three boys. Ben gives Philip a nudge and he looks back at Miss Jones feeling slightly embarrassed at being seen smiling at the enemy. A few seconds later the door opens and Richmond enters the room. The sound in the room suddenly drops as everyone stares at last year's winners in their impressive school uniform. Their burgundy blazer with a striking yellow-and-green badge sewn onto their breast pockets; make them stand out amongst their peers. They stop just inside the doorway in a unified manner and begin to scour the room like a regimental security force, looking at each individual then moving on to the next. Finally, their focus reached Harrogate.

'That's the team we knocked out last year,' their team captain informs the remaining members of her team. They all acknowledge Harrogate's presence with a condescending sneer before taking their seats at the last remaining table in the left corner.

Miss Jones, recognising the impression Richmond has had on the team, tries to spur Harrogate on. 'Children, don't worry, they may look impressive but we are better than them. Last year was last year; this year, we've got a much stronger team. We're winners and we're going to prove it tonight.'

Everyone turns back from staring at Richmond and looks towards Miss Jones who's smiling and trying to be as positive as she can.

'Listen everyone, I believe we can beat them and that's the honest truth. Just concentrate and keep focused and we can do this. What are we?' Miss Jones asks, looking at each team member.

'Winners,' Avalon quietly says. 'Yes Avalon, you are a winner, so what about the rest of you, do you feel like a winner?' Miss Jones asks.

'Yes!' all six team members called out. "That's better!' Miss Jones says.

The door opens and Miss Clarke enters the waiting area.

'Excuse me, may I have your attention please?' Everyone in the room stops talking and looks over to Miss Clarke looking all official holding a clipboard in her hand.

'The competition will begin in five minutes; the first two teams to play will be Richmond and Harrogate. If both teams could follow me, we will make our way into the auditorium and take our seats. York and Preston, please remain in the waiting area until you're called.' Miss Clarke informs everyone. Hearing the five-minute call from Miss Clarke suddenly reminds Ben how close they are to actually starting the competition. Ben slowly gets to his feet with the rest of his team and they move forward towards the doorway all feeling a little nervous about their pending performance in front of the whole school. Ben feels his heartbeat increase in pace and his palms feel a little clammy. He instinctively wipes his hands on the outside of his trousers to dry them just in case he has to shake hands with anyone as he wouldn't want them to know how anxious he's feeling at the moment. Richmond, reach the door first and file out into the corridor following Miss Clarke. Avalon joins the back of the queue and the rest of her team tag on the end as the two teams are led down the corridor and through the next door on the right into a small annex next to the stage. Miss Clarke quickly organises each team in the order they will go onto the stage, with Richmond on the left and Harrogate on the right. A large heavy curtain to the right side of the annex screens the audience from view. Ben stands behind Philip as the last person in their team listening to the hubbub from all those in the audience chatting away, totally unaware that the two teams are patiently waiting behind the screen. Miss Clarke, having received a signal from the judging panel, motions both teams to walk onto the stage and take their respective seats behind the two banks of desks.

The noise from the audience suddenly stops when they catch sight of the two teams making their way across the stage to their team starting positions. Avalon leads the way to the far bank of six desks positioned in a line. She walks around the back of the desks and takes the seat on the nearest desk to the judging panel. The rest of her team file in behind her, occupying the remaining seats, with Ben seated at the far end nearest the audience. The desks are normal desks found in school classrooms. Each desk has a buzzer with a red domed light next to a name plate. Ben notices his name printed on an A4 sheet of laminated paper folded down the middle, positioned so the judges and the audience could see. The buzzer consisted of a short wooden plank with a push-button doorbell, wired to a red plastic dome that covered a small light bulb.

Two wires run from each buzzer along the bank of desks to the judges' desks, where there are twelve small light bulbs affixed to another plank of wood. Ben can only assume whoever presses their buzzers first their light will flash and the corresponding light on the relevant judge's desk will light up so they know who pressed first.

The man sitting in the centre of the judges' desks picks up his gavel and bangs it down on his wooden block to get everyone's attention. The whole auditorium falls silent.

'Good evening everyone. My name is Mr Hodge; I will be acting as the judge for this competition. I have with me Mr Wilkinson on my left and Mrs Evans on my right; they will act as adjudicators and keep score. Welcome all, to the 2019 Inter-School Competition.'

There's a short round of applause from the audience and a few names cheered before Mr Hodge continued. 'This evening, we will have four of our best schools compete against each other from years eight and nine. They will be asked questions from a wide range of subjects covered in the school curriculum. Each round will consist of twenty questions. The first person to press his buzzer will be allowed to answer the question raised. If they get the question right, their team will score two points. If they get the question wrong, the opposing team will have the opportunity to answer the question and steal one point for a correct answer.'

Mr Hodge pauses for a second, to allow everyone time to process the initial part of his instructions.

'There will be two knockout rounds for each year and the winners will play against each other to determine who will be the Inter-School Competition winners. We will start the competition as you can see with the year eight students from Richmond High competing against Harrogate High.'

There's a short round of applause from the audience and a few names being called out from excited parents. Ben hears his mother call his name, which seems to be louder than all the other parents causing Ben to feel totally embarrassed. He quickly turns his head to the left and having spotted his family in the centre on the second row back, gives them a quick smile before turning back towards Mr Hodge.

'The second round for this year will be between York and Preston.'

Another short round of applause sounds out from the audience before Mr Hodge concludes.

'Does everyone understand the rules?'

Everyone in both teams nod in agreement.

'Right, let the competition begin,' Mr Hodge announces and bangs his gavel down for emphasis. Ben surreptitiously reaches inside his trouser pocket and slips out the watch and holds it in his lap with his left hand, while his right hand is held poised above the buzzer on his desk in readiness for the first question. Ben glances across the bank of desks to his right and sees the rest of his team doing the same with their hands at the ready held over their buzzers. He notices Avalon's hand in particular because it's shaking. Ben looks up at Mr Hodge as he holds up the question sheet in front of him and reads the first question.

'Question one: What is the capital of Madagascar?' Mr Hodge asks.

'Buzz.' The light on Thomas's desk along with the corresponding light on Mr Hodge's desk lights up showing everyone which person pressed their buzzer first.

'Yes, Thomas?' Mr Hodge asks.

'Antananarivo,' Thomas replies.

Mr Hodge checks the answer on his sheet before replying.

'Correct. Two points to Richmond,' Mr Hodge confirms. Mr Wilkinson jots down the score for Richmond as a rapt round of applause sounds out from the audience. Ben looks down at his watch in his lap and pulls the adjuster knob out with his right hand and turns it just a fraction.

'Right, let the competition begin.' Mr Hodge bangs his gavel down.

'Question one: What is the capital of Madagascar?' Ben presses his buzzer down as soon as Mr Hodge asks the question. *Buzz!* The light on Ben's desk lights up with the corresponding light in front of Mr Hodge informing everyone that Ben pressed his buzzer first. Ben, in his peripheral vision, can see all five team members turn their heads towards him looking shocked and angry, that he pressed his buzzer when it was up to Avalon, or Philip to answer.

'Yes, Ben?' Mr Hodge asks.

'Antananarivo' Ben answers.

'Correct; two points to Harrogate.'

There's a loud applause from the audience to Ben's left so Ben turns his head slightly to see his family who are all smiling and clapping; no doubt, feeling very proud of their flesh and blood answering the first question, and getting it right. Ben gives them a smile before turning back towards Mr Hodge. In the corner of his eye, he can still see all his team members staring at him but their expressions seem to have changed from anger to big smiles of relief as Mr Hodge confirms that Harrogate are ahead of Richmond two to nothing.

'Question two.' Mr Hodge says and everyone quickly turns with their fingers on their buzzers in readiness. 'What are the two letters on the periodic table that represent mercury?'

Buzz!

'Yes, Ben?' Mr Hodge asks.

Seconds earlier, Ben had watched Avalon answer that question correctly but seeing Avalon gloat over her successful answer and then recalling the threat he received from Tony really annoyed him. He also remembers the conversation he had with Tony and specifically telling Tony that he would win the competition on his own. Ben knows it's not right to cut short any winning answers from his team members but to be honest, they've all treated him as an outcast and basically looked down their noses at him, except for Philip, that is. Ben decides to win this competition on his own, just to prove a point.

'Hg.'

'Correct; two more points for Harrogate.'

Having answered the first two questions correctly, Ben relaxes a little, feeling a lot more confident in himself. He knows the rest of his team members are glaring at him, but he doesn't care; he's on a mission and nobody's going to stop him.

'Question three.

What battle took place in October 1415?'

Buzz!

'Yes, Ben?'

'The Battle of Agincourt.'

'Correct! Another two points to Harrogate.'

There's a wave of loud applause from the audience which quickly dissipates as Mr Hodge holds up his paper to read the next question.

'Now for question four: who wrote the novel, entitled *The Catcher in the Rye*?'

Buzz!

'Ben.'

'It was written by J D Salinger.'

'Correct again; another two points to Harrogate.'

Ben hears a few cheers from the Harrogate school pupils in the audience above the roar of the applause.

'Question five. In mathematics, what is the number of Pi to the eighth decimal point?'

Buzz!

'Ben.'

'Three point one… four… one… five… nine… two… six.' Ben waits for a few seconds before adding, 'Five.'

'Well done; another correct answer,' Mr Hodges confirms trying to make himself heard above the roar of the applause.

'Come on Richmond!' Mr Hodge says in an endeavour to encourage Richmond to fight back. 'Question six. Who was the 16th —'

'Buzz, Abraham Lincoln!' Ben answers

Mr Hodge, Mr Wilkinson and Mrs Evans all stare at Ben in disbelief. There's a chilling silence in the room and Ben notices that everyone is staring at him with opened mouths. Ben can't understand it, why are they staring at him? Why hasn't Mr Hodge acknowledged his successful answer? What's going on? Ben looks around at his team members as they glare at him, looking extremely angry. Avalon looks like she's fuming and about to explode. Ben quickly turns his attention back to the judging panel as they're deliberating between themselves over something. The three members of the judging panel turn towards Ben and Mr Hodge says, 'Ben Chapman, you answered the last question correctly; that is, before I had the opportunity to ask the question. For this reason, we believe you are cheating and therefore your team is disqualified.'

The word "disqualified" echoes around Ben's head like a klaxon sounding. Disqualified! What does he mean disqualified? In his excited state, Ben hasn't fully grasped the meaning of what he's just been told; all he heard was the word "disqualified", which, to him, didn't make any sense at all.

'Cheat! Cheat! Cheat!' is heard from the audience as the rest of Ben's team all stand with their heads bowed. Ben stands up as Miss Clarke quickly comes over to escort them off the stage. It's only then that Ben realises what he'd done. He looks over towards his family in the audience and sees his mom with her hand covering her mouth, looking totally shocked. His dad sitting next to her, is shaking his head in disgust with his eyes fixed on Ben, as he leaves the stage. Ben quickly glances at Jessica sitting next to Dad and notices tears running down her cheeks.

Chapter Twelve

Ben follows Miss Clarke off the stage and through the annex door into the corridor to the sound of boos and people calling out 'Cheat.'

To Ben, it all feels so surreal; he's never upset his family in his life, so seeing them sat in the audience looking so upset and angry feels like it's all part of a vivid nightmare and he's going to wake up any second. Ben slows his pace down in the corridor as he tries to piece together what led to this crazy situation he's in when Andrew and Simon barge past him, shoving him from both sides. Miss Clarke opens the door to the waiting room and Andrew and Simon step inside. Ben steps inside the room and is immediately shoved in the back by someone behind him which sends his body sprawling forward and crashing into a chair. Ben tries to step past the obstacle but his foot entangles with the chair leg, causing him to crumple down onto his side and partially slide underneath an empty table.

'What have you done?!' Avalon screams at Ben looking like a deranged lunatic. Suddenly the other team members crowd around Ben in a half circle all yelling abuse.

For a moment Ben feels paralysed; his brain doesn't want to work except to register the five irate faces staring down at him. 'Do you know what you've done Ben? We're disqualified. We've worked so hard to win this competition and you've ruined it for us!' Alexis says looking so angry.

Being scolded by Alexis is devastating. The one person Ben wanted to impress; now hates him. Ben clambers to his feet and becomes all too aware of the other two teams all staring at him, possibly wondering why he's now the outcast. Avalon steps forward and stands right in front of him and shoves him in the chest. 'You're an idiot, that's what you are,' she screams at Ben. The other team members crowd around him forcing him back against the side wall. Seeing everyone's face, inches away from his, is making Ben feel claustrophobic. A sense of panic starts to build inside him and all he can think is how he desperately needs to break free.

'*Get away!*' Ben hears himself scream at the top of his voice. Those surrounding him immediately stop what they're doing for a second, which gives Ben an opportunity to force his way through the crowd to the door leading to the outside. Ben reaches for the door handle and pulls the door open just enough to squeeze through the gap and into the corridor. Fortunately, there's nobody around so Ben sprints down the narrow passage to the entrance lobby and then out through the main door and into the playground. There's a slight drizzle and the cold evening air refreshes his flushed face. Ben runs across the playground and out through the main gate before turning left along the pavement. He's got no idea where he's heading, all he knows is that he needs to get as far away from the school as possible. Ben sprints along the pavement to the end of the road and turns right, just avoiding a passing car. He focuses his eyes on the furthest point along the pavement, not even looking at pedestrians as he passes them. Ben hears the pounding of his feet on the paved path in time with his arms as he swings them forward and back, allowing the slapping of the pavement to fill his mind. He senses his breathing becoming more laboured as he runs and then the pounding in his chest sounding within his ears, intermittently falling in time with his feet. Suddenly a stabbing pain strikes at his left side and he finds himself abruptly coming to a halt outside a furniture shop. Ben bends over grasping his side with his right hand while resting his left hand on his knee as he tries to catch his breath. The stabbing pain from the stitch in his left side suddenly spasms; sending electric shock waves up his ribcage, making it difficult to breathe. Ben grimaces as the pain escalates inside him. He looks up and catches sight of his reflection in the shop window, and seeing his image, reminds him of the pain he's caused so many others. Suddenly a wave of guilt washes over him at his prideful attitude and his arrogant conduct at the school competition. He realises how stupid he's been and what damage it's caused. He's alienated the girl he's had a crush on for years and now all the school is going to hate him. His parents must hate him, he thinks. Well, his dad certainly does, from the look he gave him. Ben stares at his reflection in the window as the rain starts to pour, soaking his bent over body. Rain droplets run down the sides of his head and link up with his tears as he begins to cry.

'I wish I was dead,' he cries out, feeling sorry for himself. He forces himself to stand up and his left hand briefly touches the bulge in his pocket.

Ben stares at his image in the window and reaches inside his pocket and pulls out the bronze watch and chain and lifts it up to his chest, as though it was an answer to his prayers.

'Right, let's do this right' he says to himself. Ben opens the watch case and pulls out the adjuster knob. He pauses for a second as he formulates what he plans to do. He wipes the tears from his eyes so he can focus properly on the watch and slowly turns time back.

Chapter Thirteen

'Good evening everyone my name is Mr Hodge; I will be acting as the judge for this competition. I have with me Mr Wilkinson on my left and Mrs Evans on my right who will act as adjudicators and keep score.'

Yes, I timed that perfectly, Ben thinks as he recognises the scene in front of him. He glances to his left at the audience who are all listening to Mr Hodge as he explains the rules. Ben turns to his team members who are equally listening to the instructions from the judge and looking nervous at facing Richmond in the first round. Ben smiles to himself, feeling so relieved that he's now got a second chance.

'Does everyone understand the rules?' Mr Hodge asks. Everyone nods in agreement and the room falls silent again.

'Right, let the competition begin.' Mr Hodge bangs his gavel down.

'Question one: What is the capital of Madagascar?

Buzz!

'Yes, Thomas?' Mr Hodge asks.

'Antananarivo,' Thomas replies.

'Correct; two points to Richmond.'

Avalon turns to the rest of the team and says quietly, 'Sorry'

'Question two. What are the two letters on the periodic table that represent mercury?'

Buzz!

'Avalon?'

'Hg,' Avalon says.

'Correct; two points for Harrogate,' Mr Hodge confirms. Avalon looks round at the rest of the team and smiles.

'Come on, we can do this,' she says to spur her team on.

'Question three. What battle took place in October 1415?' Mr Hodge asks.

Great, this is a history question Ben thinks and quickly presses the buzzer. For a moment there, he thought he was too late, because he was thinking that he didn't need to answer every question, so he was just enjoying the moment, listening to others answer.

Buzz! The light in front of Ben lights up, with the corresponding light on the judges' desk. 'Yes, Ben?'

'The Battle of Agincourt.'

'Correct. Another two points to Harrogate.'

Ben hears loud applause from the audience to his left and knowing that the applause was for him gives Ben a real buzz. Ben looks to his team members who are all smiling at him and giving him a thumbs-up as a sign of their approval. Avalon catches Ben's eye and mouths the words 'well done.' Being acknowledged by his team members is something Ben never expected and a sudden feeling of being overwhelmed washes over him, making him feel quite emotional. Ben knows it's not the right time to get caught up in the moment as they have a long way to go, so he clears his head and concentrates on Mr Hodge as he begins to read out the next question.

'Now for question four: who wrote the novel entitled *The Catcher in the Rye?*'

Buzz!

'Alexis?'

'J D Salinger.'

'Correct; another two points to Harrogate.'

Alexis looks around at her team members and they all give her a big smile. For a second Alexis's eyes connect with Ben's and for a brief moment, Ben feels a strong urge to kiss her. Fortunately for Ben, Alexis is not next to him, else he may have leant forward and pressed his lips against hers. Alexis turns back around to face Mr Hodge in readiness for the next question. Ben, still seeing Alexis's beautiful smile in his mind, can't take his eyes off her. His eyes follow the contours of her profile paying particular attention to her soft lips with the trace of her white perfect teeth on display as she maintains her smile.

'Benjamin Chapman, are you ready for the next question?' Mr Hodge asks, seeing Ben looking across at one of his team members. Ben, hearing his name being called, quickly turns towards Mr Hodge half expecting to give an answer.

'Sorry, what was that?' Ben asks, feeling totally out of it.

'Are you ready; can I ask the next question?'

'Oh, er yes,' Ben replies.

'Thank you. Question five. In mathematics, what is the number for Pi to the eighth decimal point?' Mr Hodge asks.

Buzz!

'Milly.'

'Three point one, four, one, five, nine, three, two, five,' she answers.

'Sorry, that is an incorrect answer; can anyone from Harrogate give me the correct answer?' Mr Hodge asks.

Buzz!

'Yes, Simon?'

'Three point one... four... one... five... nine... two... six... five.'

'Correct; one point for Harrogate.'

The questions keep coming and Ben does his best to allow his team to answer as much as he can while keeping a mental note on how many points Richmond have. Ben hears Mr Hodge inform everyone. 'Now for the final question for this round, the scores as it stands; Richmond has seventeen points and Harrogate has sixteen points so it's all to play for.

'Question twenty: what year did Gaius Julius Caesar die?'

Buzz!

'Ben?'

'He died in the year... forty-four BC' Ben replies. Everyone on his team stared at him with their mouths wide open. The terror on their faces at the thought that Ben may have gotten the question wrong is a sight that Ben will never forget. They all turn towards Mr Hodge in anticipation of being told if the answer was right or wrong when he says.

'*Correct!* Harrogate wins this round. Congratulations Harrogate.'

There's a huge round of applause from the whole auditorium. Ben and the rest of his team stand up and go across the stage towards the exit. Ben glances over towards the audience and sees his family all waving and smiling. Ben gives them a quick smile before disappearing out of sight behind the large stage curtains with the rest of his team. They go out into the narrow corridor and along the passage to the door to the waiting area. As they enter the room, Miss Jones is the first to congratulate everyone on their win.

'That was fantastic, well done, I knew you would win,' she quickly shakes everyone's hands and pats them on their shoulders as they go into the room. Ben moves to the side to allow room for everyone to enter.

Avalon, after receiving her commendation from Miss Jones, approaches Ben.

'Ben, that was brilliant, well done,' she says, giving Ben the biggest smile. Ben is taken back for a moment having been praised by the least expected person on the team.

'Thank you,' Ben replies feeling a little embarrassed.

Andrew steps around Avalon and says, 'Well done Ben.' He gives Ben a pat on the back before taking his seat at the table. Alexis sidles between Avalon and Philip and stops in front of Ben and smiles.

'Well done Ben,' she says as she shakes his hand.

'Well done to you too, you were great.' Ben returns the compliment while still holding on to her hand. 'Thanks Ben.' She looks down at her hand, held tightly in his, before looking back into his eyes. Suddenly Ben realising that he's still holding on to her hand, quickly lets go and gives her an awkward look in a kind of apology. Alexis smiles again, before moving to her seat at the table; Ben turns and takes his seat.

'Great job everyone,' Miss Jones says before giving them a short round of applause. The door opens and Richmond begins to file into the room led by their team captain. 'Well done Harrogate; you played well,' Milly says as she goes to their table. The rest of her team follow suit and congratulate Harrogate on their win before joining Milly at the table. Miss Clarke enters the room and asks for the next two teams to go into the auditorium.

Chapter Fourteen

While York and Preston battle it out in the main auditorium; Richmond and Harrogate have an opportunity to relax and eat during their break. Fortunately, the catering staff have provided a small buffet for the competitors which prove to be a godsend as Ben and some of the other team members are starving, having skipped their evening meal. Ben goes to the buffet snack table and picks up a paper plate before scanning the selection of food on offer to see what he fancies eating. Ben picks up a pork pie and forces the whole thing inside his mouth just as Alexis steps up beside him.

'This is nice,' Alexis says as she picks up a paper plate. Ben quickly covers his mouth with his free hand and tries to say 'Yes it is' which came out as 'Bethis diz'. Alexis giggles a little at seeing fragments of pork pie fall from Ben's mouth. Alexis quickly places a few items on to her plate before returning to the table. Ben shakes his head feeling annoyed with himself; he can't believe that he's botched another opportunity to speak to Alexis. He picks up another pork pie, two sausage rolls, a packet of crisps and a handful of peanuts and walks back towards their table, while casually glancing over at Alexis to see if she's still laughing at him.

Fortunately, Alexis appears to be unperturbed by Ben's ungentlemanly conduct and is in what seems to be a serious conversation with Avalon. Ben pulls out his chair and sits down making sure not to look over at Alexis.

Philip and Andrew go to the buffet table leaving Miss Jones, Avalon, Simon and Alexis sitting with him at their table. Ben continues to keep his head down so as not to make eye contact with Alexis. He picks up a sausage roll and takes a small bite so as not to embarrass himself again if Alexis suddenly strikes up a conversation.

'So, who do you think will win between York and Preston?' she asks.

'I think York will win; although I'd prefer it if Preston won. I'd much rather play Preston in the final,' Simon says.

'Me too; I think Preston would be easier to beat,' Alexis adds.

'I know; that's what I was thinking,' Avalon says.

'Don't worry; whoever you face in the final, I'm sure you'll do just fine,' Miss Jones says, having noticed that everyone seems to be a little nervous about the final. Philip and Andrew arrive back at the table with their plates of food. Avalon and Simon stand up and head towards the buffet table and return with food for themselves so for the next ten minutes or so, they all sit in silence while they eat during their break. Ben is the first to finish his food so to pass the time he takes out his watch and stares at the pattern on the cover, not because he was interested with the pattern; rather, he just needed a distraction to while away the time. His eyes follow the spiral engraved track around the casing as it curves around the randomly positioned etched stars.

'I wonder if these markings mean anything,' he quietly asks himself. Suddenly the door opens and the victors walk in looking jubilant at their first-round win. They walk past Harrogate and smile, to suggest that they're going to beat them in the next round as they did with Preston. York makes their way over to their table and sits down. Preston appears in the doorway looking totally defeated. They sheepishly go past Harrogate and Richmond and congratulate York on their win, before taking their seats in the corner. Miss Clarke next enters the room.

'May I have your attention please?'

Everyone stops what they're doing and looks over towards Miss Clarke.

'Congratulations to Harrogate and York for your impressive victories. Commiserations to Preston and Richmond, you both made a valiant effort. The final round will commence in ten minutes so if you need to use the bathroom, please do so during your short break.' Miss Clarke makes her exit and Harrogate and York, having been reminded that they're soon to battle it out in the final, begin eyeing each other over, trying to size each other up. Miss Jones tries to reassure her team that they don't need to worry, and not to be intimidated by York's condescending stare. Before long, Miss Clarke returns and asks both teams to follow her into the auditorium, as she'd done before. Ben stands up and waits for the rest of his team to exit the room, before tagging on at the end. They wait in line in the annex just off stage out of sight from the audience and wait until Mr Hodge announces the two winning teams to take their seats. Avalon leads her team across the stage and around the back of the chairs to take their seats to the sound of a huge applause from the audience. Ben, feeling really anxious now that it's the final, manages to turn his head to his left to see his family smiling and cheering in the audience. Ben gives them a quick smile before looking back at Mr Hodge as he bangs down his gavel to get everyone's attention.

'Ladies and gentlemen, this is the final round for year eight students. May I remind you of the rules and during the question-and-answering; please may we have total silence in the auditorium to allow the students to concentrate on the questions being asked, and we can all hear the answers being given. Thank you.'

Avalon looks towards the rest of her team and gives them a confident smile, she holds her clenched hand out in front of her with her thumb up to signal that she's ready. The rest of her team does the same, before turning to face Mr Hodge for the competition to start.

'Can we have silence please?' Mr Hodge asks. The room falls silent while everyone listens out for the first question to be asked.

'Are you ready, York?' Mr Hodge asks. Douglas, their team captain, says yes and nods. 'Harrogate, are you ready?' Avalon nods. 'Let's begin.'

Ben feels his heart pounding in his chest as it did before the start of the first round. He knows, he just has to answer one question correctly to steady his nerves. With his finger poised over his buzzer, he turns his attention to Mr Hodge waiting for the first question to be asked.

Buzz!

Ben sees the light on his desk light up with the corresponding light on the judges' panel. Mr Hodge along with everyone else looked over towards Ben. 'Sorry!' Ben realised his hand was shaking and he had accidentally pressed his buzzer. "Sorry, it was an accident.'

'That's all right Ben,' Mr Hodge says. 'I know it's the final and you're all nervous so I recommend that you all place your hands next to the buzzer rather than having your finger resting on it to avoid accidentally pressing the buzzer and having to give an answer. Luckily for you Ben, I hadn't asked the question.'

Everyone, realising the consequence of accidentally pressing the buzzer, immediately rests their right hands on the desk next to their buzzers.

'Okay, let's continue, Question one. In which city would you find the famous Hanging Gardens?'

Buzz!

'Ben, I hope that wasn't another accident?' Mr Hodge asks.

'No, sir.'

"Good, so what's the answer?"

'Babylon.'

'Correct; two points to Harrogate.'

Loud applause sounds out from the audience as Harrogate takes the lead. Avalon, Alexis, Simon, Andrew and Philip quickly give Ben a smile, to say thanks for getting that one right and setting them off to a great start. Ben smiles and mouths the word 'Thanks' before they all turn back towards Mr Hodge in time for the second question.

'Question two: what is the formula for carbon dioxide?'

Buzz!

'Andrew?'

'C O 2'

'Correct; two more points to Harrogate,' Mr Hodge announces. More cheers sound out from the audience. And Andrew gets a complimentary smile from his team members.

'Question three; who wrote the novel... '

At the halfway point, York had come back and overtaken Harrogate to leave the scores at Harrogate seven and York ten. Harrogate answers the next two questions correctly bringing them to eleven but gets the next question wrong leaving York to steal a point bringing the total to Harrogate eleven; York eleven with seven questions to go. York successfully answers the next three questions correctly and jumps ahead with the scores now standing at: York seventeen; Harrogate eleven. Ben can't believe his team is crumbling under the pressure and from the looks on their faces, he knows they've already given up. There are four questions left and he knows if he doesn't intervene now, they're going to lose. He takes one last look at Avalon's face and recognises that sullen look of despair and defeat.

'Question seventeen; Name a country where star fruit is native to?' Mr Hodge asks.

Buzz!

'Ben?'

'Indonesia.'

'Correct; two points to Harrogate. A huge wave of applause rings out from the audience as they see a glimmer of hope being restored to Harrogate.

Avalon and the others stare at Ben in amazement wondering how on earth he knew that answer. Ben gives them a faint smile before turning back towards Mr Hodge.

Question eighteen; who wrote the music score to the musical *The Phantom of the Opera*?

Buzz!

'Yes, Ben?'

'Andrew Lloyd Webber.'

'Correct; two more points to Harrogate.' Ben looks over to his team members and smiles at their expressions of shock. He wonders if they're trying to work out how on earth he knew the last two unrelated questions that are not in the slightest way connected with history.

Ben gives Alexis a wink to say, 'It's all right I've got this.'

Alexis can't believe Ben's confidence; she smiles back at him, wishing she had the same confidence he had.

'Question nineteen; what is the name of the nearest star to earth?'

Buzz!

'Ben'

'Its two stars actually: Alpha Centauri A and Alpha Centauri B.'

'Well done, correct on both counts; unfortunately, I can only give you two points,' Mr Hodge replies.

Ben gives the judge a smile and says, 'That's all right.'

Ben hears a few nervous giggles from his team mates as they can't believe they're only one question away from winning the competition.

'This is the last question. Can we be reminded of the score as it stands?' Mr Hodge asks his assistants. Mrs Evans reads out the scores.

'York has seventeen points and Harrogate has also seventeen points.' There's a loud cheer and applause from the audience.

'Thank you everyone; can we be quiet while I read out the final question.'

The sound in the auditorium drops to a total silence as all ears are turned to Mr Hodge in anticipation of the final question.

'Question twenty: who was the father of Mary, Queen of Scots?' Mr Hodge asks.

Buzz!

'Yes, Ben?'

'James the Fifth of Scotland.'

Ben looks across at his team members who are all looking worried. They've probably worked it out in their heads that if he answered the question incorrectly; York would still have an opportunity to answer the question correctly and steal one point to win. All eyes become fixed on Mr Hodge as he looks down at his question sheet to check Ben's answer with the answer written down on his sheet for question twenty. There seems to be an extended pause; whether it's to add to the drama and suspense of the situation or that he just wants to be sure in his mind that he's going to respond correctly to his answer. Ben looks around to his left and sees the whole audience wide-eyed with their mouths open. He doesn't expect anyone in the audience to know what the correct answer is because most of them are older parents and have probably forgotten most of what they learnt all those years ago. Ben turns back to Mr Hodge knowing all too well what his reply will be; because he's already heard it six times over.'

'*Correct!* Harrogate are the new Inter-School Champions'

'*Yeahhhhhhhhh!*' The sound of cheers and whistles erupt throughout the vast space becoming almost deafening. Ben looks round to his teammates and notices the boys with their arms in the air cheering while the girls are screaming with excitement. It all feels so good to be able to bring so much happiness to his team members, particularly to Alexis.

Mr Hodge, Mr Wilkinson and Mrs Evans go down from behind the judging panel and walk around to the front of their desks. Mr Hodge reaches across Avalon's desk and congratulates her on her win with a firm handshake. He moves to his right and congratulates each member of the team before stopping in front of Ben.

'Well done Ben; that was a very impressive performance you put in. You're going to go far, I'm certain of that.' He shakes Ben's hand. Mr Wilkinson and Mrs Evans follow in Mr Hodge's footsteps and congratulate the winning team. Miss Clarke asks the two year eight teams to go off stage to an area at the side of the stage where a bank of fifty-six chairs are positioned for the teams and their mentors to sit and watch the final match for year nine between Richmond and Preston. Twenty minutes later Richmond year nines are declared the winner. Both year nine teams file out from behind their desks and join the others sitting at the side of the stage.

Mr Hodge goes to the podium to introduce the heads of the winning teams forward to say a few words. Miss Clarke is invited up first.

'I just wanted to say what a pleasure it was to witness a marvellous competition. Certainly the best so far and the standard of questions answered were just outstanding. We at Harrogate High School endeavour to educate our children to the highest standards and I'm sure you would all agree on seeing that hard work shine through. Well done to all the teams competing but a special well done to year eight; we're proud of you!' Miss Clarke says before turning to face the winning year eight sat on the side and gives them a round of applause.

Mr Appleby from Richmond follows Miss Clarke in congratulating his team on winning the year nine competition. Finally, Mr Hodge returns to the podium and invites the year eight team forward to accept their awards. Avalon leads her winning team to the centre of the stage and gracefully accepts a silver-plated trophy of a student reading a book, to a round of applause.

Avalon holds the trophy up in the air in a jubilant pose before passing the trophy to Alexis so she can feel the silverware for a moment. Finally, the trophy reaches Ben at the end of the line; he holds it out towards his family sitting in the audience to the sound of his laudation. Mr Hodge invites the winning Richmond team forward and they're presented with a slightly larger memento for their achievement. Miss Clarke escorts the year eight team back to the side of the stage and takes the winning trophy from them, so it can be duly displayed in the school achievement display in reception. Then they're congratulated once more and told they can go home now with their families.

Chapter Fourteen

Ben wakes up from his contented night's sleep, that sense of achievement from the night before still fresh in his mind. The morning sun shines in through his window blinds making his bedroom bright. He stretches his body out to the sides of his bed and lets out an enormous yawn as his body awakens and revives itself from lying in the same position for the past ten hours. He casually looks over at the alarm clock to see what time it is and is immediately reminded that he's slept in. Paul is coming round this morning at eight forty-five so they can all go to the fun fair which is in town for the weekend. He remembers mentioning it to his mum over two weeks ago when they first saw the posters advertising the fair, stuck to every noticeboard, telegraph pole and vacant shop front in town. The collage of images on the front of the poster advertising the array of events at the fair, had a photograph of a family sitting in a roller coaster car as it sped down a steep slope. The family appeared to be enjoying themselves with their arms raised in the air. There were other images highlighting other activities but Paul and Ben had decided that the roller coaster would be their first ride when the fair came to town.

Feeling excited that in less than an hour, he could be speeding down the roller coaster slope, Ben throws back the duvet and quickly gets into his jeans and tee shirt before dashing to the bathroom to use the toilet. He's too excited to have a complete wash, so, after washing his hands, he splashes a handful of cold water onto his face and quickly dries himself off with the hand towel before making his way downstairs to grab some breakfast. Ben walks over to an empty breakfast table and sits down feeling a little confused as to where everyone else is.

He hears his mum in the kitchen and calls out, 'Mum, where's everyone? Aren't we all going to the fair in five minutes?'

Mum appears at the door holding a tea towel in one hand and a wet coffee cup in the other.

'Sorry, Dad had to go somewhere this morning so it's just going to be you and Jess going to the fair,' Mum tells him before disappearing back inside the kitchen.

Ben picks up the cornflakes box from the table and proceeds to fill his cereal bowl. He glances up at the wall clock, only to realise that he's literally got three or four minutes before Paul will be knocking at his door. He unscrews the lid off the litre bottle of semi-skimmed milk and tips the white liquid over his cereal until the milk covers the flakes. With his left hand he stands the plastic three-quarter-filled container back on the table and replaces the cap while hurriedly eating his breakfast to save time.

Ding-dong. The doorbell rings just as Ben puts the last spoonful of cereal into his mouth. Without waiting to finish chewing, Ben rushes to the front door to let his friend in.

Paul gives Ben a smile and, having noticed a drip of milk running down Ben's chin, kindly reminds him of the fact. Ben wipes his chin with the sleeve of his coat which is hanging on a coat hook to the right of the door. 'Come in,' Ben tells his friend with the last few flakes still in his mouth.

Paul steps into the entrance hall.

'Good morning, Mrs Chapman,' Paul says as he sees Anne walking towards them holding her purse. 'Good morning Paul.' She gives him a smile before turning to face Ben.

'Here you are, take this so you can go on a ride and have something to eat.' She hands Ben five pounds in coins.

'I've given Jess the same, so she can pay for herself, so that money's just for you. Now don't forget Jess is coming with you,' Mum reminds him.

'Ah Mum, can't Paul and I go on our own?' Ben asks, knowing all too well that Jess is going to take ages to get ready and they really want to get to the fair before anyone else does, so they can be the first to ride on the roller coaster.

'No. Anyway, Jess is meeting Debbie so the four of you can stick together; it's safer that way.' 'Oh Mum, do we have to?' Ben protests.

'Yes. Dad told me to remind you this morning.'

Ben realises that if his dad said they had to stick together, he'd better do as he's told. Paul and Ben, wait impatiently by the opened front door for what seemed to be forever but in reality was probably five minutes. 'Come on Jess, we're going to be late.' Ben pleads with his sister to get a move on.

Jess appears at the top of the stairs and intentionally descends the steps as slowly as possible just to antagonise her brother; she knows only too well that Ben would be desperate to get to the fair because he'd been talking about the fair coming to town for the past ten days. Ben notices the smirk on his sister's face which really annoys him and in his desperation, he quickly turns and walks out, closely followed by his friend.

The fun fair normally turns up around the same time every year and sets up their rides and stalls on the recreation ground, at the back of Tesco's superstore. The poster advertising the funfair stated that the fair would be open all day Saturday and Sunday from nine o'clock in the morning until eleven at night. Ben looks down at his watch and sees it's already turned nine o'clock.

'I don't believe it, it's nearly five past nine.' He loudly complains to himself, hoping Jess would hear as she's now caught up with them. Jess ignores her brother and walks past them along the pavement.

'It'll be all right; I'm sure it won't be that busy.' Paul reassures his friend and signals that they should speed up their pace. Jess is at least two inches taller than her brother and her stride is slightly longer giving her an advantage when walking quickly, but today she's in one of her annoying moods, so she's just ambling along just to be awkward. Paul and Ben quicken their pace and pass Jess with ease from either side of the pavement; they smile at each other as the gap increases from five metres to ten metres as they get further away. 'Hey, what's the rush?' Jess calls out, feeling a little left behind. She watches the two boys move slowly further and further away, passing an older couple just ahead and then another couple all heading towards the funfair, until she can't see them. Jess realises it's futile to try to annoy her brother today because he's adamant that he's going to enjoy himself at the fun fair. Jess gives in, and quickly extends her pace to catch them up before they arrive at the entrance to the fair. The nearer the boys get to the fun fair, the more crowded the pavements become as most of the town have decided to do as they're doing and spend the day at the fun fair. Ben recognises two boys from school across the other side of the road. A gap appears in the traffic and the two lads cross over to their side.

'Hi Ben: Paul,' Alan Briggs says as he and Tom Weaver join them.

'Hi, are you going to the fair?' Ben asks.

'Sure. You did really well yesterday,' Tom tells Ben.

'Oh, thanks.' Ben smiles.

'Yes, you were brilliant; everyone thought we were going to lose, and then you answered all the questions at the end on your own and won it for us,' Alan says.

'Thanks,' Ben replies feeling a little embarrassed from receiving such complimentary remarks.

'Anyway, we're meeting some others so we'll see you later,' Alan tells them.

They immediately break into a jog and disappear out of view as they pass a crowd of people walking just ahead.

'So, you made a good impression then?' Paul jokingly asks.

'Oh, you know how it is when you're super intelligent,' Ben tells Paul, they burst out laughing just as Jess appears by their sides.

'What's so funny?' Jess asks.

'You wouldn't understand; it's a guy thing,' Paul tells her. They come to a standstill behind a mass of people ahead as they start to filter in through the narrow entrance to the field. Jess notices Debbie standing just off to the side on the other side of the entrance. 'Debbie' Jess calls out to get her friend's attention as they move closer. Debbie gives Jess a wave as she waits for the three of them to pass through the narrow entrance.

'Have you been waiting long?' Jess asks.

'No just about ten minutes,' Debbie replies.

'So, what do you fancy doing first? We could all go on the roller coaster or we could get something to eat?' Ben asks, hoping the consensus would be to ride on the roller coaster.

'It's too early to eat, let's go on the roller coaster,' Paul says excitedly.

'What about you two?' Ben asks the girls.

'I don't mind; we could go on the roller coaster first,' Debbie agrees.

'Okay,' Jess says.

The four of them begin walking towards the roller coaster ride in the distance with its metal structure rising high above all the other attractions at the funfair. They go through the busy thoroughfare of people passing a variety of interesting stalls and stands situated on either side from a coconut shy, shooting range, burger bar, crazy golf, Ring-a-Duck which all look good but Ben's eyes are focused on the high-rise roller coaster in the distance. Suddenly something over to Ben's left catches his attention. A bright coloured sign with the words: *Bet One Pound,* Win *Ten Pounds* above an image of three upside down cups next to a solitary pea, makes him think for a second. Ben immediately changes direction and heads towards the small crowd followed by Paul. 'Where are you going; the roller coaster's this way.' Ben hears Jessica's voice behind him. Ben goes around the side of the small group of spectators to a gap where he can see what's going on. The proprietor of the stall is a short stocky man in his early fifties with an upturned black moustache wearing a brown suede bowler hat and tartan waistcoat. He's standing on the other side of a bar table which has three small cups and a small wooden pea placed on the flat surface.

'Ladies and Gentlemen, the game is simple. Just keep your eye on the pea.' He turns one of the cups over and places it on top of the wooden pea. He turns the other two cups over and places those next to the one in the middle. Slowly he rotates the cups around themselves on the tabletop once or twice, all the while looking at the audience.

'All you have to do is tell me which cup the pea is under.' He gives everyone a smile and lifts up the cup in the middle to reveal the small round pea. 'If you can do that, you can win ten pounds. So, who would like to win ten pounds?' the gentleman asks. Ben realises that he and Jess only have five pounds each to spend on the fun fair and after spending three pounds to go on the roller-coaster ride and two pounds for a plain burger at the stall; they won't have any money left.

'This could be an opportunity to win more money, so they could go on more rides, and have more to eat,' Ben reasons to himself. He looks over at Paul standing next to him and is about to ask him what he thought, when he notices Paul's facial expression confirming exactly what he'd been thinking.

'Go on Ben.' Paul encourages his friend to have a go.

'Ben, I thought you wanted to go on the Roller coaster?' Jess asks, sounding irritated that Ben's changed his mind. Ben looks back at his sister now standing right behind him with Debbie by her side and calmly says.

'I'm just going to have a quick go at this first.'

'Suit yourself, but don't complain to me when you don't have enough for something to eat later,' Jess tells him.

'So, who would like to try to win ten pounds?' The stall owner asks. A young man standing right in front of the man quickly holds out a one-pound coin.

'I want to have a go,' he tells the man. The stall owner takes the young man's money and places it in his money pouch strapped to his waist. The young man steps forward so he can keep his eyes on the three cups. A pretty brunette stands close behind him, puts her arm around his waist.

'Come on Lee you can do this,' she says to encourage her boyfriend.

'Are you ready?' the stall owner asks.

The young man nods then leans forward to concentrate on the three cups. The stall owner picks up the pea again and shows it to the audience before placing it down on the table.

'Keep your eyes on the pea,' he says before covering it with one of the cups. He quickly places the other two cups either side and begins to move the cups clockwise and anticlockwise around each other moving from left to right. He's obviously very skilled at what he does because his hands move the cups around at lightning speed. Finally, he comes to a stop with the cups positioned in a line.

'Which cup has the pea under it?' he asks the young man. Lee hesitates for a second as he confirms in his mind which of the three cups the pea is under. He points to the left-hand cup.

'It's under there,' he says feeling confident. The stall owner lifts the cup up to reveal nothing underneath.

'Sorry, bad luck.' He then lifts up the centre cup to show where the pea really is. 'Do you want another go?' the stall owner asks.

'No thanks,' Lee replies feeling out-skilled.

'Ah Lee, that was really hard; I thought you did really well,' his girlfriend tells him. He shrugs and gives his girlfriend a half smile before they turn and walk away through the crowd. 'Anyone else, want to chance their luck?' the stall owner asks.

'Yes I do!' Ben quickly calls out from the far right of the crowd and immediately squeezes between the table and the front row of people so he can take his position in front of the stall owner.

'Hi there son, are you sure you want to risk losing your money?' the man asks, looking concerned probably thinking that Ben's a little younger than his usual clients and he's possibly feeling guilty at the thought of taking money from a child.

'Don't worry about it; I don't intend on losing,' Ben confidently tells the man to the sound of giggling from the crowd. The man gives Ben a smile before taking the one-pound coin and slipping the money in his hip bag.

'Okay, are you ready?' he asks.

'I'm ready,' Ben tells him and leans forward with his eyes fixed on the small round object on the table. He knows he doesn't need to concentrate on where the pea ends up because he can just select any one of the rested positions and if it's wrong, go back in time and pick another; but for everyone standing around, he wants them to think that he's just a normal kid. The man quickly goes into his rehearsed spiel as he's probably done a thousand times. He picks up the pea to show everyone and then places it down on the table and covers the pea with one of the cups. He positions the other two cups on either side.

'Keep your eyes on where the pea is,' he tells Ben before quickly moving the cups around the table top using both hands as he did before. Ben immediately senses that the man is moving a lot slower than he did with Lee. Maybe he's feeling sorry for Ben because he's just a young child or maybe he just thinks that Ben hasn't a chance in winning and wants the audience to notice that he's a fair businessman and not someone who would take advantage of a minor. Finally, the cups come to a stop positioned as before, all in a line. The man straightens up from his slightly bent over position and asks, 'So, which cup is the pea under?' 'Come on Ben you can do it!' Ben hears Jess and then Debbie call out from behind him. Suddenly Ben feels a sense of accomplishment having his sister now rooting for him. He raises his right hand and slowly moves it from left to right in front of the cups to give the impression that he's not sure which cup to choose; with his finger pointing between two of the cups, Ben looks up at the stall owner with an undecided look on his face. 'Just touch the one you think the pea is under,' the man tells him. Ben looks down at the three cups again before resting his finger on the base of the right cup. The store owner reaches forward and lifts up the small terracotta pot to reveal a small wooden pea underneath. 'Yeeeaaaaah!'

A cheer sounds out from the crowd including Jess, Debbie and Paul.

'Well done lad,' says a gentleman standing to the right of Ben. Ben turns and looks up at the well-dressed man in his seventies.

'Just a good guess, that's all,' Ben tells him with a slightly raised voice so that the stall owner could hear. 'Here you go son, well played.' Ben hears the voice of the businessman as he hands Ben a slightly crumpled ten-pound note. Ben takes the money and shoves the note inside his trouser pocket.

'Did you want to try your luck again?' the man asks, sounding confident that he'd be taking back some of his money.

'Why not? I don't mind if you don't mind,' Ben tells the man, before handing over another one-pound coin. The man picks up the pea and places it back in the centre of the table before covering the pea with a cup and placing the other two cups either side.

'Are you ready?' he asks and without waiting for a response, his hands move the cups around the table but this time at lightning speed.

Ben stares at the moving cups being sped around the table, almost in a blur. He watches with admiration at the speed and accuracy of the stall owner as he manoeuvres the cups around the small wooden surface; almost feeling guilty that he'll be taking what rightly belongs to the man, because he's honed his skill to such a high standard. The man finally stops with the cups all in a line and steps back from the table.

'Was it a bit harder that time?' he sarcastically asks, knowing all too well that no one on earth could have followed along. 'Which cup is the pea under?' he asks feeling a hundred percent confident that he'll be keeping the one-pound coin. Ben lifts up his hand and moves it again from left to right. 'Erm… I'm… … not sure.'

The man smiles and folds his arms to indicate that he's got nothing more to do with the game, and that the choice is solely down to Ben as to whether he wins or loses.

'Take your time son; just touch one of them when you're ready' he says.

'Eeny meeny miny moe,' Ben says as he moves his finger across the top of the row to indicate that he's about to guess.

'This one.' Ben touches the centre cup with his finger.

Ben looks up at the man just as his smile disappears. Everyone standing can't be sure whether Ben's selected the right cup or if the man is just putting on an act with a subdued appearance. The man steps forward and reluctantly lifts the centre cup to reveal the small pea beneath. 'Yeeeaaaahhhhhhhhh!' Everyone on either side of Ben begins to cheer and applaud.

'Well done Ben that was amazing,' Jess tells him. Ben looks at Paul, who doesn't say a word but gives a big smile, knowing all too well what he's been up to. The stall owner places the cup back down on the table and counts out ten-pound coins from his money bag and drops the coins into Ben's cupped hands. Ben carefully places the coins inside his trouser pocket and looks up at the store owner to tell him that he's won enough for the night and to give someone else a go; when he catches sight of Alexis and Avalon in the corner of his eye approach the small gathering to his right. 'Does anyone else want to try their luck?' the man asks the audience.

'Wait a minute, what if the lad wants another go?' the elderly gentleman asks the stall owner.

'Sorry son; did you want another go, or would you prefer to keep what you've won and not risk losing any of it?' he asks hoping Ben would take the hint. Ben looks over towards Alexis and is greeted with a smile.

Ben's heart begins to swoon and he's taken away for a second before being nudged by Paul.

'Oh er... yes, I'll play one last time,' Ben tells the owner before handing over his one-pound coin. The man quickly positions the pea on the table and covers it with one of the cups as he did before. Ben looks over at Alexis and smiles before looking down at the table as the man positions the two other cups so they're all in a line.

'Are you ready?' he asks. Ben gives him a cursory nod and leans forward to focus on the cups. The man covers the ball as he did before and begins to move the cups faster than he's ever done before and Ben is taken back by the speed of his hands. He tries to keep his eyes on the cup with the pea under but within seconds, he's lost sight of the cup.

This guy is brilliant, Ben thinks as the cups are rapidly moved around the table. Ben turns his head to the side to look at Alexis and gives her a wink and a smile to everyone's disbelief. Alexis lifts her hands to her face in shock, thinking that she's going to be the cause of Ben losing his money, so she quickly points towards the table and the moving cups to indicate that he should be paying attention to what's going on and not be looking in her direction. Ben looks back at the moving cups just as they come to a stop, positioned all in a line in front of him. The stall owner, having noticed that Ben had turned away for a second, reasons to himself that it's now going to be impossible for the lad to guess which cup the pea will be under. He confidently steps back from the table and folds his arms convinced that he won't be paying out to the lad again. 'So, any idea, which cup the pea is under?' the man asks, with a self-assured smile. 'I think the pea is under…' Ben slowly moves his hand forward. 'This one.' Ben rests his finger on the right-hand cup. The stall owner looks down to where Ben's finger is placed and begins to shake his head in disbelief. He slowly lifts the cup to reveal the small round object beneath.

'I don't believe it! That was amazing,' the elderly gentleman says, sounding astonished.

'Well done Ben,' Jess tells her brother. Ben gives her a thumbs-up sign and then looks over towards Alexis who's clapping and cheering. Her eyes lock on to him as she mouths the word 'wow.' Ben looks back at the stall owner who's still shaking his head in disbelief. He reaches inside his pocket and takes out a wad of tens and twenties and proceeds to peel one of the crisp notes from the wad and hands it over to Ben. He takes the ten-pound note and slips it inside his trouser pocket.

'Well done lad!' Many of the crowd continue to applaud him as he squeezes through the throng of onlookers to an open space to wait for the others. Paul, Jess and Debbie arrive by his side and again congratulate him on winning before he notices Alexis and Avalon go around the crowd to join them.

'Wow that was incredible; I still don't know how you picked the cup with the pea under,' Alexis says.

'I have an acute hearing which means I can hear the faintest sounds, so I just listened to the pea rolling around under the cup. It wasn't that difficult,' Ben nonchalantly tells her.

'Well, I think you were brilliant,' Alexis tells him. 'And I just wanted to say, about yesterday. I thought you played really well and I was pleased that you were in our team.'

'Thanks.'

'Yes, thanks Ben, you really won it for us,' Avalon adds.

'It's all right; anyway, it was a team effort and we all contributed,' Ben tells the girls. Alexis smiles and asks. 'So what rides were you planning on going on?'

'We're all going on the roller coaster; did you two want to come? I'm paying,' Ben offers. Alexis and Avalon look at each other for a second.

'What do you think?' Alexis asks Avalon.

'Sure, why not?'

Paul standing just behind the girls; having heard Ben invite them to join them, gives Ben an excited smile and a thumbs-up because apart from Ben's sister and on this occasion Debbie, he's never hung around with girls before.

'Okay, let's go on the roller coaster.' Ben tells them. The six of them go through the crowd to the far end of the fairground.

Chapter Fifteen

The six of them wait in line as the roller coaster cars come to a stop at the platform and the passengers all get out and exit through a gate on the far side. The line of people start to move forward as the cars are being filled for the next ride when the ride owner holds out his arm in front of Ben.

'Sorry, you'll have to wait for the next ride.'

Ben looks back at his group. 'At least we know we're next on the ride,' he excitedly tells them. Paul looks just as excited as he is and seems to be hopping from one foot to the other. Ben suddenly notices Alexis and Avalon whispering to each other and looking invariably nervous about going on the ride.

'Are you two girls all right?' Ben asks. Alexis and Avalon look towards Ben and Paul before glancing to their right as the roller coaster car speeds down a steep slope to the sound of girls screaming.

'We... erm... ' Ben senses the girls are not overly excited about going on the ride.

'I'll tell you what, why don't you ride with me, and Paul can sit behind us with Avalon,' Ben hears himself say before realising what came out his mouth. '

He thought, *I don't believe it. Jess and Debbie must have heard me, and now the whole school is going to find out. What if Alexis turns me down. This has got to be the most idiotic idea of the century. Why didn't I just think before speaking.*' Ben angrily scolds himself for letting on to his sister that he fancies Alexis. Alexis turns back towards Avalon and they start whispering something between themselves, so Ben quickly turns back towards the roller coaster as the car slows down on its final approach. Paul looking at Ben pulls a nervous expression having heard what Ben had suggested to the girls. The roller coaster cars finally stop in front of them and the passengers all climb out.

'Okay first two in the front seat.' The owner beckons the group forward. Ben steps forward along the platform and steps down inside the first car and slides along the wooden bench to the far seat. He looks over to his left just as Alexis steps down into the car and takes the seat beside him, shaking like a leaf. Paul gets down into the car behind followed by Avalon, while Jess and Debbie take their seats in the third car. The ride owner quickly checks that the safety bar in each carriage is pressed down securely before stepping back to the control panel and pressing the start button. The sound of dramatic music is heard from the oversized speakers next to the control box as the carriages jerk forward along its track. Alexis instinctively grabs hold of Ben's hand at the sound of their car hooking onto a massive chain that runs the length of the steep slope in front of them. The motorised cogs beneath the control panel churn away as the now laden cars are slowly pulled up the ramp towards the highest point of the ride. Ben is a little taken back with excitement at having the girl of his dreams hold on to his hand. He looks down at Alexis's small soft hand holding on to his and in that moment his heart is reeling with exhilaration. In his wildest imagination, he could never have thought that Alexis would like him, and here they are on the roller coaster, holding hands. Ben smiles to himself at feeling so happy and wished that time would just freeze, so he could enjoy this experience for ever. Ben looks up at Alexis's face in the hope that she would see his huge smile, but her head is tilted forward and her blonde shoulder length hair is covering her face. A gentle breeze brushes her hair causing the neat curtain of hair to part, revealing her mouth before being pushed back so that her side profile is hidden from view again. The carriage reaches the apex and their car slowly edges over the ridge.

'Look, we can see our school.' Ben points to the rooftops of the school building over to their left in the distance. He looks at Alexis's face again hoping to get some acknowledgement but her head is still tilted downwards and as their carriage leans forward the breeze wafts her hair back away from her face to reveal her eyes squeezed tightly shut. The carriage starts down the slope and quickly picks up speed as it races to the bottom before rising again up the next incline. Alexis lets out a scream and her grip on Ben's hand gets tighter. Ben can't believe he's talked Alexis into riding the roller coaster with him, while all the time she's probably been terrified. In his guilty conscience, he quickly takes hold of Alexis's hand and reaches his arm around her shoulder to reassure her that he's there for her. Alexis immediately responds, by sliding herself closer to him so their bodies are pressed together while leaning her head into Ben's chest. The carriage rises up the next incline, banks over and speeds down the next slope. Alexis's body tenses at each turn and Ben squeezes her tightly to reassure her. The change in direction and movement causes Alexis's hair to billow in front of his face; filling his nostrils with the sweet smell of her perfume. Feeling Alexis's soft body pressed against his and breathing in her rose-scented perfume is all too much for him and in that moment, Alexis becomes the most precious and valuable thing to him. Ben can't remember the rest of the ride because his mind is fixed on Alexis and before they realise it; they hear the braking system being engaged and the cars start to slow down. Alexis quickly sits upright and lets go of Ben's hand as their car comes to a complete stop next to the short platform. The attendant steps forward and releases the safety bar across their laps so they can exit their cars. Alexis and Avalon are the first to get out, they immediately give each other a quick hug before hurrying off towards the exit. Ben steps onto the platform and is distracted by the two girls chatting to each other as they leave through a wooden turnstile.

'I can't believe it. I saw you put your arm around Alexis!' Paul excitedly says. Ben nervously looks around to see where his sister is and is shocked to see her and Debbie not three feet behind them. Ben quickly hurries Paul along towards the exit.

'I know; I can't believe it!' Ben whispers back to Paul. 'Do you know if Jess saw us?' Ben nervously asks.

Paul shrugs. 'I don't think so, but who cares. Alexis is the prettiest girl in school so I wouldn't worry about it,' Paul tells his friend. As they walk out through the exit, Ben sees Alexis and Avalon waiting for them over to the right in a small clearing so they head over towards them. Ben's feeling a little unsure of the situation, because it could all change if his sister saw him put his arm around Alexis. For one thing, the whole school will know about it on Monday and to be honest, Ben doesn't exactly know what all this means. *Okay, he sat next to Alexis on a ride and, okay, he put his arm around her shoulder, so what, what does that prove?* he thinks. He's never had a girlfriend before so does this qualify them as boyfriend and girlfriend? He doesn't think so, so what's the problem? Ben nervously looks round to see where Jess and Debbie are, only to realise they're right behind them. Ben tries not to panic as they all merge on each other. He eases himself back so he doesn't become the focal point of people's attention and gradually slides in behind Paul so he can listen to the topic of conversation.

'That was brilliant," Debbie exclaims. "I know, I think I screamed most of the way round," Jess says, which surprised Ben because he never heard his sister scream. Alexis and Avalon remained quiet, so Paul quickly steps forward and asks, 'So, what does everyone want to do next?'

'I wouldn't mind something to eat,' Alexis says. 'Okay, what about everyone else?' Paul asks.

'Yes, I wouldn't mind a burger or something, either,' Jess says.

'I think there's a burger stall near the bumper cars, we passed on the way here, what about getting a burger there. Is that okay with you Ben?' Paul asks while pointing in the general direction of the burger stand.

'Sure, and I'm buying,' Ben tells everyone. They walk through the crowd of people towards the food stand. The white kitchenette style trailer is set back behind a small seating area set up with eight tables with two long picnic benches either side of each table. Ben tells the girls to find an empty table while he and Paul order the food at the Burger stand. They attach themselves to the back end of a small queue of people at the burger stand and wait their turn to be served.

'I can't believe Jess hasn't said anything,' Ben tells Paul and glances over towards the girls as they all sit down on an empty table.

'I know, I was surprised too. But what if she didn't see anything; she did say she was screaming the whole way round, so who knows, she may have had her eyes closed the whole time.'

Ben recalls Alexis's face with her eyes closed the whole time so Jess may have done the same. He looks back at the table to see if Jess is telling Alexis anything but they seem to be looking over to see what they're doing. The queue moves forward and Ben gives his order to a young girl behind the counter and pays with his winnings. Suddenly they smell of savoury fried burger meat wafts in front of them causing their gastric juices to ignite, making them feel extremely hungry. 'Mmmm I'm starving!' Ben tells his friend. The delicious smell of food is a welcome distraction for Ben so he fixes his eyes on the chef as he prepares their food. They step forward next to the counter with their hands placed on the ledge, looking like begging dogs waiting for their master to feed them.

'Here you are: six cheeseburgers with fries, and six Cokes.'

The man behind the counter hands over six brown individual bags; each containing a burger and chips alongside a cardboard pressed cup holder with six plastic cups positioned in their individual places. Ben takes the food bags and Paul picks up the drinks from the counter. They eagerly go across the seating area to their table and notice that Alexis, Avalon and Jess are sitting on the far side of a table with Debbie opposite Jess at one end. Ben takes a seat opposite Alexis at the other end while Paul sits next to Ben, opposite Avalon. Ben passes the brown paper food bags to everyone, while Paul hands out the Cokes from the tray.

'Bon appetit!' Ben says in his best French accent. 'Thanks Ben!' the girls chorus.

Ben opens his food bag and lifts out the hot cheeseburger in its bread roll and takes a huge bite.

'This was really nice of you Ben; you know, to buy all this food,' Alexis says before lifting up her burger and taking a small bite from the bread roll. Ben can't believe that Alexis has made a comment and he's got his mouth full again. He frantically chews the food that's in his mouth so he can respond but his mouth is so full of meat and bread; he's now struggling to swallow any of it. Alexis notices Ben's dilemma and gives him a sympathetic smile.

'Sorry, I'm always biting too much of my burger; I know I shouldn't but I can't help it.' Ben tries to apologise for his uncouth behaviour, which is graciously accepted by Alexis, with a slight giggle and a smile.

Given the situation, Alexis decides to keep the conversation to a minimum until they've all finished their food, which is probably a good thing for Ben. Avalon and Paul are the first to finish their food so they volunteer to take the rubbish over to the rubbish bin at the far end of the seating area. Jess and Debbie, spot a couple of boys walking past, they recognise so they decide to join them, leaving Ben and Alexis alone at the table. Ben watches the girls go over to the two boys standing near the bumper cars. They say something to the boys, who respond with smiles and waves before the four of them join the queue for the bumper cars.

'Where's Jess and Debs gone?' Paul asks.

'Oh, they're over there with a couple of lads; I think they're going on the bumper cars,' Ben explains and points in the direction of the girls.

'I still have plenty of money if you fancy doing something else,' Ben says to the girls.

'Sure,' Alexis says, looking towards Avalon to see if she agrees.

'Okay,' she replies.

They all decide to take a wander and see what's on offer. For the next few hours, the four of them try a variety of rides. First was a giant carpet slide then the merry-go-round and the last ride they went on was a Wurlitzer which made them all feel a little unsteady on their feet. To steady themselves, they venture to stick with the skill stands on offer. The boys tried their luck on the coconut shy but failed miserably. The girls didn't fancy throwing a heavy wooden ball at five coconuts on individual stands to try to knock them off so they chose the rifle shooting range next. They all made a fair effort but didn't win any prizes. As they walk away from the stand; Alexis catches sight of a cuddly white rabbit displayed as one of the prizes at the *Hoop the Bunny* stall and makes the comment that she loves rabbits. Ben decides to win the rabbit for Alexis. 'I want one too,' Avalon says.

'If Ben's going to win one for Alexis, I'll win one for you,' Paul tells Avalon. The boys walk up to the short counter that has two playing positions and the girls stand to one side to watch.

'Two please,' Ben tells the stall owner and hands over the correct money for them to play. The man gives Ben three yellow hoops and Paul three blue hoops so that they can start the game. There are eight rabbits perched on eight wooden posts randomly positioned at the far end of the stall. The idea of the game is to throw a hoop from the other side of the counter, so it lands centred around a rabbit, to win. Paul and Ben hold up their first hoop and take aim. The girls look on, feeling excited that they could be receiving a prize of a white rabbit within the next minute. The boys throw their hoops towards the white rabbits and embarrassingly miss by a mile. Their second attempts are both equally rubbish and their third throw, seems to be even worse.

'If you want to do a job properly, you have to do it yourself,' Alexis tells Ben. She holds out her hand for some money. 'Okay girls; if you think you can do better.' Ben gives them a pound each so they can have a go. They pay the stall owner the money and each receive their three hoops.

Alexis and Avalon hold up their first hoop in readiness while the boys stand to the side half expecting the girls to fail as they did. Avalon casts her hoop across the space and completely misses all the rabbits. Alexis throws her hoop high into the air and they all watch with anticipation as the hoop rotates around and around, finally coming down and clipping the side of the head of one of the bunnies and drops to the ground.

'Oooh nearly!' Ben tells her.

Alexis holds her next hoop out in front of her and lines it up with the target. She throws the hoop towards a white rabbit over to the right side and the hoop drops down around the rabbit's head.

'Yes!' Alexis screams.

'Well done Alexis, good throw,' Ben says feeling totally outplayed.

'Come on Avalon, you can do it.' Alexis encourages her friend. Avalon holds out her hoop and tries to do the same as Alexis by aiming for one on the right. She casts her hoop towards the rabbit, and misses.

'Arrrgh.' Avalon scowls. She holds out her last hoop and lines it up again. She throws the hoop and this time clips a rabbit while the hoop deflects off to the side.

'Ah, you nearly had one then. Maybe I could win you one with my last hoop,' Alexis tells Avalon. Alexis holds her hoop out in front again and focuses on where she wants it to go. She pulls back her hand and then thrusts it out towards a rabbit just to her left. The hoop rotates round and round in the air before looping over the rabbit's head. The four of them all scream in amazement as Alexis wins her second rabbit.

'Yeahhhhhhhhh!'

Alexis chooses the fluffy white rabbit she had her eye on, as her winnings and Avalon chooses a mottled brown rabbit. The four of them walk away from the stall feeling excited at having won something. Ben looks at the time on his watch and realises it's time to head home. 'Sorry guys, my mum's expecting me home at four so I need to get going,' he tells the others.

'That's all right Ben, I think we're about ready to head home too,' Alexis says. They all live in the same area so they go out of the fairground and along the pavement towards the park. The pavement is too narrow to walk four abreast, so Paul and Avalon drop behind so Alexis and Ben can walk together.

'This has been great, Ben; it's been really good fun,' Alexis says as she hugs her rabbit.

'Yes, it's been really nice and I've enjoyed your company,' Ben says and gives Alexis a smile.

They've only been together for the past few hours but it's been really nice and Ben feels so much closer to her now. She's funny and sweet and really good to be with. They reach an open gate that leads through the park, which happens to be a shortcut.

'Shall we go through the park?' Ben asks.

'Yes, I live on the other side too,' Alexis tells him. They slowly walk through the park and chat about what they've done and the funny things they've seen; especially the moment when the man with the cups, realised that Ben had picked the right cup for the third time in a row and his expression was a picture; he looked so annoyed. They laugh. They reach the far side of the park and walk through the gate.

'My home's this way,' Ben tells Alexis while pointing to his right.

'Oh, I live that way.' Alexis points in the opposite direction.

Ben notices a cyclist riding towards them along the pavement so he steps closer to Alexis standing next to the railings to allow the cyclist room to ride past. A second later he watches the cyclist pass by them before turning back to face Alexis, when he becomes all too aware of their close proximity. Ben stares at Alexis's face with a new appreciation of how pretty she is. His eyes look deep into her eyes, seeing the light brown shades with speckles of green around the iris with the dark pupil in the centre reflecting back his image. He glances down past her cute button nose to her perfectly shaped mouth and beautiful white teeth as she says.

'Thank you for all the food and, well, paying for everything.'

'That's all right; thank you for... going around with us,' Ben replies, not knowing what to say as the closeness of Alexis is making him feel overwhelmed.

'Oh, and thanks for looking after me on the roller coaster,' Alexis says as her eyes lock onto his again.

'That's all right,' Ben manages to say before Alexis leans forward and kisses him on the lips. It all happened too quickly for Ben, one moment he was just talking to her and the next her soft lips pressed against his and then she was gone. Ben stares at Alexis and Avalon as they walk away along the pavement in the opposite direction, feeling totally shocked and in limbo. 'What?! I don't believe it!' Paul says looking really surprised that the prettiest girl in school kissed his best friend. Ben, still reeling from the experience, can only stand with his fingers touching his lips; trying to recall the incident that happened moments ago. They watch the girls reach a turning on the right; Alexis looks back towards them and waves before disappearing behind a building with Avalon by her side.

'This has got to be the best day of my life,' Ben tells his friend.

'I've had a pretty good day too. Avalon's been chatting to me for the last couple of hours, and you know me, I never get to speak to girls,' Paul says.

'Alexis kissed me!' Ben reminds his friend.

'I know; I saw you.' Ben reaches inside his pocket and pulls out his watch.

Chapter Sixteen

If it weren't for Paul; Ben knows he'd still be reliving that moment over and over. Paul told Ben to stop although he didn't know exactly what he was up to; he just knew Ben had travelled back in time.

'So how many times have you kissed Alexis?' Paul would ask.

It started off with Ben saying, 'That was the second time.' After half an hour in real time, Ben told Paul that he'd kissed Alexis seventeen times already; that's when Paul told him to stop. Having travelled back in time seventeen times in the last half an hour, really embedded the memory of Alexis kissing him by the park gate. Ben recalls the image of Alexis saying, 'Oh, and thanks for looking after me on the roller coaster.' And then Ben would see her head move forward as in slow motion and press her lips against his. It feels so real to him now that he replayed that moment. The images are fresh and clear and it feels like he can recall that scene and play it over and over in his mind as easily as playing a DVD. The best thing about it; he can still smell her perfume and feel her soft skin next to his, making the experience so real and vivid.

'Ben, are we walking home; it's nearly four.' Paul reminds his friend that he needs to get home before four o'clock.

'Oh yes.' Ben checks the time on his watch, which tells him that it's five to four.

'I think we'd better run.' They jog along the road to the end, then turn left to another junction where Ben needs to turn left and Paul to the right.

'See you tomorrow,' Paul says.

'Okay, seeya.'

'And no more going back and kissing Alexis!' Paul shouts as he jogs in the opposite direction. Ben slows up at the end of his street and decides to walk the last hundred metres to his front door, to get his breath back. 'Hi Mum, I'm home,' he shouts through to the kitchen as he knows his mum will be preparing dinner at this time.

'Hi Ben, did you have a nice time?' his mum asks. Ben quickly takes his shoes off and closes the door. 'Yes thanks, just going to my room,' he tells his mum feeling that if she sees him at that moment, she would know something was up and start questioning him about why he looks so elated. He closes his bedroom door behind him and lies down on the bed.

I'm in love, he thinks. He can't seem to think of anything else but Alexis. Images of her begin streaming into his mind; her smiling face after she answered a question in the school competition, the way she looked at him in biology; then on the roller coaster when she buried her head into his chest. More and more images flood into his mind, from as far back as he can remember leaving him no time to think about anything else. He doesn't know how long he'd been laying there but he knows it's been a while, because the next thing he hears is his mother's voice.

'Dinner's ready!' his mum calls out from downstairs. Ben sits up and slides his feet off the side of the bed. Suddenly that cramping feeling inside his stomach reminds him that he's hungry, so with a bit more urgency, he stands up and goes downstairs to the welcoming smell from the kitchen. 'Hello Ben, how was your day?' Dad asks with a huge grin on his face.

'Jeeessss!' Ben calls out feeling angry that Jess has told his parents all about Alexis.

'What? I didn't know it was a secret!' Jess says defensively.

'What secret?' Mum asks, knowing all too well what went on earlier.

'Okay, I kissed Alexis,' Ben says, hoping that would be the end of it.

'You did *what*?' Jess asks. Ben suddenly realises what an idiot he is; she obviously didn't know *that* part and now he's gone and told her. Ben winces, knowing that, for the next few minutes, he's going to have to explain everything to his family. Ben reluctantly slides into his seat at the dinner table next to Jess and gives her an angry stare to show his annoyance. Mum carries a large earthenware dish containing a freshly baked cottage pie and places it down in the centre of the table. 'Wait till I've finished serving food before you tell me all the intimate details,' Mum says sounding all excited. Ben, seeing all the grinning faces turned in his direction, knew this was going to happen, so he resigned himself to just get it over and done with. He waits until everyone is seated with their food in front of them before he relates the events of the day, leaving out the parts where he travelled back in time to win the money, and when he relived the experience of kissing Alexis over and over.

'That's lovely Ben, Alexis sounds like a really nice girl,' Mum tells him.

'I'm surprised you want a girlfriend; I didn't get a girlfriend until I was fifteen,' Dad says.

'Fifteen! I thought, I was your first girlfriend?' Mum asks, sounding perturbed.

'I... er... well she wasn't that nice and I think we only went out once,' Dad says trying to dig himself out of a hole.

'That's all right darling, don't you worry; I know all about Veronica Hardcastle.' Mum tells Dad who still looks all flustered and unsettled.

'Who told you about Veronica?' he asks.

'Now; that would be telling and you know me, I'm not a gossip.' Mum pats dad on his arm to indicate that it's all okay. For the next ten minutes, everyone stops talking and concentrates on eating, which seems to suit the boys sitting around the table. After dinner, Ben tells his parents that he's going to his room because he has to finish off some homework, which is partially true as he does have some homework but the real reason; he wants to avoid being asked further questions about his so-called girlfriend.

Ben usually does his homework straight after school each day but as he had to attend the school competition on Friday, he didn't have time to do Friday's homework. He slides his schoolbag out from under his desk and takes out three folders with his homework assignments in, and places them down on the desk. He opens the uppermost folder and reads the homework assignment for his art class: *Draw something in an impressionistic style.*' He takes his drawing pad from his desk drawer and finds a clean page to draw on. It doesn't take long for him to decide on what to draw, because his incomplete matchstick ship is positioned right in front of him. Ben picks up a sharp pencil and quickly sketches the hull of the ship in an impressionistic style. After a few minutes, he places his pencil down and holds up the book to admire his artwork.

'It's all right,' he tells himself. The half-built hull of a ship drawing looks a little like a crumpled slipper, to him. He's not the best artist in the world, so Miss won't expect a masterpiece and, to be honest, it's supposed to be an impressionistic piece of art anyway. Ben closes his art folder and opens the next folder containing his history assignment.

Ben completes all his homework by eight o'clock which happens to be half an hour before his bedtime. He looks around the room for something else to do but nothing jumps out at him, so he decides to have an early night instead and just go to sleep. He heads into the bathroom, has a quick wash, and brushes his teeth before making his way downstairs to say goodnight to his family. As he enters the lounge, the sound of gunfire and explosions blaring out from the TV speakers tell him that his family are watching an action movie. It must be good because his parents don't acknowledge the fact that he's standing in the doorway.

'Goodnight,' Ben says to his parents sitting next to each other on the sofa.

'Goodnight,' his mum replies without taking her attention away from the screen. Dad doesn't say a word except for the raising of his left hand in a partial wave. Ben goes back upstairs to his room and gets into bed.

* * *

Alexis squeezes Ben's hand as they look out through the front bay window of his granddad's house. The afternoon sun brightened up the clear blue sky with the few isolated white clouds randomly spaced across the blue vista above the park tree line.

'Come on you two, have a seat,' Granddad says as he enters the lounge carrying a tray with two glasses of lemonade, a cup of tea and a plate with a chocolate sponge cake positioned in the middle. Alexis and Ben quickly let go of each other's hand at the sound of his grandfather entering the room and take a seat together on the sofa as Granddad places the tray down on the coffee table.

'Here you are,' he picks up both glasses of lemonade and positions them down on top of two coasters in front of them.

'Would you like a slice of chocolate cake Alexis; I made it myself just this morning?'

'Yes thank you, Mr Chapman.'

'Just call me Joe,' Granddad reminds her. Granddad cuts a slice of cake and passes it to Alexis. He cuts two more slices; one he gives to Ben and the other he takes for himself. He sits down in his armchair and picks up his cup of tea. Ben takes a large bite from his slice of cake just as Granddad asks, 'So, what have you been up to today?'

'Mmwee beh zto,' Ben tries to say with his mouth full.

'We were at the park near Nelson Street and Ben told me that you lived nearby, so I persuaded him to bring me round to see you,' Alexis quickly replies to save Ben's embarrassment from talking with his mouth full.

'And I'm glad you did else I wouldn't have had this opportunity to meet such a pretty young lady,' Granddad says, trying to charm Alexis.

'Thank you Mr Chapman. I mean Joe,' Alexis replies.

'You know Benjamin's never brought any of his girlfriend's round to see me.'

'I've not had a girlfriend before Granddad.' Ben immediately tries to defend himself.

'Well, I'm glad to hear that! What are you now; twelve?' Granddad asks.

'Yes, I'll be thirteen in May.'

'Still, when I was your age, I wasn't interested in girls. I had a lot of exploring to do,' Granddad says before taking a bite from his slice of cake.

Alexis and Ben both take the opportunity to join him so there's a natural pause between their conversations. They sit in silence for a couple of minutes while they finish their cake and drinks, which Ben is only too pleased about; because he was starting to feel a little uncomfortable with Granddad's conversation about girlfriends.

'I've got a few photographs of Ben and Jess when they were younger; would you like to see them?' Granddad asks Alexis.

'Yes please Joe.' Alexis gives Granddad a smile. 'I'll just find them; they're in one of my photograph albums.' Granddad stands up and walks over to a large bookcase that's tucked away behind the opened lounge door. Ben doesn't particularly want to look through hundreds of photographs of him as a young lad playing with Jess in the conservatory so he decides to wash up the empty plates and cups. Granddad walks back to the sofa carrying a thick red photograph album and noticing that Ben's now carrying the tray with their dirty crockery through to the kitchen; takes the seat next to Alexis on the sofa.

Granddad's kitchen could be described as immaculate; which is amazing, because all the other rooms in the house seem to be disorganised and cluttered. The kitchen work surface is clean and empty, except for an electric kettle, plugged into a wall socket and a neatly folded up dishcloth positioned centrally between the hot and cold taps. Everything has been put away in its rightful place inside the cupboards. Ben places the tray down on the work surface and opens the base cupboard below the sink in the hope of finding the washing up liquid. He hears Alexis laughing in the front room, so he assumes she's seen a photograph of Ben pulling a funny face or doing something embarrassing. Ben cringes at the thought knowing all too well that she'll remind him of what she saw later on when they're on their way home. Ben locates the washing up liquid in the cupboard above the sink and squeezes a little into the bowl. He puts the bottle back in its rightful place and turns the hot water tap on, to fill the bowl. He places the crockery in the bowl and begins washing the dishes. A few minutes later Granddad walks into the kitchen just as he's putting the clean plates back inside the cupboard.

'She's a lovely girl, Ben.'

'Thanks Granddad, she is.'

'So how long have you two been going out?'

'Oh, only a few weeks now.'

'Does she know about the watch?' Granddad asks. Being asked about the watch really catches Ben off guard. He doesn't know why because Granddad gave him the watch so why shouldn't he ask? Maybe it's because nobody has ever asked him that, or maybe he still feels reticent about his precious possession.

'No,' Ben nervously says, feeling a little guilty that he'd not told Alexis now that Granddad had mentioned it. 'That's good, whatever you do, *don't tell anyone,*' Granddad emphasises. Immediately, Ben's mind recalls the moment he told his best friend Paul and a sudden feeling of dread falls over him.

'So why shouldn't I tell anyone?' Ben nervously asks.

'I'll just say if others know, your life could be in danger.' Granddad puts his hands on Ben's shoulders and looks him straight in the eyes. 'Ben, I'm going to give you a few words of advice and I want you to remember them; this is very important. The first thing is this: whenever you have a memorable time that you'd like to come back to, make a mental note of the time and date. The second thing to remember...'

'Ben, wake up; Mum's making a cooked breakfast for everyone.' Ben hears his dad's voice inside his head.

Chapter Seventeen

'Ben!' the sound of dad's voice again calling him, but this time, in a much firmer tone, causes Ben to open his eyes to the familiar sight of his bedroom. One moment, Ben was in front of his Granddad, and was about to be told something important, and now he's lying in his bed, feeling a little disorientated and concerned. What was Granddad about to tell him, he wonders. It all seemed so real and apposite to his situation. An uneasy feeling surrounds him leaving him with that sense of foreboding. He knows he can't do anything about it, because it was all a dream; he pushes the thoughts to the back of his mind, for now. Ben gives his eyes a rub before throwing back the duvet.

When he eventually gets downstairs, he's surprised to see his dad still sat at the dining table because he always plays golf on a Sunday.

'Morning,' Ben says to them as they're all eating their cooked breakfast. Ben notices his dad's breakfast plates is almost empty, while his mum's plate and Jessica's have hardly been touched.

'Another minute and your food was about to disappear,' Dad tells him.

'Chris, if you're still hungry there's two more sausages and a rasher of bacon under the grill,' Mom informs him. Dad picks up his empty plate and rushes into the kitchen. Ben quickly takes his seat at the table and looks down at his cooked breakfast comprising of a sausage, rasher of bacon, fried egg, hash browns, beans and a few mushrooms. "Mmmm this smells nice.' Ben tells his mum as he picks up his knife and fork. 'That's good, enjoy it because we won't be having it again for a while,' Mum tells him.

'Okay' Ben replies before placing a section of sausage covered in beans into his mouth. Dad returns from the kitchen holding a sausage in each hand while chewing on what appears to be a rasher of bacon. 'Chris, where's your plate?' Mum says sounding annoyed that Dads holding two greasy sausages in his hands. Dad smiles and shoves one whole sausage in his mouth and begins chewing as fast as possible so he can make room to put the second sausage in.

'Children, don't ever copy your father.' Mum warns them as Dad takes his seat at the table. Dad forces the last sausage in his mouth and then smiles at Ben revealing the meaty finger as a mouth guard covering his front teeth. Ben giggles to himself at seeing his dad get into more trouble with Mum.

'Did you say Paul was coming round this morning?' Mum asks.

'Oh yes, sorry I forgot. His parents have to go into work this morning for a couple of hours so they asked if it was all right to drop him off at ten,' Ben says, having just remembered.

'Well, you'd better finish your breakfast, because he'll be here in about ten minutes.' Mum points to the clock on the wall just behind Ben. Ben quickly turns around to check on the time and notices the digital display telling him it's 9.48.

' Dad, don't you always play golf on Sunday ?' Ben asks his dad before quickly placing a hash brown with some mushrooms into his mouth.

'Yes, I would normally play but I can't afford it at the moment.'

There's a knock at the front door so Ben's mum goes to let Paul in while Ben finishes his breakfast. Ben shoves the last of his sausage into his mouth and carries his plate through to the kitchen to be washed up later before rushing through to meet his friend at the door. Linda thanks Mum for looking after Paul and tells her that they'll pick him up just after two o'clock. Paul and Ben wait until the door is closed before they go upstairs to Ben's room and close the door.

'I can't believe you kissed Alexis seventeen times!' Paul says.

'I know and the strange thing is; I dreamt about her last night.'

'Did you, and what happened in this dream of yours?' Paul asks, sounding all excited.

'Well, it was really odd, because in my dream I took Alexis round to visit my Granddad.'

'So, what's strange about that?' Paul asks.

'I only started to go out with Alexis yesterday but in my dream Granddad knew about it and he died weeks ago; so how did he know?'

Paul thinks for a few seconds before saying. 'Dreams are not real; they're just random thoughts and memories that your mind pieces together to form dreams, so they don't mean anything.'

'I know that. But if my dream is just memories of things I've done, then why did I remember taking Alexis round to see Granddad when I've never done that?'

'I don't know. Why don't you use the watch and go back in time and ask him?' Paul suggests.

Ben suddenly remembers the advice Granddad told him in his dream: *Whatever you do, don't tell anyone*. Knowing that he's already told Paul about the watch starts to make him feel a little uneasy and he begins to worry about what he meant when he said, "don't tell anyone". Is something bad going to happen now that he's told his best friend? Ben wonders.

'Are you all right Ben? You look like you've seen a ghost,' Paul says.

'I'm all right.' Ben walks over to his bedside cabinet and picks up the watch.

'So are you going to go back and ask your granddad?'

Ben turns around and faces Paul.

'Granddad said something strange that I can't work out.'

'What did he say?'

'He said whenever I have a memorable time, I should write it down.'

'What's strange about that?' Paul asks.

'I can only travel back in time up to one hour so what's the point; if I can only go back one hour, why do I have to write it down because I can remember what happened an hour ago?'

They sit down on the side of Ben's bed as they contemplate and try to make sense of what Granddad said.

Paul asks, 'Why can you only go back in time for just one hour?'

Ben looks at Paul and then down at the watch and then back at Paul again.

'I'll show you,' he tells Paul and holds up the watch. Paul slides over towards him so he can see what he's doing. Ben opens the case to the watch and shows Paul the watch face.

'See the black hands telling us it's 10.17?'

'Yes.'

'So that's the time and it's the same as my alarm clock.'

They look over at the alarm clock on the bedside cabinet, which displays the time as 10.17. Paul looks back at Ben and then down at the watch face again.

'Right, see the gold hand that's on the four?'

'Yes.'

'When I turn that hand back, that's when I move back in time and there's only twelve numbers on that dial,' Ben explains.

'Have you tried winding it back further?' Paul asks. 'No,' Ben replies feeling a little foolish that he'd never thought of that.

'Go on then; what have you got to lose?' Paul tells him.

'Okay, how far back should I wind it?'

'Go round the dial twice and see what happens.' Paul sits closer and holds the lid of the watch so he can see. Ben pulls out the winding knob.

'Are you ready?' Ben asks. Paul, feeling excited to see the watch work, gives Ben an affirmative nod and they look down as Ben quickly turns the adjuster knob so the gold hand moves from the four back around to four and then again to the four. Ben opens his eyes and notices the sunlight streaming into his bedroom. He looks over at the alarm clock on his bedside cabinet and notices the time on its face is now showing 8.18 a.m. Ben throws back the duvet cover and sits up feeling excited that his watch allows him to travel further back in time.

'Yes!' he shouts and holds out his arms in a victory pose.

Suddenly his bedroom door flies open and his dad rushes in.

'Are you all right Ben?' he asks.

Ben quickly lowers his arms and sheepishly replies, 'Oh yes thanks.'

'What was that scream for?' his dad asks.

'Oh… I think I was dreaming… sorry.'

Dad's eyes glance around the room for anything suspicious before he asks, 'Are you sure everything's okay?'

'Yes, everything's fine, thanks,' Ben reassures his father.

'Don't forget, Mum's making us all a cooked breakfast this morning at nine thirty,' he tells Ben before stepping out onto the landing and closing the bedroom door behind him.

Great, that means I've got to eat another breakfast, he thinks.

Chapter Eighteen

Ben, having only eaten two hours earlier, makes a good attempt at eating his second breakfast by devouring one sausage, one hash brown and a few beans. Fortunately for him, his dad was hungry and finished what he couldn't eat. Paul arrived at one minute past ten, exactly as before and they dashed upstairs to his bedroom and closed the door.

'I don't believe it,' Paul says.

'I know; I kissed Alexis King seventeen times,' Ben responds.

'Forget about that; I travelled back in time. One second I was sitting with you on your bed and then the next moment, I was in bed at home and it was eight eighteen,' Paul excitedly tells him.

'You've got to be kidding me. Are you serious?' Ben asks while half expecting his friend to burst out laughing and tell him that he was joking. But then how did he know Ben travelled back in time if he didn't experience it himself?

Ben is suddenly overcome with a wave of dizziness and excitement all rolled into one and quickly sits down on his bed before he falls down.

'That means whoever touches the watch when you turn back time, travels with you,' Paul tells him.

'And… we can travel back, further than one hour,' Ben says looking up at Paul's smiling face. The revelation of finding out that they can both can travel back in time, causes them both to grab each other and jump up and down in celebration.

They hear Ben's dad's voice, shouting from downstairs. *'Ben. Stop banging!'*

Paul and Ben immediately stop what they're doing and stare at each other, waiting for any other sound coming from downstairs but they don't hear anything. Ben sits down on the side of his bed and Paul joins him as they excitedly stare at each other.

'Paul, you can't tell anyone about this and I mean *anyone.*'

'That's all right Ben, I haven't told anyone and I won't, I promise,' Paul says.

'Ben!' They hear his dad's voice calling him.

Ben looks at Paul feeling that his dad's just about to tell him off.

He says, 'I'll be back in a minute,' and slowly walks out onto the landing and descends the stairs to face his punishment.

'Ben, there's someone here for you,' he hears his dad say as he enters the lounge.

'Alexis! Hi! I didn't know you were coming round,' Ben says seeing Alexis standing by his father's side. 'Hello,' Alexis says.

'Erm… did you want to come upstairs to my bedroom…

Paul's here,' Ben quickly adds, so his invitation didn't sound a little forward for a twelve-year-old.

'Okay. Nice to meet you Mr Chapman,' Alexis says.

'Nice to meet you too; have fun,' Dad says.

Ben and Alexis slowly ascend the stairs and stop on the landing outside Ben's bedroom. Ben turns to face Alexis looking a little agitated.

'Sorry, this might sound strange but I just wanted to check something. Are we going out now? I mean, are you my girlfriend?' Ben looks at Alexis feeling a little embarrassed for asking.

'Well officially you haven't asked me,' she replies and gives Ben a smile. Ben can't believe it. For a second he half expected Alexis to tell him that he's got no chance at ever becoming her boyfriend but instead she suggests that he only needs to ask. Fighting back the exhilaration he now feels in his heart, he tentatively asks. "W-w-ould… y-you be my girlfriend?'

As soon as he got the words out, he immediately lowered his gaze so as not to look at Alexis in fear that all of this is going to be some sort of cruel trick and that she's about to shoot him down in flames. Waiting for a response seemed to last an eternity for Ben. He so wishes her answer will be yes, but he's still not a hundred percent sure she even likes him. Ben can feel his heart suddenly pound inside his chest because he'd never asked a girl out before and now knowing how hard it's been; he thinks he'd never do it again.

'Okay,' Ben hears Alexis reply and immediately a weight of uncertainty falls from his shoulders. That sweet sound of her voice means the world to him. He looks up and stares into Alexis's eyes feeling on top of the world as

Alexis moves her head towards his and puckers her lips. The last time she kissed him he didn't have time to react and here she is poised in front of him with her eyes closed and her lips ready to receive a kiss. Ben's eyes stare at Alexis's beautiful lips for a second and although feeling nervous about kissing her, his instinct kicks in and he finds his head moving towards hers when their lips touch. Ben closes his eyes and tries to remember the moment. No sooner had their lips touched, they departed again and Ben quickly opens his eyes to the sight of Alexis looking back at him with the biggest smile on her face.

'Okay, so that's great,' Ben tells her and reaches for the door handle. Moments ago, Ben left his friend in his room feeling like a single loner about to be reprimanded by his father and now he's returned feeling elated knowing that he's got a girlfriend. They enter Ben's bedroom holding hands and catch sight of Paul looking at Ben's selection of PS4 games.

'Hi Paul,' Alexis says. Paul nearly jumps out of his skin at hearing Alexis's voice.

'Oh hi, sorry, I didn't know you were here,' Paul replies and nearly drops a computer game on the floor. Suddenly the realisation hits him, seeing the two of them holding hands.

'What! Are you two going out now?' Paul asks although the fact that Alexis has come round to see Ben and they're both holding hands is self-explanatory.

For the next hour and a half, the three of them play on one of Ben's racing games and to everyone's surprise Alexis beats Paul to take second place, with Ben winning as usual as he's had more practice playing his own games. Mum brings a tray of refreshments into them, nearer lunchtime. Ben thinks she just wanted to spy on them, to see if everything was going all right.

After they finished eating, they all decided to go to the pocket park for something else to do. The weather is a little colder today because of a thick blanket of cloud overhead, so the park is empty when they arrive. The large, grassed area bordered on three sides by the backs of terraced houses with a copse of trees near the entrance to the field separating the park from the main road provides a nice safe enclosure for children to play. The pocket park consists of a large field with a metal A-frame with three swings, a climbing frame, a slide and a round-a-bout. The three of them immediately head towards the swings and Ben sits down on the left one; Alexis takes the middle swing and Paul sits on the right. Ever since the park was built, just over four years ago, the children realised that if you swing high enough, you can see over the copse of trees at the bottom of the park and admire the vast panoramic view of the valley extending into the distance. It becomes even more spectacular when the sun begins to set and the whole landscape is painted in hues of oranges and reds. It's too early in the day to see the sunset, but it's not too early to find out who can swing the highest and see the radio mast beyond the copse of trees first. The three of them quickly kick their legs forward in sync while leaning backward to move the swing forward then immediately at the top of their forward swing; tuck their legs under their seat and lean forward to generate a backwards swing. Ben being taller and heavier has the weight advantage and so quickly takes the lead, followed closely by Paul, and then Alexis as they race to see who can see the mast first. Ben swings forward and reaches the highest point of his swing, then quickly lifts his head to see above the trees but can't quite see the mast; his momentum brings his body swinging down and backwards again. He catches sight of his girlfriend swinging forward and to his surprise, seems to be swinging much higher than he did, when she suddenly calls out, 'I can see it.'

Ben and Paul can't believe it. They stop thrusting their legs forward and sit upright on their swings as their momentum slowly slows down the swing until they all come to a complete stop with their feet resting on the ground.

'How did you swing so high?' Paul asks.

'Yes, I thought I was going to win,' Ben says feeling robbed.

Alexis gives Ben a self-assured smile.

'It's basic physics, that's all, just good old basic physics.' Ben and Paul stare at Alexis not understanding a word she's said, while looking totally confused.

Alexis refuses to elaborate so they all sit in silence for a few minutes and enjoy the peace and quiet, while gently rocking forward and backwards.

Ben notices two boys appear through the narrow park entrance between two oak trees. It takes them only a few seconds before they all recognise Tony Vernall and Simon Dicks walking towards them.

'Hey four eyes, who said you can use the swings?' Tony shouts over towards Paul. Ben, feeling somewhat shocked that anyone would be so aggressive towards his friend, looks over towards Paul to reassure him that he's there for him. Paul stops rocking on his seat and looks back at Ben with a slightly worried look on his face. 'Anyone can use the swings; they're free to use,' Ben quickly tells Tony, now only four metres away.

'I'm not talking to you,' Tony replies and immediately walks up to Paul and pushes him backwards. Fortunately, Paul's grip on the chains prevented him from falling off his seat.

'Hey. Leave him alone,' Ben and Alexis jointly say. Ben quickly jumps to his feet and steps forward towards Tony who's now turned towards him.

'So what are you going to do about it?' Tony says in a threatening manner with Simon by his side. Alexis stands up and squeezes between Ben and Tony to stop the confrontation.

'Tony, stop being an idiot,' she shouts at him. 'So what's this then, are you two going out or something?'

'For your information, yes,' Alexis confirms, staring right into his eyes. Tony's expression suddenly changes from a mild annoyed look to an incandescent seething. He looks up at Ben standing behind Alexis and screams, 'You're dead Chapman,' pointing straight towards Ben. He turns and walks away with Simon towards the exit shaking his head and saying something to Simon but the conversation becomes too muted to understand. Ben, Alexis and Paul watch Tony and Simon walk out through the copse of trees before Ben turns to Alexis and asks.

'What was that all about, why is Tony so angry that we're going out?'

Alexis sits back down on the swing seat. 'Sorry Ben, Tony asked me to go out with him last year and I told him, no. Ever since then, he's basically threatened every boy that liked me, to frighten them away. Sorry I should have told you.' Ben crouches down in front of Alexis and holds her hands. 'That's all right, Tony doesn't scare me. In fact, I think it's the opposite, I think he's scared of me.' Ben reassuringly tells Alexis. 'I know he doesn't scare you; I saw you the other day stand up to Tony in the playground. That's why I said I'd be your girlfriend because I knew he wouldn't be able to scare you away.'

'Oh really, is that the only reason why you said you'd be my girlfriend, because I'm not scared of Tony? Don't you fancy me then?' Ben asks, giving Alexis a suave gallant smile.

Alexis smiles back. 'Of course I fancy you.'

Alexis suddenly becomes aware that Paul's listening and her cheeks begin to turn pink.

'Don't worry about Paul. I think he fancies someone else we both know,' Ben quickly says to redirect the attention onto Paul.

'What do you mean; who do I fancy?' Paul protests. Ben looks over at Paul on the far swing, looking slightly embarrassed because he's gathered Ben already knows who he likes.

'It's all right. I won't tell anyone. Anyway...' Ben looks back at Alexis. 'So when did you know you liked me?' he asks, feeling intrigued at her reply.

'Well, I've liked you for a while but I just didn't know that you liked me.'

'You didn't know I liked you?' Ben says, sounding shocked.

'Well you basically ignored me in biology and you've never spoken to me.'

'I agree with you Alexis,' Paul says. 'I've been trying to get Ben to talk to you for the past year.'

Alexis, now looking intrigued, asks, 'So why wouldn't you talk to me. Am I that scary?' She pulls a scary face at Ben.

'No you're not scary; but you are the prettiest girl in school... and... I-I'm shy,' Ben reluctantly says, while averting his gaze.

She places both her hands on Ben's cheeks and leans forward and kisses him.

'I'm glad you don't think I'm scary and I'm glad we're going out together,' she tells him. They decide it's probably time to head back home, so they all start walking across the grassed field towards the entrance.

'What did Tony mean when he said, "You're dead, Chapman"?' Alexis asks.

Ben thinks for a moment. He's never said that before and he's never heard him say that to anyone else as a matter of fact, so he's not exactly sure on what he meant by it. Would he try to kill him? He's sure he didn't mean it. He's heard people say things like that on TV before, but it doesn't mean they're literally about to kill someone. It's all talk, that's what it is, he concludes.

'It's nothing; I wouldn't worry about it,' he tells Alexis, although from the look on her face, he knows she's not convinced that he's telling the truth.

To be honest, Ben's not totally convinced himself either. If Tony's had a crush on Alexis for the past year and he went through all that effort to scare everyone away; maybe he's crazy enough to do something stupid. In any case, Ben decides there and then, to keep an eye on Tony and his faithful followers and not put himself in an awkward situation. Ben takes hold of Alexis' hand and gives it a slight squeeze as they walk out between the two large oak trees.

Chapter Nineteen

'Are you excited about your visit to the British Museum?' Mum asks Jess.

Jess swallows her mouthful of cereal before replying. 'Yes Mum, Debbie and I can't wait to see a real mummy!'

'So just remind me again; what time is the school coach leaving and what time do they bring you back and are they dropping you all back at school?' Mum asks.

'Miss Philips said we'll be leaving on the coach at nine fifteen from the school car park and we should get to London by lunchtime. Then we get picked up outside the museum at two thirty and should be back outside school by six o'clock.' Jess explains before scooping another spoonful of cornflakes coated in cold milk into her mouth. Mum begins calculating something inside her head for a few seconds as she formulates a plan of action.

'Okay, I'll get Dad to wait at the school for you at six. Don't worry, if your coach is a bit late because I'll be cooking a stew in the slow cooker for dinner; so it won't matter what time we eat. I've made up your lunchbox and I've put in a few extra bits just in case you get hungry on the journey,' Mum informs Jess from across the breakfast table.

'Thanks Mum,' Jess says.

'So does that mean we're not having dinner at five o'clock?' Ben asks, having caught the end of the conversation.

'No Ben, we'll all eat when Jess gets home.'

'But that means I'll be starving,' he protests to his mum.

'If you can't hold on till six, you can always help yourself to an apple or an orange.' Mum points to the fruit bowl in the kitchen. Ben ignores his mother's suggestion as he'd much rather eat a cake as opposed to something healthy. He notices his dad sitting in the lounge reading what appears to be a newspaper.

'Is Dad dropping us off at school today?' Ben asks as his dad's usually at work at this time in the morning. ' Yes, your dad will take you today,' Mum tells them. 'Chris, it's time to drop the kids off,' Mum informs him.

Dad folds the paper and lays it down on the coffee table before making his way to the side cabinet where his car keys are kept. Ben quickly finishes the last spoonful of cereal and takes his bowl into the kitchen to be washed up later. 'Right is everyone ready?' Dad asks, sounding not quite himself. Jess and Ben give each other a concerned look before collecting their school bags and go out through the front door and into the back seats of Dad's car parked on the drive. Dad gets in behind the wheel and closes his car door. He fastens his seatbelt, starts the car and reverses out of the driveway in silence just as Mum steps out of the front door to wave them off. Jess and Ben give Mum a wave before Dad pulls away, heading towards school. They sit quietly in the back seats as the atmosphere in the car seems a little frosty for their liking. They assume something is on Dad's mind at the moment so they think it best just to be quiet and not annoy him in any way. As they near the school grounds, Ben lets his father know that he won't need a lift home after school because he's going to walk home.

'Why don't you want a lift?' Jess asks, just to be nosey.

Ben glares at his sister and mouths, 'It's none of your business.'

'Oooh you're walking Alexis home are you?' Jess annoyingly says.

'Shut up Jess,' Ben tells his sister and gives her a prod with his elbow.

'Ow that hurt!' Jess overreacts to being prodded. 'Children, be nice to each other,' Dad tells them with a slightly raised voice unlike his usual tone.

Ben and Jess immediately sit back in their seats sensing that they need to do as they're told. Dad moments later pulls the car over next to the kerbside to allow them to get out, as they're outside the school grounds. Jess opens her side door and gets out onto the pavement while Ben slides himself across the back seat so he can exit the car on the same side. Ben closes the car door and thanks his dad for the lift. His dad gives Ben a cursory wave before driving the car back into traffic and disappearing into the distance. Ben slowly walks towards the school entrance feeling a little concerned about his father as he notices Jess meeting up with Debbie Parker at the school gate before they turn and head into the school grounds.

Ben walks in through the entrance gate and heads over to the climbing frame to wait for his friend Paul and girlfriend Alexis to arrive. Less than three minutes later, Alexis walks through the gate and goes over to Ben as he's sat down on the lower rung of the climbing frame.

'Hi,' she says as she nears and gives Ben a huge smile.

'Hi to you too,' Ben says while looking up at Alexis now standing in front of him. For the first time in his life, he's so happy to be at school, because he has a girlfriend. Alexis sits down next to him on the low bar of the climbing frame and they look over towards the entrance for Paul to arrive. Suddenly Tony, Simon and Brian walk in through the main entrance and head towards them, barging past a group of younger boys standing between them in the process. They come to a stop a few feet away before Tony raises his hand and points directly at Ben in a threatening manner and tells him, 'You're history Chapman, just you wait till after school.'

Ben, feeling threatened, immediately senses his heartbeat speed up as he's all too aware that his girlfriend is right by his side.

Suddenly, he latches on to the words "after school" that came with the threat from Tony so he knows he's safe for the time being. So he takes the opportunity to act as though he's not concerned so his girlfriend is not worried for him.

Ben stands up and steps towards Tony so they're face to face and tells Tony. '

Whatever.'

The three lads turn and walk away to the sound of Tony saying, 'Just you wait and see'.

'He looked really angry,' Alexis says, sounding a little concerned as she stands by his side.

'Don't worry about it; it's going to be all right.' Ben tells her and wraps his arm around her shoulder. He's not exactly one hundred percent convinced of the fact, because he's never been threatened before. He is however concerned that other school children overheard the threat, so it would be difficult for Tony not to go through with his threat because by the end of the day, the whole school will expect something to happen and Tony's reputation is on the line.

Ben looks down at Alexis' face and she smiles up at him. He gives her a gentle squeeze to reassure her again that he's okay about what happened but deep within her smile, he can sense that she's worried. Ben's glad that nothing happened moments ago, because although he's had plenty of fights in his karate classes, he knows Alexis would have tried to help and the thought of her getting hurt would be the worst feeling in the world. If anything did happen after school, he would hope that Alexis wasn't with him for that simple reason that he would hate anything to happen to her. They sit down together on the climbing frame and look over towards the main entrance for Paul to arrive. Moments later, Paul walks in through the main entrance and heads over towards them.

'Hi guys, so what's happening?' Paul asks, sounding all cheerful.

'You just missed it; Tony and his gang gave us a visit,' Alexis says.

'Oh yes, and what did they want?' Paul asks.

'Nothing really; he was just in his usual bad mood,' Ben says trying to make light of the experience.

'Isn't he always in a bad mood?' Paul replies. The three of them begin to laugh. Then the school bell sounds, so they all go over towards the main building with Paul just ahead and Ben and Alexis a few feet behind.

Ben leans in towards Alexis and says, 'Don't tell Paul about what Tony said; I don't want him to worry.'

'Okay,' Alexis whispers back. They walk in through the main door and head to their first lessons.

During the lunchtime break the three of them notice Tony planning something with his menials over by the bicycle shed.

'What are they up to?' Paul asks, pointing over towards the shed. Ben knows it has something to do with getting him after school but he doesn't want Paul to know that.

He gives Alexis a wink and says to Paul, 'They're probably planning on stealing a bike or something, you know what they're like; they're a bunch of idiots.' 'You're not wrong.' Paul concurs.

'Anyway, I was thinking, the three of us should walk home together after school,' Ben suggests.

'Sorry I can't, I've got a dentist appointment and Mum's picking me up straight after school,' Paul tells them. Ben realises that his original plan for the three of them to stick together might have put Tony off from doing anything stupid has failed at the first hurdle. 'That's all right. Alexis, why don't we meet up by the school road sign straight after school, then I could walk you home from there?'

'Okay, I'll go straight there after my last lesson,' Alexis tells him.

Ben reasons to himself that if Tony and his gang are planning to get him after school; they'll need to find him first. If he meets up with Alexis by the school sign outside the school grounds, they won't see them and by the time they realise that they're not on the school premises, they'll be home safe and sound.

Ben's last lesson that afternoon is history, which is not his best subject, although he did excel at the subject during the school competition. During class, Miss Havelock decides to give everyone another question-and-answer test. Ben sits at his desk and finds himself staring into space as his mind is on other things at the moment. *What's Tony up to; what's he planning? He's definitely planning something but I can't quite work out why they were all standing next to the bike shed? Does he have a plan that involved a bike? Why would he need a bike? Did he think I might make a run for it, so he'd need a couple of bikes to catch me up?* The idea seems a little absurd but who knows what's going on in Tony's crazed mind. Ben's eyes glance over at the clock on the classroom wall and immediately realise that it's nearly home time. Suddenly his mind automatically thinks about meeting up with Alexis by the road sign outside the school premises. He giggles to himself as he imagines Tony and his gang desperately searches all the exit doors to the school building, while he and Alexis amble home with all the time on their hands.

'Benjamin Chapman,' Miss Havelock calls out on noticing Ben staring up at the clock and sniggering to himself. Ben immediately looks down at his book to make out that he was thinking about a history question. A few seconds later and with no further sound from Miss, Ben assumes he must be in the clear. He raises his eyes and looks towards Miss Havelock whose busy marking paperwork on her desk so he relaxes a little knowing he's only got a few minutes before the end of class. The next seven minutes seem to drag on and on and Ben finds it hard, just staring at his history book; making out that he was studying. Finally the sound of the school bell reverberates throughout the school corridors indicating the end of class and the end of another school day.

Immediately there's the clatter of chairs being slid back, scraping on the linoleum flooring as pupils talk and lift their bags, putting them on desks as everyone begins packing their things away. Ben eagerly begins packing away his history books into his school bag when he hears the sound of Miss Havelock above the noise in the classroom.

'Benjamin can I have a word.'

Ben looks up and sees Miss Havelock staring right at him. He can't believe it, he thought he'd gotten away with it but now it looks like Miss wants to tell him off for not concentrating in class. He quickly zips up his rucksack and lifts it up onto his shoulder.

I wonder what she wants,' he thinks as he goes forward to where Miss Havelock is standing.

'I've got to meet someone outside, Miss,' Ben tells his teacher, hoping that she'll let him go because he's made prior arrangements with someone else.

'Don't worry, I won't keep you long,' Miss informs him as she waits for all the pupils to leave the classroom so she can have a private moment with Ben. Ben looks round and is not surprised to see Jonathan Baker still putting his books inside his rucksack when everyone else has vacated the classroom. For some unknown reason, Jonathan has to have all his books neatly stowed away in size order with all the spines facing outwards. It may be because his father is in the navy and he's just copying his dad.

Come on, get a move on, Ben thinks, willing Jonathan to hurry up, when finally Jonathan zips up the bag and lifts the heavy navy-blue canvas bag up onto his shoulder. 'Jonathan can you close the door behind you please?' Miss Havelock asks. Jonathan slowly walks out and closes the door behind him.

'Benjamin, please take a seat.' Miss asks while pointing to the nearest chair. Ben tentatively sits down feeling a slight uneasiness about being kept behind. Miss Havelock sits back against the next desk.

'Am I in trouble Miss?' Ben asks, feeling that he's about to be told off.

'Not exactly, but I do have a concern,' she says. Ben averts his eyes by looking down at the floor for a second. 'Benjamin, I was very impressed with your efforts last week during our question-and-answer session and then again at the Inter-School competition which you did remarkably well.'

'Thank you Miss,' Ben quietly replies.

'I have noticed though, that your participation in our question-and-answer sessions since the competition has taken a rapid decline.' Ben suddenly realises that he should have partaken in the test to validate his new-found knowledge; so it now looks like he's been cheating all along. Ben raises his head and gives Miss Havelock a guilty look as a criminal would to his arresting officer.

'Are you all right? Are you having problems at home?' Miss asks, sounding concerned for Ben's well-being. Hearing Miss ask how he is comes as a big surprise as he was half expecting Miss to send him to Miss Clarke's office for cheating. The sudden relief at not being found out puts a smile back on his face; although he knows he can't show it at the moment.

'No, everything's all right Miss,' Ben quickly replies.

'Are you sure? If you want to talk to me about anything and I mean anything, just say,' Miss Havelock says and leans forward so she can look directly into Ben's eyes.

'I'm fine Miss, really. Can I go now?' Ben gives Miss Havelock a half smile, and glances up at the wall clock, to indicate that he needs to get going. 'Okay Ben, but don't forget that I'm here if you need me.'

'Thanks Miss.' Ben quickly picks up his rucksack and goes out of the classroom door.

By this time, the corridor leading to the outside is empty except for a girl and a boy standing outside the geography classroom holding hands. Ben runs past them and through the main doors and out into the playground which is now deserted. He sprints to the school gate and squeezes past a crowd of mothers with their children chatting away and oblivious to anyone wanting to get past. Ben reaches a clearing and tries to see Alexis up ahead but his view is suddenly blocked by a large mother crossing between them. He tries to step to the side but the pavement is crammed with people. Suddenly the large woman moves to his right and crosses the road, allowing Ben to see the road sign thirty metres ahead and notice Alexis surrounded by a crowd of boys.

'Alexis!' Ben calls out at the top of his voice to get her attention but the sound of his voice is drowned out by the noise of mothers and children blocking the pavement between them. Ben forces himself between another group of mothers to an open space where he can see clearly and to his horror, he immediately recognises the group of boys standing next to Alexis. Tony, Simon, Brian and Andrew all surround Alexis and appear to be shouting at her. Ben's anger begins to flare up inside him at seeing his girlfriend being bullied by a group of idiots.

'Alexis!' Ben screams out to reassure his girlfriend that he's coming as he struggles to get to her through the mass of pedestrians. He knows it's all going to end up badly for him because there are four of them, but he doesn't care about himself. His only concern is for Alexis. 'Alexis!' Ben calls out again and this time Alexis and Tony both turn towards Ben having heard his voice. Tony looks back at Alexis and grabs her shoulders. She tries to retaliate by slapping him across the face but his reaction is quicker and he leans back just out of reach. Tony pushes Alexis away from him, causing her to stumble backwards, off the kerb and into the road before disappearing out of view as a delivery van passes. *Bang!* The large brown van screeches to a halt alongside the kerb causing other vehicles to squeal to a stop, backing up along the street.

'Where's Alexis?' Ben asks himself as he glances up from navigating his eyes from the congested pavement to the road sign where Alexis was only seconds ago. One second she was just in front of him and now he can't seem to make out where she's gone. Tony is standing motionless with his cohorts as though they're mannequin dolls in a shop window, waiting to be repositioned for a shop display. Ben stops three metres away from Tony at the back end of a parked delivery van and stares at Tony trying to work out what happened to Alexis. Tony slowly lifts up his hand and covers his mouth. His eyes seem to widen as if in shock as the colour in his face suddenly drains away, leaving his complexion pale and drawn as though he's just about to throw up. Ben looks at the parked delivery van next to him and can't understand why Tony is staring at it. Suddenly a woman screams from across the street just as the delivery driver appears at the front of his van and crouches down to look under the chassis.

'Oh my God!' the van driver cries out as he's overcome with grief.

'Alexis, Alexis!' Ben hears himself call out while trying to process the unnatural scene in front of him with everyone standing motionless, staring at the front of the van. *What's going on, where is Alexis?* Ben thinks. Ben notices movement to his left and turns his head to see Tony and his gang running as fast as they can in the opposite direction.

'That's strange, why are they running away?' Ben asks himself. He had half expected to be fighting the four of them about now, so what made them suddenly run off?

Ben looks back at the driver as two other men crouch down by his side; one man reaches under the chassis of the van and grabs hold of something. He pulls what appears to be a girl's arm out from under the wheel when Ben recognises Alexis's coat sleeve. *'Nooooooo!'* Ben screams at the realisation that his girlfriend has just been run over. His legs immediately give way and he finds himself crouched on the pavement looking through floods of tears at the two men trying to help Alexis. Something inside him is saying that she's dead but deep in his heart he's wishing she'll be all right.

Ben wipes the tears from his eyes, feeling totally drained and unable to do anything. His body starts to shake and he can only watch as more and more people gather around the front of the van to see if they can help. His eyes focus on the sleeve of Alexis and her soft lifeless hand slightly grazed from the rough tarmac; willing it to move; only to confirm that she'll be all right. Ben hears a woman call out.

'Oh my God! Is she all right?'

Ben strains his ears to hear the reply, hoping someone will say, "Yes, she's fine," but nobody does. 'Somebody, call an ambulance!' Ben hears a woman cry out but he can't quite make out who said it. Suddenly the man who reached under the van to help Alexis, stands up.

'Sorry, we're too late; she's gone.'

The sound of the man's voice echoes around Ben's mind like a klaxon: *Sorry, we're too late, she's gone* replays over and over. Knowing that an adult has confirmed his greatest fear causes a deep pain in Ben's heart that he's never experienced before. He was upset when his Granddad died, but nothing like this. Alexis was everything to him and he just can't accept that she's gone. Ben slowly gets to his feet; feeling as though his world has suddenly crumbled around him, leaving him in a dark bottomless void. His mind has shut down and he can't think of anything except the sorrow in his heart. Suddenly he gets a panicky feeling that he needs to escape from the tormented scene in front of him. Without any conscious thought, Ben finds himself running in the opposite direction along the pavement past hordes of spectators to the accident behind him. Ben swings his arms forward in time with his feet to give himself momentum until he's sprinting further and further away. He can hear a siren in the background as an ambulance makes its way to the scene but he knows it's too late. He passes more and more people lining the pavement as many are wondering why the traffic has suddenly come to a complete stop. Ben, still crying, continues sprinting along the pavement, turning left and then cutting across the road in front of a taxi cab just pulling out from a side street. He continues on, not thinking of where he's running to, only that he needs to get away. He races past a mother pushing a pram with a baby in it. He reaches up to wipe his eyes so he can see where he's going. *Crash!* Ben's body lifts up into the air, spiralling around and around, as his mind tries to comprehend why he can't feel the ground any more. *Thud!* Ben crumples down onto the pavement landing slightly twisted onto his left side and slides to a stop against a bus shelter.

He lies there for a few seconds as his mind tries to work out what just happened. A searing pain rips across his right shoulder as he tries to turn over and sit himself up followed by a blinding pain thumping at his temples. Ben can just manage to prop himself up against the clear plastic side panel of the bus shelter when a drip from his forehead runs down into the corner of his eye, causing him to wipe the liquid away. He looks down at his hand and sees it is now covered in blood. He automatically reaches up and feels the gash just above his left eye socket as the blood starts to flow down his face.

'Are you all right, son?'

Ben looks up at a nice older lady standing next to a basket on wheels loaded up with groceries from the local supermarket. He presses his left palm against the cut on his head. 'I think so,' he replies to the lady in a grey tweed jacket and pencil skirt. He notices that she's holding out a clean handkerchief for Ben to use. He reaches up with his right hand, takes the white cotton cloth and presses it onto his forehead. 'Thank you.'

'I've already told the council that these road signs are too low and that someone will hurt themselves one of these days,' she informs Ben and points to an election campaign sign protruding out from a telegraph pole just about head height. Ben looks at the sign and realises that he must have run headlong into the sign, which sent him flying. 'I think you might need stitches.' The lady says bending forward and offering her hand to help him get to his feet. Ben takes the lady's hand and clambers to his feet feeling like he'd just gone ten rounds with the heavyweight champion of the world. 'I'll be all right,' he says and turns to walk off in the opposite direction.

'Excuse me young man, is this yours?' the lady asks. Ben turns to see what the lady was referring to, when he notices the small shiny object in her hand. 'I think you dropped this?'

Ben staggers back towards her and takes the watch from her hand.

'Thank you very much; my Granddad gave me this,' he says and gives the lady a smile to show his appreciation.

'You're welcome; now take care and no running,' she instructs him.

'I won't,' Ben replies.

Chapter Twenty

Ben watches as the lady walks away pushing her basket on wheels. He waits until she's some distance away before he walks around the bus shelter screen and takes a seat inside the enclosure on what appears to be a wooden shelf, designed for passengers to sit on. The shelter is empty so it affords Ben time to himself to think. The pounding headache now forming in his head alongside the pain in his shoulder is making him feel a little nauseous, so he's forced to bend over and put his head between his legs to prevent himself from throwing up. He breathes in a couple of deep breaths to stem the feeling of wanting to be sick, until his mind clears a little and the queasy feeling subsides a little. He closes his eyes for a moment and thinks about the watch.

'How far back do I need to go?' he asks himself. He opens his eyes and looks down at the watch. *I need to get to Alexis before Tony,* he thinks as he opens the watch cover and pulls the adjuster knob out ready to travel back in time. He slowly turns the small metal winder around, keeping his eyes fixed on the gold hand moving around on the watch face. The scene around him changes in a blur and he finds himself sat in his history class just as Miss Havelock asks the last question in the question-and-answer session.

He would like to answer the question so Miss Havelock wouldn't have an excuse not to hold him back after class but his heart isn't in it, he's more focused on getting to Alexis before Tony and his friends do. Ben keeps his eyes locked on the clock on the wall wishing the time would move faster so he can get out and save Alexis. *Come on; come on; come on,* he thinks.

Ben sees Miss Havelock staring at him in his peripheral vision which is not surprising because he's the only one looking to his right, instead of looking forward.

'Ben Chapman; do you have somewhere you need to be, other than in this classroom?' Miss asks with a slightly raised voice so that everyone can hear. Immediately, everyone in class stops what they're doing and turns to look at Ben, wondering why he's suddenly being told off. Ben looks over towards Miss Havelock and not wanting to get into more trouble; he apologises before looking down at his notebook and pretends to continue working. In the corner of his eye, he surreptitiously watches the other pupils turn back to their notebooks and continue with their assignments. He knows he doesn't need to wait long before the end of class bell sounds, so he thinks it best just to keep his head down and wait so he doesn't get into any more trouble. Ben waits patiently, staring at the blank page in his notebook and poised ready to quickly pack away his stuff as soon as the bell rings. *'Bbrrrrriiiiiiiiiiiiiinnnnnnnnng'* the sound of the school bell breaks through the silence telling everyone that class is over. As soon as the school bell sounded it was quickly joined by the noise in the classroom as students began sliding their chairs away from their desks and quickly packing their books into their bags. Ben leads the way and is already packed within seconds of the bell sounding when he hears Miss Havelock call his name.

'Benjamin, can I have a word?'

This is exactly what happened before. Ben thinks. He looks over at Miss Havelock and swings his loaded rucksack up onto his shoulder.

'No!' The bustling sounds in the classroom from everyone packing away their things suddenly drops to a complete silence as everyone must have heard Ben's reply.

'Benjamin Chapman; come here immediately!' Miss Havelock demands, having never experienced a pupil refuse to do as she's asked before. Ben steps one pace forward towards Miss Havelock, before darting right towards the opened classroom door and disappearing out of sight to the sound of loud cheers from his classmates.

The history classroom is possibly the furthest classroom from the main entrance, located at the far end of the main corridor and at this time, is teaming with school children bustling towards the exit. Ben's exit from the school is now hindered by a hundred or more noisy children blocking his route.

'Excuse me, let me through,' Ben calls out in the hope that the children just in front of him might move to the side to allow him through, but nobody does. The main corridor at home time is possibly the noisiest enclosure a child has to endure during his or her time at school.

Being cooped up in a classroom all day, keeping quiet is so unnatural for a child, so stepping into a large empty space at the end of the day; which has the best acoustics is encouragement for children to talk, scream, sing and make noises to their heart's content without being told off. Ben realises how futile his efforts are to get the attention of those just ahead of him, so he endeavours to squeeze past the mass of people as quickly as he can.

Finally he bursts out through the main entrance into the busy playground, desperately looking for Alexis. The sun is low in the sky, shining right into his eyes, so he finds it difficult to see anything. He lifts up his hand to shield his eyes and quickly scans the mass of children all walking towards the school entrance gate. Alexis is nowhere to be seen, so Ben decides not to waste any more time and breaks into a sprint for the exit. A large group of children have slowed up to a stop as they queue up to exit through the wrought iron gate leading to the outside of the school. Ben sees this as another unnecessary delay, so he runs across the grassed verge to the school fence and quickly cuts into line just in front of the gate to sounds from older boys voicing their disapproval. Ben forces his way past a couple of women blocking the exit and heads left along the pavement, darting left and right as he passes more and more mothers with prams, waiting for their children to come out. He finally makes his way past the last of the waiting mothers and reaches a clearing and is shocked to see Alexis, thirty metres ahead, standing by the sign and walking towards her twenty metres away, Ben recognises the backs of Tony and his mates.

'Alexis!' Ben calls out at the top of his voice to get her attention.

Alexis looks up and for a moment their eyes meet. She raises her hand and gives Ben a wave when she notices Tony and his gang closing in on her. Tony quickly turns around to see who she's waving at and sees Ben appearing from behind a group of waiting mothers.

Tony turns back towards Alexis and makes a dash for her. He grabs her arm as she tries to walk past him and she's suddenly swung around with her back towards Ben.

'Get off her!' Ben screams and begins sprinting towards them. Alexis tries to push Tony away but he's just too strong. She steps to the side but is blocked by Andrew and Simon. Brian moves around to the far side of Alexis almost surrounding her from going anywhere. 'Alexis!' Ben calls out again to reassure her that he's coming. She swings her right hand around and slaps

Tony across the face and for a second, it looks like she's free. Alexis turns towards Ben but finds her exit blocked by Andrew and Simon.

'Ben!' Alexis cries out, realising she's trapped. Suddenly Tony grabs her shoulders and shoves her backwards in retaliation.

'Noooooooooo!' Ben screams as he sees Alexis being pushed off the pavement and into the road just as a bright-red saloon car slams on its brakes. Ben watches in horror as his girlfriend crashes into the car windscreen and then is flung up over the roof and disappears out of view on the far side of the car. *'Noooooooooo!'* he hears himself screaming again. His legs immediately buckle under him and he finds himself on the ground crying in disbelief.

'Why?' he manages to call out between sobs. Ben notices a large crowd converging around Alexis's body lying in the middle of the road and he hears voices calling out for an ambulance amid a few screams from onlookers. The traffic has come to a complete stop on both sides of the road stretching as far as he can see and Ben notices a few people get out of their cars to see what's causing the hold up further down the road, that are unaware that a fatal accident has ensued. Ben slowly gets up onto his feet watching as more and more people close in around the red saloon car to take a look. He wipes his eyes and slowly turns away from the crowd and begins walking along the pavement in the opposite direction. He's already experienced a traumatic event earlier so he can't bring himself to go through another one in the space of a few minutes. He seems to be in a daze because nothing in his mind is registering. He doesn't know where he is or where he's going or even what he's thinking. He just knows that he needs to get as far away from there as possible. Ben hears the sound of an ambulance as it makes its way towards him. The blue flashing light of the approaching ambulance is clearly seen in the distance meandering between vehicles that have pulled over to either side of the road. It squeezes through small gaps in the road past Ben towards the scene of the accident in the hope of saving a life. Ben knows it's too late, but the ambulance crew don't know that yet. He continues on his journey away from the scene as the sound from the ambulance fades into the distance. He finds himself walking through the park which is deserted at this time of day. He passes a park bench under a large maple tree and decides to sit down for a while. He sits down in the

middle of the bench and rests his head in his hands as he tries to make sense of it all.

What good is it that he can go back in time but can't help the one person he wants to help? He asks himself. He keeps seeing the image of Alexis under the van and then being hit by a car and flying over the bonnet. 'This is the worst day of my life,' he thinks as he stares down at a broken paving slab beneath his feet. His eyes catch sight of two black ants roaming across the pale cement slab as they converge on a small fragment of crisp dropped by someone sat there earlier that day. More ants appear and give the first two a hand as they lift up the small potato crisp and transport it back towards where they came. Ben's glad of the distraction to take his mind off what happened to Alexis even if it's only for a few moments. He sits there in the quiet for what seems like forever trying to rationalise the events taken place and whether he could have done anything different, when a sudden chill shivers down his body. He quickly folds his arms tightly around him to squeeze out the cold before standing up. It takes a few moments for him to realise where he is and to get his bearings as to which way he needs to walk in order to get home. He knows he has to go home at some point but the thought of having to tell his family about Alexis is just too upsetting. He puts his hands in his pockets and begins walking towards home.

Chapter Twenty-One

Ben walks in through the front door and puts his school bag down next to the shoe rack.

'Hi Ben!' he hears his mother say from the kitchen as she's preparing the dinner for tonight. 'Hi,' he calls back so as not to ignore her and quickly heads upstairs so he's not drawn into any conversations about how his day's been. He enters his bedroom and closes the door behind him, shutting out any chance of someone asking him questions he doesn't want to answer. It's not that he doesn't want to tell someone about what happened today, but he knows, the way he's feeling at the moment; he'll just burst into tears at the slightest mention of Alexis name. Just thinking about it upsets him so he goes over towards his bed and lies down. He remembers his mum telling him that morning; that they won't be having dinner until Jess comes home sometime after six o'clock, so he's got a few hours to compose himself and to prepare for what may well be a bombardment of questions later on. Ben closes his eyes and almost immediately, his mind is filled with images of Alexis flooding back, causing him to well up all over again. After a few seconds he opens his eyes and stares at the blank ceiling; looking for any distraction. The large blank canvas above him had been recently painted just over a month ago, and yet he can still see areas not quite the same colour. He scans the large surface looking for blemishes and imperfections to fill his consciousness, when he hears the sound of faint ringing from a telephone in the distance. He's not sure whether it's coming from his house or a neighbour's house. The sound suddenly stops and he hears his mother's voice say 'hello.' Although the voice is muffled, he knows it's his mother's voice because Dad never answers the phone at home. Dad always says, 'If someone wants me, they'll ring me on my mobile, so it won't be for me.' Ben can see his dad's logic and nine times out of ten, when the house phone rings, it's usually for Mum, or it's one of those 'annoying canvas callers' as

Mum describes them. There's silence for a few seconds then he hears Mum's voice again.

'What!' Ben hears his mum shriek.

A few seconds later, Ben hears the pounding of footsteps coming up the stairs and his bedroom door flies open.

'Ben! Come on, there's been an accident; we have to go right now,' Dad informs him, in his strictest voice.

Dad suddenly disappears out of sight and Ben can hear him enter his bedroom. 'I'm just getting my wallet and car keys,' he shouts down to mum. Ben sits up on his bed, wondering why dad's acting strange all of a sudden, when his dad reappears in his doorway.

'Ben, now!' Dad shouts before making his way downstairs. Ben's never seen his dad sound so serious before and seeing him now was a little frightening so Ben quickly stand up and goes downstairs to see what all the commotion is all about, when he catches sight of his mother standing near the front door, crying as she puts on her coat. Ben senses that it's not a good time to ask questions so he quickly puts his shoes on and follows his mother out of the house and into their car parked on the drive. Ben takes his usual seat behind the driver's seat and straps himself in at the back. His mum gets in on the passenger side and attaches her seatbelt before using a tissue to wipe the tears from her eyes.

'Are you all right, Mum?' Ben asks wondering why his mum is so upset. Mum blows her nose in her handkerchief and then slowly turns to look at him.

'Ben, we've just been told; there's been an accident,' she says.

'I know Mum, I was there.' Ben quietly replies.

'What do you mean, you were there?' Mum asks, sounding all abrupt.

'Outside school; Alexis's been run over.'

As he tells his mum he hears his voice starting to break as the emotions come flooding back and the tears start streaming down his face.

'Oh Ben, you poor thing; we were talking about your sister,' Mum informs him. Ben can't quite understand what his mum just told him.

Did she just say my sister? His mind tries to make sense of what his mum said.

'Don't you mean Alexis?' Ben asks, sounding a little confused.

'No Ben, the school coach that Jess was on has crashed on the M25. We don't know much at the moment except that several people have been injured and they're taking everyone to the City Hospital in St Albans.'

Ben stares at his mum in disbelief thinking how the day couldn't get any worse. Alexis is dead and now something has happened to Jess. Dad gets in the driver's seat and starts the car and for the next few hours they drive south towards St Albans in total silence.

For most of the journey, Ben just stares out of the side window watching the landscape change from urban areas to clear open spaces and greenery of the countryside. It all seems much like a dream to him. His girlfriend and sister were involved in an accident on the same day. How does that happen? How much bad luck can a person have? He starts thinking about Jess and the coach accident, trying to visualise what might have happened. Did the coach crash into other cars or did it career off the motorway and crash into a tree or something? Was Jess sat at the front of the coach, or at the back? He tries to recall Jess getting on the coach that morning to see where she may have sat, but he can't quite remember. His mind creates lots of scenarios of what might have happened and he finds himself feeling more depressed at the thought that his sister may be dead also.

'Come on Ben, Jess is going to be okay,' he tells himself, trying to be more positive about the situation. Dad indicates left as he takes the slip road off the M1 Motorway, following the signs for St Albans. Ben stares out of the window as they enter a built-up area with high-rise buildings and industrial estates lining their way. Within a minute they see the sign for City Hospital to the left, so dad indicates and slowly decelerates ready to turn off. Ben knows they'll reach the hospital in a few minutes; then they'll find out about Jess. The very thought that they'll know one way or the other is making him nervous because in his heart he knows something bad has happened. The anxious wait starts to take its toll on Ben and with what's already happened today, he starts to feel very sick.

'Mum, I don't feel well,' Ben tells his mum who immediately opens the windows to let the rush of cold air wash over his face. Ben closes his eyes and rests his head back against the headrest and allows the cold breeze to soothe him. The constant flow of air across his face wafts his blonde fringe over his forehead causing the ends to gently stroke his skin. It's a nice relaxing sensation that transports him to a far-off place and for a few moments his mind is somewhere else.

'Here we are,' Mum says to reassure him that the journey's come to an end.

Ben opens his eyes as dad turns into the hospital car park. He takes a ticket from the ticket machine at the barrier and they all watch as the red and white barrier lifts up into the air to allow them to enter. Dad drives the car along the directional route until he sees a vacant free space to park the car which he does in one attempt not like his mother, who's taken up to three attempts to park her car before. They all get out and head for the Accident and Emergency entrance.

Chapter Twenty-Two

The reception to the A and E department is packed with people. Every seat is occupied in the waiting area and there are a few people standing. It's the first time Ben's ever been in a hospital except for the day he was born; so seeing all the sick and injured people sitting around is a little frightening for him. He notices an old workman with bandages around his hands and head; another man is holding a patch over his eye. A young man standing next to the toilet is holding what appears to be a wastepaper bin under his chin so Ben assumes he's using it to throw up in. He spots a group of children huddled together near the back of the seating area and from what he can see, he thinks they're from his school. Suddenly he recognises one of them.

'Mum, Mum over there,' Ben tells his mother while pointing to the group in the far corner.

'Ben wait, we've got to ask at the reception desk and there's a queue,' his mum informs him.

'Mum, I can see Debbie Parker,' Ben replies, still pointing to the group. Mum looks round to see where he's pointing and recognises Debbie. She taps dad on the shoulder.

'Chris, we're just going to pop over there and speak to Debbie to find out where Jess is.'

Dad looks over at the group of schoolchildren and says, 'Who's Debbie?'

'You know, Jessica's friend,' Mum informs him. Dad suddenly remembers.

'Okay, I'll wait here and ask at the reception desk.' Ben and his mum rush over towards the group through the rows and rows of waiting casualties. Before they get to the group, Debbie recognises them and immediately stands up.

'Mrs Chapman, hi,' Debbie says, looking pleased to see them.

'Hi Debbie, do you know where Jess is?' Mum asks.

'Sorry, I don't know. We were the first and second group they picked up in the ambulances that brought us straight here. Maybe they'll pick Jess up next?' Debbie suggests.

Ben and his mum look at the other school children all sitting around in their small group, all with minor cuts and bruises to their faces and arms. Seeing the minor injuries to the children reassures Anne and Ben that everything may be all right with Jess because the injuries are only superficial. 'I'm sorry Debbie; this must be a nightmare for you all. Are you all right? Can we call your mother for you? Mum offers.

'That's all right Mrs Chapman; I managed to telephone home over an hour ago so Mum and Dad should be here soon.'

'That's good, so does anyone know exactly what happened?' Mum asks.

'I'm not sure. We were talking and singing on the coach one moment and then the next thing we know, the coach suddenly swerved to the side and we heard a loud bang and we ended up rolling down a bank on our side.' 'You poor thing, that sounds horrendous; was anyone seriously injured?' Mum tentatively asks.

'I'm not sure. We're all okay except for a few cuts from the broken glass, I think.'

'I thought you and Jess would have sat together on the coach?' Mum quickly asks, as Jess and Debbie usually sit together whenever they go on a school trip. 'We did; Jess was sat next to me by the window,' Debbie explains.

'Sorry, how is it that you were the first ones to be brought in here then? If Jess was sat next to you, surely, she'd be in this group too, wouldn't she?' Mum's voice begins to crack as she asks Debbie. Debbie notices Mum sounding emotional.

'Did you want to sit down Mrs Chapman?' Debbie asks while pointing to a vacant chair next to her.

Mum quickly sits down next to Debbie. She takes out a tissue from her bag and wipes her eyes. Still clutching the tissue, she says, 'Can you please tell me exactly what happened, just tell me everything; I need to know what's happened to Jess.'

Debbie looks nervously at Mum.

After the coach swerved across the road, there was a loud bang and our chairs were pushed into the centre aisle. The coach then hit something and started to tip over onto its side. Everyone was screaming. Then the coach stopped moving and we were like; upside down and it suddenly went all dark. I remember undoing my seatbelt and climbing out through the broken window.' 'Why did it go dark?' Ben asks not quite understanding how it was dark, when the accident must have happened around three o'clock.

'The coach was on its side down a bank and the windows were all covered over with branches or something.'

'So let's get this straight. You said your chairs were pushed sideways into the centre aisle?' Mum asks.

'Yes, Jess was by the window and I had he aisle seat. Suddenly my chair was next to the chair on the other side of the aisle,' Debbie explains.

Mum suddenly looks really upset and covers her mouth with her hand. She stands up and quickly walks over towards dad still waiting in the queue.

'Is your mum all right?' Debbie asks.

Ben looks over towards his mum now talking to Dad.

'Yes, she'll be okay,' he tells Debbie who's looking a little upset after explaining everything to Mum. Ben sits down in the empty seat left by his mum and turns towards Debbie.

'Does anyone know what caused the accident?' Ben asks the rest of the group.

'I do,' says one of the boys sitting at the back. Ben can't remember the lads name but he's seen him before at school.

'So what happened?'

The boy leans forward so he can be heard. 'We sat just behind the driver,' he says, pointing to his friend next to him. He continues.

'I noticed the driver took a drink from a bottle he had tucked down by his feet, then he lost control and then a big lorry ran into the side of us and pushed us over the barrier.'

'Do you know what he was drinking?' Ben asks.

'I do,' his friend says. 'It was whisky. I recognise the bottle because my dad drinks the same stuff at home.'

Ben feels the anger slowly build up inside him at hearing that it was the driver who caused the accident. Fortunately for him, he hears his mum call him before he has time to say something, he'd probably regret.

'Ben, we've got to go.' Ben quickly thanks his school colleagues before heading back towards his mum. Ben notices his dad talking to someone in a medical uniform who's pointing towards the far end of the corridor.

'What's happening?' Ben asks his mum.

'They've taken Jess to another part of the hospital, to Plover Ward. Dad's just being told where that is.'

They turn towards Dad just as he's finished talking to the nurse who was giving him directions. He tells them, 'Come on, it's this way.'

The three of them head down the corridor to the end and turn left along another main corridor to the second turning on the right through a set of double doors. They go up two flights of stairs and then through another set of double doors. They turn left along the corridor for about thirty metres and then right through another set of double doors into Plover Ward. Dad leads the way to the nurses station positioned on the left of the ward, with two women in uniform behind the desk. One nurse is behind a computer screen and the other is doing something to a machine attached to a tall metal stand.

'Excuse me, we're the parents of Jessica Chapman,' Dad informs the woman behind the computer screen. She looks up at Dad and then types something on her keyboard while staring at the computer screen. They anxiously wait a few seconds for the nurse to retrieve whatever information she needs. She stops typing and looks round at the nurse standing behind her.

'Jackie. These are the parents of Jessica Chapman.' The nurse stops what she's doing and goes around the reception desk before coming to a stop right in front of Dad.

'Mr and Mrs Chapman?' she asks.

'Yes' Mum replies.

'My name is Jackie and I'm the staff nurse in charge of the ward.'

'Oh hi' Mum and Dad say nervously.

'Jessica came into us a few hours ago. I don't know what you've been told but Jessica was involved in an accident and has received some injuries, I'm sorry to say.' Mum quickly covers her mouth in shock at hearing the news that her daughter was injured and quickly grabs hold of Dad's arm for support.

'Is she okay?' Dad asks.

'Yes Mister Chapman; however, the X-ray revealed that her pelvis was crushed and she also received a break to her right femur and her right ulna. That's her upper right leg and her right wrist along with a few facial cuts from the broken glass.'

'Oh my word, how is she; can we see her?' Mum asks with a slight trembling to her voice.

'Of course you can Mrs Chapman. Just so you know, we've set her wrist and thigh in plaster to help her bones to heal. Unfortunately, she'll need an operation tomorrow, to place her in traction because of her crushed hip. We've sedated her with a morphine drip for the pain so she's comfortable,' Jackie informs us. Hearing the list of injuries Jessica has incurred comes as a huge shock to all of them, especially after seeing Debbie and the other school children having only sustained minor cuts and bruises, so it takes them a few moments just to register what they've been told.

'Sorry, erm, I mean; it's a lot to take in,' Dad explains as we all appear to be speechless for a moment. 'That's all right Mr Chapman; did you want to see her now?' Jackie asks.

'Yes please,' Mum quickly intervenes.

'Okay, please follow me; I think she's awake.'

Jackie turns and leads the way down the ward and into a small room off to the side which accommodates four hospital beds. Jackie points towards the furthest bed on the right partially hidden behind a floor-to-ceiling partitioning curtain.

'Jessica's there,' she informs them.

They all slowly walk over to the end of Jessica's bed and look at Jessica for the first time after the accident. The right side of Jessica's face is bruised and swollen; she has a plaster just above her right eyebrow. A plasma bag suspended off a metal frame with a clear plastic feed tube stretches down and feeds into the back of Jessica's left hand, no doubt providing vital medication. The lower part of Jessica's body is covered by a single sheet draped over a metal frame to prevent anything touching her injured pelvis. Jessica's right wrist is encased in a white plaster of Paris cast, supported by a triangular bandage wrapped around the back of her neck, so her arm is nicely secured against her chest. Mum is the first to speak.

'Jess you poor thing, how are you?'

Mum quickly takes the seat next to the bed so she can be closest to her daughter. Dad slides a chair from the vacant bed next to Jessica's and positions it just behind Mum's chair and sits down. Ben moves forward and stands behind Dad. Jessica's eyes fully open when she hears Mum's voice and she tries to smile but her bruised face prevents her.

'Hi Mum, hi Dad,' Jess says.

'What happened sweetheart?' Mum asks and gently takes Jessica's hand in hers.

'I can't remember,' Jess replies

'Don't worry darling. I'm sure the doctors will make you all better in no time,' Mum says. Ben notices a single tear appears out of the corner of Jessica's right eye as it makes its way down her cheek. Mum grabs a tissue from her handbag and wipes the tear away before she starts to cry. Dad puts his arm around Mum's shoulder and gives her a squeeze.

'It'll be all right darling, don't you worry. The doctors can perform miracles, you'll see,' Dad tells Jess. He reaches over and grabs Jessica's hand protruding from the cast and gives it a gentle squeeze. Jess tries to smile again. 'I'm all right, really,' she tells everyone.

The sight of seeing his sister in hospital all bashed and bruised is too much for Ben especially after experiencing what happened to Alexis so he decides to leave his parents with Jess for a while.

'Mum, Dad, I'm just going to wait outside,' Ben says. Mum and Dad look up at Ben and, knowing how upset he was earlier, tell him that it's all right and that he can wait outside the ward if he wants. Ben holds up his hand and gives Jess a brief wave before making his way out of the ward and into the corridor where he notices a bank of four chairs against the wall opposite the ward.

Chapter Twenty-Three

Ben sits down on the right-hand seat opposite the entrance to the ward and rests his head in his hands looking like a moody teenager. He's not bothered by what other people think and how upset he looks because he's had a lot to contend with today. A young couple in their early twenties appear around a corner further along the corridor and go towards where he is sitting. As they get nearer the girl notices Ben looking over towards her and gives him a smile; he forces a smile back as they go past him and disappear through the double doors leading to Plover Ward. She was a pretty girl and on any other occasion her smile would have made his day, but today, he's got too much on his mind and he really needs to think about what happened to his sister. He decides it's probably best if he lowers his gaze and stares at the floor so as not to be distracted by other people coming in or going out of the ward. He looks down at the linoleum flooring and focuses his eyes on the indentations caused by trolleys and possibly stiletto heels that women wear. He tries to recall what the lad on the coach told him earlier about the coach driver.

Why would a coach driver be drinking alcohol while he's in charge of driving school children to and from the museum? he asks himself. *It's against the law to be drinking and driving.* Ben suddenly remembers the TV ads showing a group of teenagers drinking and driving and then crashing the car. Everyone knows it's illegal so why was he drinking? Then he remembers that two teachers were on the coach with Jess. Why didn't one of the teachers say something?

They should have stopped him and called the police. He tries to understand why nothing was done, when the comments from the lad come back to his mind. He said he saw the driver take a drink from a bottle of whisky, when they were on their way home, just before the accident. If that was the only time he saw the driver take a drink; maybe the driver wasn't drinking on the journey to London; maybe he bought the whisky when he was waiting for the children to board the coach for their homeward journey. The more Ben thinks about what happened, the more angry he becomes.

'He should be jailed for what he did. They should lock him up and throw away the key,' Ben tells himself. 'So how am I going to stop this?' he asks himself but his mind is a complete blank. 'Come on Ben… Think!' He feels agitated that nothing is coming to his mind. 'Talk the problem through; break it down,' he reminds himself. He gives his eyes a quick rub.

'Okay, I've got to help Jess and I've got to help Alexis. I tried to help Alexis earlier but it didn't work. Why couldn't I help her?' he asks himself, trying to visualise the two failed attempts at saving his girlfriend. He remembers on both occasions calling Alexis's name and then seeing Alexis being pushed by Tony into the road.' Just thinking about what happened is starting to make him upset, but he knows he has to persevere otherwise he's not going to save her.

'Okay, what would happen if I didn't call out Alexis's name?' he asks himself. 'Would that help? The first time I was held back in class and Tony and his mates had already surrounded Alexis so calling out wouldn't have made a difference. The second time Tony hadn't quite reached Alexis but he still got to her before I did and I wasn't held up in class that time. He knows he really needs to get to Alexis before Tony does, but how could he do that if the second time he wasn't delayed and yet Tony still got to Alexis before he did? He decides to concentrate on Jessica's situation for a while.

'Right, let me think how I can help Jess. Someone needs to find out about the driver and his drinking problem. What if I tell a teacher before they set off from school. But what would I say? Excuse me Miss, I think the driver is a drunkard and shouldn't be driving. What if they called the police and they gave the driver a breathalyser test and the test showed that he was sober? I'd look really stupid then and that wouldn't help. The two boys on the coach said they saw the driver take a drink just before the crash; so, let's assume that he didn't drink on his journey to London but started drinking on his journey home. Jess told them that the coach would arrive at the museum at lunchtime and they'd all be picked up by the coach driver after two thirty to bring them back. If that was the case, the driver could have bought the whisky while everyone was wandering around the museum. It would have been too risky to buy whisky before they set off from school just in case someone saw the bottle and questioned him. This way the driver could have bought the whisky and stashed it in the driver's door compartment or something and maybe kept it concealed in some way. So basically, I need to be there in London at lunchtime so I can watch the driver take a drink and I also need to be back home at school to save Alexis. How on earth am I going to be in two places at once Ben wonders. Suddenly the answer comes to him in a flash: 'Paul.'

If I get Paul to meet up with Alexis after school instead of going to the dentist; I could come here and save Jess. Ben starts to formulate a plan in his head. He quickly takes out his watch and holds it in his hand; checking that no one can see him, he opens the lid and looks down at the watch face, calculating in his mind the precise time he needs to travel back, when something occurs   to him. 'Wait a minute if I go back in time now, Paul's not going to know anything about the accident outside school. I'd just be telling him about a future event that won't have the same impetus. He won't even know about Jess either. I really need to speak to Paul first and explain everything, for this to work.' He slips the watch back inside his pocket and stands up, feeling a lot happier, knowing that he's now got a plan. He walks through the double doors back inside Plover Ward and heads over towards Jessica's room. Mum and Dad are standing up now by the side of Jessica's bed saying their goodbyes.

'We'll come back tomorrow bright and early. Don't worry darling, we'll book into a hotel or something so we can see you every day until you're ready to come home,' Mum tells Jessica. Jess gives Mum a smile just as she leans forward and kisses Jess on the forehead. She steps back and Dad does the same.

'Bye Jess, we love you,' Dad says. Mum and Dad slowly step away from the bed and turn to walk out when they see Ben standing just in front of them.

'Ben, we didn't see you there. We're just about to go. Did you want to say goodbye to your sister?' they ask. Ben gives them a nod and walks around to the left side of Jessica's bed and leans in towards her so she can hear him.

'Jess I'm going to make you all better. I promise,' he whispers into her ear while gently squeezing her hand. He straightens up and turns to follow his parents as they wave to Jess and exit the room. Ben knows his sister won't really understand what he told her, but it doesn't really matter. What matters is that Ben has a plan and tomorrow, he's going to save his sister and his girlfriend with the help of his best friend Paul.

Chapter Twenty-Four

By the time Ben meets Paul at school, it seems that everyone in school has already heard about Alexis. The whole playground seems to be talking about how Alexis flew over the top of a car and died in the road. Ben takes his usual seat on the climbing frame as Paul goes over to him and sits down.

'I'm sorry Ben; I should have stayed with Alexis and told Mum not to take me to the dentist,' Paul tells his friend.

'Don't worry Paul. It's not your fault, it was Tony Vernall. I saw him push Alexis into the road, right in front of a car.'

Paul looks physically shocked that Ben saw the whole thing.

'Why didn't you go back in time and save her?' he asks.

'I did, but it didn't work.'

'What do you mean, it didn't work?' Paul asks, looking confused that the time machine may have not worked.

' The first time, Tony pushed Alexis into the road, she was run over by a delivery lorry, so I travelled back in time to try to save her but Tony got to her before I did and pushed her in front of a car.' Ben's voice seemed to break as he tried to get his words out. Paul realises how upset Ben is and looks down at his feet, so Ben doesn't feel he has to continue until he's ready.

They sit there in silence for a few seconds when Paul asks, 'Why was she killed by two different vehicles?'

'It's because the first time, I was held up in stupid history class by Miss Havelock. The second time, I just dashed out of class but it still took me ages to get from my history classroom to the road sign where Alexis was waiting. By the time I got to Alexis, it was too late, Tony and his gang had already surrounded her, that's when Tony pushed her into the road.'

Paul looks down at his feet again feeling upset that his friend couldn't save his girlfriend and had to see her being run over twice. His mind desperately tries to think of some words of comfort but at that moment, he's lost for words.

'Have you heard about Jess?' Ben asks.

'No, what about Jess?' Paul asks sounding confused as to why Ben is mentioning his sister at a time like this.

'The school coach crashed coming back from the museum trip yesterday and Jess is in hospital,' Ben explains. Paul can't believe it. He sits there in total shock, shaking his head in disbelief.

'I don't believe it Ben, that's terrible.' The sad news about Alexis and Jess is obviously having an effect on Paul, because Ben notices Paul's eyes start to water and his voice becomes a little shaky.

'It's all right Paul; I think I've worked out a plan to fix this,' Ben says. Paul looks up at his friend and quickly wipes his eyes.

'What are you going to do?' he asks, sounding hopeful.

'Actually, my plan involves the two of us,' Ben tells his friend.

'Okay, what do you want me to do, I'll do anything to help?' Paul offers, feeling good that he can help, but a little apprehensive because he doesn't know exactly what's involved.

'I need you to save Alexis and I'm going to save Jess,' Ben tells him. Paul leans in closer and looks intently at Ben as he explains his plan in great detail. Once he finishes, Paul gives his friend a smile, feeling quite excited that he'll be playing a key role in saving Alexis. They shake hands and promise to do their best to save the two girls. Ben reaches inside his pocket and takes out the watch and opens the lid.

'So how far back are we travelling?' Paul asks. 'This time yesterday, remember when we met up by the climbing frame,' Ben says.

'But you and Alexis got there first didn't you? Will I be with you or will I still be walking to school?' Paul asks, sounding a little nervous.

Ben is a little surprised that Paul's sounding nervous about travelling back in time so he says, 'You've travelled back in time before, what are you nervous about?'

'The last and only time I travelled back in time, I went back to my room, alone,' Paul says.

'So, what's that got to do with anything?' Ben asks. 'If I'm travelling back in time and I suddenly appear in my own body while I'm walking, won't I fall over? And won't everyone see me?' Paul nervously asks. Ben bursts out laughing at Paul's preconception of what might happen.

'No, nobody will see you and, no you won't fall over,' Ben tells him.

'But if I suddenly appear as I'm stepping off a kerb, it might take me by surprise and I might trip or something,' Paul says not sounding too convinced at Ben's explanation.

'Paul, don't worry about it, you'll be fine. So are you ready?' Ben asks, having finally composed himself. Paul gives him a nod and takes hold of the lid of the watch with his left hand while crossing his fingers with his right just in case it doesn't go as well as planned.

Ben and Paul look down at the watch face as Ben slowly turns the time back twenty-four hours.

Suddenly Ben finds himself sitting on the low bar of the climbing frame with Alexis sat by his side. Just having Alexis next to him once more is the best feeling in the world. Ben can hardly control his emotions; he doesn't know whether to cry, laugh or just give her the biggest hug.

It takes him a moment to remember what he was doing this time yesterday; which is the exact moment he's now reliving, when he remembers they're waiting for Paul to arrive. Suddenly Tony, Simon and Brian walk into view and barge through a group of younger boys heading towards them; they stop just in front of Ben and Alexis and Tony says, 'You're history Chapman. Just wait till after school.'

Ben looks up at Tony, knowing all too well what he's planning and says, 'Whatever, loser.' Tony glares at Ben and for a second Ben thought he'd overstepped the mark and forced Tony to react to his comment. Ben holds his stare and after what seemed like ten or fifteen seconds, when in actuality was only about three seconds; Tony shakes his head and turns away.

'Ben you've got to be careful, Tony's not going to let you off for saying that he's a loser,' Alexis tells Ben. Ben gives her hand a gentle squeeze, followed by a smile.

'Don't worry, I know what I'm doing.'

Just then, they notice Paul walking towards them from the direction of the school entrance having just seen Tony and his mates walking away.

'Hi guys; is Tony in a bad mood again?' Paul asks.

'How did you know?' Alexis replies.

'Déjà vu,' Paul says and gives Ben a wink. Alexis and Ben stand up from sitting down on the climbing frame and the three of them head over towards the main school entrance just as the school bell sounds. They walk in through the main door and walk along the corridor to Alexis's classroom where Ben gives her a quick kiss before she disappears inside. They quickly move along the corridor and dart behind a set of lockers out of view from the few stragglers still making their way to their first class.

'Don't forget what we said,' Ben reminds Paul. 'Don't worry I won't and I hope it goes well in London,' Paul replies before they separate. Paul rushes across the corridor to his first class while Ben heads back out through the main entrance and into the playground.

Chapter Twenty-Five

Paul tries to concentrate on his lessons during his morning classes because for one thing, he can't do anything at the moment anyway, and Ben specifically told him to wait until lunchtime to tell Alexis that he'd gone home because he wasn't feeling well. He didn't want Alexis to worry about him or even try to telephone his house to see how he is; so that's why he told Paul to wait until just before they need to go back into class for the afternoon lessons so she wouldn't have a chance to ring. Ben assumes that if Alexis knows that Ben has gone home early, she wouldn't be waiting for him at the road sign and Tony wouldn't have another opportunity to push her into the road as he's done twice before. Paul looks up at the wall clock in his music class knowing that he's literally got a few minutes to wait until the lunchtime break starts. He reasons to himself that if he finds Alexis straight away, they could hang out together so if she suggests telephoning Ben's house, he'd give her some excuse so she doesn't let the cat out of the bag and cause problems for Ben. Paul patiently waits as Stuart Cummings plays his practiced music piece to the class on the keyboard. "Well done Stuart.' Mr Plummer commends him as he finishes his piano recital and goes back to his seat. "That was excellent fingering but you still need to improve on your tempo. You drifted out of time just near the end. But well done, you're definitely improving, so keep practising each day and we'll get you in for your level three next month.' Stuart smiles from ear to ear at the praise. Paul looks back at the wall clock just as the second hand counts down from ten seconds until it reaches the twelve to the sound of the school bell blearing just outside the music classroom, letting everyone know that it's lunchtime. Paul quickly stands up and begins packing his two music books away inside his rucksack.

'Don't forget children, I want you all to write down a simple melody consisting of eight bars by next week,' Mr Plummer says. Paul picks up his bag and joins the long queue of children making their way to the door. Eddy

Ringer is possibly the biggest and fattest boy in school and because he finds it difficult to walk; the teachers always assign him the nearest seat in the classroom next to the door; just in case he needs to use the bathroom. Eddy's massive body standing right in front of the doorway is preventing anyone from leaving. 'Come on Eddy, some of us need to have our lunch,' Phil Drake cries out.

'Eddy, get a move on.' Brian Hillock joins in. 'Children, don't be impatient. It's not a race,' Mr Plummer reminds everyone. Eddy squeezes through the door and into the corridor, allowing the other children in his class room to pass him. The rest of the class quickly makes their way around Eddy and speeds along the corridor to the dining room before Eddy gets there. Paul manages to squeeze past Eddy as his massive frame labours along the corridor, swaying from side to side. He rushes out through the main entrance only to be held up by two smaller children just in front of him; he quickly swerves around them at the top of the steps and leaps down the steps onto the playground as he jogs towards the science lab, situated at the far left of the main school building. He knows Alexis has chemistry for her last lesson that morning so she should still be in the science lab he reasons to himself. As he near the entrance to the science lab, he notices a group of girls leaving the building through the blue fire door. They stop in their small group and begin chatting about something all huddled together. Paul immediately recognises Avalon stood to the side of the group.

'Avalon, have you seen Alexis?' Paul quickly asks as he runs up to the small gathering.

'Hi Paul, I'm not sure.'

More girls start to file out through the door so Avalon and Paul stare at those coming out from the building in the hope of seeing Alexis. The girls all exit the building, but there is no sign of Alexis. Avalon notices Paul's anxious disposition, so she stops Susan Davis.

'Sue have you seen Alexis anywhere?'

'Oh I think she's gone to the auditorium for the rehearsal.'

'What rehearsal?' Paul asks.

'I think it's for the play at the end of the month; she's playing the part of Ophelia,' Susan tells Paul. 'Thanks,' Paul says before quickly dashing off in the opposite direction.

'Please, please don't already be in rehearsals,' Paul murmurs as he runs towards the other end of the school grounds. Paul dodges around pockets of children milling around in the playground moving quickly left and right as he tries to avoid colliding with anyone on his way to the auditorium. He passes the last group of children when his mind drifts off to the thought that he might be too late, because if he is, he won't have another opportunity to tell her about Ben.

Damn it! Paul gets annoyed with himself knowing that he should have asked her this morning what she was doing during lunch break, but how did he know that she was rehearsing a school play; she never said? Paul rushes past the main entrance doors just as two boys suddenly step out in front of him. *Thud!* Paul's shoulder crashes into the nearest boy, sending him flying through the air and crumpling down in a heap on the ground. Immediately Paul's shoulder begins to ache along with his bruised knee and elbow. It takes him a few seconds to comprehend where he is as the side of his face is pressed up against a couple of daffodil stems, now ripped out from the neatly arranged flower bed. Paul quickly sits up and wipes the dirt from his cheek to the sound of the uninjured boy shouting at him.

'Hey, what do you think you're doing?'

Paul looks up at the boy who shouted and immediately recognises Simon Dicks.

Suddenly all thought of Alexis escapes him at the shock of seeing Simon and he's all come over with a sudden feeling of dread as he watches the other boy help his friend Brian Philips to his feet not two metres away. The two boys quickly advance on Paul and together they grab both his arms and yank him to his feet.

'Hey, let go,' Paul hears himself call out.

'Where do you think you're going?' Simon asks as both his hands tighten around Paul's arm.

'Let go of me, I need to go somewhere,' Paul tells them.

'You're not going anywhere. You just knocked me over, you geek!' Brian screams into Paul's face. 'Look at my shoes, they're scuffed.' Brian points to the tip of one of his black lace-up shoes, now with a white scuff mark across the top. 'How much money do you have on ya? These shoes cost ten quid and you're gonna buy me a new pair, now cough up.'

Paul senses a sliver of hope that he could escape if he just gives Brian ten quid, when he remembers that he only has five pounds for his lunch. Paul quickly reaches inside his pocket and pulls out a crumpled five-pound note.

'Here, have this and I'll give you another fiver tomorrow.'

Brian snatches the money from his hand and shoves the note inside his pocket.

'Can I go now?' Paul asks, sounding relieved that he'd paid him off.

'Not so fast bozo, that's for my shoes but you knocked me over and you're not gonna buy your way outta that.'

Paul starts to protest.

'Shut up loser. Where's your friend Ben?' Brian asks while twisting Paul's left arm behind his back, causing a shooting pain to run up his arm.

'He's not here; I-I think he's sick,' Paul tells him. They start to push Paul backwards towards the side of the building. Paul feels his feet clambering backwards searching for solid ground beneath him as his body is transported backwards. Suddenly Paul's head crashes into the brickwork just below an office window to the sound of a loud thud.

'Arghhh!' Paul cries out.

'You haven't got your friend here to protect you,' Simon says as he holds Paul against the wall with his left hand and proceeds to punch him in the stomach with his right.

Paul hears a voice call out. *'Simon Dicks, Brian Philips!'*

Simon and Brian quickly let go of Paul's arms and turn around to an angry Miss Clarke standing not five metres away. 'You boys go to my office right now; I'll deal with you in a moment.'

Miss Clarke points towards the main entrance. Simon and Brian slowly slope off past Miss Clarke and into the main building. Miss Clarke walks towards Paul who's now bent over from the pain in his stomach. She stops by his side and rests her hand on Paul's shoulder.

'Are you all right Paul?' she asks.

Paul feels a little winded from the punch and the pain in his shoulder, knee and elbow are manageable so he slowly straightens up and gives Miss Clarke a courageous smile.

'I'm okay, Miss.'

'Now don't you worry about them; I'll be having a word with their parents and they will be staying behind on detention tonight, you can be assured of that. We do not tolerate bullying in this school,' she informs Paul. Paul gives her an approving smile.

'Thanks Miss. Can I go now?' Paul asks, all too aware of the time ticking away and the need to see Alexis before she goes into rehearsals.

'Are you sure you're all right or do you want to see the school nurse?' Miss Clarke asks, looking concerned.

'I'm fine, really, thanks Miss,' Paul tells her. Miss Clarke knows he's putting on a brave face, but she can't force him to see the school nurse, so she lets him go. Paul slowly walks away from Miss Clarke until he turns the corner of the building, before breaking into a sprint for the auditorium. He pushes his way in through the double doors and enters the large lobby area, which extends around both sides of the building, enabling patrons to access the inner auditorium on three sides. Paul runs towards the nearest door and reaches for the door handle just as his eyes catch sight of a sign next to the door handle saying, *Do Not Enter – Rehearsals in Session"*.

'Nooooooo!' Paul shouts in frustration at not being able to speak to Alexis. 'Arghhhhh! if it weren't for Simon and Brian!' Paul angrily mutters.

"Ssshhhhhhhhhhhhh!'

Miss Donaldson, standing near the noticeboard, signals to Paul to keep the noise down as rehearsals are in progress. Paul apologises and heads back out of the building feeling annoyed with himself.

By the time the afternoon lessons start, Paul is so wound up that he finds it difficult to concentrate on anything. He reruns the events during the lunchtime break to see if he could have done anything differently but each time he comes to the same conclusion. If only Alexis had told him about her rehearsals, it would have turned out much better. What's he going to say to Ben when he sees him? Ben's going to be furious and he'll probably never speak to him again. Paul looks down at his history book lying open on his desk in front of him, when his eyes are drawn to a vivid photograph of what appears to be a battle scene, with two cavalry men in the centre of the picture with their sabres held out in front of them while a group of Native Americans riding on horseback encircle them, when suddenly an idea pops into his head.

I wonder if I've changed anything? Paul asks himself. *Ben told me that Tony, Simon, Andrew and Brian all surrounded Alexis after school when Tony pushed Alexis into the road. Miss Clarke told me earlier that Simon and Brian would be held back on detention so they're not going to be with Tony and Andrew to surround her…* he thinks. Paul feels a glimmer of hope rise up inside him, knowing that he has changed something, so maybe things might turn out all right after all. He knows he's clutching at straws, because Tony could still push Alexis into the road without Simon and Brian, but he's hoping that with Simon and Brian not around, things might work in his favour. Paul anxiously looks up at the wall clock to see how long he has before the end of school.

'Please, please, please God, help me save Alexis,' he quietly prays. He looks back at the clock on the wall and watches as the final seconds tick down. *Briiinnnnng, briinnnnng.* The school bell reverberates throughout the school building. Everyone in class begins packing away their history books into their bags as they prepare to leave the classroom.

Paul is usually meticulous when it comes to packing his rucksack, but at this time, the only thought in his head is saving Alexis. Paul throws his books into his bag and makes a dash for the door. Eddy Ringer stands up and steps towards the open doorway leaving just a sliver of space for someone to slip through. Paul swings his rucksack forward towards the gap and his weighted bag clips Eddy on his hip which causes Eddy to yelp a little and step to the opposite side, leaving just enough room for Paul to squeeze through. Fortunately for Paul the main corridor has just a few children making their way towards the main exit at that moment, so Paul sprints along the corridor and out through the main doors before anyone has a chance to get there first.

Paul lifts up his hand to shield his eyes from the winter sun and quickly scans the few children that are already walking across the playground heading for the exit gate where a mass of parents and other family members are patiently waiting. His eyes dart from one school child to another in the hope of identifying Alexis but he's finding it difficult because he's looking at the backs of their heads.

This is a stupid idea, he tells himself and makes a dash towards the main gate. He reaches the gate and quickly turns so he can see all the faces of those exiting the main school building. Paul finds it easier to move his eyes from one pupil to the next, because they're walking out in groups of two or three and the sun is now behind him, making it easier to see their now illuminated faces. His eyes flick from pupil to pupil as they appear from the doorway when his eyes catch sight of Tony and Andrew as they exit the building.

No, damn it. Where's Alexis? he asks himself as he watches the two lads go down the steps and onto the playground. His eyes are transfixed on Tony and Andrew as they head towards him. But then they stop and look towards the science building at the far side of the school grounds.

What are they doing? Paul muses. He glances back at the main entrance just as Alexis appears. *No, no, this can't be happening. Alexis is going to walk right past them in a second and there's nothing I can do about it.* He holds his hands to his head in disbelief sensing that everything that could go wrong today has gone wrong and he can't do a thing about it. His eyes begin to water in despair at having to admit that he's failed. If he were Ben, he could rush down there and take Tony and Andrew on in a fight but he's not; he knows that if he even attempted to fight Tony on his own, it would be over in seconds. The utter frustration of knowing how helpless he feels, causes him to turn around and walk towards the main gate feeling totally defeated. He doesn't want to be an eyewitness to Tony and Andrew grabbing hold of Alexis when he can't do anything about it. He reaches the main gate and glances over his shoulder for one last look at the playground when he catches sight of Tony and Andrew walking towards the science building.

Suddenly a spark of hope ignites inside him, as he sees his two arch enemies wandering off in the opposite direction.

Why are they walking towards the science building? Paul asks himself; then he remembers that Simon and Brian are in detention and Tony and Andrew don't know.

Maybe they're just slow at coming out of their last lesson which must be biology or chemistry. Tony and Andrew slowly move across the playground just as Alexis walks behind them, heading towards the exit gate. Suddenly Paul is on tenterhooks as he watches Alexis head his way while keeping an eye on Tony and Andrew, hoping they don't turn around. Paul wants to call out to Alexis to speed up, or something but he knows if he shouts her name, Tony will definitely hear. Paul quickly goes towards Alexis hoping she doesn't see him until he's right next to her, for fear that she'll call out his name. Suddenly Paul's right in front of Alexis and links his arm around hers.

'Hi, Alexis,' he says with a smile.

"Oh hi! Have you seen Ben?' she asks.

Paul glances around her to see how far away Tony is before he quietly tells her that Ben went home early because he wasn't feeling very well. They walk out through the front entrance together and squeeze their way past a large group of mothers waiting for their children to come out.

'I'll see you tomorrow then,' Alexis tells Paul.

'Wait Alexis, as you don't have to wait for Ben, why don't I get my mum to drop you off as we're going that way anyway?'

Alexis shrugs. "Okay, if that's all right with your mum.' Paul can't risk Tony catching up with Alexis now that they're safely outside the school grounds. He would feel so much better if he knew that Alexis was safely at home, so that's why he wants to get his mum to drop her off. They step towards the kerb and look along the road for Paul's mum's car.

'There she is,' Paul tells Alexis and points to a silver Audi A3 parked fifty metres down the road between a red Nissan and a black new-style Mini. They quickly walk along the pavement towards his mum's car.

'Are you sure it's all right for a lift home; I could still walk home on my own, if it's easier?' Alexis asks, feeling that it might be putting Paul's mum out to drop her home.

'No it's fine, really,' Paul replies. They reach the silver Audi and Paul opens the back door. 'Mum, can we drop Alexis off at home on our way to the dentist?' Paul asks his mum. She checks the time on her watch and looks back at Alexis standing next to the car.

'That's fine Alexis, jump in.'

Alexis gets into the back next to Paul and closes the door. Paul's mum slowly pulls out into the road and drives past the school entrance. Paul glances out of the side window at the crowd of mothers standing on the pavement as Tony and Andrew appear around the side of a group of mothers, frantically looking left and right for someone. Paul looks at Alexis next to him and smiles.

Chapter Twenty-Six

Fortunately Ben came up with his plan last night after arriving home from the hospital. He knew then that he'd have to travel to London to save his sister. He'd never travelled to London before; in fact, he'd never travelled anywhere on his own before so the thought of travelling to London was a little daunting. *How would I get there? What mode of transport should I use?* To be honest, it wasn't difficult to plan. He sat at his computer and used Google Maps to find out where London was and where he was, so he could get a bearing on where he needed to go. He knew London was the capital of England and he knew the city was located south of where he lived but that was all he knew, except that the queen lived in London. He entered London on the search bar in Google Maps and then entered his home town on the travelling from text box and the website came up with three alternative routes for travelling to London. The first route directed him straight down the A1 to London, the second route directed him down the M1 and then the third option was mostly the A1 and then the M11 for the last part of the journey. All three routes took approximately four hours to get to London.

The next question Ben needed to work out was how he intended on travelling to London. It was too far to walk and that would certainly take too long. He thought, even if he took his bicycle and cycled the route, that would still take too much time so he really needed a mode of transport that would get him there quicker. Jess told them that the coach they're travelling on would take about four hours to get there and as he'd be leaving after Jess, he'd need something that would get him there even faster than a bus or a coach. Ben stares at his computer screen wondering what type of transport he should use when a pop-up advert flashes across the top of his computer screen advertising Virgin Trains.

'That's it,' he says to himself. Ben enters the words "Train travel" into his search engine and a list of possibilities fills the screen. He looks down the list and selects "National Rail enquiries" then presses the enter button on his keyboard. The screen quickly changes to the National Rail website where it asks him to enter where he wants to travel from.

Ben enters the word "Harrogate" in the small box and then types in the word "London" in the destination box. The next box on the screen asks him when he wants to travel. Ben selects ten o'clock the following morning and presses the enter button. Within a second the screen changes and the details of the possible train journeys appear in front of him. *Harrogate [HGT] to London King's Cross [KGX] platform 1 Leaving at 09.42 arriving at 12.40,* with the price of the ticket listed below.

'Okay, at least I know there's a train that'll take me straight into London, so that's good,' he says to himself and notices the "Buy Now" button on the screen for those who want to pay for their tickets using a credit card.

Ben knows he can't pay for his ticket online because he doesn't have a credit card. He looks around his bedroom for inspiration when he catches sight of his piggy bank on the windowsill. He immediately walks over and picks up the small round ceramic piglet from its resting place and carry's it over to his desk. The pig feels heavy and it should be, because Mum's told him for years to save his pocket money because some day, he'll need money for something important.

Saving his sister is definitely the most important thing he can think of at the moment, with the exception of saving Alexis; but he's already planned for that. Ben turns the little piglet over and removes the plastic cap under its belly. He turns the piglet back over and allows his savings to spill out over his desk top. He gives the piglet a little shake just to make sure all the coins have dropped out before putting the piglet back down on the desk.

The mass of coins piled up in the centre of his desk, looks impressive and appears to be a lot of money, but he knows it's not. He hopes it's enough to pay for his ticket to London and maybe a little extra, just in case. He eagerly begins to organise the coins into piles of the same monetary value. He stacks all the ten pence pieces in one pile; the twenty pence pieces in another pile, then the fifty pence pieces and finally the one-pound coins to form four separate piles. He begins counting the pound coins and then the fifty pence pieces while jotting the total sum down on a piece of paper. It suddenly dawns on him that he'll never have enough for a return journey to London but he does have enough for a one-way single fare.

I don't need to come back on the train; if I can save everyone from disaster, someone will bring me back home, he thinks, trying to be positive.

He puts the pound coins and fifty pence pieces that he'd counted inside his trouser pocket so he doesn't forget them in the morning.

* * *

Ben tells Paul 'Don't forget what we said,' as they wait by the lockers.

'Don't worry and I hope it goes well in London,' Paul replies. Just hearing Paul wishing him well really gives Ben the confidence to do his part. He turns around and walks back out through the main school entrance.

His initial thought about leaving just after the bell sounded that morning was that everyone should be in their classes and all the teachers would be focused on what was inside the class and not on what's going on outside. Ben nervously walks along the path leading to the school gate half expecting to hear the sound of Miss Clarke's voice calling his name and telling him to come back into school. The pounding in his chest as his heart beats louder and louder begins to ring inside his ears. He's never bunked off from school before and the fact that he's actually doing it now is possibly the most nerve-wracking experience of his life. He reaches the outside gate undetected and quickly steps around the fence so he's out of view from the school building.

Ben stops for a moment, to calm his nerves and to allow his heart to slow down a little. He notices a few of the mothers slowly walking away from the school while chatting among themselves. They seem to be more interested in talking than they are in walking because they're not moving very quickly. Ben doesn't want to be noticed by one of the mothers just in case they recognise him and then, report him to the school or even his parents. The annoying thing is that the women are walking in the same direction that he needs to go and if he stays behind them all the way, he'll miss his train. He walks slowly forward while keeping his distance until the women pass a side street. He thinks, *I know going down the side street will take me around the long way, but it's still going to be quicker than staying behind these two.*

Ben decides to take the longer route else he'll never make it to the train station on time. He slips around the corner and immediately breaks into a sprint along the side street. He's not the most athletic of people and running is not his thing so the journey becomes a real struggle. He must have sprinted for two hundred metres before he needed to slow down into a slightly quicker walking pace. He reaches another side street to his right and heads down that, at a comfortable jog before turning right again which then brings him back out onto the main road leading to the train station, but thirty metres ahead of the two slow-moving mothers. Ben walks along the pavement towards the train station conscious that it looks a little suspicious that a young lad is travelling the street all on his own while every other child is in school. His eyes scan the route up ahead as he approaches his destination, with the occasional ducking down behind a wheelie bin or parked car to avoid being seen by anyone. This part of the journey was never his main concern; it was the part where he needed to buy a ticket, because that would put him face to face with the ticket operator at the station.

He knew a single schoolboy travelling to London by himself would draw attention from others, so he devised a plan so as not to be stopped and questioned. He just hopes it works. Ben enters the train station building and sees the train ticket booth over to his right where a man and a woman are queuing to buy their tickets. He quickly goes into the toilets to prepare himself. The mens toilet has three cubicles over on the left and a bank of urinals right in front with two sink units with mirrors above, to his left. The room seems to be empty except for one of the cubicle doors being closed so he assumes someone must be using it. There's a strong smell of disinfectant mixed with urine wafting around the room, which is typical of public toilets. Ben doesn't mind the smell because it smells similar to the school toilets. He suddenly thinks of school and he wonders how Paul is doing. *He's probably studying hard in his first lesson right about now,* he thinks.

Suddenly, there's a groaning noise from the occupied cubicle and the sound of a splash as something is dropped into the toilet bowl. Ben realises he'd better get a move on, so he goes over to the sink unit and looks at his reflection in the mirror. He's never really stared at himself before so it seems a little weird. He knows girls look at themselves all the time; his sister is always looking at herself in the mirror, either fixing her hair or just admiring herself. He does remember seeing his mum stare at herself in the mirror once before as she applied some lipstick to her lips. She doesn't wear lipstick now as she's getting older but he remembers thinking how weird it was, to smear sticky red stuff over your mouth. He vaguely recalls how his parents had arranged for a babysitter to look after them because Dad was taking Mum out on a date; well, it was an anniversary meal or something. Mum looked really nice with her hair all tied up and she wore a pretty red tight-fitting dress. It was the red lipstick that gave him the idea. Ben reaches inside his pocket and pulls out a small tube of red lipstick belonging to his mother.

After glancing round to check that no one else has suddenly entered the toilets, Ben removes the lid to the lipstick and twists the plastic end to raise the glossy lipstick out of its sheath. Ben begins dabbing his face with the end of the tube, applying small red dots all over his face and the back of his hands. He looks at himself in the mirror to see if he'd applied enough dots when an older gentleman walks into the toilet and looks over at Ben as he goes towards the urinals. Ben quickly tucks the tube of lipstick back inside his pocket and glances up at the man's reflection in the mirror to see what reaction he's getting. The man must have noticed the red dots over Ben's face because Ben can see him continually looking around as he stands in front of the urinals while trying to unzip his trousers. Ben smiles to himself as he exits the toilet area and walks back into the main lobby when he notices the ticket kiosk is now clear. He quickly goes over to the glass window feeling a little apprehensive at presenting himself in front of the ticket clerk. Ben looks up at the ticket salesman before coughing into his left hand to get the gentleman's attention.

'A single, to King's Cross, please, Sir.'.

The man looks down at Ben with a suspicious look probably thinking 'Why aren't you at school?' when he notices Ben's face covered in bright red spots and his expression immediately changes.

'Sorry son, where do you want to go? he asks again.

'A single, to King's Cross please,' Ben repeats before coughing again into his hand.

'Certainly!' He quickly types something into his computer. 'That will be seventeen pounds and forty-five pence.'

Ben holds up a handful of coins and deposits them individually into the small stainless-steel tray. The man behind the kiosk window doesn't make any attempt to pick the money up to count it; he just prints out Ben's ticket and hands it over while holding the very farthest tip with his finger and thumb so as not to make physical contact. Ben takes the ticket from him.

'Thanks mister.'

Ben steps back away from the booth just as the ticket clerk covers the mound of coins with a cloth and then gently slides the coins out of the tray and onto the side of his counter, where he'd probably have them washed and dried before endeavouring to count them. Ben goes out of the building and on to the train platform to wait for his train to arrive. The time on the platform clock tells him that it's 9.40 so his train should arrive in two minutes. He looks down along the track half expecting to see the train in the distance, but all he can see is clear tracks as far as his eyes can see. He wonders if the train will arrive on time as he's often heard of people complaining about the trains and saying, how they're usually never on time. Ben notices the platform is empty, except for three other people waiting for the same train as himself. He expects most commuters would have taken the earlier train at eight o'clock so they could get to work for nine assuming their place of work is less than an hour away. In any case; Ben's feeling a little better knowing that the platform is not crowded and that he won't have to spend the whole journey crammed on a train with everyone staring at him. Ben notices a black object moving towards him in the distance along the rail tracks. *It's got to be my train,* he thinks as he looks over at the platform clock which is now showing the time as 9.42. He feels a sense of relief, knowing that the train is on time, which means that he should theoretically arrive in London at twelve forty, which also means that he'll have about an hour and fifty minutes to get to the museum and expose the driver. The sound of metallic squealing slowly gets louder and louder as the train approaches the platform. All three waiting passengers remain transfixed in their positions away from the nearside edge of the platform until the huge carriage comes to a complete stop in front of them.

The electronic doors automatically open to allow the passengers to exit the train and for new passengers to get on. Ben steps forward towards an open doorway and stops to allow a young couple to get on ahead of him. He steps inside the carriage and looks for an empty seat. As expected, the train carriage is only half full so Ben moves along the aisle and sits down in a seat adjacent to a mature professional looking gentleman in a dark blue pin striped suit. Ben looks over at the man who's totally engaged in reading *The Times* newspaper held in his well-manicured hands. Ben notices that the gentleman is probably in his late fifties and from the look of him, Ben assumes he's a solicitor or bank manager from his clean-shaven, well-groomed appearance. It's a little frightening, travelling on a train all alone, but having this man nearby makes him feel a little happier. The train starts to pull out of the station on its straight journey towards London King's Cross so Ben relaxes into his seat.

Ben spends most of his time looking out of the window at the ever-changing scenery as the train speeds past towns and cities between stretched out countryside. After two and a half hours, the scenery dramatically changes from lush green countryside to grey urban built up areas consisting of high-rise buildings and large commercial factories. Grey walls with graffiti and dilapidated buildings littered with rubbish. The grim, depressing sights causes Ben to worry about his decision to travel into London alone. Suddenly the world outside of the train becomes a scary place to be and the thought of having to leave the train when it finally stops at London King's Cross is becoming more and more unappealing. The train slows down a little as the train enters a dark tunnel. The sound from the wheels running along railway tracks is suddenly heightened by the enclosed space. Moments later the sound drops as the train emerges from the tunnel and they're cast into bright sunlight again. Ben continues to stare out of the window as the carriage continually rocks from side to side, feeling slightly comforted by the movement of the train as a baby would be comforted by their mother as she would rock the child to sleep. The thought of sleep did cross Ben's mind because of the long journey, but the idea of sleeping on a train with people he didn't know was a bit scary, so he pushed back the thought and decided to keep his wits about him. The train's made a couple of stops along its journey to London and more and more people got on, so the carriage is nearly full. Nobody sat in the seat next to Ben, but a youngish man and woman took the seats opposite. Ben felt relieved when they sat down in front of him, that he washed his face not long after leaving Harrogate. He would have hated the thought that a nice young couple would be staring at him for the whole journey thinking that he was contagious and had some rare disease or something.

They appeared to be really nice as Ben listened in on their conversation to pass the time. When they noticed Ben looking their way, they would give him a courteous smile, before continuing on with their conversation. Ben tried to work out what they did for a living but having no knowledge or experience of work in London, he could only conclude that they must be artists or worked in the theatre because of the way they were dressed in their bright, colourful, stylish clothes. Ben checks the time on his watch and realises that they must be nearing King's Cross as they're only minutes away from the scheduled time of arrival. He looks out of the window and notices that the scenery has changed again. Large style town houses and historical buildings fill the void outside. It's much cleaner and not so run down. He hears the train engines roar as the brakes are applied and the train starts to slow down on its final approach into King's Cross. Suddenly the train enters what appears to be a huge hangar with several platforms on either side, some with stationary trains, while others with trains now heading out in the opposite direction as they go out of the station and on their way to somewhere up north. The noise from the train applying its brakes gradually fills the carriage as the sound rises with the increased pressure to slow the train down. The train slows down to a walking pace as it nears the end of the line and pedestrians appear in view as they walk along the platform all rallying for position to board the train as it comes to a complete stop. Ben notices all those sat in his carriage now standing as they ease towards the doors. Ben stands up and joins the back of the queue as people start to exit the train. Ben steps down off the train onto the long, crowded platform and is overwhelmed by the mass of people all around him. People are moving quickly from left to right, rushing to get on the train or get out of the station and for a moment, the scene in front of him seems so busy and manic that he's not sure on what to do next. Ben begins to feel a little panicky with the proximity of everyone all around him and his eyes search for something or someone who could help; when he catches sight of the two younger artist types just up ahead.

They must be heading for the exit, Ben thinks. Without hesitation, he quickly follows the young couple in the hope of escaping the overwhelming intense environment he finds himself in. The couple suddenly disappear around a corner so Ben finds himself squeezing past a crowd of slow-moving people to try to catch up with them; he turns the corner into what appears to be a long pedestrian tunnel leading to the bottom of the biggest escalator he's ever seen in his life. Ben spots the artists now halfway up the escalator standing on the left of a large queue. Ben joins the queue of people on the escalator standing behind a lady in a trouser suit as they slowly ascend the steep incline. A young man steps past him on his right as he jumps the queue.

Hey, what does he think he's doing; were in a queue! Ben thinks.

Suddenly there's another man and then a woman walking up passing him on the right. Ben notices the artists nearing the top of the escalator and about to disappear over the ridge, so he decides to do as everyone else is doing and make a dash up the right-hand side. Ben quickly steps up the right-hand side feeling a burning sensation in his thighs as his muscles begin to ache from the sudden exertion. He finally reaches the top of the escalator and quickly steps off onto solid ground and follows the artist as they exit through a gateway into a large hall with thousands of people standing around. Ben notices right in front of him, what appears to be an exit, so he starts to walk in that direction when he sees another exit to the left which causes him to stop in his tracks.

'Two exits?' he says to himself while wondering which exit he should go through.

He quickly checks the time on his watch to confirm how long he has to save his sister and with a minor calculation, he confirms that he has one hour and forty-three minutes, assuming Jess told them the correct time of departure. He looks at both exits not knowing which one to go out, and reasons to himself that even if he went out of the wrong exit, it won't make that much of a difference; it might only add another fifteen seconds onto his journey. He dashes towards the exit right in front of him and for the first time in his life, he steps out onto a London street.

The first thing Ben notices is the noise. There's a continuous noise from engines revving, car horns beeping, music playing in the background from street performers and the sound of feet stomping the pavement with the hum of chatter as crowds of people go left and right. Ben's not sure exactly where he is; he's finding it difficult to get his bearings because he can't see any road signs for the mass of people wandering in front of him. He steps back against the outside wall to the station and tries to remember looking at Google Maps on his computer last night. He worked out that he needed to walk south from King's Cross and head towards Covent Garden where he should then see signs for the British Museum. From what he can remember there was a busy main road right next to King's Cross Station and by crossing that road, he should be travelling south and in the right direction.

Ben realises the road right in front of him is the busy road he needs to cross. He notices a crossing just to his right and the green walk sign has just appeared on the light box. He quickly joins the mass of people walking in that direction and manoeuvres his way across the pavement and onto the crossing in one piece. He turns right on the other side of the road and walks along the pavement until he reaches Judd Street. Ben turns left heading south down Judd Street.

The first thing he notices about the streets in central London is how spacious they are. Judd Street is no exception. The houses on either side of the street are large Georgian houses, all well preserved and grand in design. The warm sun is shining which makes his experience of walking the streets of London a pleasant experience and kind of makes him feel like he's on holiday. Ben sees an older lady walking alongside a younger girl around Jessica's age just up ahead, which instantly reminds him of the time, and that he needs to get a move on. Ben starts to jog a little along Judd Street until he reaches the end when he comes to a stop, trying to decide which way to go as he can't quite remember the rest of the journey. An Asian couple appear around a corner and head towards him, stopping every couple of steps to take photographs of passing London taxis and any landmarks they want to remember.

'Excuse me, can you tell me the way to the British Museum?' Ben asks the lady, hoping she speaks English. They stop and look at Ben, possibly trying to decipher his northern accent.

'Ah Bwittish Moozeum.'

They quickly take a London street directory from a hip bag and begin to open the paper map out, so they can check where they are. Ben steps to the side of them and recognises the aerial view. He points to Judd Street and follows the road with his finger to the end, when he works out that he needs to continue along the road until he gets to Russell Square. Once he's past Russell Square he just needs to turn left, which should take him to the museum.

'Thank you, thank you!' Ben tells the couple before jogging in the right direction for the museum.

Before he reaches Russell Square, Ben sees a road sign up ahead for the British Museum telling him that it's less than a mile away. Seeing the sign, knowing it's not too far away now, is such a relief. He's travelled so far and at the back of his mind, he was always worried that he wouldn't make it there on time, he takes a couple of deep breaths just to catch his second wind before checking the time on his watch. One twenty-five his watch tells him, which leaves him just one hour and five minutes left. Ben breaks into a jog towards the little bit of greenery he can see up ahead over to the left.

That's got to be Russell Square, he tells himself as he gets nearer and nearer. Finally he rounds the corner of Russell Square and continues along Montague Street for a few hundred metres, when he catches sight of a large grey stone building on the right with its impressive tall columns. Ben slows down a little as he nears this magnificent building feeling in awe at seeing such a huge edifice. It's one thing to see historic buildings from pictures in books, but to see them up close is just breathtaking.

As he nears the building, he starts to wonder if the inside is as impressive as the outside. He slowly goes up the short flight of stone steps and enters the building through the large glass door. The imposing lobby immediately takes his breath away. The marble floors and walls are a marvel to walk on and see. A mass of people are walking in all directions and mostly staring up at the architecture and décor. Some are carrying what appears to be information brochures of some sort which they casually look down at and read now and then. Ben notices a small reception desk off to the side, so he goes over to the young woman in a smart uniform.

'Excuse me, can you tell me where the school coaches are parked?' Ben asks.

'Are you all right, son? Have you been separated from your school party?' she asks. 'No... I... err left something on the coach so I was going to get it and then join the rest by the café,' Ben says hoping that his explanation sounded believable.

The lady smiles at Ben.

'Okay, the coaches are usually parked around the side of the building; it's best if you go out through the main entrance and then walk around to your right,' she points towards the exit.

'Thank you.' Ben smiles at the lady and heads out through the door he came in. He makes his way around the side of the impressive building to what appears to be a low dividing wall overlooking the coach parking area. Ben looks across at the allocated parking area and sees three coaches parked up.

I don't believe it; which one is Jess on? Ben asks himself. *Why didn't I pay more attention to the coach when it was parked outside our school this morning?* he angrily thinks as he stares at the three coaches while trying to recognise any distinguishing marks he may have remembered. It's no use, he can't remember anything about the coach Jess got on that morning except that it was whitish in colour, but that's about all, and the three coaches in front of him are all whitish. Ben walks down towards the parked coaches, all the while hoping that something will spring to mind but nothing does. He sees two of the drivers standing on the pavement smoking cigarettes so he decides to speak to them.

'Excuse me, I can't remember which coach I came on,' Ben says to the two men.

The taller of the two turns to face Ben, having just taken a puff of his cigarette; he slowly exhales a waft of smoke from his mouth before asking, 'Which school are you from?'

'I'm from Harrogate high.'

They look at each other and shake their heads; not recognising the name of the school.

'Sorry we didn't pick you up, you must have come in Steve's coach; he's just nipped off to the shops. He won't be long.'

They point in the direction of the furthest coach with the words "Travelline Coaches" written along the side of the coach.

Ben thanks them and wanders over towards the last coach and sits down on a low concrete wall bordering the museum. He must have waited a good ten minutes before seeing Steve in the distance approach the coach park wearing his Travelline uniform. As he nears, Ben recognises the all too familiar McDonald's takeout bag in one hand and a plastic carrier bag in his other as the driver steps towards the locked door to his coach. He looks over and smiles at Ben as he sits all alone on the concrete wall. He takes out his keys and opens the coach door, he steps up inside and sits down in the first passenger seat.

Ben is probably about six metres away from the front of the coach which wouldn't have been a bad spot to watch the driver but the sun is now reflecting off the coach windscreen and the glare from the sun's rays is preventing Ben from seeing anything inside the coach. He wonders if the driver is actually staring at him, trying to work out why a boy is sat all alone on the perimeter wall, away from everyone else. 'What am I going to do?' Ben thinks. He can't just sit there waiting for something to happen because time is running out and he can't see anything anyway.

He thinks about moving over to the side so he could look directly into the coach through the opened doorway, but that would look suspicious especially if the driver's been watching him all this time. Finally, Ben decides to "take the bull by the horns" (as he's heard that expression before) and go for it, but he's not entirely sure how he's going to go about it. First he needs to psych himself up.

Come on Ben! He looked friendly enough, he tells himself still feeling a little nervous. *Don't be a wimp, just get on with it.*

Ben knows he needs to find out if the driver is drinking alcohol and the only way he's going to do that is by getting on the coach and seeing for himself.

What if the driver doesn't recognise him from being among the students he picked up that morning? Ben nervously asks himself. Don't be stupid, he won't remember individual faces, all he'll remember is the number. Who'd recognise fifty kids' spotty faces; he certainly wouldn't, so how would a driver be expected to remember everyone on his coach? Anyway what's one extra face going to matter. Ben decides to bite the bullet and just go for it, so he slides himself off his concrete perch and stands up. He knows he's committed himself now because the driver can clearly see him staring back at the coach, so he has to go through with it. Ben starts to feel like a nervous wreck now that he's committed himself. He can sense his whole body nervously shaking as he slowly walks over towards the open doorway. Ben pops his head around the doorway so the driver can see him and says in a greeting he'd rehearsed more than thirty times as he waited for the driver, 'Hello, I think I left my phone on the coach, can I just grab it?' Ben speaks in a positive manner and gives the driver a confident smile. The driver looks down towards the opened doorway from his seat having taken a big bite from his burger and holds up his hand to indicate that he can't talk for a second. Ben can sense his heart pounding in his chest feeling that any moment, the driver is going to tell him to clear off. He maintains his forced smile and watches the man quickly chew and swallow what food he had left in his mouth. Ben notices the furrows in the man's forehead and his eyes narrow as he tries to recall seeing Ben from the group he picked up that morning. Ben quickly says, 'You picked us up from Harrogate High this morning' and pointed to his school motif on his school jumper. Hearing the name Harrogate High and seeing the badge must have cleared away any doubt in his mind and he waved Ben on.

'Thanks, I won't be a sec,' Ben tells the driver as he goes up the steps feeling like a fly entering a fly trap.

What am I doing? Ben silently asks himself while thinking what an insane situation he's putting himself in. He fights back the urge to turn around and rush off the coach by keeping the image of his sister at the hospital clearly in mind. Ben goes past the driver while casually glancing over at the McDonald's bag on the drivers lap and the white carrier bag tucked down the side of his seat next to his leg, which happens to be covered over. He continues along the aisle towards the back of the coach wondering what the hell he's supposed to do now as he didn't see the driver actively take a drink or see any evidence of a whisky bottle. Ben stops one seat from the back and proceeds to look down at the seat he's supposed to be sitting in for his phone. He figures that he's got to pretend to be doing something, else the driver might suspect something. Ben holds on to the back of the seat and turns his head from side to side to give the impression that he's looking for his phone. After a few seconds of turning his head, he glances towards the front of the coach without moving his head to see if the driver has taken a drink from the contents enclosed in the carrier bag. The driver is still holding a half-eaten burger near his face and seems to be continually chewing on what he has in his mouth. A wave of panic washes over Ben because he knows he needs to hang around until the driver takes a drink and he's running out of ideas as to what to do next. Ben notices the overhead storage above the seats which gives him an idea.

'Where did I leave that stupid phone?!' Ben calls out so the driver can hear him. Ben proceeds to check the over seat storage space and lifts down a carrier bag with what appears to be a waterproof raincoat. He doesn't know who it belongs to but he needs to stretch out his time until the driver takes a drink. Out of the corner of his eye he can see the driver take another bite of his burger. Ben pulls the coat out of the plastic covering and looks inside the empty bag. *Damn it!* He quickly shoves the raincoat back inside the bag and places it back on the over seat shelf. Running out of options Ben starts to panic even more and can feel sweat trickling down the back of his neck as he tries to think what else he could do to waste time when another thought springs to mind. He crouches down between the seats to give the impression that he's checking to see if the phone may have dropped down and is lying on the floor.

'Where is it?' Ben says out loud so the driver can hear him. He glances back at the driver just as he turns his head to see what's holding Ben up. Ben quickly gets down onto his knees and begins looking under the seats for his phone.

'There it is!' he calls out. The driver turns back towards his food and continues eating, having heard that Ben's found what he's looking for. Ben lies down in the aisle and reaches under the seat with his phone held tightly in his right hand. 'I can't quite reach it... ' Ben says sounding like he's straining to reach his phone. He looks forward along the aisle of the coach in his prone position and notices the driver bending down and retrieving something from the plastic bag. *Gotcha!* Ben thinks and waits a few seconds until he knows the driver must be taking a swig from the bottle.

'Got it!' Ben immediately stands up holding his phone out in front of him and quickly walks back towards the front of the coach. The driver, sensing Ben striding towards him, tries to screw the lid on the bottle and hurriedly places the bottle back down inside the plastic bag. Ben quickened his pace and got level with the driver just as he leaned over trying to slot the bottle inside the crumpled plastic bag.

'Thanks mister,' Ben tells the driver and holds up his phone to show the driver. Without thinking, Ben's eyes drift to the plastic bag and immediately he sees the whisky bottle with the word "Bells" clearly on the label. The driver looks up at Ben and immediately notices Ben's eyes staring down at the whisky bottle. Ben looks back at the man's face and notices the sudden change in his facial expression to one of anger. In that instance Ben realises that he'd been caught out and in his defence he quickly says.

'I just fancy a burger; is it nice?'

The driver looks down to his lap and notices that the last cheeseburger he bought is clearly in view. He quickly changes his mind, picks up the wrapped burger and offers it to Ben when he realises that the young lad must be hungry.

'Here you are, you can have this. I've already eaten two burgers already and I don't think I could manage this one as well,' the man says. Ben takes the burger and thanks him. He goes off the coach and heads back towards the front of the museum thinking what a narrow escape he's just had. It must have taken a good few minutes for his hands to stop shaking and his heart to calm down.

Chapter Twenty-Seven

Ben takes a seat on a low wall near the front of the museum out of sight from the driver and looks down at the cheeseburger wrapped in its greaseproof paper. 'That was really kind of the driver to give him a burger,' he thinks. He is hungry and the aroma from the burger is making his stomach rumble, but the thought of eating something from the man he's about to report to the police is making him feel a little guilty. Ben allows the rumbling in his stomach to help him decide on what to do. He slowly un-wraps the burger and the smell from the warm cooked meat combined with the cheese and relish is all too much for him so he lifts the burger up to his mouth and takes a large bite.

Mmmmmm this is delicious,' he thinks and for the next few minutes the burger becomes his main focus as he's seduced by the very thing his stomach is craving. The sun is nicely positioned to the right of where he's sitting and he can feel the warmth of the sun on the right side of his face making him feel totally relaxed. He watches the passing traffic of people from all walks of life making their way in all directions and in that second he's lost in time; just enjoying the moment, people watching. Ben places the last of the burger into his mouth and screws up the grease proof paper wrapping from his burger and looks for a waste bin to deposit his rubbish. Fortunately there's a bin near a level crossing just thirty metres away, so Ben casually walks over to the concrete square column with its metal bin positioned inside half full of rubbish and deposits his wrapper. What to do now? Ben asks himself. Suddenly he's overcome with a wave of guilt as he begins to feel ashamed at the thought of having to turn the man over to the law.

What should I do? He seems like a really nice man.

Ben decides to double-check that the man is really the cause of Jessica's accident by seeing if he's had another drink from the whisky bottle. Ben goes back around to the far side of the coach park on the other side of the

187

perimeter wall bordering the museum. He's further away from the coaches so he knows even if the man sees him in the distance, he won't recognise him. Ben looks down from his vantage point and can just about make out the driver still sat in his seat. Ben knows the driver has eaten all the food he had, so if he sees him lift anything to his lips, it has to be the whisky.

He leans on the low wall and stares at the opened door to the coach as the driver sits in his seat. Without blinking, Ben focuses his attention on the man's right arm. Within seconds, he lifts what appears to be a bottle of liquid and drinks.

'Gotcha!' Ben says to himself, feeling vindicated for his decision to involve the police. He quickly stands up and heads back around to the front of the museum in search of a police officer.

'Where's a policeman when you want one?' Ben asks himself as he scans the area for a uniformed officer. The front of the museum is crowded with people, all shapes, sizes, and colours; but can he see a policeman? No.

'Where can I find a policeman?' Ben asks himself, feeling desperate. He begins wandering through the crowd of people in the hope of seeing an officer mixed in with the crowd but all he's seeing is tourists and young lovers kissing. He reaches the main road and looks left and right, hoping to see a police car with the intention of flagging it down but there's not a car in sight.

Ben takes a look at his watch again to check the time and notices it's already eleven minutes past two.

'Damn it, I'm running out of time!' Ben mutters knowing all too well that the coaches will be heading back up north at two thirty so that only leaves him nineteen minutes to find a policeman and stop the driver. He desperately looks left and right again scanning the streets, moving his focus from parked car to parked car hoping to see someone in uniform but there's literally no one around. 'Excuse me' Ben desperately asks a passing gentleman in a pinstriped suit but he's ignored by the man. Ben can't believe it; he stares at the back of the man's head in disgust as he walks away from him. He then spots a CCTV mast next to the roadside with its camera pointing towards the road.

'That's it, if I can't go to the police, I'll get them to come to me,' he tells himself. Ben squeezes past an elderly couple talking to themselves next to the kerb and runs into the middle of the road swinging his rucksack around his head. A car squeals to a halt causing other vehicles to slam on their brakes behind them. Ben runs into the next lane causing a taxi driver to slam on his brakes. Suddenly car horns begin sounding from irate drivers behind them. Ben continues running around in circles in the road swinging his rucksack in the air like a crazed lunatic.

'Oy clear off!' Ben hears the taxi driver call out to him from inside the taxi. More shouts are heard from others as they step out of their cars wondering what's causing the hold-up. Crowds of people gather along the kerbside and watch in amazement at a crazy child with a death wish. Ben glances up at the CCTV camera that's now pointing directly at him. Ben decides it's time to make his way back towards the museum.

He runs towards the crowd of people lining the road, who instinctively move to the side to allow him through, thinking that he may attack them if they don't move. He quickly passes the two elderly couple still talking to each other and probably unaware that anything unusual has happened. Ben glances back at the CCTV camera and notices the camera tracking his movements.

Good, I should see a police officer soon, Ben thinks as he runs past crowds of tourists towards the stone steps at the front of the museum. Suddenly a dark figure appears from the right of the building and Ben immediately recognises the familiar uniform of a policeman walking towards him. Ben changes direction and heads towards where the police officer is standing, causing the officer to stare at Ben in bewilderment.

'Good afternoon, Officer' Ben says.

The officer, not expecting a suspiciously behaving youth to suddenly present himself, stops in his tracks. He can't quite understand why the lad hasn't tried to make a run for it.

'Hello son, did you want to tell me something?' 'Yes, Officer. I need your help.'

'Do you now? Is that help with stopping traffic?' he asks and gives Ben a smile.

'Sorry, I only did that so I could find a policeman.'

'Why do you need a policeman?' he asks, sounding a little intrigued.

'I'm with fifty other school children from Harrogate High School. We came here on a school coach this morning. However, I noticed the driver of our coach is drinking alcohol and he's meant to be driving us home at two thirty,' Ben quickly blurts out.

The policeman continues to look at Ben as he slowly processes the information Ben's just given him. 'You're saying the driver of your coach has been drinking and he's supposed to be driving you back home?' the officer asks.

'Yes, yes. He's supposed to pick us up in ten minutes, so that's why I needed you to come and arrest him.'

The policeman takes his radio in one hand and begins to say something to those on the other end. Ben waits anxiously while the person on the other end of the police radio talks back to the officer. The young officer replaces the handset back on his vest.

'Okay son, this is a serious allegation you're making. Do you have any proof that your driver has been drinking?'

'Yes, Officer, I saw him drink from a bottle of whisky; Bells, I think,' Ben informs him, now sounding desperate. The officer notices how impatient the lad appears; shuffling from one foot to the other as though he's urgently in need of the toilet.

'Are you all right son; do you need the toilet?' he asks Ben.

'No.' Ben looks down at this watch and then looks at the officer. 'He'll be leaving in eight minutes.' Ben says and pleads with the officer to do something. The officer realises that the situation requires immediate action so he asks, 'Where is the coach now?'

Ben points in the direction of the coach park and says, 'It's parked just around the corner.'

'Okay son, can you show me?'

Ben quickly turns and briskly walks across the front of the museum to the far perimeter wall overlooking the coach park on the side of the building closely followed by the young officer.

They stop at the low perimeter wall and look down at the coach park, which now has just two coaches parked up. For a second, Ben was shocked to see one of the coaches missing, thinking that it was his coach; but then he recognises the Travelline logo on the side of the far coach still in its parking bay.

'There it is,' Ben quickly tells the officer. Within seconds of pointing to the parked coach, the coach engine roars into life and the headlights suddenly come on.

'Nooo!' Ben shouts.

Seeing Ben's reaction, the officer quickly asks, 'Is it the one at the end with its lights on?' He looks at Ben for confirmation as he starts moving towards a flight of steps leading to the coach park.

Ben calls out, *'Yes!'* and quickly follows the officer as he goes down the flight of steps towards the coach park. Within seconds the officer arrives at the bottom of the steps and jogs towards the furthest coach. Fortunately, the coach hasn't pulled out yet because it needs to wait until the engine has built up enough pressure in the hydraulics for the brakes to work. Ben goes down the steps towards the coach park and glances up to see how the officer is doing. The policeman seems to have passed the first parked coach and is heading towards Jessica's coach at the end as it starts to reverse out of its space. Ben keeps his eyes focused on the furthest coach until it disappears behind the first coach, when his eyes lock on to the officer as he darts around the parked coach, now disappearing out of view. Ben reaches the first parked coach just as the policeman runs around the side of the moving coach to get to the closed door. The coach reverses as far as he can and stops leaving the officer twenty metres in front of the coach. The driver shoves the transmission into first and starts to drive the coach forward. He mustn't have seen the officer while he was reversing, but now the man in uniform is standing right in front of him, holding his hand out to indicate to the driver that he needs to stop. Without warning, the driver presses hard down on his accelerator and the coach shoots towards the standing policeman. The police officer quickly dives out of the way, narrowly being run over as the coach speeds past him and clips the tail light of the parked-up coach, smashing the plastic glass cover. Ben quickly steps back as shards of glass splinter out from the impact just metres away. Suddenly the policeman is up on his feet with his handset in his hand speaking to anyone and everyone as he runs after the coach as it speeds out of the parking area and towards the busy main road. Ben, not wanting to miss a thing, rushes around the parked coach to see what happens and watches in disbelief as the coach speeds headlong into the busy main road, crashing into two cars before careering across the carriageway and hitting a metal barrier. Ben stands there open mouthed, not quite believing what's just unfolded before his very eyes. The scene seems to be something you would see in an action movie with people nearly being run over, a coach speeding into traffic and taking out two vehicles, then crashing into a barrier and now the policeman is sprinting to the door of the coach to arrest the driver.

Ben jogs forward so he can get a closer look. Suddenly everything seems to have come to a complete stop. The traffic on both sides of the carriageway has all stopped and all the people that were walking have all stopped in their tracks to watch the drama unfolding in front of them. The policeman tries to open the door on the side of the coach when all of a sudden the coach starts to reverse backwards. The policeman runs alongside the coach and somehow manages to open the passenger door just as the coach crashes into a removal van and comes to a complete stop.

Immediately the policeman jumps onto the coach through the passenger door and within seconds is followed by two men from the removal van. Ben hears the sound of a siren in the distance and then sees a police car squeeze its way through the crowded street towards the damaged coach.

The police car stops with its lights flashing and two officers get out and immediately enter the coach. A few seconds later, two officers appear out of the coach supporting the driver with his hands handcuffed behind him. A crowd of people standing near the kerbside all cheer and clap as the man is arrested and bundled into the back of the waiting police car. Ben takes a seat on a marble stone wall feeling exhausted from witnessing the whole thing but feeling pleased with himself for saving his sister.

He continues watching as the police car with the arrested driver, slowly manoeuvres its way through the crowded street on its way to the police station. Ben's eyes return to the coach as more officers arrive and take charge of the scene. Just then he hears his name being called. *'Ben... Ben!'*

Ben turns around wondering who would be calling his name, when he sees Jess with the rest of her class standing right behind him.

'Ben, what are you doing here?' Jess asks. 'You wouldn't believe it if I told you,' Ben tells her.

Chapter Twenty-Eight

Ben goes downstairs for breakfast still feeling a little wearisome from his busy day yesterday. He wanders into the dining room where the rest of his family are sat around the dining table staring at him. *This is different,* Ben thinks.

'Good morning, my school hero!' Mum says and the three of them begin giving Ben a round of applause. Ben feels his cheeks begin to redden a little as he pulls out a chair from the table and sits down.

'I'm not a hero,' Ben humbly tells his family while feeling a little overwhelmed at seeing three smiling faces trained on him.

'You are a hero; well, at least that's what the newspapers are saying,' his mother tells him.

'What newspapers?' Ben asks, sounding a little shocked that his local paper has heard what happened. He stares at his mum waiting for an explanation.

'We received a telephone call late last night and *The Times* newspaper wants to write an article about how you skipped off school and travelled all the way to London to prevent what could have been a serious accident.'

The words "prevent a serious accident" certainly ring true in Ben's mind because he knows what previously happened.

Suddenly the images of Jess in the hospital bed floods back into his mind and he gets an irresistible urge to tell the rest of his family the truth. Ben leans forward in his chair to tell them when his mum gets up and goes into the kitchen. Mum reappears carrying two breakfast plates loaded with a traditional English breakfast of eggs, bacon, sausages, mushroom, tomato, beans and a round of toast. She places one of the plates in front of Jess and the other she gives to Ben. The wonderful aroma rising from Ben's breakfast, breaks his concentration and he finds himself thinking only of his breakfast and how hungry he is. Ben picks up his knife and fork and begins eating.

'I can't believe you travelled all the way to London by yourself. How did you know our coach driver was a drunkard?' Jess asks just before taking a bite from her sausage. Ben looks across at his sister, somewhat surprised at being asked two important questions so early in the morning when he's not fully woken up. He notices his mum and dad staring at him as they appear to be interested in knowing the answer too. Ben makes out that the food in his mouth is taking a little longer to chew, to allow him a few extra moments to get his story straight.

Suddenly Ben recalls the police officer asking him that very question yesterday so Ben repeats his answer to his sister.

'I noticed a bottle of whisky next to the driver's seat on the coach before he picked you up.'

'Why didn't you tell the teacher?' Dad asks. 'Well I didn't think too much of it at the time; it wasn't until later after the coach had left that I began wondering if the alcohol was for him, like for the journey?' Ben takes another mouthful of food and begins chewing to allow himself more time to think of the rest of the story.

As soon as he swallows, his mother quickly asks. 'Go on, so you wondered if the alcohol was for him…' 'Oh yes, then I started to worry that if he starts drinking on his journey down to London, he could cause an accident. Then I remembered Miss Philips and Miss Havelock were on the coach and I think they were sitting right behind the driver, so if he took a drink whilst driving, they'd see him straight away,' Ben explains.

'Yes, you're right, that was good thinking, Ben,' Mum says. 'You obviously take after your father, he's analytical too.'

'What do you mean, Mum?' Jess asks. 'What's ana… ?'

'Analytical darling, it means that your dad and Ben are logical, systematic in their thinking, that's all.' 'Okay.' Jess replies now having understood what her mum was explaining.

'So, if the driver had a drink, Miss Philips and Miss Havelock would have noticed,' Mum continues. 'So why did you decide to go to London?' she asks.

Ben hadn't anticipated that question, so he quickly cuts a strip of bacon, covers it with mushrooms and beans and places it in his mouth, while he thinks. Mum, Dad and Jess all stare at Ben waiting for him to finish his mouthful so he can continue with his story. Ben swallows the food and continues. 'Well, I thought, what if he starts drinking at lunchtime when everyone's looking around the museum. He's brought the bottle with him so he must be intending on drinking from it sometime; so why not have a drink when nobody's around.' Ben explains.

'I tell you something Chris, Ben should be a detective when he leaves school, the way his mind works is just incredible; he's like that famous detective... You know the one, the one with a deerstalker,' Mum says.

'What, Inspector Clouseau?' Jess asks.

'No you idiot, Mum means Sherlock Holmes,' Dad says.

'Yes that's the one; Ben's just like him, he's really good at working stuff out,' Mum says.

'Yes you are Ben; that was really insightful of you. Well done,' Dad tells him. Ben gives his parents a smile before eating some more of his breakfast.

'I just wondered why you didn't tell a teacher in the morning; they could have telephoned the coach company and complained about the driver,' Dad says. 'I did think of telling a teacher, but who would have believed me? I mean, they'd probably used the coach company for years and never had a problem before, so why would they listen to the accusations of a twelve-year-old, over the reputation of a coach company,' Ben explains. 'You're right, Ben; you did the right thing. I don't think teachers really listen to children anyway. I remember when I was in school—' Dad tries to say but is cut short by Mum.

'We're not interested in what happened to you thirty years ago darling; we want to know what happened to our brave son. Now carry on with your story, Ben.'

Ben looks over towards his father, feeling a little sorry that Mum had cut him off; Ben would have liked to have known what happened to Dad thirty years ago; but he expects that his dad could relate that story to him any time. Ben turns to his mum looking so excited and carries on with what happened.

'So I slipped out of school and walked to the train station and bought a ticket to London King's Cross. I knew the museum wasn't that far away from the train station, so I walked to the British Museum and then found out where the coaches were parked up. I wanted to make sure that the driver had been drinking so I pretended that I was one of the school children that came down on the coach that morning. I asked the driver if I could check my seat because I thought I'd left my phone on the coach.'

'What did he say?' Jess excitedly asks.

'He was fine with it; he was eating his lunch at the time. That's when I saw him drink from the whisky bottle.'

'I would have been really scared,' Jess tells her brother.

'So what did you do next?' Mum asks.

'Well I tried to find a policeman but couldn't so I…' Ben starts to giggle to himself for a second.

'What is it? What's so funny?' Mum asks.

'Well I couldn't find a policeman and I knew I was running out of time.'

'So what did you do?' Mum asks.

'You know those CCTV cameras you find in town centres?'

'Yes, we've seen them,' Dad says sounding worried.

'Well, I thought that whoever's monitoring the camera would report anything unusual to the police. So I ran into the busy road waving my bag around my head.'

'You did *what*! *No*, Ben you could have been killed!' Mum shouts, sounding alarmed.

'Sorry, I was running out of time and I needed a policeman, like fast because the coach was about to drive back to Harrogate.'

'That's okay son; at least you're safe. But never and I mean *never* do that again!' Dad says in his stern voice.

'Okay Dad.'

'So what happened next?' Mum asks, sounding a little calmer.

'I ran back towards the museum and met up with a policeman. I told him everything. He asked me where the coach driver was, so I took him around the building to where the coaches were parked. Just then our coach driver began to reverse out, and you should have seen it. It was crazy.'

'What! What happened?' Mum asks, sounding all excited again.

Ben looks at both his parents, looking wide-eyed and exhilarated at what they've been told; so Ben decides to milk it for all its worth. 'The police officer… ran to the front of the coach to stop him. And you wouldn't believe it… the driver. He suddenly… pressed down on the accelerator and nearly ran the policeman over.'

'Nooo!' Mum and Dad shout in unison

'The coach clipped the back end of another parked coach, smashing its indicator and nearly running me over, then it sped off out of the car park… and right into the busy road taking out two or three cars.'

Mum and Dad don't say a word; they just stare at Ben with their mouths open.

'Anyway, the coach can't go anywhere and the policeman I spoke to ran to the coach and jumped on.' Ben glances down at the last bit of toast and egg on his plate and digs his fork into it.

'No you don't. Tell us the ending first,' Mum says while grabbing hold of Ben's arm to stop him from eating.

'Okay, let me see. Oh yes, the driver tries to reverse and crashes into a removal van and the two men from the van go and help the first policeman to arrest the guy, then more police arrive and they bundle the man into a police car after they handcuff him, and like everyone was cheering and clapping,' Ben explains.

'Wow; that sounds like it was really exciting,' Mum says.

'You're so brave Ben,' Jess tells her brother.

'Thanks,' Ben replies.

'Yes, well done, son,' Dad says and pats Ben on the shoulder. Ben picks up his fork and stabs the last piece of sausage and puts it in his mouth.

Mum looks up at the clock on the wall.

'Come on everyone, we've got to go.'

She stands up and grabs their empty plates. Mum rushes into the kitchen with them before rushing back into the dining room.

'Come on, we've got to get there before nine.' 'Don't we usually get to school for nine?' Ben asks, feeling a little confused.

'The newspaper reporters are going to meet us outside your school so they can do this article I mentioned earlier.'

'Argh Mum, do I have to? That means the whole school is going to be there,' Ben complains, feeling a little nervous about the thought of talking to a reporter with hundreds of children all gawking at him.

'Don't you worry Ben, you're a hero and everyone's going to hear about it,' Mum proudly says. Ben slowly gets up from his chair and wanders over towards the front door feeling ambivalent at the whole idea of talking to the press in front of the whole school. He doesn't want to be a hero and it's bad enough that his family thinks he's a hero but having the whole school think he's a hero is going to be unbearable.

Oh Ben, you're my hero! Ben can just imagine everyone at school sarcastically telling him, just to wind him up. Suddenly, the thought of school brings Alexis to mind. He still doesn't know whether Paul was successful or not at saving Alexis as they all arrived home late last night so he's not had an opportunity to talk to Paul.

'Please God, I do hope Paul managed to save my girlfriend,' Ben quietly prays to himself as he collects his coat from the coat stand and picks up his rucksack. The thought that he might see Alexis in the next fifteen minutes seems so exciting that he finds it difficult concentrating on anything other than Alexis. Ben, now in his new enlivened state, steps out through the front door and pauses next to his dad's car with his head fully in the clouds looking like a lost soul.

Jess walks around Ben and gets into her seat behind mum while Dad locks the front door and goes around the car to the driver's side door and opens the door ready to climb in.

'Ben are you coming with us or are you walking to school?' Dad sarcastically says. Ben looks over at his dad and realises that he needs to get inside the car. 'Sorry, I er… ' Ben thinks better not try to explain, so he opens the rear passenger door and slides himself in the back seat next to Jessica who's staring at him. Mum turns around in her seat and looks at Ben. 'My son's going to be in the news,' Mum says sounding all excited and gives Ben a big smile. Ben reciprocates with an agitated smile before turning his head to the side, so he can look out of the side window. He hopes his mum will get the hint that he doesn't really want to be interviewed by the press and he doesn't want to be famous; well, not in that way.

Ben tries to remember the last time he saw Alexis. It was yesterday morning before he set off on his journey to London. He remembers how she looked in her school uniform with her blonde hair tied up in a ponytail. She wore a cute pair of purple dinosaur earnings which he'd not seen before. He knows he should have commented on them but at the time he had a lot on his mind. He vividly remembers the kiss they had before she entered her classroom, it was one of those quick unassuming kisses that is usually performed when others are around. Thinking back now, he wished he'd given her a better kiss.

'I wonder if that's the last time I'll ever kiss Alexis?' Ben quietly asks himself, feeling crushed at the thought that Paul may have failed. Ben's eyes start to glaze over at the realisation that Alexis may still be dead. Ben's churning thoughts are interrupted by Dad reversing the car off the driveway and onto the road; he quickly puts the car into first gear and accelerates along the street towards Harrogate High school. The sudden change in movement brings Ben back to the present and he quickly wipes a tear from his cheek before Jess notices. He casually glances over to his sister and notices she's texting on her mobile phone; which is a relief because he didn't want Jess to see him crying. He knows Jess kinda likes him now, after he saved her from what could have been a serious accident; as far as Jess is concerned, but he would still feel vulnerable if she realised how much he liked Alexis.

Ben turns his head away from his sister again and tries to focus his mind on anything other than Alexis. A few minutes later, Dad pulls the car over and parks in the first available space next to the kerb about a hundred metres down from the school gate. Mum and Jess climb out of the car on the left side and go around the car to join Ben and his dad, now standing on the pavement. Dad locks the car and they all turn towards the school gates up ahead when they notice a suspicious looking black van parked near the entrance. 'Is that the newspaper?' Mum excitedly asks dad while pointing to the black van, not fifty metres away. Dad doesn't say a word; he just starts walking towards the entrance so the rest of his family quickly follows. As they near the black van, they all notice the writing on the side in bold silver scroll print, *The Times*. Mum turns towards Ben and gives him an excited look, which doesn't help. He was quite emotional in the car, when he was thinking of Alexis and now seeing the van, has suddenly made him feel sick. The thought of talking to a reporter in front of the whole school fills him with dread. Ben automatically slows down a little as his nerves start to take over his body causing his legs to feel like lead weights. His dad and Jess seem to be extending their lead and are about to walk in through the entrance gate when his mum notices Ben lagging behind.

'Ben, what are you dawdling for? Come on, the reporters are here,' Mum tells him. She waits for a second to see if he quickened his pace but the effort he's making could be compared to a ninety-year-old pushing a Zimmer frame. Mum steps towards Ben and takes him by the hand and pulls him towards the entrance. By this time, Dad and Jess have already walked in through the gate so they know what sort of welcoming party awaits Ben. Ben realises it's too late to back out now because everyone must now know that Ben's dad and sister have arrived. Mum walks in through the gate still holding Ben's hand to prevent him from making a run for it to the sound of a loud cheer.

At least the reception sounds promising, Ben thinks after hearing the cheers. He steps around his mum to see the whole school standing in a large half-circle around the school entrance where the news reporter and cameraman are talking to Miss Clarke. Dad and Jess slowly go through the crowd, as the mass of pupils split to form a pathway leading right up to the school entrance where the news reporter is standing. Ben nervously looks at his mum in his last desperate attempt to avoid talking to the reporter and says pleadingly.

'Can't we just turn around and go home?'

Mum gives Ben a reassuring smile and squeezes his hand knowing that he's feeling really nervous. They continue walking towards the school entrance through the corridor of pupils with their faces all turned towards Ben. Ben's initial instinct is to keep his eyes lowered so he doesn't have to look at anyone, but he's desperate to find out if Alexis is alive.

Ben lifts up his head and scans the line of faces on his left and right as he nears the school entrance but doesn't see either Alexis or Paul. He wonders where they are.

Did something happen to Paul? He thinks. Suddenly he finds himself standing at the bottom of the steps in front of the school entrance with Miss Clarke and two men he's never seen before.

'Here he is,' Miss Clarke informs the news reporter and points to Ben.

The news reporter quickly steps down the five concrete steps to join Ben and his family at the bottom of the school steps. He holds out his hand towards Ben. 'Good morning Ben; it's a pleasure to meet you,' the reporter says.

Ben reaches out and shakes the man's hand.

'Hello,' he replies and forces a smile. The large crowd of pupils that had separated to form a pathway for them to reach the school steps have now closed in around them, blocking any hope of trying to escape. Ben suddenly feels a little claustrophobic from the wall of students gathered around him and a wave of panic washes over him making it difficult to speak. Fortunately for him, Ben hears his dad speak up.

'Hi, I'm Ben's father and this is his mother,' Dad tells the news man.

'Hello, my name is Dave Plummer. I spoke last night to Mrs... ... Chapman.'

Dave expectantly looks across at Mum.

'Hello; call me Anne.' Mum says and tucks a curl back behind her ear. 'And my husband's name is Chris.' Mum points to Dad.

'Chris and Anne, we would like to set up just outside the main entrance where I'll introduce Ben and set the scene for the story, if that's all right?' Dave asks.

'Sure, whatever you think is best,' Mum quickly says and gives Dave a big smile.

'Right, come on then.'

Dave turns around and walks back up the steps to the main entrance and positions himself over to the right; he directs Ben and his family to stand slightly to his left with Miss Clarke in between them as she'll be interviewed first.

The cameraman steps back away from the doors so he can get a good angle on the shot.

'Children, can you all move to the sides please?' Dave asks. 'We just want to get Ben and his parents and the headmistress in this first shot. Thank you,' Dave says to the hoard of children standing almost within arm's reach. There's a slight movement within the crowd of pupils and the front row of faces seem to have only moved less than a few inches backwards when Miss Clarke's booming voice informs the children.

'If you don't want to remain behind on detention after school today, I suggest you do as you're asked.' Suddenly the crowd moves back a good two metres giving the cameraman plenty of room to film the interview. Miss Clarke smiles at Dave and takes her position as before.

'Thank you Miss Clarke,' Dave tells the headmistress. Dave turns to the cameraman and indicates that he's ready. The cameraman gives Dave a thumbs-up and then points to Dave to say he can start now.

'Good morning, I'm here at Harrogate High School to talk to one of its pupils. He's no ordinary pupil: he's a brave and courageous pupil.

'Before we interview Ben Chapman, we'll have a few words from the school's headmistress, Miss Clarke.' Dave turns to his right and looks at Miss Clarke standing right next to him. 'As headmistress of Harrogate High School, what are your thoughts on the actions of Ben Chapman?' Dave asks.

'Well, what Ben did was against school policy and we do not condone skipping school under any circumstances; however, Ben did á brave and courageous thing and because of his actions, he may have saved many lives.'

Suddenly all the school children that travelled on the coach begin to clap and cheer, showing their appreciation to what Ben did.

'Thank you everyone.' Dave turns towards the camera. 'As you can hear, everyone here at Harrogate High School feels the same way and consider Ben to be their hero,' Dave says into the camera. He waves his hand in a slicing movement across his neck to indicate to the cameraman to stop filming.

'Okay everyone, I'd like to continue this interview on the school premises if I may?'

'Yes of course; come with me,' Miss Clarke tells the reporter and cameraman.

Everyone follows Miss Clarke as she goes around the building and into the auditorium which has already been prepared for the interview by enthusiastic school staff; either late last night or very early this morning. The stage has several adult chairs positioned centrally in front of a large banner advertising the school between two Corinthian pedestal plant stands, supporting a terracotta flower pot tastefully decorated with lilies, tulips and roses.

'Will this be all right for you?' Miss Clarke asks Dave.

'Yes, this is perfect; thank you, Miss Clarke. Now could I have a quick word with Ben's parents?'

Mum and Dad take a seat next to each other while Dave sits to one side so the cameraman can capture the three of them in one shot. Most of the pupils crowd into the auditorium and grab a seat so they can listen to what's being recorded. Ben looks across at the audience to see if he can spot Alexis and Paul when he catches sight of Tony and Andrew sat on the front row, just over to the left-hand side. Ben averts his gaze and looks back at Dave as he's about to interview his parents. Dave indicates to his cameraman that he's ready and the room falls silent.

'This is Mr Chris Chapman and Mrs Anne Chapman, Ben's parents.' Dave introduces Mum and Dad.

'Hello' they say.

'When did you first hear what a courageous thing your son Ben did?' Dave asks.

'We didn't know anything until our daughter returned home from her school trip to London around about six o'clock on Monday evening,' Dad says.

'Yes, Jessica travelled to London to see the British Museum on the school coach and we were all supposed to collect Jess from school at six but Ben hadn't come home.'

'Did you wonder where Ben was?'

'Yes, Ben told us that morning that he was going to walk home with his girlfriend ,Alexis, so we knew he would be later than usual. But when he hadn't arrived home when it was time to pick Jess up. We were worried that something may have happened to Ben.'

Dave continues to interview Ben's parents, giving Ben an opportunity to look for Alexis or Paul in the audience.

His eyes begin randomly searching the large seating area in the auditorium in the hope of seeing those two familiar faces, when he hears his Mum mention Alexis's name again. Ben quickly looks back at Tony to see if he can detect any sign on his face to indicate that he'd killed Alexis but Tony's expression remained the same. Tony notices Ben looking over at him and his eyes break from watching Dave on the platform and stares directly back at Ben with the utmost venom. Ben suddenly feels uncomfortable at Tony's stare and quickly averts his eyes by looking down at his feet. If he could describe Tony's stare; it would be like Medusa. The sheer hatred in his eyes was undeniable, and if he had the ability, Ben knew he'd be instantly turned to stone.

I've never seen him look so angry, Ben thinks. *Does that mean Alexis's alive? He wouldn't look that angry if she was dead, so maybe she is alive and Paul managed to save her.* Ben's heart begins to soar with the hope that his girlfriend may still be alive, he immediately tunes out the conversation going on beside him and begins focussing on the audience. He systematically begins searching every face in the auditorium, starting with the front row to his left. He looks at the first person's face, then moves on to the next one to his right and so on until he reaches the far side before looking to the second row on the right and moving steadily along the row to the left.

'So there you have it, Ben Chapman was so humble about his heroic exploits, that he never told his parents. Let me now introduce the man of the moment; Ben Chapman.'

Ben, not hearing Dave's voice on the platform, continues searching the audience, when his mind tells him that something is wrong as everyone in the audience seems to be looking right back at him. 'Why are they all staring at me?' Ben thinks as his eyes continue along the third row, when he hears Dave's voice.

'I think Ben must be a little stage struck. Let's give him a round of applause.' Ben is a little taken aback by the audience suddenly cheering and clapping when he remembers where he is and glances over at Dave smiling at him.

'So Ben, tell us, what led to this heroic journey of yours to London and to prevent what could have been a major disaster?' Dave asks.

It takes Ben a few seconds to compose himself and to register what he's just been asked.

'Like I told my family this morning; I noticed a bottle of whisky next to the coach driver's chair… ' Ben starts to relate the events of the previous day to Dave and the cameraman standing to his right.

Dave turns to the camera.

'What an incredible young man we have here. Not only does he travel to London on his own, but he buys a ticket out of his own money to save all those on the coach. How old are you, Ben?'

'I'm twelve.'

'That's incredible; people much older than yourself would be far too scared to do what you did.' Dave gives Ben a brief round of applause and is joined by the whole school. After the applause, Dave continues. 'Tell us what happened when you arrived at the Museum Ben?'

Ben continues with his story with the occasional glance out to the crowd to see if he can spot Paul or Alexis but without any joy.

'Were you nervous, Ben?' Dave asks after being told that Ben had slipped onto the waiting coach in the hope of catching the driver drinking.

'Yes; I thought he would recognise that I wasn't part of the class he picked up that morning and kick me off.'

'So what happened?'

'I went to the back of the coach and pretended to look for my phone; I waited until I noticed the driver take a drink from what appeared to be a bottle and I quickly walked towards the front of the coach so I could see if it was whisky.'

'And was it?' Dave excitedly asks.

'Yes, and the driver looked really angry.'

'So what happened next?'

'Well, I had to think quickly, so I pretended that I was looking at his burger that he'd just bought from McDonald's. I just said how much I fancied a burger as I'd not had anything to eat.' The audience begins to laugh at Ben's comment.

'So presumably, you left the coach and told a police officer?' 'Yes.'

'I understand that it wasn't a straightforward arrest?' Dave asks. Ben looks at the audience and then back at Dave before relating the rest of the story.

'No, the driver saw the policeman and tried to run him over. He then drove right into a busy road and crashed into two cars, then when the policeman reached the coach, the driver reversed the coach into a delivery van, and then two men from the van helped the policeman as they arrested the driver; it was like crazy.'

'Thank you, Ben, for relating your story. We can confirm that the two injured passengers only received minor injuries and are back home, safe and well. The driver of the coach, a Mr Steve Huskova was arrested at the scene and taken into custody. He was found to be twice over the legal limit for alcohol consumption and will be brought before a judge pending charges. Once again we'd like to thank Ben for his foresight, and courage in averting what could have been a tragedy for many here. I think we can all agree that Ben Chapman is a hero.'

Suddenly a loud applause erupts from the audience. Dave turns to the camera and says, 'This is Dave Plummer for *The Times*.'

Dave indicates to the cameraman that the interview is over and stands up from his seat.

'Thanks again Ben for allowing us to report on your story. You're a very brave young man,' Dave says to Ben and shakes his hand before turning to face Miss Clarke. Ben stands up and looks towards the audience in the hope of carrying on with his search for Paul and Alexis when he vaguely recognises a voice calling his name from amongst the crowd.

'Ben, Ben, over here!' Ben hears Paul's voice again above the noise of continued clapping. Ben turns his head and looks to where he thought the sound came from over on the far right and catches sight of a small arm waving right at the back. Ben's eyes trace down the arm to the torso and immediately recognises Paul waving and smiling. He points with his other hand to the person standing beside him and to Ben's delight, he sees Alexis smiling back at him.

Chapter Twenty-Nine

Alexis and Ben take a walk through the park after school to get away from all the attention he's been receiving since the interview that morning. It's the only opportunity they've had all day to be together and although it's nice for Alexis to spend time with her boyfriend, it means so much more for Ben, knowing what he knew about what happened in the past. He can't thank Paul enough for what he did. Paul would have come with them, but he understood that Ben needed to be alone with Alexis, at least for today. The warm afternoon sun has brought out several dog walkers, walking their dogs through the park. One walker has at least five dogs on five different leads and seems to be struggling to control the dogs as they pull him along. Ben holds Alexis's hand as they walk side by side along the footpath that meanders through the large, grassed area of the park. The park is quite picturesque in the afternoon sun and they catch sight of the sun's rays streaming through the branches of a large oak tree near the centre of the park. Several other trees are speckled throughout the grounds with small well-kept flowerbeds and wrought iron benches equidistant along the footpath.

Ben and Alexis stop at one of the park benches near the oak tree and sit down to enjoy the nice weather and the peaceful surroundings.

'It's nice here,' Alexis says.

'I know; Jess and I always came here with Granddad when we used to visit him.'

'Sorry to hear he died,' Alexis says and squeezes Ben's hand to show her concern. Ben returns a smile 'Me too; I used to enjoy going to his house, we always had fun and he'd show us lots of unusual stuff he'd collected over the years.'

'Did he live near here then?' Alexis asks.

'Yes; his house is just over there.' Ben points towards where Granddad lived. 'Did you want to see where he lived?' he adds.

'Sure.' They stand up and start walking towards the east side of the park towards Granddad's house. Ben tells Alexis all about the visits he and Jess had and the things they used to get up to. They go out through the park gate and cross the road. 'It's just around this corner,' Ben says. They turn the corner and continue along the road a little, when Ben says, 'See that "For Sale" sign? That's Granddad's house. They walk along the pavement and stop next to the picket fence, bordering Granddad's front garden.

'Is your grandmother still alive?' Alexis asks.

'No she died years ago.'

'So who's living in the house now?' Alexis asks. 'Nobody, the house is empty,' Ben replies. Alexis stares at Ben in confusion.

'What's wrong?' Ben asks. 'I can see someone inside your granddad's house.' Ben immediately looks at the front window hoping to see what Alexis just saw; but the sun has just come out from behind a cloud, and the bright sunlight is reflecting off the glass, making it impossible to see into the house. Ben squints at the bright reflection, straining to see when another cloud moves in front of the sun allowing Ben to see into the front room and is taken back by the outline of a man standing inside the room waving back at them.

'Crikey! Who's that?' Ben says. They continue staring at the window as the figure standing deep inside the room, moves forward towards the glass and his appearance suddenly becomes clearer.

'I don't believe it! It's Granddad!' Ben calls out and without thinking, runs around the picket fence and up the driveway to the front door. Alexis quickly follows and joins Ben who's now standing on the doorstep with his arms by his sides.

Alexis looks at Ben half expecting him to knock or ring the bell, but he just stands there.

'I thought you said that your granddad died?' Alexis asks. Ben glances over at Alexis and gives her an anxious smile before returning his gaze to the closed door in front of him; possibly waiting with bated breath to see whether his dead granddad will open it. Ben heard what Alexis asked him about his granddad but to be honest, he's got no idea what to tell her. They hear a key being turned in the lock and then see the door slowly open in front of them.

'Ben, good afternoon and who's this?' Granddad asks while holding out his hand. Instinctively Ben shakes his granddad's hand feeling like he's in some kind of dream.

'Hi, I'm Alexis,' Alexis says.

'Hello Alexis, nice to meet you. Call me Joe.' Granddad shakes Alexis's hand and invites them both in. He steps to the side so they can enter the hallway before Granddad closes the door.

'In you go,' he tells them, pointing to the lounge. They slowly step inside the lounge and Granddad follows.

'I'm just about to make myself a cup of tea; would you both like a glass of lemonade?' Granddad asks. Alexis looks to Ben to see what he was going to say, but he stands there completely speechless with his mouth slightly open.

'Yes please Mr... I mean Joe,' Alexis says. Alexis takes Ben's hand and gives it a tight squeeze. Ben immediately looks at Alexis not quite comprehending the situation he's found himself in; is it all a dream? He wonders to himself, then he senses the pain in his hand and realises that it can't be. Ben gives Alexis a smile before looking around the room to see if anything is different from the last time he was there. The room looks the same. He catches sight of Granddad staring at him. 'Lemonade?' Granddad asks.

'Yes, thanks,' Ben tells him.

Ben can't believe that he's just spoken to his granddad weeks after the good man died. *What's going on?* He tries to work it out.

They watch Granddad walk out of the room and into the kitchen to make the drinks.

'Are you all right?' Alexis whispers, feeling concerned about Ben's unusual behaviour. To be honest, he just doesn't know what to think. *Is this real? Am I dreaming? Am I hallucinating?* he thinks. He can still feel the dull ache in his hand from Alexis squeezing it, so it must be real.

Could he be hallucinating? Is the image of Granddad all in his imagination or is he a hologram created by some elaborate trick? He doesn't know why he's asking such questions because in his heart and mind, he knows Granddad died. But why does everything seem so real? He looks back at Alexis.

'I'm okay,' he tells her although he doesn't think she believes him. Ben looks at where he is with Alexis and for some unknown reason, this whole scene seems so familiar, but he doesn't know why.

'Your granddad has a lovely view from his window,' Alexis tells Ben.

Ben looks out of the window with the sun just above the skyline of trees and houses and it does look nice. They continue to admire the view while feeling the warmth of the sun shining in when they hear Granddad come back into the room from the kitchen.

'Come on you two, have a seat,' Granddad says as he enters the lounge carrying a tray with two glasses of lemonade, a cup of tea and a plate with a chocolate sponge cake positioned in the middle.

Ben and Alexis sit down on the sofa as Granddad places the tray down on the coffee table.

'Here you are,' he picks up both glasses of lemonade and positions them down on top of two coasters in front of them. 'Would you like a slice of chocolate cake Alexis? I made it myself just this morning,' Granddad asks.

'Yes thank you, Mr Chapman.'

'Just call me Joe,' Granddad reminds her. Granddad cuts a slice of cake, places it on a side plate and passes it to Alexis. He cuts two more slices; one he gives to Ben and the other he takes for himself. He sits down in his armchair and picks up his cup of tea. Ben takes a large bite from his slice of cake just as Granddad asks, 'So what have you been up to today?'

'Mmwee beh zto,' Ben tries to say with his mouth full.

'We were at the park near Nelson Street and Ben told me that you lived nearby, so I persuaded him to bring me round to see you,' Alexis quickly replies to save Ben from speaking with his mouth full.

'And I'm glad you did, else I would not have had this opportunity to meet such a young pretty lady,' Granddad says, trying to charm Alexis.

'Thank you Mr Chapman. I mean Joe,' Alexis replies.

'You know Benjamin's never brought any of his girlfriends round to see me.'

Ben looks over at Granddad knowing they've had this conversation before.

'What are you now, twelve?' Granddad asks.

Ben makes out that he's still chewing his food so he doesn't have to continue with this repetitive conversation.

'Yes he is Joe; we're both twelve,' Alexis tells Granddad.

'Still, when I was your age, I wasn't interested in girls. I had a lot of exploring to do.'

Granddad takes a bite from his slice of cake so they all sit in silence for a minute or two until they finish eating. Granddad wipes his mouth with a napkin to remove any crumbs from his cake before adding, 'I've got a few photographs of Ben and Jess when they were younger; would you like to see them?'

'Yes please Joe.' Alexis gives Granddad a big smile which he really appreciates. It's not often an old man gets a beautiful smile from a pretty young girl. 'I'll just find them; they're in one of my photograph albums.' Granddad stands up and walks over to a large bookcase that's tucked away behind the opened lounge door. Ben sees an opportunity to disappear for a while, so he picks up the empty plates and cups and takes them through to the kitchen as Granddad carries the thick red photograph album over to the sofa and sits down next to Alexis.

Ben puts the tray down on the work surface and places the plug in the sink before turning the hot water tap on to fill the bowl. He squeezes a little drop of washing up liquid into the water and watches as the clear water foams into a bubbling bed of suds that spreads immediately out to the sides of the sink. Once the sink is half full, Ben turns the tap off and lowers the dirty dishes into the water. Ben hears Alexis laughing in the front room which sounds so familiar and for a moment, he feels like he's already lived this moment before.

This is so weird, why am I reliving this moment? Ben asks himself. *Everything that's happened feels like it's happened before and I don't know why. I've never been here with Alexis before, so why do I feel like I have? I only started going out with Alexis after Granddad died so being here with Alexis shouldn't feel so familiar, because I've never experienced it before.* Ben desperately tries to understand why he feels like he's reliving this moment, when something springs to mind. Ben suddenly remembers having a conversation with Paul about a dream he had that freaked him out a little. He closes his eyes for a second to help him remember the small fragments of the dream that are slowly coming back to him. He remembers sitting with

Alexis and drinking a glass of lemonade and eating cake with Granddad. *Am I living that dream now? How is that possible?* Ben wonders. He quickly washes the plates and cups and places them on the draining board to drain before pulling out the plug and allowing the water to slowly drain away. He can hear Granddad talking to Alexis so he knows he's got a few moments to try to remember the rest of the dream; he tries to concentrate. *From what I can remember in my dream, Granddad will come into the kitchen in a few seconds and I think we will chat about something,* Ben tells himself. *What were we talking about? Was it important?* Nothing seems to come back to him, so he picks up a tea towel and begins drying the plates hoping that if he takes his mind off trying so hard to recall the dream, it just might come back to him. Just then the door opens and Granddad walks in.

'She's a lovely girl, Ben,' Granddad tells him. 'Thanks Granddad, she is.' Ben finishes drying a plate and places it back inside the cupboard.

'So how long have you two been going out?'

'Oh, only a few weeks now.'

'Does she know about the watch?' Granddad asks which takes Ben by surprise.

'No,' Ben says feeling like he's done something wrong. 'That's good, whatever you do, *don't tell anyone!*' Granddad emphasises. Ben's heart suddenly sinks knowing that he's already told Paul.

'So… why shouldn't I tell anyone?' Ben tentatively asks, feeling even more nervous about the answer Granddad might tell him; he hopes whatever he says won't be so serious, like his life will be in danger. Ben stares at Granddad's mouth, trying to visualise the words as they come out.

'I'll just say that if others know about the watch, your life could be in danger,' Granddad tells him. Suddenly, Ben's legs turn to jelly and he finds it difficult just to remain standing. He reaches for the corner of the sink just to stop himself from collapsing. Being told that his life could be in danger hits him with the greatest severity; it feels like someone's slapped him across the face whilst wearing a gauntlet.

Why would my life be in danger? Would Paul try to kill me? What does he mean by that? Is someone I don't know going to kill me? Should I tell Granddad that I've already told my best friend? So many unanswered questions spring to Ben's mind causing a brain overload which triggers a nervous reaction, sending his whole body into an uncontrollable shaking.

'Ben, I'll give you two words of advice: whenever you have a memorable time that you'd like to come back to, make a note of the time and date. The second thing to remember is never travel more than four weeks in either direction,' Granddad tells him. Ben, in his overwrought condition, only catches the last part of what his granddad said.

'Sorry Granddad, what was that again?' Ben asks thinking what Granddad had just told him must be important. Granddad repeats his advice.

'Whenever you have a memorable time that you'd like to come back to; make a note of the time and date. The second thing to remember is never travel more than four weeks in either direction.'

'Sorry Granddad, what do you mean four weeks in either direction? I'm really confused at the moment. How I'm able to talk to you, considering that you're...' Ben looks down as his voice tapers off and he can't quite get the last word of the sentence out.

'Dead?' Granddad finishes the question. Ben lifts his head and looks into his Granddad's eyes, feeling sorry that he must know that he no longer exists. 'Granddad, you died a few weeks ago,' Ben tells him. As soon as the words came out, Ben can't control himself and he finds himself crying. Granddad steps towards Ben, wraps his arms around him and gives him a firm hug. His warm embrace and the smell of his skin and clothes bring back so many wonderful memories that Ben longed to have back. He buries his head into Granddad's chest and sobs. Granddad holds him tight for a few moments without saying a word. He knows it must be hard on Ben, so he lets his grandson let it all out. Ben feels his Granddad's embrace ease off, when Granddad steps back from him.

'There, there. Dry your tears; it's okay; really it is,' Granddad tells Ben. Granddad rests his hands on Ben's shoulders. 'Ben, don't worry. I knew I was going to die; that's why I gave you the watch.' He crouches a little so he's the same height as Ben and looks him right in his eyes.

'Ben, I'm really proud of you and I know you're going to have a wonderful life as I have. I was given this watch from my father and he told me the same thing. We have something very special that nobody else has. If we use it wisely, we can have a fulfilling life and we can benefit so many people. So going back to the question you asked me about either direction. You know about the secret don't you? I mean you've worked it out?' Granddad asks.

Ben wipes his eyes with the sleeve of his jumper before saying, 'The secret that I can travel back in time with someone else as long as they're holding on to the watch; yes I worked that one out.'

'What? You travelled back in time with someone else?' Granddad asks, sounding surprised and alarmed. *Oh no, I've just told him that someone else knows about the watch*, Ben thinks.

He quickly says, 'It was an accident. I didn't know Paul was going to jump back in time.' He hopes his granddad won't mind because it was an accident.

'Well I never! That's a new one to me,' Granddad says, looking bewildered.

'Oh, is that not the secret then?' Ben asks.

'No, but it's a secret to me. I wish I knew about that when I was alive. I'll tell you what. Me and your grandmother could have had a whale of a time, if we'd known about that. Ha-ha-ha.' Granddad begins to laugh.

The sound of Granddad laughing brings a sense of joy to Ben's heart. He suddenly remembers the times when he, Jess and Granddad used to dress up in all kinds of disguises; they would play the parts of leading explorers finding treasures around the house. Granddad always fashioned the best moustaches which sprang out to the sides of his face, looking as though he'd been electrocuted. He was so funny. Ben joins in laughing with Granddad for a few seconds.

'That's better,' Granddad tells Ben.

'So what's this secret then, Granddad?' Ben excitedly asks. Granddad looks at Ben and smiles. 'How is it that I'm talking to you?'

'I don't know; I mean, I was thinking about that earlier,' Ben replies.

'When did I die?' he asks. Ben thinks for a moment, and it suddenly starts to make sense. The secret must mean that we can travel into the future!

'I don't believe it. You've travelled into the future?' Ben excitedly asks.

'Look Ben; when I said you mustn't travel more than four weeks in any direction, it was for your own protection.'

Yes! I can travel into the future, Ben excitedly tells himself.

'Ben, Ben, don't get carried away. This watch gives us unbelievable abilities and we mustn't under any circumstances abuse that privilege,' Granddad tells Ben in his serious voice.

'Okay, okay, Granddad. So how does it work, how do I do it? I mean I've only been able to move back in time.'

'Have you got the watch with you?' Granddad asks.

'Yes, here it is.' Ben retrieves the watch from his trouser pocket and hands it over to Granddad. Granddad turns the watch over to show Ben the casing on the back. 'What can you see?' he asks. Ben looks down at the bronze casing and notices the two engraved circles. The outer circle has a small etched star near the winder knob and the inner circle has a small etched star to the left of the outer star.

'I can see two circles and two stars,' Ben tells his granddad.

'That's right; the outer circle represents this time and the inner circle is the direction in which we want to travel,' Granddad tells him.

'So how do I travel forward?' Ben asks, still not entirely sure as to what Granddad had just told him. Granddad places his thumbs on the inner circle and twists it around clockwise. The inner circle rotates round to the right a little. Granddad lifts his thumbs away from the watch surface to reveal the star on the inner circle has now moved to the right of the outer star.

'Wow, I didn't know that it moved,' Ben tells his granddad.

'Yes Ben. If you turn the gold hand on the front now, it will move you forward in time and not back.' Granddad hands the watch back to Ben so he can see properly what had just happened. Ben lifts the watch closer to his face and examines the outer casing. He'd never noticed that the inner circle on the back was a complete separate part of the watch that moved; he thought the back was a complete solid brass plate with two circles engraved on it. Ben places his thumbs on the back of the watch as his granddad did and after applying a little pressure, he twists the inner circle back to its original position with the inner circle star to the left of the outer circle star.

'This is amazing! Thanks Granddad.'

'Ben! You've got to see this.' Alexis calls from the front room.

'Won't be a second,' he calls back to Alexis. Ben looks at Granddad.

'So what's going to happen to you now that you're in the future? I mean you're in the present but again in your future, I mean... you know?'

Granddad places his hands on Ben's shoulders again.

'Ben I only wanted to make sure you were all right. That's why I travelled into the future. I knew I was going to die and the doctor told me I only had literally days to live. So when I go back, my time will be up.'

Ben looks deep into Granddad's eyes. Those strong emotions begin to flood back and he senses his eyes starting to well up.

'Ben, don't worry about me; I've had a wonderful life. Promise me that you'll do as I asked. Never go beyond four weeks forward or back. It's safer that way and less likely to change the world.'

'I promise,' Ben hears himself say.

'Good, now let's dry those tears and get back in there with your girlfriend before we both get into trouble.'

Ben wipes away the tears and they go back into the lounge.

Chapter Thirty

Ben and Alexis walk down the drive towards the pavement. They turn and wave goodbye to Granddad who's still standing in the opened doorway. He waves and gives them a big smile before stepping back inside the house and closing the door.

'I like Joe, he's nice,' Alexis says.

'I do too!' Ben tells her and they turn and start walking towards the park.

'I'm a little confused; who is Joe again?' Alexis asks. Ben realises that he can't tell Alexis the truth so he quickly makes up a story in his head.

'Joe is my granddad's half-brother. I haven't seen him in like, ages.'

'So why is he at your granddad's house?' Alexis asks.

'Granddad I think, borrowed some money from Joe to buy the house years ago as he didn't quite have enough at the time; I think Joe was just checking the house to make sure that everything's okay before it's sold,' Ben explains.

'Okay.'

Ben glances back towards the house and a wave of sadness washes over him as he now knows that this is the last time he'll ever see Granddad. Alexis looks back for a second which gives Ben an opportunity to wipe a tear away from his eye before she notices.

'I think I need to get home; Mum's sister's coming over for tea and Mum said I need to be home by five thirty and its ten past five already,' Alexis tells Ben.

'Come on then, let's run.'

Ben takes hold of Alexis's hand and they jog along the street towards the other side of town. Ben drops Alexis off outside her house, before making his own way home.

'Hi Mum, I'm home! You wouldn't believe who I saw today' Ben excitedly calls out to his mum as he takes his shoes off at the front door.

'Hi Ben, you're just in time; I'm about to serve dinner,' Mum informs him. Ben quickly heads into the downstairs toilet to wash his hands.

'So who did you see?' Dad asks as he takes his seat at the dining table. Ben feels a surge of panic sweep over him as he realises what he's just said. He can't tell Mum and Dad that he just saw Granddad; that would really upset them. Ben turns the hot water tap off and quickly dries his hands on the hand towel before making his way over to the dining table.

'So who did you see?' Jess asks, wondering why Ben hadn't replied to dad's question.

'Oh you know… that footballer who plays for one of the premier sides; the black guy with the short hair.' Ben rambles on not knowing what he's saying.

'The black guy with the short hair? Do you know his name?' Dad asks.

'Ermm… I'm not sure.'

'So which team does he play for?'

'Ermm I'm not sure.' Ben replies feeling like a total idiot.

'Ben, you're an idiot,' Dad tells him. Ben takes a seat at the dining table and gives his father an apologetic smile. Mum enters the room carrying two dinner plates and places them down in front of Jess and Ben before returning to the kitchen to get dad's food and her own. Ben decides it's probably best to remain quiet for the duration, just so he doesn't get into any more trouble. After dinner Jess and Ben go to their rooms to finish any homework they have. Ben closes his bedroom door and takes a seat at his desk. He opens his maths homework book and looks down at the twenty equations on the left page that he needs to work out by tomorrow. Ben glances up at his bedroom window and notices the beautiful bright orange sun, slowly moving into view as it appears in the top left corner of his window. The bright round shape, partially veiled behind a grey cloud looks like it's creeping across the rooftops way into the distance. The sky all around reflects bright hues of oranges and reds with a hint of purple, giving the houses a warm glow. For a moment, Ben feels the warmth on his face and with the beautiful view before him, his mind is transported to somewhere exotic for a short while. A bird suddenly flies across his view breaking his concentration and causing his mind to return to the present. Ben looks down at his maths homework book and for some reason, doesn't feel motivated to do it. He's had such an exciting day so far, that he finds it difficult to concentrate on anything, especially boring old maths. Ben picks up an empty glass that's been left on his desk and decides to take it back down to the kitchen and maybe fill it with Coke from the fridge. He opens his bedroom door and steps out onto the landing to the sound of voices coming from downstairs. Usually, he can stand on the landing and not hear a thing because Jess is always quiet in her room and Mum and Dad are either relaxing on the sofa and reading something or they're just listening to classical music with the volume turned right down, so it's strange to hear them talking. Ben slowly goes down the stairs and although he knows, it's rude to eavesdrop on other people's conversations, because he can hear slightly raised voices from his parents, he feels concerned that something is wrong and he wants to help. A thought suddenly occurs to him: they may be talking about politics or something that's just as boring so he decides he should try to ignore the voices in the front room. Ben reaches the bottom of the stairs and walks across the hallway towards the kitchen when he hears Mum tell Dad, 'Don't worry Chris; I'm sure you'll find another Job.'

Ben continues walking towards the kitchen and passes the lounge open doorway when his parents see him and their conversation immediately stops.

'Hi, I'm just getting some Coke,' Ben tells his parents.

'Okay,' his mum replies. Ben goes into the kitchen and opens the fridge door. He half keeps an ear out for the conversation to continue in the lounge, but it doesn't. He pours his glass of Coke and puts the bottle back inside the fridge door. Ben again listens out for his mum and dad to carry on with their conversation but they remain silent. He wanders back through the dining room and into the hallway, passing the lounge doorway again then slowly walks up the stairs towards his bedroom to the sound of more silence. Ben opens his bedroom door and places his glass of Coke on his chest of drawers, then closes the door again while standing on the landing. He hears his mum and dad continue with their conversation. Ben decides he wants to know what they're talking about so he crouches down on the landing and presses his head against the banister. With his eyes closed, he concentrates on the faint sounds from downstairs where he can now just make out what they're saying.

'I'm forty-two, darling, nobody wants to employ someone in their forties when they can employ someone in their twenties and pay them half the money,' Dad says. 'We'll be all right; we have a little money saved, don't we?' Mum asks.

'Our savings will only keep us for a month and that's all. If I can't find another job before then, we'll have to sell the house and move further north, where the properties are cheaper. We literally can't stay here darling, it's far too expensive,' Dad says. Ben opens his eyes in shock at hearing his father say that they may have to move away. They can't do that; he's only just found a girlfriend and it's taken him twelve years. If they moved away, what would happen to his girlfriend? He can't drive, so how would he see her? This was a disaster. Ben concentrates on the conversation again.

'What will we tell the children?' Ben hears his mum ask.

'I don't know; maybe we should just tell them the truth. They're going to find out sooner or later and to be honest, I think it's best if we just tell them now. At least they could get used to the idea that we may have to move at the end of the month.'

'When did you want to tell them?' Mum asks.

'Tell them to come down now and we'll tell them together.'

'Okay, I'll give them a call,' Ben hears his mum say. Ben quickly stands up and moves back towards his bedroom door; he quietly turns the handle and opens the door.

'Children, can you both come down for a moment; dad wants a word with you?' Ben hears his mum call up the stairs. He waits in his doorway for a second until he sees Jessica's door open, then he quickly closes his door and walks along the landing followed by Jess; they go down the stairs to their mother waiting at the bottom of the steps. Mum directs them into the lounge.

'Children, have a seat,' Dad says pointing to the sofa. The two children take their seats on the sofa and look up at their parents staring back at them.

'What's going on?' Jess asks.

'Children we've got some bad news to tell you. You may have noticed that Dad's been home a lot recently. the reason for that is, Dad lost his job with Onyx Solutions a few weeks ago, which means we don't have any more money coming in,' Mum tells her children. 'Oh, Daddy can find another job can't he?' Jess asks her mum then looks over at her father with a slightly worried look on her face.

'Well that's the problem, Jess; it's not that easy to find work when you're our age,' Dad explains. 'I've already applied for what jobs there are available at the moment but I've had no response to my letters. The reason we wanted to tell you guys now is that if I can't find work in the next couple of weeks, we may have to sell the house and move up north,' Dad tells them. 'Move up north?! I don't want to move up north! I want to stay here,' Jess protests.

'We're sorry Jess but if we don't have the money, we can't stay here.'

Mum tries to reassure her daughter. She sits down next to Jess and places her arm around her shoulder. 'Dad, please find another job so we don't have to move,' Jess begs.

'I'll try sweetie, I really will but if I can't then we'll have to move. We've told you now so you know the situation and if we have to move, it won't come as a massive shock. Now don't worry too much about it, we've still got till the end of the month before we need to make a decision,' Dad explains.

Jess and Ben head back upstairs to their bedrooms so that they can process the information in their own time. Ben closes his bedroom door behind him and walks over to the desk and sits down. Hearing his father tell him the bad news face to face was still a shock, even though he knew what was coming. The thought of moving away and leaving his friend and girlfriend behind is unimaginable and unacceptable. This is got to be the worst news ever, Ben thinks. He looks down at his maths homework book. 'What's the point in doing homework for a school that I'll be leaving in a few weeks?' he angrily calls out. In his rage, he swipes the book away to the side with his arm and watches it fly through the air, before landing on the floor in the corner of his room. Ben buries his head in his hands feeling totally sorry for himself that all the good he's achieved over the last few weeks has all come to nothing. Nobody's going to know what a hero he's been and how he'd saved all the children on the coach and how he won the school competition, when he gets to wherever they move to. Ben instinctively reaches inside his trouser pocket, takes out the watch and places it down on the desk in front of him. He stares at the bronze object, thinking what a useless piece of equipment it is, because it can't get his father's job back.

Mind you, I wonder if I could use it to get Dad a new job, Ben thinks but the idea of using the watch to get Dad a new job is ludicrous. *Actually, Dad doesn't need a new job, he just needs money,* Ben reasons to himself. *If Dad had money, he could pay his bills and they could stay where they are.*

Ben picks up the watch in his hand and an idea starts to form in his mind.

Chapter Thirty-One

Ben's alarm clock begins to ring next to him as he lies in his bed. He reaches across and turns the alarm off and although he knows what time it is, he instinctively glances at the time displayed on the clock face to confirm in his mind that it really is seven thirty in the morning. Ben spent a good few hours last night devising a plan to help his parents which is why he's feeling a little weary because he's not quite had the ten hours of sleep he usually has. Although feeling tired, he knows he's going to have a brilliant day. He throws back the covers and sits up, giving his eyes a quick rub before sliding his legs over the side of the bed. He stands up, ready to put his plan into action. Ben opens his bedroom curtain and looks out at the morning sky.

Everything seems so much brighter today and life seems good, now that he can see light at the end of the tunnel. Yesterday was such a shock and for a brief time he really thought it was the second worst day of his life, with the exception of what happened to the girls. Now that he's devised a plan, today is going to be brilliant. Ben knows his mum religiously plays the lottery twice a week; from what he can remember, she normally spends five pounds for tickets on a Wednesday and another five pounds on a Saturday which, to his mind, isn't too bad if she actually won something one day. He expects most people think the same; they must feel that they may win the jackpot one day so it's got to be worth spending a couple of quid each week to have the chance of winning. The problem is that millions of people play the lottery and sometimes nobody wins the jackpot; that's why they have a rollover.

I wonder how much Mum's already spent on lottery tickets, Ben muses. She plays every week and he knows she's done that for years. He doesn't think his mum's ever won anything as far as he can remember. So if she's spent ten pounds every week, that's five hundred and twenty pounds every year. Ben realises that he's going to need a calculator to do the maths, so he wanders over to his desk to get one. Ben begins to enter the details of how much his mother has spent.

'So that's ten pounds a week for fifty-two weeks.' Ben taps the numbers on the keypad. 'That equals…' he presses the "equals" button and the total shows as 520. 'Okay, so if she's played for seven years…' he taps the multiply button with his index finger followed by a seven and then the equals. *Mum's spent about three thousand, six hundred and forty pounds already and never won; that's terrible. I think Mum deserves to win something for spending all that money and I've got a feeling it's gonna happen tonight,* Ben tells himself. He gets dressed and washed and heads downstairs for breakfast. His father was already sitting at the breakfast table, reading the local newspaper as Jess takes a seat next to him while texting someone on her phone. Ben goes over to the table and takes his usual seat next to Jess.

'Good morning Ben, sorry we only have cereal for breakfast this morning; well, it's going to be every morning until Dad gets a job.' Mum informs Ben.

'That's all right Mum; I only wanted cornflakes anyway,' Ben tells her.

'What about you Jess, have you decided what you're having?' Mum asks. 'Jess!' Mum says with a slightly raised voice, showing her annoyance at being ignored.

Jess looks up from her phone. 'Oh sorry Mum, I was just texting Debbie. She asked if I could go round hers after school. Can I please?'

'Yes. Will you be eating there or should I make you some dinner?' Mum asks.

'Debbie said I can eat at hers.'

'Okay, and have you decided what you want for breakfast?'

'I'll just have some toast and marmalade, thanks Mum.'

'I can't believe it; there's absolutely nothing suitable in the job section again today. What a waste of time and money, buying a newspaper that's no good to anyone!' Dad exclaims. Mum walks into the dining room carrying a bowl of cereal and places it down in front of Ben.

'Don't worry darling, I'll tell you what, why don't we drop the kids off at school and then we could go into town and take a look at the job centre; they're bound to have lots more jobs for you to look at?' Mum puts her arm around Dad's shoulder and gives him a cuddle.

'I suppose so,' Dad says as he awkwardly folds the newspaper and drops it down on the floor beside him as Mum presses her lips against his cheek. Ben pours cold milk on his cornflakes and begins eating while his eyes are focused on his mother. He wants to wait for the right moment to ask her a question, and as she's still giving Dad a squeeze, he feels it's not quite the right time.

'Sorry Jess, I'll just get your toast,' Mum says having heard the toaster popping. She goes back into the kitchen and within seconds comes back holding a side plate with two rounds of toast on it and places the plate down in front of Jess. 'There you are,' she says.

'Thanks Mum.' Jess gives her mum a smile.

'Mum have you got your lottery tickets for today?' Ben asks. Mum walks over to her handbag and takes out five blank lottery tickets. She looks down at them for a few seconds.

'I don't know why I even bothered to pick these up, we've never won and... well we can't exactly afford to play the lottery any more.' She turns and walks towards the kitchen wastebin. Ben's heart begins to race at seeing his mum about to throw away his plan to save his family.

'You never know, this might be our last chance to win something,' Ben quickly says, hoping his mother might change her mind. Ben stares expectantly at his mother as she stands next to the bin with the lottery tickets held between her thumb and forefinger, poised above the opened void below.

'Come on love; let's have one last go as a family,' Dad suggests.

Mum turns around and walks back to the breakfast table with the tickets still in hand and gives everyone a blank lottery ticket, before tearing up the spare fifth ticket.

'Okay, we've got one ticket each, and this is the last time,' Mum says. Ben's heart seems to be racing inside his chest as he looks down at the only chance he has to help his dad.

This is it; I'm going to pick the winning numbers, Ben thinks. Unfortunately he doesn't know what they are at the moment, but he will know by tonight. Mum gives everyone a pen to mark the seven numbers they want to select on their lottery tickets. Ben looks down at the lottery ticket with all the numbered boxes clearly marked; wondering which seven numbers to mark with an X. He knows it doesn't really matter which numbers he chooses now because tonight after they've announced the winning numbers, he'll travel back to this morning and mark the right ones on his ticket. Ben doesn't want to appear to be flippant about choosing his numbers, so he can't pick the numbers 1-2-3-4-5-6-7 because his mum would think he's being stupid and doesn't care about winning, so he thinks for a moment, before marking his ticket. Suddenly an idea springs to mind as he remembers learning about the Fibonacci sequence at school.

'That would work,' he quietly says to himself. From what he can remember, the sequence goes something like; 1-2-3-5-8-13-21-34-55-89. He knows he can't use all those numbers so he decides to miss out, the first number and choose the next seven numbers. Ben holds his pen above the number two and marks the box with an X; he does the same for three, five, eight, thirteen, twenty-one and thirty-four. He puts the pen down and hands the ticket back to his mum.

Dad drives them all to Harrogate High School and drops Ben and Jess off outside the main entrance.

'Have a nice day!' Mum calls out to her children as they go in through the main gate. Ben looks around and waves to his mum, just as the car pulls away, heading into town. Jessica's friend Debbie is waiting for Jess, just inside the entrance, so they give each other a quick hug before walking off towards the main school entrance. Ben goes over to the play area to wait for Alexis and Paul to arrive. He sits down in his usual spot and places his rucksack on the ground between his feet.

'So you think you're a hero do you?' Ben hears Tony's voice call out, over to his right. He turns his head towards the sound to see where Tony is when he catches sight of Tony's clenched fist heading straight for his face. *Crack!* A blinding pain strikes him right between the eyes and he finds himself falling backwards off the climbing frame and onto the ground. Ben instinctively holds his hands to his face as the pain in his forehead begins to escalate, causing flashing to appear before his eyes. He senses others are gathered around him so he moves his hands to the side so he can see what's happening when he notices Tony, Andrew, Brian and Simon standing all around him. Suddenly a sense of foreboding comes over him and he knows his troubles are not over. The four lads all begin kicking Ben as he lies helpless on the ground. Ben quickly curls up in a ball and holds his arms over his head to protect himself as best as he can until the melee ends. The onslaught must have only lasted for a few seconds but in his mind it seemed to last much longer. Pain surges from all areas where he'd been kicked: from his legs, sides, arms and back. He'd never experienced such an onslaught in his life before and as the pain continues, he hears his voice scream out, 'Arghhhhhhhhh!'

As quickly as the attack began, it ends and the four lads step back away from him.

'Don't forget, I'm the cock of this school. You do as I say or else.' Ben hears Tony's voice call out to him. 'Alexis is my girlfriend; if I ever see you talking to her again, you'll get another beating.'

Tony and his gang turn and walk away. Ben rolls over onto his back and looks up at the clear blue sky above him. The pain surging through his body is making him feel slightly nauseous, so he closes his eyes and tries to take in a few deep breaths to stop himself from fainting.

'Are you all right?' Ben hears Paul ask. He opens his eyes and sees his best friend standing over him, looking slightly confused. 'What's happened; why are you lying on the ground?' Paul asks. Tears start to run out from the corners of Ben's eyes and he quickly wipes them away with his sleeve.

'Ben, what's happened?' Paul asks again, sounding concerned.

Eddy Stewart appears next to Paul.

'It was Tony and his gang; they just came over and attacked Ben for no reason,' Eddy informs Paul. They lean forward and help Ben get to his feet.

'Let's tell Miss Clarke what happened,' Paul says. 'It's all right Paul; Tony only attacked me because he had the others with him. Don't worry, I'm gonna get him back; you can be sure of that,' Ben tells his friend.

Paul smiles before adding, 'Just make sure I'm there to give you a hand.'

Ben nods and smiles. Then he notices Alexis walking in through the main entrance gate.

'Paul, don't say a word to Alexis; I don't want her to know. You too, Eddy,' Ben tells the two lads. They give Ben a nod.

'Hi,' Alexis says.

Ben straightens up as much as the pain in his body allows him to and with the best cool look on his face he asks, 'How did it go with your mum's sister last night?'

'Yes it was good. She's bought a holiday home in Florida; she said we could all go over in the summer for a holiday if we wanted.'

'Does that invite include your boyfriend?' Ben asks and gives her a smile.

'I don't know, but I'm sure you could come; the bungalow has five bedrooms and my mum's sister lives there by herself.'

'Cool,' Ben replies just as the school bell sounds. They all turn towards the school entrance and go inside.

After school, Ben meets up with Alexis by the school gate. He knows he's running the risk of being seen by Tony but he doesn't care. For one thing, Tony and his mates attacked him when he wasn't expecting it; he'll never do that again because Ben's going to keep an eye on him, and Tony only attacked Ben because he had all his mates with him. The chances that all four of them walk out of school at the same time are probably a hundred to one, so even if he was seen by Tony he wouldn't do anything until he's with his mates. Paul comes out from the main entrance and immediately sees Ben standing with Alexis by the gate.

'Ben, Ben!' Paul calls out as he rushes over towards them. They look over at Paul looking anxious.

'Are you all right Paul?' Alexis asks. Paul ignores Alexis for a second and nods to his side, indicating that someone is about to walk out of the main entrance. Ben nods back to Paul.

'Come on then, I'll walk you home,' Ben tells Alexis and grabs her hand. The three of them walk out through the gate and turn left along the pavement towards home.

'What was all that nodding you two were doing?' Alexis asks.

'It was nothing, just boy stuff,' Paul tells her. They all turn left and head through the park. When they reach the far gate, Alexis heads home in one direction while Paul and Ben walk in the other direction. Tony's going to find out,' Paul tells his friend, sounding a little concerned that Ben's going to get beaten up again.

'Don't worry, I've got a plan.'

'What do you mean, you've got a plan?'

'It's all going to be okay, you'll see. Just wait till the weekend,' Ben tells Paul and gives him a smile.

Chapter Thirty-Two

'Hi Mum I'm home!' Ben tells his mum as he walks in through the front door.

'Hi Ben; how was school?' Mum asks.

'It was all right, same as usual,' he tells her; he knows he can't tell her what really happened else she'd freak out. Ben walks into the kitchen and sees his mum peeling a potato and then placing it in a pan of cold water.

'What are we having for dinner?' Ben asks.

'I'm making a shepherd's pie,' his mum tells him. 'Mmmm that sounds nice.' Ben watches his mum place the last potato into the large saucepan and then picks up the peelings and deposits them into a separate pot that appears to consist of scraps of vegetable bits.

'Yuk, what are those for?' Ben asks, looking disgusted at the mound of rotting scraps. Mum looks round at Ben wondering what he's talking about, when she catches sight of his face with his nose turned up at the pile of peelings.

'That's not for eating; it's for the compost bin, silly.' Ben looks at his mum not fully understanding what she means; he did however understand the bit about not having to eat it, which was a relief.

'Mum did you manage to put the lottery numbers on?' Ben asks.

'Yes, it's all done. The ticket receipts are under the clock on the mantle.'

Ben quickly walks into the lounge and slides the receipts out from under that clock positioned centrally on the mantelpiece. Feeling a little apprehensive that his mum may have entered the wrong numbers, he quickly scans the four entries just to check.

'Mum, who selected the numbers 1-2-3-4-5-6-7?' Ben calls through to the kitchen.

'That was your father. He said any number sequence could win. I didn't tell him what I thought of his choice of numbers, and I wouldn't recommend you saying anything either,' Mum cautions Ben.

He looks down at the other numbers on the tickets. He recognises his mum's numbers because she always uses the same numbers every week, she always picks all their birth dates 4 – 15 – 16 – 22 and her wedding anniversary on the 24th then there's Christmas on the 25th and Halloween on the 31st for some unknown reason. Ben glances at the next receipt with his numbers listed. He checks the numbers to see if they're all listed correctly saying the numbers as he reads them: 'Two, three, five, eight, thirteen, twenty-one and thirty-four… perfect,' he tells himself. He knows it's not important which numbers he's selected because he'll go back in time later on tonight and change the numbers, but for some reason, he just wants to use the Fibonacci numbers. Finally he glances down at Jessica's numbers just out of curiosity: 4 – 8 – 12 – 16 – 20 – 24 and 28. Ben immediately recognises the sequence in her numbers; they're all multiplications of the number four. 'She's a strange one,' Ben says to himself. 'Why would you pick only numbers that are multiples of four? Then it suddenly dawns on him. *She likes Star Wars. She thinks she's a Jedi. Let the force be with you; or should I say let the fours be with you.*

Ben giggles to himself at having such a strange family. He replaces the receipt back under the clock on the mantle and heads upstairs to his bedroom to catch up with some homework before dinner. Twenty minutes later Ben hears the front door open, followed by dad's voice telling Mum that he's home. Hearing his father's voice gets him to wonder how he got on today, looking for a job. Personally, he's never had to experience applying for jobs because he's a child so he wouldn't know what it's like to attend an interview. He doesn't like the idea of asking people to employ him; it all sounds so belittling. It's like imploring people to employ you; just the thought of it doesn't sound appealing, so he knows he couldn't do it, he couldn't take the rejection. Ben checks the time on his alarm clock and sees that it's only twenty past four. He still has forty minutes or so before dinner's ready so he packs away his homework books and picks up a new tube of glue he found lying next to his model ship. He assumes that his mother must have bought it for him, having seen Ben's half-finished ship on his desk and no glue to finish it. Ben decides to glue a few matchsticks to pass the time.

'Dinner's ready!' Ben hears his mum calling him. He fits the last matchstick to the central mast on his HMS *Victory* model ship and replaces the cap on the tube of glue. He moves back away from the desk so he can have a better look at his achievements today.

'Well, it's looking good,' Ben proudly says to himself; he has finished the hull and started the main mast. He goes downstairs and joins his dad at the dining table.

'Hi Ben, have you been doing your homework?' Dad asks.

'Yes, all done. I only had a bit of English homework,' Ben informs his father.

'Well done son. I wonder what we're having for dinner,' he adds.

'Shepherd's pie,' Ben quickly replies. Dad looks at Ben somewhat surprised that he knew what they're having for dinner, considering he's been upstairs all the time.

'How did you get on with finding a job?' Ben asks. His dad frowns and says, 'Not so good, but tomorrow might be a better day; we'll just have to remain positive.' He gives Ben a hopeful smile. Ben gives his dad a confident smile back. He admires his father's attitude; he always considers a glass to be half-full, rather than, half-empty and from what he can remember, he thinks his dad's favourite song is that one from the Monty Python film *The Life of Brian* where they all sing 'Always look on the Bright Side of Life'. He can't remember ever watching the film but it did make him laugh when his dad sang it to his mum a while ago. Ben's mum returns from the kitchen carrying a steaming dish of shepherd's pie.

'Here we are,' she says and places the dish down in the centre of the table then returns to the kitchen to collect the warmed plates from the oven. After dinner, Ben helps his mum with the washing up and putting away, while his dad relaxes in his armchair in the lounge.

Mum challenges everyone to a game of Scrabble, so they all sit around the coffee table and play. Dad usually wins but tonight Mum won with seventy-four points; dad came second with a score of fifty-two points while Ben managed a rubbish score of just thirty-eight. Ben assumes Dad probably lost because he wasn't fully concentrating on the game; maybe his mind was on other things, like finding a job. Mum packs the Scrabble board away and then returns to the sofa and sits down next to Dad to read for a while; Ben turns the TV on with the sound turned down low so as not to distract his mum and dad, he sits on the floor in front of the screen with his game controller in hand and plays one of his PlayStation games, Tomb Raider, for a while until Jess arrives home at seven thirty.

'What time's the lottery result on TV?' Ben asks his parents.

'Eight o'clock,' Mum tells him. The children don't usually watch the lottery because they're normally in their bedrooms getting ready for bed at that time, but as Mum allowed them all to pick out the numbers, she thought it would be exciting for them all to sit and watch the results together.

'Did anyone want a drink before the lottery comes on?' Mum asks.

'Coke please,' Jess and Ben reply. Dad decides to have a cup of coffee, so he goes into the kitchen to make one for himself. Mum walks back into the lounge carrying two glasses of Coke and places them down on the coffee table for Ben and Jess and takes her usual seat on the sofa between them. Mum turns the TV on and flicks over to the right channel using the remote control.

'Where's the numbers, Mum?' Jess asks.

'Oh, oh, yes they're under the clock.'

Mum quickly gets up and fetches the small receipt with the list of selected numbers. She sits down again just as Dad returns with his coffee.

'I can't believe you picked 1-2-3-4-5-6 and 7,' Ben tells his dad.

'What! Is that what you picked?' Jess asks, laughing.

'Just wait and see, I might have the winning numbers!' Dad confidently says before sipping from his coffee cup.

'In your dreams,' Mum quickly replies and they give each other a teasing stare. Just then the programme starts and they all turn towards the TV screen to watch the image of the lottery machine with the long glass tube appear in the opening credits with the introductory music playing.

'Okay, quiet everyone,' Mum says, sounding very serious. 'Just to remind everyone of the numbers we've picked; we've got to listen out for 1 – 2 – 3 – 4 –5 – 6 –7 – 8 – 12 – 13 – 15 – 16 – 20 – 21 – 22 – 24 – 25 – 28 – 31 and 34.' Mum is standing holding the receipt tightly out in front of her so she can look at them when the winning numbers are announced.

'Do you expect me to remember all those numbers; you're having a laugh ain't ya?' Dad tells Mum.

'I only said it so you've got an idea of what numbers we've picked, that's all.'

'Don't worry, darling, I only need to remember my own numbers,' Dad says. Everyone looks across at Dad with his confident look on his face.

'Okay, it's starting,' Mum informs everyone. Ben glances over to his dad and then looks left at his mum and Jess as they focus their attention on the TV screen. Ben doesn't know why, but he's also feeling nervous as they wait for the lottery balls to be selected. He knows it doesn't matter which numbers are picked tonight, because in about ten minutes, he'll travel back in time and change his numbers to the winning numbers. Even so, the nerves start to kick in, making his heart start to race a little. He reaches forward and picks up his glass of Coke and takes a sip hoping that the cold liquid will calm his nerves a little. The effervescent liquid runs down his throat and for a moment soothes his disquieting thoughts. Ben puts his glass down, just in case his mother jumps when listening to numbers being called out. They all watch as a celebrity pulls a lever, letting all the different numbered balls drop down into the machine that will select at random each ball. The tension in the room feels so high that Ben's palms begin to sweat.

'The first number for tonight's lottery is... 8,' the TV announcer calls out. The TV screen displays a white lottery ball, roll down a clear plastic tube and coming to a stop at the bottom left of the screen, clearly showing the number eight.

'Yes, Jess and Ben's picked that number. Sorry darling we haven't won,' Mum gladly informs Dad.

Dad casually picks up his coffee cup. 'I might have picked all the other numbers; just you wait and see.' He takes a sip from his drink and turns towards the TV again.

'Quiet, the next ball's coming,' Mum says, calming everyone down.

'The second ball chosen for tonight's lottery is... 2!'

'Yes!' Mum shouts. 'Ben, you've picked that one as well. 'I don't believe it. Did anyone else pick that number?' Ben inquisitively asks.

'Only Dad, but he didn't pick the first number,' Mum says.

Ben can't believe it! *What's the chances of randomly picking the first two lottery numbers,* he thinks. *I wonder what number's going to be next.*

'The third number for tonight's lottery selection is... 34.'

'Yes, yes! Well done, Ben! You've picked the third number as well,' Mum calls out.

'I don't believe it; does that mean we've won something?' Dad asks.

'I don't think so but if he gets another number, we must win something,' Mum informs Dad. Everyone's so excited that they've accurately picked three balls already and they've got four more chances to pick one more number to win something. All eyes quickly focus on the TV screen in anticipation of the next ball being drawn. 'The fourth number is… 3!'

'*What!* I don't believe it!' Mum screams. 'You've picked another one, Ben!'

Mum covers her mouth with her hands looking so surprised. The room suddenly falls deathly silent as they await the next number.

'The fifth number in tonight's lottery is… 21!'

'Yeahhhhhhhhhhhhhhhhh!'

Mum Jess and Dad immediately stand up, screaming with excitement at getting another number and as quickly as they stood, they're back in their seats staring at the TV screen ready for the next number.

'The sixth number in tonight's lottery is… 5!'

'Bloody hell!' Dad calls out. Ben looks over at his dad's face held between his hands, looking totally shocked. Mum stares at Dad with an equal expression of shock but holding her hand over her mouth as though she's about to throw up.

'Does that mean we've won the jackpot?' Jess tentatively asks.

Dad looks at Jess. 'No Jess, but we've won a lot of money, that's for sure.'

Everyone notices they're just about to announce the bonus ball, so all heads quickly turn towards the TV. Ben glances at the side of his mother's face as she looks towards the TV screen and in the reflective light, he notices a tear running down her cheek. He's never seen his mother cry before and the sight of her crying with joy nearly sets him off. He finds himself having to focus on the TV so as not to burst into tears.

'The bonus ball for tonight is … Thirteen!'

The noise in the room suddenly erupts with shouts of joy, hugs and crying from Mum, Dad and Jess. Ben stands up feeling totally amazed that his Fibonacci numbers were all the correct numbers drawn.

I didn't have to travel back in time anyway, I did it all by myself. Why didn't I pick the lottery numbers years ago? he thinks. He had it all worked out in his head, how he was going to remember the seven winning numbers and then travel back in time twelve hours to breakfast that morning and mark the numbers on his lottery card; but he doesn't have to do it now. It all seems so surreal. It's like it's not really happening. He can see his mum, dad and Jess jumping up and down and screaming, but it all feels like his mind is outside his body, in a different realm. He feels numb and confused. Suddenly Dad grabs hold of Ben and lifts him up into the air above everyone as they dance around the room. Dad slowly lowers Ben down towards his chest and wraps his arms around Ben and gives him a huge hug, almost squashing all the air from his body. Dad presses his head against Ben's cheek as he gives his son a kiss, then, in a soft voice, he whispers into Ben's ear, 'I love you, son.'

Ben can't remember the last time his dad told him that; in fact, he can't ever remember hearing his dad say that to him.

He knows his dad loves him and he loves his dad, but it seems that they've never had an opportunity to tell each other. Ben's glad his dad told him; it means so much to him hearing his dad actually say it. Dad lowers Ben down to the floor.

'Yahoo!' Dad screams out, thrusting his arms in the air. The four of them begin jumping up and down in celebration of winning the lottery. It seemed like they were cheering and "yahooing" for ages but in reality it probably only lasted twenty seconds or so. Suddenly they're all slumped down in their seats to the sound of heavy breathing as Mum and Dad try to get their breath back. Ben sits there for a few seconds in complete silence as the realisation slowly sinks in. He looks over at Mum and waits until she opens her eyes, before asking, 'So when do we get our winnings?' Mum quickly sits up from her sprawled out position and looks at Ben.

'I don't know; we've never won before,' Mum says. 'What does it say on the receipt?' Dad immediately asks. Mum, realising the piece of paper is missing, frantically stands up and screams, 'Where is it, I've lost it!' Everyone starts looking around the room for the small priceless piece of paper when Jessica bursts out laughing. Mum glares at Jess, thinking this is not the time to laugh when they've lost something that could be worth a million pounds. Jess, seeing Mum's face, immediately stops laughing and points to Mum's bottom.

'You sat on it!' Jess exclaims. Mum twists round and pulls at her skirt to see the small piece of paper stuck to her backside. She quickly retrieves it and begins to giggle to herself.

'That was a relief,' she tells everyone.

'So what does it say on the ticket?' Dad asks.

Mum holds up the receipt and examines the small print. 'There's a telephone number we have to ring.' Mum looks over at Dad.

'You ring them; I'm too nervous,' she says. Mum quickly passes Dad the slip of paper and he begins reading the information.

'Okay,' Dad says and takes out his mobile phone. He taps in the numbers on his keypad with one hand while holding the phone to his ear.

'Hello, hello? We've got a winning ticket for tonight's lottery,' he says. 'Yes... Yes our numbers are 2 - 3 - 5 - 8 - 13 - 21 and 34,' Dad tells the person on the other end of the phone.

'Yes, my name is Chapman; Chris Chapman and we bought our ticket at the Spar shop on Albert Street in Harrogate.' He waits a second before continuing. 'Okay... Yes. That's fine. Thanks.' He ends the call and looks at Mum.

'What is it; what's happening?' Mum asks, sounding nervous.

'They just need to wait to see if anyone else claims the winning numbers but they've confirmed that we've got the winning ticket.'

'So how long do we have to wait and when will we know how much we've won?' Mum excitedly asks. 'The jackpot is a little over six million,' Dad informs everyone.

'*Six million pounds!*' Mum screams and jumps up and down.

'Don't get too excited; if a hundred people all have the same numbers as us, we'll only get sixty thousand,' Dad tells everyone.

'So when will we know?' Mum asks again.

'They said we should know by the weekend—' 'Mum, Dad,' Ben interrupts. 'I'm going to bed now.'

'Are you all right Ben?' Mum asks looking a little concerned that her son wants to go to bed after having won the lottery.

'Yes, I'm just tired, that's all,' Ben explains.

'Okay son, off you go, and well done for picking the winning numbers,' Dad says.

'Yes, well done, Ben; I love you,' Mum tells him as he goes out though the lounge door and slowly ascends the stairs towards his bedroom. He's not really tired; he just told his parents that so he could go to his bedroom to be alone. Knowing that they've won the lottery and having to wait until the weekend is unacceptable, he can't do that, and why should he, when he has the means to find out exactly how much he's won in the next few minutes. Ben enters his room and closes the door behind him. He sits down on the side of his bed and takes the watch out from his trouser pocket and holds it out in front of himself.

So should I go forward in time to the weekend to find how much we've won? Or should I go a bit further? he thinks. He turns the watch over and twists the plate on the back to allow the winder out.

Suddenly, Ben recalls the advice his Granddad gave him to only travel four weeks in either direction.

'Four weeks should be enough to see what happens,' he tells himself. He places his index finger and thumb on the winder and rotates the dial quickly forward. Ben immediately notices his surroundings change in front of him in a blur: the scenery rapidly moves from light to dark back to light then dark as the days move forward. He stops turning when he notices the gold hand on his watch moves four weeks ahead. Ben finds himself in a comfortable white leather armchair with thick raised sides and back rest. His head is resting against what he imagines to be a soft leather pillow positioned nicely behind his head and shoulders. He slowly lifts his head from the pillow to see exactly where he is but doesn't recognise anything.

'This is weird,' he says to himself feeling like he's been transported into another world. He notices what looks like a white leather sofa next to the left of his chair with an identical chair next to that, all positioned around an oblong solid marble coffee table. In front of where he's sitting, is a large fireplace with pantheon-styled columns either side, supporting a grand plinth with scrolled ends in what could be marble carvings. A large carriage clock sits centrally above the plinth and he immediately notices the time on the clock. Twenty past eight, which is the exact time he sat on his bed, moments ago. The room has two large Georgian style windows with thick cream curtains that hang down from the ceiling and stop just above the floor.

The light streams into the room through the windows and reflects off all the white surfaces, giving the room a bright appearance. Ben's not sure if it's morning or evening because everything seems so bright. 'Hello, is anyone here?' Ben calls out. He listens for any response but all he hears is total silence, except for the faint sound of cars driving outside. 'Where am I and where's the rest of my family?' Ben mutters, feeling vulnerable and all alone. He quickly stands up and walks to the large Georgian windows and looks out through one of the small panes of glass hoping to identify his surroundings. He sees an unusually busy road outside with people walking up and down along the pavements. It all seems strange and alien to him. He doesn't recognise the house or the street outside.

'Hello, is anyone home?' Ben calls out again in a slightly louder voice this time, hoping someone will answer but nobody does. Feeling all alone and a little frightened, he decides to investigate and take a look around. He turns around and heads towards the opened door in the corner of the room. The doorway leads to a large entrance hall with stone tiled flooring and a staircase rising up to the second floor with an ornate sweeping banister rail; all highly polished and clean, with its curved, rounded end. There's a large mirror in a decorative frame mounted near the front door to his left and what appears to be a crystal chandelier hanging from the ceiling. A door opposite is partially open and he can see part of a dining table through the gap.

Ben crosses the hallway and pushes the door to the dining room open. He steps inside the room and gazes at the highly polished, large oblong table positioned centrally in the room with eight chairs around it. Against the right side of the room stands a large free-standing cupboard with a shelving unit above, filled with the finest crockery he's ever seen. He walks over to the cupboard and slides the top drawer open to find silver cutlery laid out in their individual settings on a velvet cushioned base all neatly in their assigned places. He closes the drawer and thinks, *This can't be our house; it's far too posh.*

Ben begins to feel a little overwhelmed at being alone in such a grand house and half expects a lord or baron to suddenly barge into the room holding a double-barrelled shotgun and say, 'Who the hell are you and what are you doing in my house,' before pointing the rifle in his direction and pulling the trigger.

'Hello, is anyone here?' Ben anxiously calls out again with a crackly voice, fighting back the urge to cry. Again, there's no response. 'Where is everyone?' he shouts at the top of his voice. He can't believe he's here all alone and there's no one to tell him what the hell is going on.

He stops for a moment and thinks. *If this is somebody's house, then there ought to be some kind of evidence to prove they live here, like a photograph or something.* He decides to search for evidence of who lives there, so he goes past the dining table to the far end and walks through a doorway leading into a large square well-equipped kitchen with the most up-to-date kitchen appliances. He glances around the room looking for photographs, letters, receipts of any kind to show him who lives there but can't see anything; the kitchen is immaculate. Ben decides the best place to look would be in the lounge, so he goes back into the dining room, when he hears a noise coming from the hallway. He stops in his tracks. Ben listens for the sound again and he hears the front door open. His heart starts to beat rapidly at the thought that an intruder or the owner is about to enter the house. Ben forces himself forward towards the doorway leading to the entrance hall and peers around the door frame at the front door.

'Ben, give us a hand with the shopping,' Mum asks as she struggles through the front door with a grocery bag in each hand. Ben instinctively steps towards his mother, still feeling confused about why she's walking into a strange house with groceries in her hand.

'Take those through to the kitchen; I'll just give Dad a hand with the other bags,' his mum tells him and gives Ben both shopping bags. Ben finds himself staring at the opened doorway as his mum disappears through the opening. Jess walks in carrying two more shopping bags and has to stop because Ben is blocking the entrance hall.

'Go on, take the bags into the kitchen; they've got frozen stuff in them and they need to go in the freezer,' Jess tells Ben. Jess, realising Ben must be having an episode or something, quickly squeezes past him and goes through the dining room and into the kitchen. 'Ben, come on,' he hears his sister call out. He goes through the dining room and into the kitchen where Jess is slowly unpacking the shopping from her two bags and placing the items inside a cupboard.

'What's going on?' Ben asks.

'Isn't this great; we've never had it so good,' Jess tells Ben.

'What do you mean? Where are we?' Ben asks.

'Der… we won the lottery!' Jess sarcastically replies.

'I know, but what are we doing in this house?'

'We live here.'

'What, in Harrogate?'

'No stupid; this is London!'

Hearing the word "London" sends shivers down Ben's spine.

Why are we in London? What about my friend Paul and what about my girlfriend? Ben thinks.

Jess notices that her brother is not helping so she takes the carrier bags from him and carries them over to the large chest freezer and begins to unpack the bags and deposit the frozen items into the empty chest.

'So when you said we live here, do you mean we're on holiday?' Ben musters up the courage to ask.

'No; don't you remember? Dad bought this house for three million; well actually three million, two hundred and ninety-three thousand to be precise and we moved in yesterday… hello!'

'Three million; how much did we win?' Ben asks in a slightly panicky voice.

'We won six million, two hundred and fifty-three thousand. That's how much.'

Jess made a point of emphasising each numerical word.

'Six million, two hundred and fifty-three thousand pounds,' Ben slowly tells himself.

'Yes, isn't it brilliant? We can buy whatever we want and we can go on holiday whenever we please and to any destination. I'm definitely going to get Dad to take us to Disneyworld in Florida and then we could go to Venice or Rome. I learnt all about Rome at school; it's where all the millionaires go. Wouldn't it be wonderful to go there?' Jess asks.

Ben's mind suddenly drifts from what Jess was saying to thinking about Alexis.

'What about Alexis?' Ben asks.

'You broke up last week,' Jess tells him.

'Broke up? What do you mean we broke up?'

'Because we bought this house and moved to London and Alexis lives in Harrogate… der. Do you have a brain freeze or something?' Jess asks.

Why can't I remember any of this? I don't want to live in London and I want my girlfriend back, Ben thinks. Mum and Dad walk into the kitchen carrying the last of the shopping bags and deposit them down on the long work surface just inside the room. Mum reaches inside one of the bags and takes out a bottle of Champagne. 'Anyone fancy a glass of champers? Mum asks. Dad looks at the bottle and says, 'Why not darling?' He opens a cupboard and lifts down two crystal Champagne flutes and places them on the work surface in front of Mum.

'Isn't this wonderful; don't you just love it here?' Mum rhetorically asks and gives Dad a smile as he begins to uncork the bottle.

'Erm, it's all right,' Ben replies feeling at a loss as to what to say.

'We knew you'd come around to liking the house,' Dad tells Ben and gives him a comforting smile.

Ben, noticing his mom and sister putting the shopping away, decides to give them a hand while he thinks about his new life in London. He's not exactly sure where everything is supposed to go because he can't ever remember seeing the insides of the kitchen cupboards before, so he finds himself asking his mum every time the item he has in his hand needs to be stored somewhere else. Finally the shopping is stored away and his mum and dad take their glasses of Champagne through to the lounge to relax. Ben decides to explore the rest of the house and to find his bedroom for one thing. He walks up the first flight of stairs and immediately finds his parents' bedroom with an on-suite bath and shower room. There's another bedroom on the other side of the landing to Mum and Dad's room, but it has a double bed and chest of drawers and nothing else in the room; so Ben assumes that that room would probably be used for guests that might want to stay the night.

Feeling a little impatient at not finding his room yet, Ben quickly dashes up the next flight of stairs to the second floor and on seeing two closed doors, he decides to go through the one on his right, which happens to be the right room. Ben immediately recognises a few items of clothes sprawled across the floor belonging to him. The second thing he sees is his half-built ship positioned on his desk in the corner, next to what appears to be a brand-new computer with speakers. The room's different to how his room was in Harrogate. For one thing, he's got a large double bed, which he's never had. There's a massive TV screen mounted on the wall to his left, above a base cabinet with stacks and stacks of games next to what looks like a new PlayStation Console. His eyes quickly scanned the room and identified things he never noticed when he first walked in. It looks like everything in the room is brand new except for his model ship.

'I don't believe it. This is amazing,' Ben tells himself. Ben closes his bedroom door and lies down in the centre of his king-sized bed feeling spellbound by all the amazing stuff he has. He lays there for a few seconds; trying to decide which game to play first when the sight of his TV screen reminds him of something. Images of dad holding him up in the air in front of their old TV, suddenly floods back into his mind. It was literally only twenty minutes ago when they announced the winning numbers and here he is weeks later in a new house in a new city without his best friend or his girlfriend.

He was just starting to enjoy his life in Harrogate; he became popular at school having won the Inter-School Competition and he finally found a girlfriend and not to mention how he became the school hero; life was good. Ben closes his eyes so he can fully concentrate and evaluate what's happened to him. Sudden images and conversations from the past four weeks start to fill his mind. He remembers seeing Alexis's face smiling at him and looking so happy; then her expressions changed as he told her the news of moving away. He remembers how brave she was, as she told him, that it was all right and that he didn't have to worry about her and that she'd be all right. Ben knew she didn't mean it because she was crying and he didn't know what to say. He knows now that she only said what she said, so it would be easier for him to leave without feeling guilty. She must have known in her heart that winning six million pounds would change them; it would change anyone. He remembers how excited his whole family was when they were presented with the cheque on national TV and how they told the TV presenter that the money wouldn't change them, they would still be the same old family. 'Has it changed me?' Ben asks himself. He knew how excited he had been when he walked into his bedroom moments ago, seeing all the amazing stuff he had, but that was momentary excitement.

'Has the money really changed me; is it the most important thing in my life?' Ben asks himself again. He suddenly remembers the journey down to London when he was feeling totally miserable. You would have thought that being a millionaire would make anyone happy, but deep down in his heart, he missed his old life; he missed Alexis and his best friend, Paul. He remembers his dad telling him on the journey down here that it's all going to be fine, he'd make new friends and find another girlfriend; however, he doesn't want a new friend and he definitely doesn't want a new girlfriend. He loves Alexis.

Ben opens his eyes and calls out, 'I don't want this life. I want my old life back.' He sits up on his bed and takes the watch out from his pocket. He twists the back plate around so he can travel back in time and open the front cover.

Chapter Thirty-Four

Suddenly Ben finds himself walking into the dining room.

'Good morning Ben, sorry we only have cereal for breakfast this morning; well, it's going to be every morning until dad gets a job,' Mum says.

'That's all right Mum; I just want a bowl of cornflakes, thanks.'

Ben takes a seat at the dining table and thinks, *This is great. What perfect timing.*

'What about you Jess; have you decided what you're having?' Ben hears his mum ask Jess. He looks at his sister still texting on her phone as she was yesterday.

'Oh sorry Mum, I was just texting Debbie.' Jess tells her mum. Ben tries to recall what happened next and thinks his dad is about to say something about the newspaper so he glances over to his father.

'I can't believe it; there's absolutely nothing suitable in the job section again today. What a waste of time and money, buying a newspaper that's no good to anyone,' Dad says sounding annoyed. Mum returns from the kitchen and places a cereal bowl down in front of Ben before moving around the dining table and standing next to Dad.

'Don't worry darling. I'll tell you what, why don't we drop the kids off at school and then we could go into town and take a look at the job centre; they're bound to have lots more jobs for you to look at?' Mum puts her arm around Dad's shoulder and gives him a cuddle exactly as she did before.

Ben pours cold milk on his cornflakes and begins eating as he tries to remember exactly what moment when he asked about the lottery tickets. Ben watches as his Mum walks back inside the kitchen and comes out carrying Jessica's breakfast and lays it down in front of her when Ben suddenly remembers that he needs to ask his mum now.

'Mum have you got your lottery tickets for today?' Mum walks over to her handbag and takes out some lottery tickets.

'I don't know why I picked these up, we've never won a thing and… well, we can't exactly afford to waste money on the lottery any more,' she says

'We might win, you never know; we could all do one card each if you want?' Ben suggests. Suddenly there's a deathly silence in the room and Ben's heart feels like it's about to stop as he anxiously waits for someone to say or do something. The moment seems to drag on and on and Ben's palms begin to sweat as he senses it's all going to go wrong. Ben pleadingly looks over towards his dad hoping that he'll come to his rescue. Dad looks at Ben, and for a moment, Ben can see his mind mulling the idea over in his head.

'That's a good idea, let's have one last go as a family.' Dad suggests.

Phew. I really thought for a moment that he wasn't going to like the idea, Ben thinks. Mum walks back to the breakfast table and hands each of them a ticket. 'Okay we've got one ticket each and this is the last time,' Mum tells them.

Ben's not bothered that his mum doesn't want to play the lottery ever again; who cares, because they're going to win tonight. Ben happily takes a pen handed to him from his mother and looks down at his blank lottery card.

What numbers should I choose? Ben thinks. *We need to win enough money to be able to stay here, but not too much that Mum and Dad buy a house in London; so how many numbers do I need to get right to give us what we need?* Ben tries to work it out for himself. *I picked the numbers two, three, five, eight, thirteen, twenty-one and thirty-four last time, so I definitely don't want to pick all those. What if I changed just one of the numbers? Thirteen is an unlucky number; so what would happen if I take that number out and pick something like forty-eight which is the next number on the Fibonacci scale.*

Ben, having decided, marks an X on all the numbers he's selected then places his pen down on the table to indicate to his mother that he's finished. Mum collects the filled-in cards and puts them back inside her handbag. After breakfast, Mum and Dad drop Jess and Ben off outside the school gate before continuing on into town. Jess sees Debbie waiting for her just inside the school entrance so they give each other a hug, before wandering off towards the school building.

Ben happily goes through the school gates and turns towards his usual spot when he has a strange feeling of foreboding come over him. Ben stops for a second and suddenly remembers being attacked by Tony and his gang the last time he was there. Ben's eyes quickly scan the school play area for his attacker but can't see him among the twenty or so pupils milling around in front of him. Ben remembers Tony attacking him from his right, when he was sitting on the climbing frame looking back at the school entrance, so that means he must be somewhere over to his left. Ben casually glances over to his left as he goes back to the climbing frame and finally spots Tony standing by the side of the school building with his buddies. They seem to be huddled together as though they're discussing a plan.

'Right that's where you are,' Ben says to himself feeling a little anxious, knowing that he's about to be attacked.

He reaches the climbing frame and turns around to face the school gate as he did before. He anxiously sits down on the low bar knowing that in a few moments Tony is going to punch him in the face.

He vividly remembers every single detail of the attack on him yesterday and the thought of reliving that experience is not something he would ever want to experience again. It was a painful and the most unpleasant experience of his life and knowing that it could repeat itself in the next few moments is making Ben feel quite nauseous. Ben tries to remember the exact moments before the attack so he can prepare himself. Ben lifts the rucksack off his shoulder and lowers the bag down so it's resting between his feet. He wraps the handle tightly around his right hand so he's got a firm grip on the bag before positioning his right foot under the low bar of the climbing frame, as an Olympic sprinter would crouch on the starting blocks, with one foot behind the other to get a good start. Ben leans forward a little to move his centre of gravity to aid his movement, in anticipation of that starting pistol; or in this case, Tony's fist flying towards him. Ben knows what he needs to do, but he's still anxious because he doesn't really know if his plan will work and the reality of failing would be another beating which he's definitely not looking forward to. Ben continues to stare at the entrance gate as he did yesterday, fighting back the urge to look to his right to see his attacker coming. He knows he can't look, because if he does, Tony would know that he knows that he's coming; which would change the outcome altogether. Ben realises that if he keeps the situation exactly as it was yesterday, he would know which direction his attacker will come from and know the exact moment when Tony will throw that first punch. All he needs to do is wait for Tony to say, "So you think you're a hero". Ben feels his body starting to shake, in anticipation of waiting for his attacker to arrive. His ears are tuned in to any sound coming from his right, when he hears the faint sound of feet walking towards him.

'So you think you're a hero do you?' Tony's voice call out over to his right. Without looking, Ben immediately throws himself forward one step and swings his school bag around to his right. Everything suddenly happens in slow motion as his adrenaline kicks in. Ben watches Tony's fist whistle past the back of his head, while his rucksack laden with books, swings around hitting the back of Tony's head. The blow sends Tony flying over the low bar of the climbing frame and crashing face first into the tarmac surface. Ben quickly turns with the momentum of his rucksack until he's facing Tony's entourage all gawping at their leader sprawled out flat on the ground with his feet hooked up over the low bar. He looks like a beached whale.

Ben follows their gaze and sees Tony as he turns his head towards them looking like a helpless casualty of war with blood oozing out from his mouth. Ben realising Tony's out of action for the moment; turns back towards Simon, Brian and Andrew and immediately drops his rucksack on the ground and takes on a Karate stance to look as intimidating and threatening as he can.

'*Hey!*' Ben calls out towards the three comrades with his clenched fists ready for action. Their eyes turn towards Ben then back down at Tony who's not moved and then back to Ben.

'Come on,' Ben shouts at his enemy.

'Sorry, we don't want any trouble,' Andrew says apologetically, holding up his hands.

'Yes, sorry Ben,' Simon and Brian reply.

The three of them immediately begin to back away having seen their leader defeated. Ben waits until they all turn and walk in the opposite direction back towards the school building before he turns round to face Tony who's managed to turn himself over and is now sitting flat on the ground looking all pathetic and helpless.

'Are you all right Tony?' Ben asks. Tony seems to find it difficult to move, so Ben steps over the low frame and holds out his hand to help him up. Tony humbly takes hold of Ben's hand and is helped to his feet.

'I think you need to see the school nurse,' Ben suggests while staring at the blood oozing down Tony's chin. Tony nods in agreement and covers his mouth with his free hand. Ben picks up his school bag and helps Tony limp over towards the main building, followed by the eyes of every other child in school. Ben helps Tony up the stairs and in through the main doors.

'Hello, we need to see the nurse,' Ben says to the receptionist. She notices the trickle of blood and quickly rushes back into an adjacent room before returning with the school nurse.

'Oh, you poor dear, what happened to you?' the nurse asks. She leads them both through to her medical room and sits Tony down in a chair. She tears off a large sheet of paper towelling from a roll and wets it under the tap before wiping away the blood around Tony's mouth and hands.

'Now let me see.' She bends forward and holds Tony's head back a little so she can see the damage. 'It looks like you're missing a tooth and you have a cut lip and some small scratches on your face. What happened?' the nurse asks.

Tony glances over at Ben and then returns his gaze to the nurse.

'I fell over the climbing frame.'

'Well don't you worry son; it's not too bad. I'll just clean those cuts with a little antiseptic and you'll be right as rain in no time.'

The sound of the school bell reverberates throughout the school grounds to indicate the start of class. The nurse looks over at Ben.

'It's all right; off you go; I'll take care of your friend,' she tells Ben. Ben gives Tony a smile and pats him on the shoulder before making his way out of the room and into the entrance hall that leads to all the classrooms.

A crowd of children walk in through the main entrance and on seeing Ben, they all say, 'Well done Ben,' and give him a big smile and a thumbs up sign to show their approval. Ben could have just continued on his way to his classroom but receiving the adulation from everyone who were eyewitnesses to what happened was something he just couldn't resist.

It was interesting at lunch time when Ben eventually met up with Alexis and Paul. They'd heard whispers throughout the school but couldn't believe it when Ben told them what happened.

They'd seen Tony earlier in one of their classes with an injured face and wondered who beat him up. Suddenly Ben notices Tony walking out from the school building. Tony stops at the bottom of the steps and looks around looking like a lost sheep. His head stops turning when he sees Ben, Paul and Alexis near the climbing frame. Ben gives him a quick wave. Tony waves back and slowly walks over towards them.

'Tony's coming over; don't say a word,' Ben tells Alexis and Paul. Tony stops a few feet away.

'Hi, Ben,' Tony says.

'Are you all right, Tony? How's your mouth?' Ben enquires sympathetically.

'It's all right, just a little bit sore. I just wanted to thank you for helping me, that's all.'

'That's all right mate,' Ben replies.

'Thanks again,' he says before turning away and walking towards the far side of the field, where his friends Simon, Brian and Andrew are standing.

'That's all right *mate!*' Paul says mockingly. 'What was that?'

'Look I know he's been a bully for ages. But look at him. I think he feels totally embarrassed having been beaten up in front of the whole school,' Ben explains. Paul looks around and watches Tony make his way towards his friends looking a little dejected.

'I suppose you're right.'

'Well done Ben, I thought you did the right thing,' Alexis tells him.

After school, the three of them walk home together and discuss how the day couldn't have been better.

'Did you see Simon, Andrew and Brian when we came out of school?' Ben asks.

'Yes, I can't believe it; they were as nice as pie to me,' Paul replies. 'You need to beat up more people.' Paul suggests before laughing.

'No, that would be horrible. Ben's nice and wouldn't dream of beating people up for no reason,' Alexis replies.

'I am nice; thanks for noticing,' Ben tells Alexis. They reach the other end of the park and Paul continues towards his home on his own while Ben walks with Alexis to her house.

'So see you tomorrow?' Ben says.

'Yes, see you at school,' Alexis replies. She leans forward and they kiss for the first time outside her home. Ben watches Alexis enter in through her front door before turning round and heading home.

Things seem to be moving forward nicely with Alexis. She was always a little apprehensive about Ben walking her home and he always had to drop her off a few doors down from her house, because she didn't want her dad seeing them together. It was really nice to be able to finally walk her to her gate and then to be kissed; well, that was certainly a nice surprise for Ben. Ben thinks Alexis's father is a solicitor or barrister and her mum is a writer or something; that's why they live in the most salubrious part of town. Maybe that's why Alexis has always felt reticent about introducing Ben to her parents, because she thinks they've always been over-protective of their little girl and the thought that she might someday like someone below their social standing would be too shocking. Ben doesn't know exactly how they feel, because he's never had the opportunity to speak to them, but he's glad she allowed him to walk her home today.

Ben starts thinking how well the day has gone and how he'd overcome two large hurdles; making friends with Tony and progressing with his relationship with Alexis. *This day couldn't get any better*, he thinks, when he suddenly remembers. *It's the lottery tonight!*

Chapter Thirty-Five

Ben takes his seat on the opposite side of the sofa to Jess and his father sits down in his usual chair. Mum retrieves the numbers from under the clock on the mantle and sits down between Jess and Ben just before the programme starts.

'Right quiet everyone. Just to remind you what numbers we want,' Mum says. She continues reading the numbers out loud so everyone can hear.

Ben, feeling so much more relaxed now about the lottery, having already experienced it once before, sits back in his corner of the sofa with his glass of Coke in hand and resolves to chill out while the lottery balls are called out. Seconds later, the rest of his family are all anxiously staring at the TV screen as the numbered balls are dropped into the clear glass mixing bowl prior to a ball being selected. A voice from the presenter announces. 'The first number for tonight's lottery is... 8.'

'Yes! Jess and Ben picked that number. Sorry darling, we haven't won,' Ben hears his mum call out exactly as she did before.

Ben smiles at the repetitious actions of his family and glances over at his father as he picks up his coffee cup. 'I might have picked all the other numbers; just wait and see.'

Ben takes another sip from his glass of Coke feeling good about this whole scenario unravelling in front of his eyes.

'Quiet, the next ball's coming!' Mum calms everyone down.

'The second ball chosen for tonight's lottery is... 2!'

'Yes!' Mum screams out. 'Ben, you've picked that one as well. 'Was I the only one who picked that number?' Ben asks knowing all too well that his dad picked it but didn't pick the first number.

'Only Dad, but he didn't pick the first number,' Mum says.

'The third number for tonight's lottery selection is... 34!'

'Yes, Yes, well done Ben; you've picked the third number as well,' Mum calls out.

'I don't believe it! Does that mean we've won something?' Dad asks.

'I don't think so but if he gets another number, we must win something,' Mum informs Dad.

'The fourth number is… 3!'

'*What!* I don't believe it!' Mum screams.

'You've picked another one, Ben!'

Mum covers her mouth with her hands looking so surprised. Ben gives his mum a smile, knowing how excited and surprised she'll be when he picks the next number as well. 'The fifth number in tonight's lottery is… 21.'

'Yeahhhhhhhhhhhhhhhhh!' Mum Jess and Dad quickly stand up and scream with excitement and within less than two seconds they're sat down again staring at the TV screen breathing heavily from their sudden exertion. 'The sixth number in tonight's lottery is… 5.'

'Bloody hell!' Ben hears his dad call out just as he did before.

'Does that mean we've won the jackpot?' Ben hears Jess ask.

'No Jess, but we've won a lot of money, that's for sure.'

Ben watches his mother's face again and sees in the reflective light, a tear run down her cheek. She quickly wipes the tear away with her hand and continues looking at the screen. 'The bonus ball for tonight is…'

'*Quiet everyone!*' Mum screams out so they can all concentrate on the TV screen.

'… Thirteen!'

'*Nooo!*' They all cry out and hold their heads in their hands feeling devastated that they've not won the jackpot. They stare at each other for a few seconds without saying a word.

'We've still won something, haven't we?' Dad asks.

'Yes, of course. It won't be the jackpot but we've won something,' Mum tells him.

'So what do we do now?' Dad asks.

'Here, you ring them. The numbers on the ticket.'

Mum hands the lottery receipt to Dad and he dials the number. Ben knows they're not going to find out how much they've won tonight, and that they'll have to wait until the weekend to find out the exact amount, so he tries to relax in his seat until his dad finishes on the phone.

Dad ends his call and turns to everyone. 'They've confirmed we've won, but they can't tell us how much we've won until the weekend,' Dad explains.

'I'm going to bed, I'm tired,' Ben tells his parents. His parents look at Ben in surprise.

'Are you all right Ben; don't you feel well?' Mum asks.

'I'm all right Mum, I'm just tired that's all,' Ben tells them.

'Okay Ben, and well done for picking the winning numbers,' Mum tells him. She quickly gives Ben a hug and a kiss before whispering, 'I love you' into his ear. Dad waits for Mum to let go of Ben before he picks Ben up in his arms and gives him an enormous hug.

'Well done lad,' he tells him before lowering him gently to the floor. Ben goes upstairs feeling a lot better; now that he knows they're not going to win the jackpot. He walks into the bathroom and closes the door behind him. He uses the toilet and washes his hands and face in the sink before picking up his toothbrush from its holder and squeezing a small amount of toothpaste onto the bristles from the half-empty tube of toothpaste. He returns the tube to the shelf above the sink and looks at his reflection in the mirror.

Suddenly he's completely overwhelmed by a wave of guilt.

'What have I done?' Ben asks himself, feeling like a piece of dirt. He drops his toothbrush into the sink and grabs hold of the sink unit and the towel rail to prevent himself from collapsing on the floor. Images of his mum and dad looking so happy in their London home suddenly appear in his mind; the sight of Jess sounding so ecstatic at being a millionaire. He can hear her voice telling him how they could go on holiday, anywhere and have anything they wanted; it resounds in his head. The realisation that he gave his family everything, and now he's taken it all away hits him like a thunderbolt. How could he be so cruel? He must be the worst child in the world to do this to his parents and his sister. Ben stares at his reflection in the mirror and all he can see is a selfish, hateful person who's committed a heinous and iniquitous act against those he's supposed to love. Ben lowers his gaze in disgust and watches the tears run down his cheeks and drip into the ceramic basin below. Ben tears a few sheets of toilet tissue from the roll and wipes his face before depositing the damp crumpled tissues in the waste bin next to him. He suddenly remembers his mother telling him only moments ago that she loved him and how his dad gave him a massive hug because he picked the winning numbers. They seemed so happy to have won with six numbers; so is it that bad that they don't remember winning the jackpot? What if they still win enough money to pay the bills and still have plenty left to live here; that way they could all be happy.

They don't know that they won the jackpot, so they don't know what they've lost. They're happy now and that's the most important thing. Ben wipes his eyes again in light of his new reasoning.

If we don't win enough money this time to live a good life, I'll just go back and change the numbers,, he thinks. Ben picks up his toothbrush from the sink unit and begins brushing his teeth. He hears Jess enter her bedroom, so he knows she'll be knocking on the bathroom door very shortly. He quickly rinses the toothpaste out of his mouth and replaces his toothbrush back in its holder before making his way back to his bedroom and closing the door behind him. With all the excitement and mixed emotions he's experienced during the day has really taken its toll on him, both physically and mentally, leaving him totally exhausted. Ben gets up onto his bed and for a brief second, he thinks about travelling into the future to find out what happens, but he's just too tired. Ben lies down on his bed and rests his head between his soft pillows. The last thing he remembers is pulling the duvet up around him and closing his eyes.

Chapter Thirty-Six

The following morning starts on a high. Ben hears his Mum singing in the kitchen and Dad seems to be pleased as punch.

Even Jess is nice to him. 'Good morning Ben, can I get you anything?' Jess asks.

Ben stares at his sister feeling ambivalent about her generous offer.

'I'm all right thanks.' Ben says and cautiously sits down on the seat next to her.

'So how about we all go shopping on the weekend. You can have anything you like,' Dad says. Ben looks up at his father thinking how strange this whole situation is.

What's going on? he thinks. Mum walks in from the kitchen, carrying a large plate consisting of two rashes of bacon, two eggs, two sausages, mushrooms and beans and places it down in front of Dad.

'Can I get you the same Ben?' Mum asks.

Ben looks at the huge, cooked breakfast his dad is having, and although it looks tempting, he knows he'd never be able to manage it all.

'I'll have the same as Dad but only one piece of bacon, one sausage and one egg, thanks Mum.'

'You can have anything you like, my wonderful boy,' Mum says as she places her hands either side of Ben's face and kisses him on the forehead.

'Did you want some Coke? I'll get it for you,' Jess offers.

Before Ben has a chance to reply, Jess is up on her feet and heading towards the kitchen to get Ben his drink.

'Okay,' Ben manages to say before Jess disappears through the kitchen door. Ben looks over at his dad who's grinning from ear to ear.

This is so weird, Ben quietly says to himself. Mum walks back through from the kitchen carrying Ben's plate of food and lays it down in front of him.

'There you are you beautiful child.' She leans forward and kisses him again before taking her seat at the table. Jess walks back to the table carrying a large glass of Coke and puts it down beside him. She sits down in her seat next to Ben and gives him a big smile. Ben smiles back at his sister before picking up his knife and fork and tucking into his food. He keeps his head down for a few seconds, hoping that his family will get the hint and stop staring at him; because seeing three faces continually smiling at him is starting to freak him out.

To Ben's relief, he notices the other members of his family turn their attention to their breakfasts which creates a few moments of silence in the dining room. Ben thinks about how happy everyone seems. He's never seen his mum so happy in years and having his dad promise to take them shopping; well, that's a first and then there's his older sister fetching him his drink without any snide remarks is definitely a breath of fresh air. Could he live with a family this nice? Ben asks himself. The answer is a definite *yes*.

Dad drops Jess and Ben off at school as usual. Jess heads off with Debbie and Ben goes over to the climbing frame to wait for Alexis and Paul to arrive. He sits down on the low bar and turns towards the school gate in anticipation of his friend arriving. A few minutes later, Ben sees Tony walk in through the entrance. He usually goes over to the school building to meet up with Simon, Andrew and Brian but this time he turns and heads straight towards Ben.

Ben immediately tenses up thinking Tony's only heading this way to try to reclaim his position as top dog again. Maybe last night, he thought about what happened the other day and decided to try his luck again but this time, one on one in front of the whole school and away from the climbing frame. Ben stares at Tony, looking for any indication as to his intentions so he can prepare himself. However, Tony smiles at Ben revealing his missing tooth and asks, 'Hi Ben, how's it goin?'

Ben, feeling a sense of relief, smiles back. 'I'm all right; how are you? How's your face?'

'Oh it's all right I've had worse.' Tony says and takes a seat next to him on the climbing frame.

Ben hasn't quite accepted the fact that Tony's friendly towards him, as he's known Tony for the past two years as the school bully; it's hard to change your opinion of someone overnight. Still feeling a little cautious because of his past reputation, Ben tries to appear relaxed but inside he's on tender hooks, ready to react if Tony suddenly flares up.

'Avalon likes your mate, you know?' Tony tells Ben.

'Does she?' Ben asks, not quite making the connection.

'She asked me to ask you if you'd ask your mate if he wanted to go out with her.'

'Ermm okay; I'll ask him when I see him,' Ben replies, still not knowing exactly who Tony's referring to. Tony gives Ben a smile and stands up.

'I'll see you later then and let me know what Paul says.'

'Okay, see you later.' Ben watches Tony walk away towards the school main entrance before he finally relaxes and lowers his guard.

That was a strange conversation,' Ben thinks. 'So Avalon wants to go out with my mate. Which mate is that?' Ben asks himself. Then it all suddenly becomes clear as he recalls Tony mentioning Paul's name. 'I don't believe it. Avalon fancies Paul. You've got to be kidding.'

Ben laughs aloud and mutters,. 'The school bully's sister wants to go out with Paul?' Ben laughs at the idea that she fancies Paul. 'Well, I never saw that coming, I mean, I knew Paul sort of liked her but he liked any girl that spoke to him. The news about Avalon and Paul sends Ben's emotions into a state of sheer exhilaration that he finds difficult to hold in. Ben quickly looks towards the main gate, willing his friends to walk in so he can tell someone. Within a minute or two, Alexis walks in through the entrance and heads over towards Ben who's now standing next to the climbing frame hopping from one foot to the other. Alexis immediately recognises that something's different because Ben's looking so excited. '

What's happened?' she eagerly asks. 'You're not going to believe what just happened?' Ben tells her. 'Tony Vernall came over and asked me to ask Paul if he'd go out with…' Ben pauses for a second.

'Who?' Alexis asks, sounding intrigued.

'Have a seat first.' Ben points to the space next to him and they quickly sit down. Ben turns to face Alexis and looks into her eyes. 'Avalon.' Ben tells her.

'Ahhhhhh. I knew she liked him. I could tell.'

'What do you mean you could tell? I didn't know, I mean I kinda knew,' Ben says, sounding surprised. 'That's because you were too focused on chatting me up!' Alexis states.

Ben tries to remember the last time he saw Paul and Avalon together, and the only time he could think of, was when the four of them were at the funfair. Ben suddenly remembers Paul telling him that he had a nice time talking to Avalon. It all makes sense now. He'd never seen a girl talk to Paul before so she must have liked him.

'I remember now... der. I certainly missed that one,' Ben tells Alexis.

'I just don't understand why Avalon didn't ask me to ask Paul because I'm her friend.'

'I suppose she might have felt nervous about asking you to ask him just in case he refused and then she'd look a little foolish or even embarrassed in front of you.'

'I suppose you're right,' Alexis replies knowing that that must have been the reason she wasn't asked by her friend. They sit in silence for a couple of minutes as they wait for Paul to arrive. Paul walks in through the main gate and heads over towards them and almost immediately recognises that something's up. 'What's happened, and why are you both smiling?' Paul asks, looking intrigued. Paul's never had a girlfriend before, so when Ben and Alexis told him about Avalon, they thought his body couldn't cope with the excitement. Paul's eyes were as wide as ever and his expression was a picture. He just stood there with an elated look on his face, displaying a huge grin. Ben tried to get him to say something but he just stared into space looking as though he was in La-La Land. The school bell sounds; informing everyone that class was about to start and Paul just stood there, oblivious to anything around him. Alexis and Ben quickly grab his arms and lead him across the playground and into the main entrance of the school.

'What class do you have for your first lesson?' Ben asks, feeling concerned that his best friend is having a breakdown or something.

Paul doesn't say a word, except to stare longingly into space; probably imagining some romantic liaison with his true love. Alexis takes his school book out of his bag and looks at his schedule for the day.

'Physics, he's got physics in Mr Benson's class,' Alexis says. They quickly rush down the corridor to the physics lab and push Paul in through the doorway before closing the half-paned door behind him. They watch Paul wander over to his seat on the third row back and sit down.

'Look who else is in his class!' Alexis says, pointing to a girl on the front row. Ben shakes his head thinking '*He's not going to survive.* Avalon turns around and looks over at Paul looking all goo-goo eyed and lost in love.

'Come on; let's leave the young lovers.' Ben tells Alexis, they giggle to themselves as they head to their own classrooms.

During the lunchtime break, Alexis and Ben collect their food in the school dining room and take their seats at one of the large dining tables that seat eight pupils. Moments later Avalon and Paul join them looking happy and in love, shortly followed by Tony.

'Hi, Avalon,,' Alexis says.

'Hi.'

'So is it official you're going out with each other?' Ben asks Paul as he sits down next to Avalon.

Paul gives Ben a big smile and says, 'Yes and you'd never guess what. Avalon's having a party on Sunday and she's invited all of us.'

Ben immediately thinks how interesting that's going to be. He can't quite imagine it; being at the school bully's house with his sister who told Ben off at the Inter-School competition is definitely going to be a party he'll never forget. He wonders what their parents are like. He's never been to their house before and to be honest, he's got no idea where they live.

'Oh, wow, that's great. What time do you want us to get there?' Alexis asks.

'Come over about twelve.' Avalon tells them.

'You'll have to tell us where you live because I don't think we've ever been round to your house before,' Ben says.

'It's 1433 Sycamore View; about a mile past the new Morrison's Superstore.'

Even after Avalon mentioned the address, Ben still can't visualise where they live. He tries to remember a council estate near Morrison's but all he can remember about the new Morrison's store is that it was built next to a new estate and not a council house estate. It might be a preconceived idea that you'd expect all school bullies to live in a deprived estate somewhere, but 1433 Sycamore View didn't sound like a run-down council address. Ben vaguely remembers the new Morrison's store when it first opened because his mum took them there, so they could see if it was any cheaper than the store they use for their weekly shopping; but that was about all he remembers. He wasn't particularly interested in where it was located or what development was around it; all he was interested in was what sort of games they had on offer.

Chapter Thirty-Seven

Saturday morning Ben wakes up feeling excited about the day ahead. It's not often when your father tells you that you can have any present you want; in fact, he did say they could have as many presents as they wanted provided he could fit them all on his credit card. Ben knows it's not going to be like Birthdays or Christmas when you're sometimes given presents you don't want and you'd never use. He remembers his dad once was given a present from a work colleague. He removed the wrapping and took one look at it and said. 'That's going straight on eBay, there's no way I'm listening to a Barry Manilow CD.' It made everyone laugh at the time and to be honest, Ben thinks it was a good thing, because ever since that day, he'd never received a present that he didn't want or like. Ben's been desperately trying to think of presents he would like; as his dad said they could have whatever they wanted but he's finding it difficult to suddenly think of stuff he wants.

He wouldn't mind getting a Millennium Falcon; not the actual thing but an eighteen-inch model of one he saw on the TV the other week. He would like a racing game for his PlayStation as well; he quite likes the game, 'Gran Turismo' because it allows you to race lots of sports cars around a track. When he's older, he'd like to buy himself a Ford Mustang. Ben suddenly realises that he needs to get a move on; else they'd be leaving for the shops without him. Ben quickly gets dressed and uses the bathroom before making his way downstairs. Jess and Dad are already sitting at the table having their breakfast when Ben walks into the room.

'Hi Ben, what do you fancy for breakfast?' Mum asks as she sees him enter the dining room.

'Just cereal thanks Mum,' Ben tells her. He never has to specify which cereal he wants, because they always buy the same cereal each week: cornflakes and it can't be any old brand, it has to be Kellogg's Corn Flakes as his dad refuses to eat anything else. Ben takes his seat at the table and Mum brings his cereal through from the kitchen.

'So have you decided what presents you'd like?' Mum asks.

'Dad, can we have two presents?' Ben tentatively asks.

'Of course you can, you can have as many as you like,' Dad tells him.

'Chris, we can't afford it at the moment; we don't have that much money in the bank,' Mum reminds him. Dad holds up his credit card.

'You can have as much as I can fit on this thing.' It takes Ben a few seconds to realise that his father didn't literally mean for the toys to fit on his credit card as they'd need to be pretty small.

'Can I have a keyboard Dad?' Jess asks.

'Of course you can, just make a list of everything you want and we'll see what we can buy,' Dad tells the children. Ben continues eating his cereal and tries to think of anything else that he'd like to get.

'Darling, what time did the lottery people say we should ring back to see how much we've won?' Mum asks Dad. 'They told me to ring after lunch.'

After breakfast, the four of them drive into town and park the car in the multistory car park, just a short walk from the large toy store. It only takes them less than five minutes to walk from the car to the large warehouse packed with every conceivable toy there is. They enter the building through a glass sliding door into the large warehouse style shop with its huge aisles running the length of the vast open space. 'This is amazing,' Ben tells his father, feeling really excited at seeing so many toys on display.

'Okay, have a wander round and when you find what you want, just give us a shout,' Dad tells Jess and Ben. They quickly rush off in different directions.

After ten minutes of searching, Ben eventually finds a Millennium Falcon that he'd been looking for. *'Mum!'* he calls out in the busy store to the surprise of other mothers looking at him and realising he's not their child. His real mum appears from around a corner and they load the Falcon into the large shopping trolley.

'Anything else you want?' Mum asks. Ben gives her a quick nod before rushing off towards the 'PlayStation' Game section he spotted earlier on the left-hand side. Within seconds, Ben sees the game he wants and grabs hold of it before anyone else does; not that it mattered, because there must have been another thirty or so copies of the same game on display. Another game just to the left of him catches his eye so he picks it up and begins reading the details on the back of the case. It sounds really good and something he'd definitely like to play so he tucks it under his arm with his Gran Turismo game when suddenly his eyes are drawn to another game on the display that looks just as good as the first game. Ben finds himself reaching for that game as well; when his conscience warns him.

'No, this is wrong,' Ben tells himself. 'Just because Dad said he could have anything in the shop, doesn't mean he should. He can only play one game at a time and buying more than one is just greedy. Ben puts the game back on the shelf and takes just the one game to his parents standing at the end of the aisle. 'Found it.' Ben tells them and places the game into the trolley next to his Millennium Falcon.

'Don't you want a couple more games?' Mum asks.

'No, I'm fine, thanks. I can only play one game at a time anyway,' Ben tells them. They give Ben a smile and look round to see where Jess is. Jess appears from around a corner looking sullen and depressed.

'What's wrong honey?' Mum asks, having noticed how down she looks.

'I can't find any keyboards,' Jess tells them.

'Don't worry darling, there's a music shop around the corner, we can go there as soon as we finished here,' Mum tells Jess, which cheers her up. They all head towards the checkout and join a short queue of people waiting to pay. Ben catches sight of a Paddington Bear near the exit.

'Dad, can I get one more present?' Ben asks.

'Of course you can; what do you want?'

Ben points towards the Paddington Bear.

'Okay, quickly grab it as we're next in the queue,' his dad tells him.

Ben rushes over and grabs the bear and puts it inside the trolley. Dad pays on his card and they all head out of the store and back towards the car park where they load Ben's presents inside the boot.

'Why don't you two wait in the car, while I take Jess around to the music shop?' Dad suggests to Mum and Ben. Ben didn't really want to wander around a music shop, so he's happy to wait in the car with his mum. They get inside the car and wind the windows down so the car doesn't get steamed up. 'I didn't know you liked Paddington Bear,' Mum says.

'I don't really.'

'Oh, so why did you get Dad to buy you one?' Mum asks. Ben begins to feel guilty that Dad spent money on something that wasn't for him, so he says in a timid voice.

'I got it for Avalon.'

Mum notices the change in Ben's demeanour.

'Ben, you picked the winning numbers so we're guaranteed to win a couple of thousand at least, so don't worry about it; it's nice that you've thought of Avalon especially as you're going round there tomorrow.' Ben gives his mum a smile and relaxes in his seat as he waits for his father to return. Fifteen minutes later, Dad and Jess return with Jessica's present. The box is far too big for Jess to carry, so Dad carries it and loads the large box into the boot of the car; which only just fits. Dad and Jess get back inside the car and Dad starts the engine.

'Are you all happy?' Dad asks

'Yes thanks Dad,' Ben and Jess tell their father. 'What's my present?' Mum asks. Dad thinks for a second, then smiles and looks Mum straight in the eyes and says, 'If we win more than ten thousand on the lottery, I'm taking us all on a cruise.'

'Wow! On a cruise!' Jess and Ben reply.

Mum pauses for a moment looking a little taken back.

"Chris I was only joking when I–'

Dad cuts Mum off.

'That's all right darling, I think we all could do with a nice holiday and I think we deserve one. We haven't been on holiday as a family for at least two years, so yes, if we win more than ten thousand, we're going.'

Mum prepares a load of sandwiches for lunch at one o'clock and they all sit around the dining table just picking at their food anxiously waiting for two o'clock for dad to ring the lottery people.

'What time did you say you were going to ring them?' Mum asks Dad, feeling like she can't hang on any longer. Dad looks up at the clock on the wall which tells him that it's twelve minutes past one.

'The hell with it; I was going to wait until two o'clock but I can't stand it any longer,' he says and he takes his mobile phone out from his pocket. 'Have you got the ticket, darling, with the number on?' Dad asks.

Mum quickly stands up, rushes over to the clock and retrieves the ticket receipt with the winning number and dashes back to Dad.

'Here you go.' She passes the ticket to him and quickly sits down at the table. Dad taps in the numbers on his keypad and presses the dial button. He holds the phone to his ear and waits for someone to answer. Mum, Jess and Ben all anxiously look at Dad waiting to be told the good or bad news about how much they've won. Ben wonders how much a good amount would be and how little would be bad in respect of their winnings. He thinks if they win thirty thousand for instance, that would be good, because they could live off that money for a year or so, until Dad gets another job.

'Hello, yes my name is Mr Chris Chapman and I've been asked to call this number today because we picked the winning numbers on Wednesday.'

They all stare at Dad with bated breath as he's now speaking to someone. Ben hopes his dad wins more than ten thousand, especially as he's just bought them some presents.

'Hello, yes the numbers are two, three, five, eight, twenty-one, thirty-four and forty-eight. Yes, okay. Yes. We have to go where to present our winning ticket?' Dad indicates to Mum that he needs a pen and paper. Mum quickly grabs her handbag and pulls out a notepad and pen and hands it to Dad.

'Yes, hold on a second, I'm just going to write that down...' He scribbles an address near the top of the paper and then moves the pen down to the bottom of the page ready to write something else. 'Okay, yes and can you confirm how much we've won...'

They all stare at Dad's face hoping his expression will tell them if it's good news or bad news. Dad suddenly drops the pen on the table.

'Oh my God!' he exclaims. He quickly picks up the pen and begins to write the numbers 3... 6... 5 and then pauses.

'Three hundred and sixty-five quid! Is that all?' Mum cries out in disgust. Dad holds his hand up to Mum to say for her to be quiet. He writes behind the 365 another three zeros. Dad presses his phone to end the call and they all look at him with their mouths wide open. *'Yeahhhhhhhhhhhhhhhhhhhhhhhhhhhhhhhhhh!'* they all cry out.

Chapter Thirty-Eight

Ben wakes up Sunday morning feeling excited at the thought of going to Avalon's party later on that day. Not that he doesn't feel excited, going to anyone's party but Avalon's party is a little different. For one thing, he'd never in his wildest imagination thought that he'd be invited to the school bullies sisters party because until a few days ago, he never knew she existed and the fact that she's the sister of the school bully meant that no one in their right minds would go; unless they were actually friends of Tony.

Ben still can't get his head around the fact that his best friend is dating Avalon. Apart from being a little strange, she's one of the tallest girls in their year and Paul's probably the shortest boy which is probably why he never saw it coming. To him Avalon looked like she was at least a few years older so it never occurred to him that they would like each other. She does have red hair and so does Paul, so in a sense they do look like siblings, but boyfriend and girlfriend, no. *Is she pretty?* Ben asks himself. He concludes that she is pretty but she's not his type. He likes blondes and he prefers his girlfriends to be shorter, like Alexis, who, in his opinion, is the perfect shape and size, with the right colour hair and beautiful. Not that being blonde makes any difference, but he does like blondes. Avalon's kind of strong and robust. She's the type of girl you could run into and you'd come off worse; she's not fat; she's quite slim but solid. He can only describe her as being hardened like her brother Tony in that they could take a knock and not be fazed about it.

Ben quickly gets dressed and washed and heads downstairs for breakfast. Mum's in her happy mood again; singing in the kitchen preparing breakfast and Dad's smiling while drinking his coffee at the table. 'Good morning.' Ben greets everyone.

'Good morning Ben, are you looking forward to your friend's party?' Dad asks.

'Sure, she's not exactly my friend; she's like my best friend's girlfriend.' Ben tries to explain.

'That's all right, so what time do you need to be dropped off?' Dad asks.

'Avalon said to get there for twelve.'

'And I gather you know where she lives. Did she give you an address?'

'Oh yes, it's 1433 Sycamore View about a mile past the new Morrison's' Ben tells his father. After breakfast Jess goes up to her room to practice on her new Keyboard while Ben goes into the lounge to play his new game; Gran Turismo. To his surprise, he notices his dad following him into the lounge and takes his seat in his comfortable armchair. Ben looks back at his father wondering why he's decided to sit behind him when he's never sat in the same room when Ben's playing his computer game before. Dad picks up his newspaper and pretends to read it.

Ben loads his new game into the game console and turns the TV on, fully aware that the eyes of his father are probably piercing into the back of his head. The game starts and Ben uses the money he has to buy a cheap run around car for his first race, conscious that his father must be watching him. The idea of the game is simple, and he recalls reading the blurb on the back of the cover when he bought it. You're allocated some money at the start of the game to buy yourself any car you can afford. You then enter a race and if you're successful in winning the race you receive prize money which can be used to improve the spec on your own car to make it go quicker or you can sell your car and with your combine money, you can buy a better car to race in more prestigious races with the hope of winning more money.

It's not long before Ben becomes immersed in the game, when he hears his mother say that he should finish what he's doing. Ben looks round at his mother feeling slightly annoyed that she's stopping him from playing, when he notices his mum pointing to the clock on the wall. Ben looks up at the time and sees that it's twenty to twelve. *Crikey, is that the time!* Ben mutters. He quickly puts the hand controller down when his dad tells him, "It's all right Ben, just finish this race.'

Ben notices his father sitting on the edge of his chair looking excited at his son's racing achievements.

Ben couldn't believe how quickly the time had gone when he noticed his newly purchased Mazda MX-5 sports car sat on the starting grid for the mid-engine sports car race. He remembers the clapped-out Renault Cleo he originally bought and how he won several races and changed his car more than twice to reach this point in the game. He gives his dad a smile and picks up his hand control. Within two minutes, Ben finished the race and came in second with a slightly reduced prize money.

'Don't worry Ben, you've got enough money now to buy better tyres,' his dad tells him. Ben saves the game and switches everything off before dashing to the front door to put on his shoes.

'Don't forget the present!' Mum reminds Ben as he reaches for his coat. Ben makes a dash upstairs and seconds later, comes down with the Paddington Bear tucked under his arm. Mum opens the front door and Ben quickly follows his father outside to the car and gets in the front passenger seat. Ben waves to his mum as his dad reverses the car off the drive and into the street. 'So where am I going again?' Dad asks.

'It's 1433 Sycamore View about a mile past the new Morrison's,' Ben tells his father for the second or third time.

Ben had arranged to meet up with Alexis and Paul outside Avalon's house at the same time, so they could all walk in together as none of them had ever been there before. Paul and Alexis thought that would be a good idea, so they planned to meet up outside the house at twelve o'clock. Ben checks the time on the dashboard clock and sees that it's ten to twelve already and they're nowhere near the Morrison's store. Dad notices Ben looking so he tells him reassuringly, 'It's okay, we'll be there in seven minutes.' Within a minute, they drive past the new Morrison's Supermarket on the right, so Ben reminds his dad that Avalon's house should be about a mile just up ahead. Almost immediately, they notice they're driving along the new stretch of road on the new development with modern houses on either side of the road. They all seem to be large five-bedroom houses on nice size plots of land. A bit further along they see the number 1395 on the gatepost to an even larger house on the right so they know they're getting closer. Ben keeps his eyes peeled, staring at each number as they drive past the houses on the right-hand side when he sees another number '1425' displayed on a brick gate post with a large electric gate across the drive. Dad quickly looks over at Ben.

'That looks a bit posh,' he says before looking forward again to see where he's going. They pass another two houses, so they know there are only two more houses before they have to stop. They see the neighbour's house, 1431, which is the largest house they've seen along this road and Dad looks back at Ben. 'Is your friend rich?' he asks.

'I don't think so,' Ben tells him, feeling that he must have been given the wrong address. Dad slows down a little as they see the next house just up ahead on the right with two people standing on the pavement outside.

As they approach, Ben recognises Paul and Alexis.

'That's it there Dad.' Ben points to his friends just up ahead. Dad drives up to the edge of the driveway and stops the car. Ben and his dad look past Alexis and Paul at the high brick wall with a six-foot wrought iron gate and what appears to be security cameras housed on either side of two large marble stone pillars. They see a long drive on the other side of the gate leading up to a house that must have at least eight bedrooms.

'Are you sure this is the right place?' Dad asks. 'It must be, because Paul and Alexis are here,' Ben says, although he's not a hundred percent sure. 'Okay, have a nice time and be good, and I'll pick you up around three?' Ben gets out of the car and closes the door before making his way around onto the edge of the driveway as dad drives off. Ben looks at Alexis and Paul and says, 'WHAT! Is this where Avalon lives?' Paul doubting himself says. 'This is the address she gave us.' The three of them look up at the security camera looking down at them and instantly feel like intruders.

'So how do we get in?' Ben asks.

'I don't know, I mean I wasn't expecting to be standing outside a huge security gate.' Paul says feeling at a loss. Ben notices what appears to be some kind of intercom built into one of the stone columns.

'Press the buzzer and talk into that.' Ben tells Paul.

Paul presses a green button with the word 'Talk' on it and they wait a few seconds for someone to respond. 'I hope this is the house, else we might have to make a run for it.' Paul says. They all have a little giggle.

'Paul, hi it's me, Avalon.' They hear a voice coming out of the small speaker.

'Hi, how do we get in?' Paul asks. Suddenly the large gate slowly starts to slide open and they hear Avalon's voice again. 'Come up to the house.' They wait a second until the gate opens wide enough for them to enter. They slowly go up the long drive towards the grand house set back behind semi-mature maple and silver birch trees spread throughout the garden. Just as they reach the house, the front door opens and Avalon steps out onto the marble stone porch to welcome them. 'Hi, I'm glad you could make it, come in.' Avalon says. Alexis walks up the four marble steps and enters the house. Ben follows behind Alexis and stops next to Avalon. 'Alexis and I got you this.' Ben holds up the Paddington Bear, hoping she'll like it. 'Ah Ben, that really kind of you two, thank you very much.'

Avalon takes the bear from him and before he has the chance to walk into the house; she throws her arms around him and gives him a big hug. Avalon quickly steps back and gives Alexis a thank you hug as well.

Paul walks up the stairs and gives his girlfriend a small, wrapped box with a card attached.

'You can open that later,' Paul tells her. Ben can only assume he didn't want her to open it in front of his friends, just in case the gift was something personal that would embarrass him. Paul stretches upwards, and Avalon bends slightly as they kiss each other. It's the first time Ben had seen them kiss and he knows Paul felt a little awkward in front of his friends because when they entered the house and the light was on their faces; Ben could see Paul was blushing. Ben didn't say anything and he thinks Paul appreciated him not saying anything. Avalon closes the front door and asks them to follow her. Avalon takes Paul's hand and they walk ahead through a doorway into a spacious dining room. They walk past a long solid dining table and chairs with twelve place settings to the far side of the room. They continue through another doorway into the large kitchen, breakfast room and out through the back door.

'Where is she taking us?' Ben whispers to Alexis, who shrugs and looks just as confused as Ben. Avalon walks across a large patio area and then around the side of the house to a large marquee tent next to a huge inflatable slide. The side of the tent is open and they can see a group of children inside and the sound of music playing in the background.

'Hi everyone! Alexis and Ben are here.' Avalon says.

Ben and Alexis follow Avalon and Paul into the tent and immediately recognise Philip Matthews, Andrew Perkins and Simon McDonald from the Inter school competition. They see Tony, Brian, Simon and Andrew and then a group of girls whose names he can't remember over to his left.

'Hi everyone!' Alexis and Ben say and give everyone a wave. The large marquee is laid out with three long picnic tables. Two of them have twelve chairs around them while the third table is covered with a wide selection of food. From where Ben is standing he can see chicken drumsticks, pizza, quiche, hotdogs, sausage rolls, cocktail sausages on sticks, salad, burgers and bread rolls at one end of the table and the other end. He can see jelly, chocolate cake, lemon drizzle cake, coconut macaroons, profiteroles and iced cakes. To the right of the food table, tucked in one corner is a middle-aged man standing behind a table with a tape deck and a selection of CDs between two enormous freestanding speakers. 'Wow this looks great.' Ben tells Avalon. He glances down and notices she's still holding on to Paul's hand.

'Oh, this is nothing special. When we lived at our old house, we used to have really big parties,' she tells Ben.

'Hello everyone, my name is Brenda.'

Ben hears a grownup's voice behind them. They all turn around and look at an elegant woman in her early forties wearing a blue sparkly knee-length dress standing in front of a man holding a fold-up table and a small suitcase.

'Thank you all for coming to my daughter's party. Mr Wilson will be looking after the music this afternoon.' She points to the middle-aged man in the corner. Mr Wilson gives everyone a wave. 'And Mr Treet behind me will entertain you with some magic and a little bit of sleight of hand, he kindly informs me.' Mr Treet holds up his small suitcase so everyone can read the advertising printed on the side. '*Ivor Treet for you and it's called Magic!* Brenda continues with her announcement. 'Help yourselves to the food on the table and in the fridge just outside the marquee, we have a selection of soft drinks for you; just help yourselves to anything and everything.'

Everyone thanks Brenda with a short round of applause as she turns away and heads back inside the house. Ivor Treet walks to the centre of the Marquee and sets up his table and places the small suitcase on top. 'Ladies and Gentlemen; Boys and Girls,' he begins realising his audience consists of school children. Everyone in the marquee slowly moves forward towards Mr Treet to form a half circle so they can see his performance.

'Can I have a volunteer?' he asks. 'Avalon, would you like to join me,' he beckons Avalon over. Everyone applauds as Avalon tentatively walks towards Ivor and stands just in front of him.

'Avalon, can I ask you to hold out your right hand for me?'

Avalon holds her hand out. Ivor takes her hand and turns it over so her palm is facing up. He quickly removes a red handkerchief from his pocket and waves it around in the air so everyone can see it's just a plain handkerchief. He covers her hand with the handkerchief and then places his left hand under hers and his right hand on top of the handkerchief.

'Avalon; is there anything in your hand?' Mister Treet asks.

'Err just a red handkerchief.' Avalon replies. He presses his right hand down against her right hand while supporting her hand with his left hand.

'Avalon, can you feel anything else in your hand?' She thinks for a second before answering. 'No, I don't feel anything except your hand.'

Ivor quickly removes his hands while taking off the red handkerchief to reveal a set of diamond earrings resting in her palm. Avalon holds the two earrings up so everyone can see. Suddenly everyone in the marquee begins to cheer and applaud at seeing this amazing trick. Ivor quickly takes a bow and then tells Avalon that the earrings are a gift for her. Avalon thanks Ivor and returns to the outer circle and shows Paul the two earrings.

Ivor opens his suitcase and takes out a Rubik's cube and holds it out to show everyone. Ben looks at Alexis and says, 'This guy's amazing.'

'I know, I still have no idea how he did that.' Alexis tells Ben. They continue watching while Ivor performs tricks and sleight of hand for the next half an hour. After he finishes with his best trick; he invites everyone to enjoy some food while Mr Wilson will play some relaxing music. Ben checks the time on his watch and notices it's a quarter to one. No wonder he was starting to feel a little peckish. Ben and Alexis each collect an empty plate and join the queue at the buffet table; they reach the food and begin placing a few items onto their plates before making their way over to one of the large empty tables and sit down at the end. Avalon and Paul join them and for a few minutes they all sit in silence as they eat.

'Avalon, what does your father do?' Ben asks, out of curiosity.

'He owns a couple of jewellery shops. Why?'

'Oh nothing, it's just that I don't know anyone as rich as you are.'

'He's not rich; he just buys expensive diamond necklaces and bracelets and then sells them on. I think.'

'Now that you've all been entertained and fed, I think it's time for the party girl to have a dance,' Mr Wilson announces.

Everyone looks at Avalon following the announcement of which had been totally unaware and now feeling a little embarrassed. A romantic love song starts to play and Avalon turns to Paul for support. Paul stands up and takes Avalon's hand and they walk out to the centre of the marquee. Everyone gives them a round of applause for being so brave. Paul holds Avalon around the waist and pulls her close. Avalon wraps her arms around his shoulders and the two of them begin a slow dance on the spot. Ben can't let his friend suffer alone, so he takes Alexis's hand and they join the two of them in the middle of the dance area and within a few moments; are joined by three other couples. Everyone remains on the dance floor for the next couple of up-tempo songs, to burn off the food they'd all eaten. Suddenly the music dies down and they all hear Brenda's voice again.

'Sorry to interrupt but we seem to have more entertainment for you.'

Everyone stops dancing and looks over at a strangely dressed man standing next to Brenda.

The man is wearing black trousers and a yellow jumper with the word *Mime* printed across the front. He's wearing a pair of white gloves and has a yellow beret on his head. His face is all painted white with a painted red tear just below his right eye.

'Oh, I love mime artists; they're great.' Alexis tells Ben, who can't remember ever seeing a mime artist before, so he's not sure what to expect.

The man asks Brenda to point out which of the girls is her daughter, Brenda points to Avalon standing in the centre of the marquee next to Paul. He points towards her and then slowly walks over giving her a big smile. Everyone steps back away from the centre of the dance area to give him adequate room to perform his act. The man reaches Avalon, now standing all alone. He slowly raises his left hand and softly touches Avalon on her right cheek with his fingers as he slowly steps around the left side of her. Suddenly in a flash, the man presses his hand across Avalon's mouth and pulls her head back against his chest as his right hand appears at the right side of Avalon's face with the barrel of a handgun pressing into the right side of her face.

Everyone on seeing what's happened gasps in utter shock and horror at the madman holding Avalon at gunpoint.

There are a few screams from some of the girls standing to Avalon's right who can see the gun clearly but apart from that; everyone remains motionless as if struck by fear. Ben standing slightly off to the side can see Brenda looking horrified, standing just ten feet away. 'Noooooooo. What are you doing?' Brenda cries out. '*Quiet!*' The man shouts above the sound of the music and presses the pistol into Avalon's cheek which causes Avalon to cry out.

Mr Wilson mutes the music and the marquee falls into a deathly silence as everyone waits for further instructions from the crazed lunatic. 'Everyone, move over there.' The man waves his gun towards the double garage next to the house with a single door access from the garden. Everyone in the marquee begins slowly walking over towards the closed doorway looking terrified. 'Open it and get inside,' the man demands. Tony opens the door and steps inside the darkened enclosure followed by Simon, Ben and Alexis. Ben in the semi-darkened double garage can make out a Jaguar car parked at the far side of the double garage; leaving ample space for everyone to fill the vacant car space left by Mr Vernall. Ben and Alexis go over towards the garage door to allow the others to crowd in behind them; within seconds the space is full and they all hear the gunman tell Brenda to close and lock the door. They all turn and stare at the doorway as Brenda pulls the door closed leaving all those inside the garage in complete darkness; suddenly the sound of a key turning in the lock confirms their situation that they're trapped with no way out. The gunman has Avalon and Brenda hostage and who knows what their fate will be. If they're killed then who knows what will happen; the gunman's not going to release them and God knows when Mr Vernall will be home.

'Who is he?' 'What does he want?' 'What's going to happen to Avalon?' Ben hears different children in the group ask, all sounding concerned for the two girls. Ben knows Alexis is feeling upset so he pulls her towards him and wraps his arms around her. He feels her body trembling next to his, so he whispers in her ear, 'It's going to be all right,' he's got no idea as to how he's going to fix this but he knows he's the only one who can. Ben closes his eyes for a moment, so he can concentrate on his options. *The man's obviously a professional of sorts as he's got a gun. He must have known that Avalon's dad owns a couple of jewellery shops and that he's not here this weekend. He must also have known about the party because it gave him the perfect ruse to get inside the house and wearing a mime costume is perfect; the gloves on his hands mean no fingerprints and the makeup and beret makes it difficult to identify him,* Ben thinks.

'I need to do something as he's probably robbing the place now and I dread to think what he's going to do with Avalon and her mum.' Ben reaches inside his pocket for his watch and takes it out. He looks down but can't see a thing.

'Damn it,' he says to himself.

'Are you all right Ben; what's happening?' Ben hears Alexis ask.

'It's all right, I just needed to do something but I can't see,' Ben tells Alexis.

Just then he notices a sliver of light appearing from under the garage door just behind where Alexis is standing.

'Alexis, I just need to squeeze past you.' Ben tells her. Ben reaches out and grabs her waist and they shuffle round in the darkness so that Ben is now standing next to the garage door. He crouches down and holds the watch at right angles next to the narrow beam of light so he can see. Ben can just about make out the time at 1.22 p.m. and he knows the watch is already set to travel back in time so he just needs to calculate how far back to travel.

What time do I need to go back to and what am I going to do when I get there? Ben asks himself. Suddenly a plan starts to form inside his head. Ben remembers looking at his watch when they had lunch and he's pretty sure the time was a quarter to one. He quickly calculates how far back he needs to go and slowly turns the adjuster knob around.

'Avalon, what does your father do?' Ben hears himself ask.

'He owns a couple of jewellery shops. Why?' Ben suddenly realises where he is and what's about to happen. The DJ's going to ask Avalon to have a dance any second now so he needs to be quick. Ben notices Avalon staring at him, waiting for an answer. 'Oh sorry, my mind just went blank for a second.' Ben apologises. Avalon gives Ben a smile.

'I just wondered that's all.' Ben continues. 'Can I use the telephone? I forgot to tell my father what time to pick me up,' Ben asks.

'Sure, you can use the one just inside the kitchen.' Avalon points to the kitchen doorway. Ben quickly goes out of the marquee tent and across the garden to the kitchen door. He steps inside and immediately notices the telephone hanging on its cradle next to a large refrigerator. A grocery message board mounted to the wall next to the phone with a pen conveniently placed centrally on a wooden shelf below. Ben picks up the telephone and dials the number for the local police station before his eyes casually look down the list of food items on the shopping list: *milk, cheese, cheesecake, champagne, brandy...* As he waits for someone to answer the phone he picks up the pen and writes 'squid' on the list. He laughs to himself because he assumes nobody likes squid and it would be funny if Brenda buys it and everyone refuses to eat it.

'Harrogate Police Station, Sergeant Davies speaking,' says a voice on the other end of the phone. 'Hello, my name is Ben Chapman; I'm at number fourteen, thirty-three Sycamore View. A man dressed as a mime artist is here and he's waving a gun at everyone,' Ben tells the officer hurriedly.

'Sonny, it's an offence to make bogus telephone calls,' the officer tells Ben.

'It's not a bogus call; I'm telling the truth!' Ben shouts down the phone.

'Listen son, if you persist in wasting our time, I'll be forced to send one of our officers round and then you'll be in serious trouble.'

Ben can't believe that the officer's not taking this call for help seriously. How can he make the officer understand that a criminal is just about to rob the place? *'The man has a gun and he's dressed as a mime artist and he's here now. Fourteen, thirty-three, Sycamore View!'* Ben screams down the end of the telephone, before slamming the handset down into its cradle in frustration. 'I don't believe it.' Ben says to himself still fuming at the attitude of the Police officer. Ben goes back to the marquee and notices they're just about to play the last song before Brenda brings the guy in. Ben quickly finds Alexis and leads her out into the middle of the marquee so they can dance near Avalon and Paul.

A minute later, Ben sees Brenda walking in with the gunman by her side.

'Sorry to interrupt but we seem to have more entertainment for you,' Brenda says. Ben quickly positions himself to the right of Avalon. Ben watches as Brenda indicates to the gunman where her daughter is by pointing over to where Avalon is standing. The gunman slowly walks towards her. Everyone begins to move backwards away from Avalon to allow the mime artist space to perform his act; Ben remains where he is, maybe three feet away to Avalon's right. Ben knows the man will pull a gun out from somewhere with his right hand so he focuses his attention on the mime artist's right side in the hope of seeing where he's stashed his pistol. The man smiles at Avalon and gently touches her with his left hand on the cheek, then, in a flash, his facial expression changes to a serious look as he whips around her and pulls out a gun from his pocket and holds it up to her cheek. Ben, now standing just over a metre away to the man's right, concentrates on the gun pressed to Avalon's face. He vaguely remembers the gunman pointing towards the outside garage with his gun hand as he tells everyone to get inside so he thinks it's going to be his best opportunity at disarming the gunman. Ben nervously waits for the man to move the gun away from Avalon's face, while blanking everything out from his mind so he can stay focused. Ben can feel the adrenaline rushing through his body to the point of feeling nauseous, because he knows he only has one chance and he doesn't want to mess it up.

'Everyone, move over there.' Ben hears the man say as his gun hand holding tightly onto the weapon moves away from Avalon's face. Ben immediately steps one pace towards the man and kicks his foot out towards the gun. As in slow motion, Ben watches his right foot fly up towards the man's hand and connect with his wrist. *Bang!*

A loud explosion echoes around, causing Ben's ears to start to ring. In horror Ben sees Tony Vernall fly backwards and land on the ground three metres away to his right followed by screams coming from all sides. The gunman quickly turns towards Ben looking crazed and angry and points his gun at Ben's chest.

'You idiot!' the man yells. Ben, sensing his life is about to end, musters up courage to quickly take out his watch. He drops his focus to his watch held in his hand hoping the man will wait a few moments for him to rewind time. Ben flips open the watch cover and takes hold of the adjuster knob but finds it difficult to focus on the watch face because his hand is shaking so much. In that moment, he can sense his vision becoming narrower and narrower; feeling like he's about to faint as he waits for the sound of another gunshot. Ben fractionally turns the adjuster.

Ben hears a few screams from some of the girls to his right and he sees Brenda staring wide eyed at the Gunman looking terrified. 'Nooooooooooo. What are you doing?' Brenda cries out.

'Quiet!' The man shouts. Ben, realising that he's only travelled a few minutes back in time, quickly assesses that he needs to reposition himself so he doesn't repeat what just happened. Ben slowly steps to his left so he's standing directly behind the gunman and moves into one of his karate stances. He waits ten seconds for the man to tell everyone to move over to the garage and then Ben kicks his right leg out in a frontal high kick and catches the gunman with his foot, right on the end of his right elbow causing his arm to fly upwards.

To everyone's surprise the gun falls from the gunman's hand and lands six feet in front of him. The man yelps in pain at receiving the hardest Karate kick Ben could muster. Tony, standing on the other side of the marquee on seeing the gun leave the man's hand and fall to the floor, makes a dive for the weapon. In what could be described as a commando role; Tony picks up the gun and is back on his feet in a crouched position pointing the gun at the mime artist. Avalon notices the gun dropping from the man's hand; quickly looks down and stamps on the man's foot with her stiletto heels. 'Arghhhh!' the gunman cries out and quickly lifts his left leg.

Ben immediately sees the man's vulnerable state, hopping backwards towards him, so he whips his right leg around in a roundhouse kick and takes the gunman's right leg out from under him, sending him crashing down to the ground. Within seconds Ivor Treet and Mr Wilson run in and hold the man down. Suddenly there's a huge cheer from everyone in the marquee as the crazed gunman is restrained. In the silence to follow; they all hear the faint sound of a police siren that begins to get louder and louder as a manned police car drives towards 1433 Sycamore View. Avalon walks over to the man now pinned to the ground by Mr Treet and Wilson. She stops by his side and stares at his crazed expression. "You're a lunatic that's what you are.' Avalon kicks the man as hard as she can in his side before turning around and walking back towards Paul. Tony walks over to Ben. 'That was a brilliant kick; you caught him just right.' 'And well done to you for grabbing the gun!' Ben tells Tony. They give each other a hug, as a kind of thank you for helping each other out. Avalon and Brenda walk over and thank Ben for being so brave and disarming the armed robber.

The noise from a police siren is clearly heard outside followed by the sound of the doorbell. Brenda, looking pleased that the gunman has now been restrained and feeling a sense of relief that the police are now here says,

'I wonder who that could be?' Everyone in the marquee except for the gunman gave a resounding cheer. Brenda goes back inside the house to let the police in. Alexis walks up to Ben and gives him a hug and a kiss.

'You're the bravest person in the world,' she tells him and stares admiringly into his eyes with her arms wrapped around his neck. Ben looks deep inside Alexis's eyes and for a moment the world around him fades into obscurity leaving only Alexis and him. For Ben, life couldn't get any better.

* * *